MW01132274

THE BROKEN KING

CONQUERING IMORIA'S MAGIC DUOLOGY
BOOK 2

T. B. WIESE

For everyone who enjoys DARK romance.
You're my people.

BOOKS IN THIS WORLD

- Book one - The Crown Breaker
- Book two (this book) - The Broken King

AUTHOR'S NOTE

The Broken King is a DARK adult fantasy MM romance. It contains elements of language, explicit sex, murder, graphic violence, sadism, physical & mental torture, drug use, and child abuse.

IMORIAN MOUNTAINS

JOXIS

KINGDOM OF LIEREN

MALNAR

FARDEN

KING RYDEL'S HOME TOWN

VARYEN DESERT

KINGDOM OF ADREN

KINGDOM OF TRILSEN

KINGDOM OF ESHENA

KINGDOM OF ALARA

COUNTRY OF

IMORIA

LEGEND
◆ CAPITAL
• CITY
---- BORDER

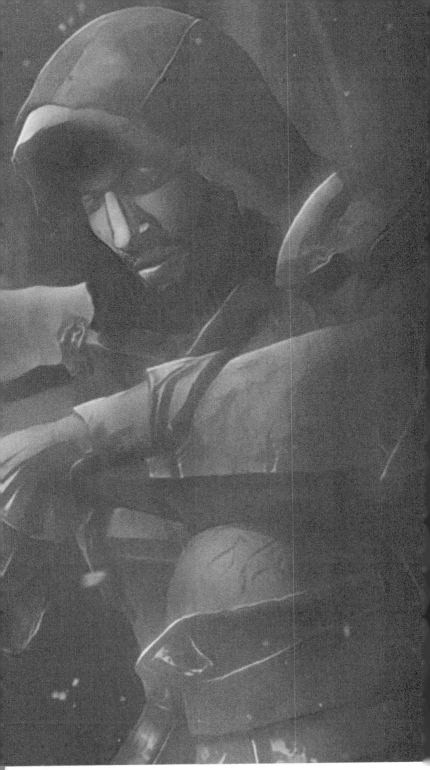

1

LUCARYN

Rydel's voice echoes a warning through my mind, and I have a split second to move. The arrow thuds into my chest, and fire spreads. Poison.

Ry is across the clearing, his rage drawing my fading vision like a beacon. He's so powerful. He's everything to me. It can't end here.

His magic drops body after body, his blade flashing to finish what his mind-power started, delivering each enemy to their death.

He's so beautiful, so deadly. As he rushes to me, the world fades, the edges of my sight turn white, the noise around me grows dim.

For a moment, I think I'm falling into unconsciousness, but my awareness doesn't fade. In fact, it gets sharper. The pain in my gut is so intense, I attempt to curl in on myself, but my limbs won't cooperate. I'm agonizingly hungry, and my mouth feels like it's filled with sand. I lick my lips, finding them raw and cracked. The room spins as I try to figure out where I am and what happened. A moment ago I was dying from a poisoned arrow. Now I'm ...

I let my head fall to the side, gasping. I'm in my bedroom in the castle laying on my back in my bed. It's cold, my breath puffing out in white vapor with each breath. It's dark. No fires, no torches. I struggle to flex my muscles, slowly bringing my hand to my face, and my heavy fingers run through my long beard. What happened? Did Rydel save me? I run my hand down my neck, barely strong enough to control that slight movement, until I find the spot below my left collarbone.

My brows pinch as my fingers meet scar tissue. Not a new or even healing wound, but a closed one. How long have I ...

Memories slam through me, and a sob tears from my throat. Oh gods. Rydel knows. He knows everything—the Stone, his family, my lies ... He locked me in my mind. How long have I been trapped in my memories? How many times have I relived my betrayal?

A shadow in the corner of the room shifts, and my body shakes with the effort of propping myself on my forearm. I squint into the dark corner. My heart jumps, and my eyes go wide as Rydel peels away from the wall, walking out of the shadows like a wraith.

His cheeks are hollow, his blond hair hangs limply over his face. His usually bright green eyes are dull, and his gaze is hard as he stares at me. I lick my lips, looking past him into the dark room beyond, half expecting a group of soldiers to come filing into the room to drag me to the dungeons. But as far as I can tell, my rooms are empty besides the two of us. My door is open to the hall, which is

2

dark as well. There's not a noise to be heard beyond our breaths and Ry's slow footfalls.

The closer he gets, the more I see of him. His pale skin is almost grey, and his lips are cracked. His clothes, which are usually neat and styled, are wrinkled. There are even a few rips in the fabric, and there are dirt smudges on his knees and elbows. He flexes his hands at his sides, drawing my attention to his bony fingers and the fake ring.

What could have driven Rydel—the King, the mighty Crown Breaker—to such a state?

I lick my lips again, swallowing around the desert that is my throat. "How—" I swallow and try again. "How long have I ... ?"

"Thirty-eight days and four hours."

Somehow, I manage to sit up, swinging my legs over the edge of the bed. My back trembles, and the room won't stop tilting one way, then the other. "How am I still alive?"

He flinches slightly, eyes pinching before he wipes his emotions from his face and stares at a spot beyond my right shoulder, avoiding my gaze. "I had the healer force feed you water and broth."

So, just like every other prisoner. Rydel has kept me in my rooms, but other than that, he's treated me like ... his enemy. That thought scrapes at my hollow insides, threatening to break me apart. I open my mouth to ask about my fate now that I'm out of the memory loop, but he sways before bunching his muscles, stiffening his spine and holding up his hand, stalling my words.

I swallow again and just stare at him as he slices his dagger across his forearm, digging his fingers into his flesh. The Heart Stone—the object that gives its owner the magic to feel and influence emotions—emerges, pinched lightly between his bloody fingers. He tosses it, and it clatters

3

quietly to the floor, bouncing a few times before it settles at my bare feet.

His eyes finally shift to mine, and his whispered words send a shiver up my spine. "You were right. Two Stones is too much."

So, that's why he's here, why I'm no longer being tortured by his magic. Anger overshadows my pain and despair. My body shakes from more than weakness as rage courses through my blood. Of course two Stones is too much! All the texts warned against taking too much magic into yourself that is not natural born—and natural born magic vanished centuries ago. Rydel knew this. We both did. We've been researching and hunting down the last pieces of magic in this world for most of our lives.

But did Ry listen? No. He believed himself to be untouchable. He raged against my betrayal, even though everything I did was for him, to protect him. My best friend punished me. The love of my life tormented me and took the magic.

Now, here he stands, what? Repentant? My eyes travel over his tense shoulders and tightly-pressed lips. No, he's not sorry.

I know he can hear every thought racing through my mind because of the Mind Stone that is sewn into his back over his right shoulder blade. And while he may have cut the Heart Stone from his flesh, I haven't taken it, so that magic is still his, meaning he feels every wave of anger beating from my heart.

I should take it. I should welcome the power of the Heart Stone back into my body and shove every scrap of despair, and pain, and horror I can muster into Rydel. I should let the magic tear apart his heart, but I'm not sure he has one.

Rydel rubs at his temples. He sighs, opening his mouth, presumably to address everything I've been thinking, but my stomach grumbles loudly. I feel completely emptied out. The room tilts again, and I almost fall onto the bed but somehow keep myself sitting upright with a shaky hand pressed to the bed. Rydel runs a hand through his dirty hair before scratching his long beard. The silence in the room and beyond presses in on me like a heavy blanket. Ry snaps his mouth closed, rolling his head side-to-side, stretching his neck.

Fine, since he's being closed lipped, I'll ask aloud. "I assume you want my help?"

His dagger spins in his hand as he shuffles to a chair and drops into it like his own weight is too much to hold up.

"Fuck!"

I jerk back at his shout as he stabs his blade into the arm of the chair.

He takes a few breaths, just staring at the hilt of his dagger before he sighs. "Yes. I should never have ..."

His words trail off, and when he doesn't continue, I inhale deeply before prodding, "Rydel?"

His green eyes meet mine. "I've lost the southern kingdom. Adastra has taken Trislen and has moved north. I've lost ... a lot."

I'm trying to process everything as he shoves out of the chair, stumbling toward me before dropping to his knees between my thighs. Heat and longing threaten to shove my anger aside. I physically ache to touch him, but I grip the sheets instead.

"I'm losing, Luc. I'm losing everything, and I never even made it close to the Trislenian capital. I never laid eyes on Adastra! Fuck!"

My eyes widen. Ry isn't used to not knowing ... everything. He thrives on control, and to see him so broken is unnerving. But before compassion can wiggle its way into my heart, my back spasms, and I'm starkly reminded of what he did to me.

I don't know what I expected when he finally learned the truth that he was not the one who killed his abusive father, his drug-addict mother, and his useless sister. I have no doubt he would have killed them had he been able, but the beating his father gave him that day knocked Rydel unconscious, so I did what he could not.

I killed his family. Then I lied. For twenty-seven years, I kept that secret ... until thirty-eight days ago.

Rydel used his magic against me. He tortured me by trapping me in the agony of my betrayal. We could have talked it through. I would have let him rant and rage against me, but we could have come out the other side. No matter how angry we got with each other over the years, we always found a way back to our friendship.

But what if we can't this time?

How can I forgive the fact that Rydel imprisoned me within my mind and locked me away? Yet somehow, I'm not surprised by what he did to me. I'm heartbroken and angry, but I'm not surprised. I always knew what I was risking by keeping my secrets, and now they've made me an enemy of my best friend.

I'm pulled from my thoughts as he rubs at his chest, no doubt experiencing the depth of my feelings. He crawls backward, folding himself until his forehead presses to the floor at my feet. "I don't deserve your forgiveness, so I won't ask it of you, but please"—His voice cracks on a sob— "please tell me I haven't completely lost you. I ... I ..."

2

LUCARYN

I can't keep the gasp from sliding past my lips at the sight of Rydel bowed low before me. My chest aches, and just as I lift my hand to rub at the pain, I stop myself, letting my eyes travel to the small pink stone covered in blood laying at my feet.

It would be such an easy thing to reach down and take the Stone, take the magic. I can help him. I can hurt him. I ... I want him. Can I forgive him?

The pain in my heart, bleeding through my body tells me no. Rydel could have faced me when he learned of my lie. He could have tried. But he didn't. He locked me away like so many of his enemies before. He used his magic on *me*, the one he claimed to love above all others.

And I love him. *Loved*.

No, that's not right. I still love him, but this anger ...

My shoulders slump as I recall the near-constant pit of

anxiety that lived in my gut for the past twenty-seven years —all because I wasn't brave enough to face Rydel and talk to him. Can I really blame him for doing the same?

No. It's *not* the same.

I ball my fists tighter into the sheets and bite my bottom lip as another wave of sorrow and rage pushes at me from the inside out. Ry groans, and I know my thoughts and feelings are battering his mind and heart. I'm causing him pain.

Satisfaction courses through me. Good. He should hurt. I've always protected Rydel. Always. I've spent years doing whatever I could to be what Rydel needed. I've let him explore, expand, and cultivate his darkness, always there to back him up. I've molded my life around Rydel. I've followed him, supported him, loved him.

He grunts, his face blanching. A thread of heartbreak spears through my smug anger. I'm causing him pain, and that hurts.

Damn it.

Ry's fingers scrape over the wood floor as he groans again. His voice cuts through my thoughts. "I hear your conflict. I feel your pain and anger."

My eyes cut to him as he pushes to kneeling before pulling his hair back at the nape with a tie, and I notice his ribs are visible through the pull of his shirt. I can't keep the wince from my face as I once again take in his thin form. There's still muscle there. Rydel has always been large– larger than life. But now his muscles seem to be desperately clinging to his bones.

Shaking my head, I drop my eyes to stare at the Heart Stone. I don't want it. That Stone lived under my skin for months while I tried to hide the magic from Rydel. I didn't want him to take it. I didn't want to lose him to the magic.

I lost him anyway.

The floor creaks as Rydel shifts, but I don't look up as he continues. "Honestly, I'm amazed you're even still listening to me, Lucaryn."

His voice wavers as he speaks my name, and longing spears through me—longing for him to smile at me, to wrap his arms around me ... longing for him to tell me everything will be alright ... longing for what we had together for one shining moment before it all fell apart. My vision blurs, and the bloody Stone shimmers with the tears that well in my eyes before falling down my cheeks.

I try to put some venom behind my whispered words. "I don't have much choice." I lift a hand, waving at myself. "It's not like I can storm out."

He sucks in a breath, and it sounds pained.

My mind tumbles. How can we ... how do we get back to ...? After I ... After he ... After we ... How?

"Luc." He barks my name, pulling me from my spiraling thoughts. I shake my head, keeping my gaze on the floor, my dark hair brushing against my face. The floor creaks again as he rocks back on his shins. I keep my gaze down but watch him through my lashes as he presses one hand to his thigh like he needs that pressure to hold himself upright. His other hand reaches forward, pausing, hovering over my hand resting on my knee.

We both stare at his hand. My heart begs me to pull away, to protect myself. But wounded as my heart is, it still beats for him.

His hand lowers painfully slowly. "I know what you're feeling. I know what you're thinking." The press of his flesh to mine is a shock. His fingers are cold and shaking as they flex against the top of my hand. I know the magic is eating away at him. I know he's in pain ... and I'm glad.

His lips pull up slightly at the corners. "You finding pleasure in my pain is ... confusing." He licks his lips, holding his hand on mine before he looks up at me. "I ..."

I may not have the magic, but I know Rydel. He's turned on. Pain and pleasure always did it for him. He thrived off the heady mix. And it seems he still does. I can't help the little tickle of arousal that kicks through my body, recalling the blissful feel of him sliding into me, of his hand fisting my hair ...

My stomach grumbles again, extinguishing the whisper of lust, reminding me of my situation and why I'm sitting here cold and starving. Rydel keeps his hand pressed to mine for another moment before sighing and pulling away. I'm immediately grateful he withdrew even as I miss his touch.

He shifts to adjust himself before pressing both his hands to his thighs ... thighs I had trembling under me mere weeks ago. I shake my head with a groan, and his groan matches mine as I force my eyes to the floor.

"Luc ..."

I know he's seeing my thoughts, so to keep the memory of his lips on mine at bay, I stare at the Stone, counting the little black splotches dotting its pink surface.

Rydel clears his throat. "Lucaryn, I know you have questions and have things to say to me, and we need ..." He lets the silence draw out until I'm forced to look up, and he continues, "We *do* need to talk. You were right, and I'm ... I ... well." His hands clench in the fabric of his pants. "Damn it." He crawls forward, his knee knocking aside the Stone until his thighs and stomach press to my shins. Reaching up, his hands frame my face, his touch firm but gentle.

I'm frozen. I want to lean into him. I want to pull back. I want to punch him. I want him to bleed. I want ... him.

I hate him.

I love him.

I stare into his soft green eyes, and he stares back. The seconds tick by before his lips curl in a half smile. "I'm sorry."

I blink a few times. Did he just apologize?

He chuckles, dropping his hands. Standing slowly, he turns. "You're hungry. Cooks are gone, but I'm sure I can find something edible for you." He pauses, glancing over his shoulder at me. "Can you stand? Do you need help?"

I shift forward, pressing more weight on my feet, testing my strength. As much as I crave his arms around me, I don't want his help. I wiggle my toes against the cold stone floor, and a shiver shakes my entire body.

Ry shakes his head, cursing, "Beatuis."

He crosses my room to my dressing closet. Since when did Ry start swearing to the gods? I hear him rummaging through my things, and it's just now I realize my bedroom is clean. There's not a wayward piece of clothing cluttering the floor. All the dishes and cups have been cleared away. Blankets are neatly folded and stacked on the couch near the cold fireplace. My weapons are clean and gleaming even in the low light of the dark room, all lined up, hanging on the far wall.

I swallow, trying once again to ease my dry throat. "I hate it."

Rydel chuckles, reading my thoughts. "I know, but I couldn't help myself."

I glance toward my closet. "Wait, *you* cleaned my rooms?"

Silence greets me in answer. I bite my lip, feeling the cracked edges against my tongue. The thought of Ry coming into my rooms to clean up while I was suffering under the punishment of his magic is infuriating. Yet, at the same time, a small knot unfurls in my chest at the knowledge that he was here with me. I hope it pained him to see me vacant and wasting away.

His voice floats from the closet. "It did. Every time."

"Then why come at all?"

Silence again. I take a deep breath, and it feels like the first big lungful of air I've taken in a long time. It stutters on the way in, and I let it out slowly, trying to release some of my pain and anger with my breath. With a shaking hand, I bend down.

"Are you sure?"

Rydel's voice stops me, my hand hovering over the Heart Stone. He's still in the closet, but he's heard my intentions. I bite harder on my lip, changing my mind at the last minute. Pulling back, I let myself sink into the mattress, releasing another deep breath. Why is it so hard to inhale properly?

Rydel says nothing as he emerges with a heavy wool cloak and my favorite pair of fur-lined winter boots. His gaze snags on the Stone on the floor before concentrating on my boots in his hands. Kneeling, he slides one then the other onto my feet, and my throat burns with the threat of tears born of both sorrow and rage, but I swallow them down.

He stands, fingering the cloak, and I take a moment to look at him. He's been suffering too, maybe more than I was stuck in my horrible memories. I think he was punishing himself by coming into my room while I was lost to his magic. And while a large part of me revels in his pain, knowing I can take some of that from him, knowing I can help him tears at my stupid, stupid heart. Rydel has been the one constant my entire life. He is and always will be a part of me. He is a part of my soul.

Longing, disappointment, rage, and fear, war within me.

Rydel grunts, stumbling back a step, hand pressed to his chest as he folds over, heaving. Bile splatters against the floor with a wet splash. He spits, wiping the back of his hand across his lips as he straightens and turns back to me.

I wince at the hollow look in his eyes. I did that to him. My emotions and thoughts forced on him by the magic made him sick. And I can't seem to keep my emotions under control as satisfaction at hurting him runs through me, quickly followed by shame at causing my best friend's pain. And then anger again for feeling that shame. He deserves it.

Rydel shakes his head with a frown. "It's fine. Think your thoughts. Feel your feelings. You're entitled to both." Moving to swing the cloak around my shoulders, I hold up a hand. "Wait."

He tilts his head in confusion, then his lips press into a hard line as he catches my thoughts. "Don't worry about it, Luc. I'll learn to control both Stones eventually. It's only been a few weeks. I learned with the Mind Stone. I'll do the same with the Heart Stone."

He takes another step toward me, but his leg buckles, and he has to catch himself against the chair. I'm going to have to take back that damned Stone.

His eyes snap to mine, some of his old fire shining through. "No. Don't. Don't take it out of pity. I can—"

"What?" He presses his lips in a tight line. "What, Rydel? According to you, things have gone to shit." I wave a hand at him. "You look like shit." He snorts a laugh, and my face pulls up into a smile. "Let me help."

His shoulders hitch, and his smile falls. "Like you helped me with my family?"

I rear back, a pulse of sorrow spearing through me at his words. He rubs his chest in reaction to my emotions. Yes, I killed his family. His father beat him nearly every day. His mother spent her days and nights lost in the haze of drugs. And his older sister did nothing, just told Rydel to be quiet and bear it. So yes, I killed them and kept the truth from Rydel. And I'm not sorry.

I hold his stare. "I'd do it again."

His shoulders slump, and he drops his gaze to the floor. "Beatuis. I shouldn't have said that."

I grit my teeth, shaking my head, biting back my own angry response. "Just ..." I hold out my hand.

"Are you sure?"

I yank my shirt over my head, noticing it's clean. Rydel made sure I was taken care of, even as he tortured me, and I hate him for it.

"No. I'm not sure, Rydel. But the magic is killing you, and we need the magic—or at the very least, we need to make sure it doesn't fall into anyone else's hands." I wave a hand at myself. "So ... " I stare him down. "I mean, this is why you woke me, yes?"

His eyes go wide, and he takes a step back as my words hit their mark. Sure, I may wish he came to me because he missed me, because he really is sorry, because he loves me. But ...

He crosses the room, disappearing into my washroom. The creak and thunk of drawers opening and closing carries across the quiet rooms, and then water splashes before Rydel comes back out. He's carrying a small bowl of water. A towel is draped over his arm, and a threaded needle is pinched between his fingers. He sets everything on the floor at my feet before yanking his dagger from the arm of my chair. Snagging a bottle of whiskey from my cabinet, I imagine his knees are getting sore as this mighty king once again kneels before me, pouring the liquor over the blade. He picks up the small pink Stone, dousing it with the alcohol as well. His arm shakes as he holds the bottle out to me, and I frown. "I'm not sure that's the best idea on a stomach as empty as mine."

His lips press together, but he nods, setting the bottle down. Pressing a hand to my shoulder, his eyes meet mine. "Same place?"

I nod, determined.

Fast and efficient, his blade digs into my skin, slicing over the twice healed wound in my chest. I hiss, then shiver as my hot blood drips down my body.

"Deep breath."

I suck in a sharp inhale at Rydel's command, and he presses the small Stone into the open cut. My teeth grind together as I grumble, "Fuck."

His fingers pinch my skin together, and the needle pierces me as he begins sewing me up.

"Beatuis, Luc. Sorry. Almost done."

My jaw aches from my clenched teeth, and I once again wonder at his new compulsion to swear in the name of Beatuis, the god of malevolence. It's so unlike Rydel. Growing up, neither of us had much use for the gods. What did they ever do for us? But before I can ask, he pulls away, and I glance down to inspect the neat stitches marching across my chest.

The room spins as the magic floods my body. I feel relief, anxiety, regret, anger, and longing ... but mostly relief. I rub my chest, recognizing the emotions as both mine and Rydel's. He sighs, visibly relaxing as the magic releases its hold on him. The Heart Stone's magic is mine once again.

Fuck.

Rydel nods, already looking stronger as he stands a little taller, and the tremor in his hands stills. "I'll catch you up on everything. But first, let's go find something to eat."

Bracing my hands on the bed, I push, trying my best to

ignore the trembling in my arms and legs as I stand. The room spins again, and the edges of my vision darken. Rydel's concern flutters through me, but then everything settles. Thank fuck it's just Rydel and me right now. I don't know if I could take more emotions on top of being near starved and dizzy.

I take one step, then two, shuffling across the room until I'm next to Rydel. Before I pass him, he sweeps the wool cloak over my shoulders, resting his hand on my back. His worry weighs down on my already heavy body, and my knees threaten to buckle under the pressure of my weakened state and the stinging magic. I step away from his touch.

"Luc—"

"No, Rydel. Your concern for me is like a slap to the face!" He jerks back, eyes wide, but I can't stop the flow of angry words. What does it matter anyway? He'll hear my thoughts. I might as well let it out. "You always said the magic works off trust, Rydel. If you truly trust someone, the magic is quiet. For the past ten years, my thoughts have been my own, safe from your magic's reach. But now, your doubt, your suspicion, your mistrust of me have my very mind at your mercy."

His guilt punches into me, but under it there's a tiny flare of anger.

I press on. "I acknowledge my part in causing this rift between us, Rydel. But you could have listened. You could have heard me out. You could have tried to understand. I hate y—" I manage to keep myself from finishing the sentence, but he knows. Stepping back with a frown, he opens his mouth, but I shake my head before he can say anything. "Now's not the time. I'm too weak and hungry to think clearly. Let's just go."

His frown deepens as he opens the door, and we step out into the dark hallway. Silence, chilled, stale air, and shadows follow us as we make our way through our wing of the castle. Our progress is slow. I pause, placing a hand on the wall, trying to hide the deep gulps of air I'm sucking down. Closing my eyes, I take one more big inhale before pushing off the wall and move forward.

Rydel says nothing, keeping his pace with mine. We walk down the stairs, and halfway I stop again. My vision darkens at the edges and sweat drips down my back. Fuck. There's too much emotion pouring through me. He stands still and silent at my side. The concern coming off him in waves pisses me off. He's the reason I'm in this state. Damn him! Why does he have to be so ... him?

Clenching my hands, I continue down the stairs. We make our way through the winding halls, down another set of stairs, and into the kitchen. The entire way, we pass not a single person.

Where is everyone?

Rydel ducks into a pantry, his voice floating out behind him. "Eat first. Questions later."

A chuckle actually bubbles from my lips, but I swallow it down, angry at myself for feeling ... happy—happy to be here with him. A quick assessment tells me that, yes, that flash of happiness was my own, not Rydel's. I've missed him.

Damn it.

He comes out of the pantry holding a loaf of bread, a jar of dark jam, a bottle of something, as well as a square package. The contents of his arms clatter to the table, and he goes about slicing the bread and smearing generous amounts of jam onto each piece. I watch his long fingers work, licking my lips with every kind of hunger.

His eyes snap to mine, and I feel his rising hunger as

well—for the food, and for me. We both ignore the others' thoughts and feelings as he holds out a piece of bread to me. "Eat. Slowly."

My eyes travel down his thin body, then back up again. "You first."

His smirk causes my heart to skip, the stupid organ shoving aside my anger and replacing it with heated desire. He takes a big bite, and I can't help but want to lick the little smear of jam from his lip. He must catch my thoughts because his gaze drops to the table, and he wipes the jam from his mouth with his sleeve before holding the bread back out to me.

I take it, carefully avoiding touching him, shoving my anger back to the surface once again. We are both in this state because he refused to talk to me, to listen. But what did I expect? That's who Rydel has always been. Reactive.

I take a bite, the sweet and sour flavors bursting over my tongue. I groan around the mouthful, not even swallowing before I take another bite.

Rydel passes me a cup of water, taking the bread from my hand. "Easy. I know it's tempting, but you have to take it slow."

I swallow, nodding, but I'm unable to peel my eyes away from the bread as he takes another bite. I feel his hunger, but it's not as sharp as mine. He smiles at my thoughts. "With the power of both Stones, I couldn't eat. The magic was ... too consuming." He rolls his shoulders. "I feel more myself now." Paper crinkles as he unwraps the small package, revealing a hunk of dried meat. He takes a big bite, and my mouth waters. I know the meat is too heavy for me to eat right now, but that doesn't keep me from wanting it, desperately. I want it all—the meat, the bread, cheese, the perfect flaky pastries that our cook, Asha would make, stews, roasted vegetables, sweet fruits ... him ...

I'm snapped from my thoughts as Rydel leans forward, making sure I'm looking into his eyes. "Thank you."

I feel his relief that I've taken the magic, that I'm helping him at all. He didn't think I would. His hope that I'll forgive him washes over me, and my shoulders involuntarily straighten for a moment before they slump with my exhaustion. Under his hope, he's uncertain ... of us, of the future.

Until the magic of the Heart Stone, I never comprehended how many emotions we carry and process at once. The magic brings forward and amplifies each feeling, each emotion, forcing me to experience them. It's amazing. It's overwhelming. It's painful.

I take another sip of water, already feeling full from the two meager bites of food.

I clear my throat. "I have a lot of questions and a lot to say." He nods, but stays silent, so I continue. "You've woken me from my torment, but you hear my thoughts, meaning" —he stiffens, and I'm punched with his anxiety—"you still don't trust me. You haven't forgiven me."

Gods. I wish it could be that simple. Forgiveness is a tricky thing. You can want it, but sometimes the heart just won't cooperate. I want Rydel back. I want us back. I want this anger at him to vanish.

I watch his face as he watches mine. He doesn't respond, so I shake my head, taking another sip of water. "So, my first question is this; why come to me? What exactly do you want from me, your Majesty?"

3

RYDEL

I flinch at Luc's formal address, his voice barely containing the scorn of his inner thoughts.

Scratching my beard, I sigh. "Honestly, I ..." The silence hangs between us like a heavy fog. What *do* I want from him? Everything, but I can't very well say that.

Luc takes a final sip of water before setting the mug on the scarred table with a soft thud. I feel his eyes on me, but when I refuse to meet his gaze, he rests a forearm on the table, dropping his head in his other hand. "Rydel, I—"

I jerk back as rushed, angry thoughts shove into my mind. Luc grunts and rubs his chest. I whip around just as Casin, my acting captain, charges into the kitchen. His pants are dirty and wet with snow. There's a blood stain along the right side of his shirt, and a bruise darkens his jaw. His disheveled hair sticks out in all directions.

Casin's long strides carry him across the room. "There

you are!" He pauses when he sees Lucaryn. He salutes with a smile. "Captain, you're awake. We've all been worried the Shinvar Fever would take you from us. I should have known better. It would take more than a mountain sickness to kill our captain. It's good to see you, sir."

Luc does a good job keeping his face blank of the questions tumbling through his mind. It hurts like hell, but I project my thoughts into his mind.

'Everyone believes I sent you north on a special mission. They were told you fell sick, and the healer has been tending you.'

Luc doesn't react, simply nods. "Thank you, Casin. It's slow going, but it's good to be up and about."

I turn my head toward Casin. "What do you need?"

He focuses back on me, his eyes losing their warmth, and his voice goes from kind to controlled anger. "Your Majesty, I've been looking all over this damned castle for you. Things are devolving in the city. Rebels are fighting our forces at the southern gate, and more have gathered at—"

I hold up a hand to silence him, but before I can say anything, Casin shakes his head, crossing his muscled arms over his chest. "This can't wait. You're needed. Now."

He holds his ground as I scowl at him. "It can wait if I say it can wait."

"No."

I raise an eyebrow, and Luc presses his hand to the table, ready to stand and berate Casin, but I wave him off. Casin barrels on, ignoring both of our scowls. "It's been a week since you came back. A week of you *hiding* in this stone fortress." I grit my teeth as anger fires through me. Casin's voice raises. "A week of your soldiers and your people being harassed, hurt, and killed! A week of—"

Luc slaps a hand on the table, his arm trembling slightly as he pushes himself upright. "Casin, you forget yourself."

24

Casin stands taller. "No, captain. This has gone on long enough." He turns to me, his lips peeled back in anger, his thoughts spooling through my mind in a rush along with his words. *'I will not be a sacrifice for your greed.'* "Your greed for power has led us to war." *'You need to fix the mess YOU made.'* "You went too far, and the magic you once wielded to protect us has driven you to abandon us." He boldly holds my gaze, knowing damn well that I've imprisoned and killed people for lesser acts of disrespect. "If you can't lead, if you *won't* lead, someone else will. Someone else has to."

Luc shifts and opens his mouth, but I hold up a hand. "The magic has been sorted."

Casin raises an eyebrow with a smirk, his thoughts doubtful. *'Just like that? Sorted? So, what's he been doing all this time?'*

Reaching for the magic of the Mind Stone, I ignore the nausea as I shove the sensation of blades slicing through Casin's temples. He grunts in pain, pressing his hands to his head, doubling over as I direct my thoughts to scream through his mind.

'What have I been doing? I've been fighting against betrayal at every turn!' I do my best to ignore Luc's small hiss of guilt as I continue my assault on Casin. *'I've been holding back Adastra!'*

Casin's thoughts leak through his pain. *No, the magic has consumed our king, and we, his people, are paying the price.*

I round the table, the sound of my boots striking stone is loud. My fingers pinch Casin's chin, lifting his gaze to meet mine. Pain flares through his eyes, and I grin as I lean closer to him, shoving my thoughts into his mind once again. *'We are all paying the price as long as Adastra's secrets remain hidden.'* My grip tightens even more, the skin of his face turning red under my fingers. I speak aloud as my voice rings in his mind. "Do you know who Adastra is yet?"

Casin remains silent, his earlier rage tempered by the pain I'm unleashing on him.

"Do you know *where* Adastra is?"

No answer.

"Do you know for certain if he does indeed have natural magic as his followers claim?"

His teeth grind together, his jaw working under my bruising grip.

"No?" I lean closer, spit flicking against his face with my next words. "Then what have *you* been doing?"

Casin drops to one knee, and I release him from my grip and my magic. I barely keep myself from rubbing the bridge of my nose as the pain of the power presses against the inside of my skull. But this magic, the power of the Mind Stone, is familiar, welcome even. I can deal with the pain now that Luc has the Heart Stone.

Wood scrapes against stone, and I turn my head. Luc has practically fallen into a chair, his broad hand rubbing his chest.

Shit. This is too much for him. Guilt floods my heart before I can rein in the emotions. Luc's eyes snap to mine. His lips press into a tight line, and he shakes his head, saying nothing.

But I hear him.

Casin's pain ... Rydel's emotions ... I'm going to throw up.

But he doesn't. He swallows a few times, breathing in through his nose and out of his mouth. Standing upright, I return to my original place at the table, palming my dagger. Casin is once again on his feet, but his eyes are downcast. His shoulders are relaxed, and his head is bowed in submission, but anger still tinges his thoughts.

I ask him, "The southern gate?"

Casin nods. "Yes, your Majesty. It's under attack." His head remains bowed, but his voice punctuates with his impatience and frustration. "As. We. Speak."

I ignore his insolent tone, calmly asking, "And the eastern gate?"

Casein sighs, lowering his voice. "There are rebels gathered at the eastern gate, but they have not attacked ... yet."

I turn to face Luc, but before I can tell him to stay here, he holds up a hand. "I'm coming."

I know there will be no swaying him. I could force him, but I won't. Never again. So I face Casin. "Go. We'll be right there."

Casin only hesitates a moment before turning on his heel and storming out. Luc clicks his tongue. "It seems you've dug quite the hole for yourself."

My shoulders tense with anger. I'm aware of the clusterfuck that my actions have caused. I don't regret killing the Queen of Trislen. I'd do it again. She tried to kill Luc, and well ... It's the mess with Adastra that I've messed up. And Luc. I handled him all wrong.

I spin on him, but a small smile turns up the corner of his mouth, and my anger bleeds away, replaced with a fierce yearning. Luc rubs his chest with a wince, bringing a frown to my face.

"I'm sorry, Lucaryn. I'll work on keeping my emotions under better control."

He shakes his head, his dark curls floating around his face, but his broad hand still presses to his chest. "We should get going."

I glance around, heading to the ice room. The door hisses open, freezing fog rolling out at my feet. Inside the room, frost crawls up the walls, and a chill shivers down my

27

spine as I quickly go through the various items ... cheeses, meats, milks ... until I find the pot I'm looking for. Lifting the lid, I take a sniff, catching the earthy smell of vegetable broth. The cold pot tingles and burns slightly against my skin as I lift it from its shelf, kicking the door shut behind me.

Luc's voice follows me as I cross the kitchen, setting the pot on the counter. "We don't have time, Ry."

I pause, mug lifted, before I dip it into the pot. That was the first time he's called me Ry since I woke him. "Time enough." I hold out the mug, and Luc wraps his fingers around it, purposely avoiding touching me as I hand it over. "It's cold but you need the nutrients."

Luc looks me up and down with a smirk. "So do you."

I wave him off, heading out of the kitchen. "I'm fine. I'll eat later."

Luc's footfalls follow me. "You'll forget."

"Not with you nagging me."

He chuckles, and my heart constricts. I'm sure he feels my pang of regret, but I ignore the awkwardness between us and keep going. Our footfalls and the occasional sipping sound of Luc drinking the broth are the only noises accompanying us through my vast castle. *Our* vast castle. Gods, I hope I haven't ruined everything beyond repair.

"Rydel ..."

When he doesn't continue, I pause, stopping in the hall that leads to the main doors. Turning, I face him. Even tired and thin, he's beautiful. His brown skin holds a warmth that contrasts stunningly with his bright blue eyes. He rubs his chest with a sad smile, and I take a step back, even knowing the small distance won't help.

I cringe. "Sorry."

He smirks. "You've gotten much better at apologizing."

I shrug, not echoing his small grin. "I've made a lot of mistakes."

"I ... I think you're doing the best you can." His thoughts reveal his reluctance to say those words, but I'm grateful he did.

I cross my arms. "No. I've been ... less than."

"It took you a week to come to me once you came home from ... Trislen?"

Taking another step back, this time in self-preservation, I bite my lower lip, nodding. "I thought I could take back the southern throne with the magics. But Adastra's troops held us at the border. Every move I made, he countered." My hand scrubs over my face, exhaustion pulling at my muscles like I'm wrapped in thick chains. "The magic was ... I couldn't use it. It just kept consuming me. There was an attack. It was chaos. So much death. So much pain." My eyes unfocus as I recall the agony of dozens of deaths screaming through the magic, slamming into me. "I was on the verge of unconsciousness. Carelle ordered Kahar to retreat." I smile thinking of the large black warhorse. But then I recall how Carelle stumbled as an arrow slammed into her back, her pain radiating through me.

Luc grinds his teeth, but remains silent, his mind focused on my story.

"When we finally made it back here, the magic ... the pain ... I was so tired, so sick."

"You sent everyone away."

I nod, moving down the hall once again. Luc keeps pace, though I know he's weak, tired, angry, and in pain. "I meant to release you that day ..."

Luc's hands clench. *'But you didn't.'*

"No. I didn't. I ..."

"Rydel. We can unpack this later. I need to focus if I'm going to be of any help at all."

I sigh. He's right, but leaving these issues hanging between us is like leaving a ball of lead to fester in my gut.

Our boots seem to tap unnaturally loud against the stone floor. There's only a slight change in temperature as we leave the frigid castle and step into the weak winter sunlight, making our way to the south gate. Snow squeaks under my boots. I lengthen my stride, and Luc ducks his head, trying to hide his smile as I add a little of my usual swagger to my steps.

How I've missed him. Even in my anger, even through the pain of his lies and betrayal, I loved Luc. I still do.

His thoughts trickle through my mind. *It seems he's quickly getting back to his old self. Taking the Stone was the right thing to do. I may get a sick pleasure in seeing him suffer, but it also tears at my heart. Why are things between us so ... complicated? I just want things to go back to how they were. But I want him to hurt. I want to hurt him. I want to chase his pain with pleasure ...*

I chuckle, and his shoulders hitch slightly. He must have forgotten that I can hear his thoughts. He spent so many years not having to worry about my power, but once he revealed his lies, my trust in him broke, and the magic pushed into Luc's mind. And now I can't stop the hum of his thoughts.

But I *want* to trust him. I want the peace that being around Luc always brought me. I feel like I've forgiven him, but his thoughts continue to buzz through me, mocking my poor choices. What will I have to do to let go and fully trust again? And more importantly, what can I do to gain his forgiveness?

The mental noise within my head gets louder when

several soldiers round a corner and approach. Men and women wearing the royal armor bearing the name, Wescaryn—my name, flank Lucaryn and me. Their weapons are drawn, determination hardening their tired faces. I try to push off their thoughts, but those closest to me push through.

'The King has finally come' ... 'He looks stronger' ... 'The captain is back' ... 'Captain Lucaryn looks awful' ... 'The King will sort this' ... 'These rebels are good as dead' ... 'Finally' ...

The south gate comes into view in the distance, and a grin breaks across my face. Finally, indeed. I'll clean up the mess here in Farden, then Luc and I will find a way to get to Adastra.

But first, it's time for some rebels to die.

4

LUCARYN

I'm hit with small waves of concern as the soldiers glance at me, but behind the concern is relief at Ry's and my presence. My spine stiffens, and I do my best to stand a little taller and lengthen my strides. I pull on the magic and push strength through myself and into my soldiers—men and women I've fought next to for the past ten years. A jolt of pride that's all my own bolsters me as I notice the soldiers gripping their weapons a little tighter, their chests expanding with the strength I've sent them. I'm doing it. I'm controlling the power and affecting the emotions of my soldiers. It hurts like a hot poker jammed between my ribs, but seeing the soldiers' exhaustion and uncertainty melt away makes me dizzy with anticipation.

So much power. So much potential. I could just as easily turn their confidence into fear or complacency or merriment or ... anything I want them to feel and experience.

Ry clears his throat, and I meet his gaze. His eyes are slightly pinched at the edges, and I shake my head. "Just clearing the cobwebs."

"Don't push."

"I'm fine. Just testing the waters before we get to the real fight."

Ry's jaw flexes as his apprehension barrels into me. His eyes dart to my chest, and when I look down, I notice I'm rubbing at the spot over my breastbone without even realizing it.

The sound of steel clashing snaps our attention forward, and we pick up the pace to a slow jog, the soldiers keeping easy pace with us. I'm amazed my legs are still holding, but I'm concentrating an embarrassing amount on the crunch of gravel under my boots, making sure I don't trip and fall on my face.

Just beyond the gate, about a dozen of our soldiers are fighting with a green and black clad group of rebels. Rydel growls, and the sound goes right to my cock. He shoots me a half smile as we burst through the gates, and I can't help but chuckle under my breath. I may be angry with him, but I also can't deny that this, with him, is exhilarating.

With practiced precision, our soldiers fan around Rydel and me, surging forward to help the fight. I stop, struggling against the urge to double over and press my hands to my knees to catch my breath. Instead, I straighten my shoulders and take a deep breath. The cold that's seeping through my boots is barely noticeable as I take a handful of moments to pick through the emotions flooding my body. Anger tightens my fists, and I have to wiggle my jaw to unclench my teeth. Fear sends a sheen of sweat across my skin. Pain pulses across my nerve endings. But none of these emotions are mine, and I force them to the background until I'm left with a low churning sensation in my gut.

Cracking my neck, I focus on the rebels. A few of them have noticed Rydel, and I smirk at their fear. Good. I grab their fear and ramp it up. The fear swirls like a dark pit of snakes within my chest. It morphs into terror—the kind of terror that ices your blood, stalls your breath, and releases your bowels. I take that terror and shove it at the rebels. Several stumble. A few drop their weapons, but most simply freeze, rooted in place, urine staining their pants.

I smile, and it feels like I'm on the edge of madness. I wonder if I look as crazed as I feel.

An eerie quiet presses against my ears, broken only by the sounds of the soldiers' panting breaths fogging in front of their mouths. Rydel holds up a hand, and our soldiers stand at the ready, weapons raised. Sure, they could easily cut the rebels down while they're immobile under my magic, but Rydel likes to show off.

He's a few paces in front of me, and as I continue to pump fear into the rebels, I do my best to ignore the pounding at the edges of my skull. I don't need to see Ry's face to know he is aiming his terrifying grin at the rebels. I feel his glee. There's exhaustion underneath, but his adrenaline is overriding it at the moment, and it's giving me a boost of energy as well.

His voice rings out in the silence. "I am King Rydel Wescaryn. You are enemies of the crown. This ends here!"

The rebels' fear explodes, even overwhelming the magic I'm pushing into them, so I pull back. Rydel stretches his raised hand forward, adding theatrics to what he's about to do. A smile lifts my lips as screams fill the air. A handful of rebels turn to run.

I laugh. "Oh no you don't." I slam defeat into their

hearts, rubbing at my chest as they stumble to a standstill, their heads hanging as their will to go on dies at my command. I wonder if I can convince their hearts to stop beating?

I'm concentrating so hard, I don't notice the world is tilting until a soldier to my right jumps to my side, grabbing my arm. "Captain?"

Righting myself, I swallow hard around the nausea that threatens to bring the broth and bread up my burning throat. I shrug out of the woman's hold, maintaining eye contact with the rebels I'm holding with my magic. "I'm fine."

Rebels at the front of the group grab their heads, their screams getting louder. One man drops to his knees, followed by another, and another, until they are all either on their hands and knees or curled up on the ground. Rydel's arm is still raised, but I catch the slight tremor in his hand. The screams slowly die off, fading to moans and mumbles of pain before Ry drops his hand and every rebel goes silent. As their minds dim under Rydel's magic, their emotions fade, and the pain in my chest lessens.

Ry jerks his chin toward the downed rebels. "Check them."

As our soldiers stride forward, the only sounds are of gravel and snow crunching under boots, fabric sliding over skin as they kneel, checking pulses, and the occasional slide of steel between ribs to finish off those rebels still breathing.

Rydel turns. Pain clouds his eyes. His exhaustion weighs me down. His green eyes meet mine before they travel down my body and back up again. I catch his concern before it dissolves into satisfaction that I'm still standing and unharmed—physically at least. He gives me a quick nod before striding my way. I turn, keeping pace, our soldiers trailing behind us as we head back toward the castle.

Rydel speaks to Casin. "Call the heads of each unit to the war room."

"And the rebels gathered at the eastern gate?"

"You said they haven't engaged yet." It wasn't a question, but Casin nods anyway. "Then we will deal with them after I speak with my unit leaders."

Casin peels away, yelling over his shoulder. "Soldiers, return to the barracks. See to the wounded. Tell Aoyin the King requires her presence at the War Room."

Rydel and I climb the steps to the castle as the soldiers veer down the path toward the barracks, the press of their emotions dissipating like mist under the morning sun. I sigh at the absence of other's feelings, leaving only Ry's presence, which is barely a brush of determination as he strides through the castle.

The shadows of the narrow stone hall leading to the War Room close in around us, and he pauses, turning to me. Before either of us has a chance to say anything, the weight of feelings and emotions not my own presses into my chest, making it hard to breathe. A second later, Casin comes around the corner, four soldiers following closely. Rydel and I turn, leading the way down the hall, pushing into the war room where we all spread out around the large, rectangular marble table in the center of the room.

One soldier strikes a flint, lighting a torch before taking it around the room, setting each torch ablaze. Once he joins us at the table, I look around. Two of the four unit leaders are new, and I wonder just how severely Adastra's rebels have culled our ranks.

Planting his hands on the cool grey marble of the table,

Rydel meets each person's eyes before landing on Casin. "Okay, report."

He mimics Ry's stance, leaning on the table. "In short, we've lost Trislen." We knew this, but my lips pull down into a frown, bracing for more bad news. Casin continues, "What's left of the ranks you took to the south retreated on your orders and returned here, your Majesty. We lost maybe thirty percent of that contingent."

"Was our army pursued?"

"Only a few miles into Adren, then Adastra's army fell back."

I lean forward. "Did Carelle make it?"

Rydel flinches, his guilt slamming into me, dragging a quiet grunt from my lips. From his story, it sounded like Carelle saved his life in Trislen. His guilt turns to shame, probably at not thinking to ask after Carelle himself. But his face remains impassive, hiding his emotions from the others in the room. I barely hold back a smirk. It wouldn't do to have your soldiers think you actually cared.

Casin doesn't notice Rydel's flinch, or if he does, he ignores it. "Yes. Carelle made it back, though her wound was infected, and she's been fighting a fever for a week. The healer is optimistic, but it's concerning that her fever hasn't broken yet."

Ry nods. "Any word on Runic?"

Casin's face falls, shaking his head. His sorrow and frustration tears at my heart, and I take a deep breath, asking, "What happened?"

Casin clears his throat, but Ry holds up a hand. "When Adastra invaded Trislen, he took Runic hostage as well as a small contingent of our soldiers that remained loyal to me. Most of the soldiers turned to serve Adastra. Unsurprisingly."

I nod, absorbing the information with practiced stoicism, easily falling back into my role as captain of Rydel's army. Of course most of the southern army changed allegiances. They did so for Rydel. And now that there's a new power in the south, they'll do what they must to live and earn coin.

I ask, "How many of ours are being held?"

Rydel looks at Casin, who says, "Twenty-three. But there has been no word from our remaining spies on whether the prisoners are all still alive or not."

Ry crosses his arms over his chest. "How many of our spies are left in Trislen?"

"Two."

My eyebrows shoot up my forehead, and Ry sucks in a sharp breath. Out of the eight spies we had planted in the south, only two remain? Casin nods at our expressions. "Three heads were dropped on the castle steps two weeks ago. Three days later, another head was left impaled on the southern gate, and two days ago two more heads were left on display in the city square."

Fuck. Fuck Adastra. Fuck this war. Rydel will choke him on his worst fears. I'm going to drown him in sorrow and depression until all he knows is pain and suffering. Then Ry and I will bathe in Adastra's blood and leave his broken body staked to the gates of the southern palace he wanted so badly.

Rydel presses his hand against the table's surface. "Any word from Mica?"

Casin shakes his head. "No word from the self-proclaimed Shadow Lord. I suspect his messages are being intercepted ... if he's sending messages at all."

Rydel's impatience rolls through me while Casin continues his report. "Adastra's fighters have wiped out our villages closest to our border with Adren"—he looks to Rydel—"as I'm sure you saw. They struck in the night, burning and killing everything and everyone before retreating like cowards. By the time we sent reinforcements to the smaller villages and towns, we'd already lost six entire villages along the border. There are many rebels already here in Farden, and the numbers seem to grow daily. It's hard to get exact numbers, but they are enough to have almost overrun the city. We have managed to hold them back from the castle, but they stormed the barracks last night. We lost twenty soldiers in that battle before we were able to push them back through the gates."

My fingers dig into the table, my knuckles turning white as the unit leaders' anger and mourning crash into me. I crack my neck. "Are the attacks well coordinated?"

"Up until last night, they operated in small chaotic groups, striking quickly with more fervor than actual skill before dispersing seemingly at random, never striking the same location twice. This attack on the southern gate was the largest scale attack so far, but I'm concerned they're building up to a similar attack on the eastern gate."

Casin's concern becomes my own. We need to crush this. I nod. "So, the rebels are growing more bold."

The head of the Annarr unit rubs a hand over the back of his neck. "Rightfully so. They've been winning."

Rydel slaps the table, startling everyone in the room, and his smile makes everyone uneasy. I keep my palms pressed to the table to keep from rubbing my chest. I don't mean to, but I grunt at the push of emotions battling inside me, and Rydel glances at me. I shake my head, trying to keep his concern from adding to the pile. I purposefully aim my thoughts at him. *'I'm fine.'*

Why do I keep saying that? I'm not. Bile burns in my

throat. There's a cold sweat slowly dampening my shirt under the warmth of the cloak, and my body feels stretched tight, like there's not enough room for all the emotions I'm being forced to feel. I'm afraid my skin might split at any second.

Ry turns back to the discussion at hand.

"Good. Confidence breeds hope." He licks his lips, his excitement trembling down my spine. His grin grows, and a small smile lifts my lips. There's the old Rydel, reveling in the pleasure of pain. He grabs his dagger, absently twirling it around in his left hand. "I'm going to dash their hope into the pain and death they deserve."

Casin raises an eyebrow. "Are you ... strong enough?" Ry presses his lips together, and Casin stiffens in fear of the magic before he quickly bows his head. "Your Majesty, you have the potential to be our greatest weapon. We lose you" —He waves a hand around the room in a vague gesture— "we very well may lose everything."

Rydel rolls his shoulder, his dagger stilling for a moment before it picks up its twirling motion again. "What are our current numbers?"

A female soldier steps closer to the table, introducing herself. "Aoyin, your Majesty. Head of the Prioi unit. In total, we have lost thirty-five percent of our ranks, and ... morale ... well ..." Her fear is like sour milk on my tongue. How the fuck did this timid woman end up the head of the Prioi?

She glances at me, and I realize I must have vocalized the angry growl that was building in my chest, but she presses on through her fear. "Morale is not great. But I'm sure a show of ... strength from their King will ... raise their spirits."

Her stilted, halting way of speaking grates on my nerves, and Rydel's annoyance with her adds to mine. But he tilts his head with a mischievous smile. "Hmm. A show of strength. Yes."

Pressing to my feet, I move to stand to his right, unable to stop the slight trembling in my hands. I'm so tired. I know I should be hungry, but I'm not, and I'm unsure if that is good or very, very bad.

Rydel looks around the table. "I have given the Heart Stone to the captain." The soldiers' shock spears through me, and I can't keep my groan from escaping as Ry continues, "Information I'd like to keep quiet from our enemies as long as possible."

Slow nods bob around the table before I lean forward, pressing a hand to the marble surface. I take a moment to let the smooth table cool my heated skin. My breath catches as sharp heartache punches into me. Rydel's guilt is going to kill me. We need to talk. We need to fix this or I'm not going to survive him.

The pain lessens as Ry takes a step away from me. It's not his physical distance that helps, it's his sheer strength of will to barricade his feelings inside himself. I take a deep breath before pushing off the table, standing tall. "What's the plan, your Majesty?"

His anticipation is infectious, and I'm smiling before he says, "I'm going to set their minds on fire. All of them."

I nod, knowing well what he's capable of. But I have power as well. I don't have to hide the magic from Rydel anymore. He knows all of me now. Shivering with anticipation and more than a bit of exhaustion, I smirk. "I'll hold them down." I tap my chest. "The Heart Stone will lull them into complacency. I'll have them as calm as baby lambs, and you can"—I wave a hand—"do what you do."

He opens his mouth to protest, but the look I shoot him

snaps his mouth closed. There will be no swaying me from this.

Rydel turns to Casin. "Let our wounded and exhausted soldiers rest. Move them into the castle if you feel the barracks are not secure enough. Assemble a contingent of able-bodied soldiers, as many as can be spared, and split them in three. One to guard the wounded, one to meet us at the East gate, and one to make sure the South Gate remains secure."

Rydel and I lay out our plans before we all exit the war room, the soldiers peeling away to carry out their orders, leaving Ry and me alone once again. We stride side-by-side toward our wing, pausing in silence before my door. My hand hovers over the handle, and Ry stiffens, muttering, "If it's too painful to be this close to me, you can set up a room anywhere else in the castle you want."

I shake my head. "It's not that." Turning to face him, his green eyes fill with worry. "*Are* you strong enough, Ry? I'll do what I can, but I don't know my limits yet. If we misstep here, this could be the end."

He smiles. "I know I'm rash and compulsive, but I *do* know my limits, and while I'm tired and hungry, I can do this." He reaches up, his desire to touch me tingling across my skin. His hand stalls in mid-air, and after a moment, I step away from him.

My anger at him flares again, like molten rock flowing through my veins. But under that is despair. I suspect in his current state, this will be too much for Rydel ... for us. Even if we win this fight here in the capital, going up against Adastra is ...

We're not going to survive this. But I guess if we're going to go out, this will be a—

With a loud sigh, Ry drops his hand to his side. "Stop, Luc."

Shit. I have to try harder to keep my rambling thoughts to myself.

He stares at me for a second, his teeth worrying at his bottom lip, revealing the uncertainty that he would only show me. Then his resolve blooms through me, and he closes the small distance between us, bracing his hands on my shoulders.

I try to shake him off, not wanting his touch—for many reasons, not all of them to do with my anger. He holds me tight, and when I still, he nods.

"I *will* do this. *We* will do this ... together. I have a lot to atone for, but first, I need to make sure all we have worked for does not crumble to the likes of Adastra, or to anyone else, for that matter." He holds my gaze, like he's willing me to read between his next words. "I will not lose what is mine."

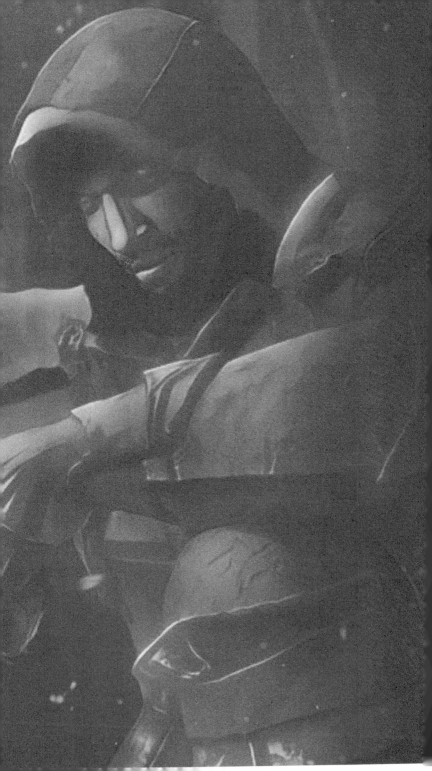

5

LUCARYN

I *was* Rydel's, and he was mine for a short time. That first time, him kneeling before me, his lips wrapped around my cock, it was bliss. Am I still his? I want to be, but every time I think about releasing my rage, it sinks its claws into me, dredging up what Ry did to me, how he so easily tossed me aside.

Rydel glances at me from the hall but says nothing even though I know he can hear my thoughts.

After grabbing a few weapons from my room and changing my boots for ones better equipped for the snow-covered grounds, I meet Rydel back outside my door, and together we make our way through the castle—our home for the past ten years. It's still hard to believe. I won't let Adastra, or anyone else, take what we've built.

I glance up at the hazy sun as we step outside, heading toward the eastern gate. Despite the cold, I'm hot, too hot. I fling one side of the wool cloak over my shoulder, sighing as the crisp air hits my skin. Rydel's distress slams into me, and I grunt. He reaches toward me, stopping short of touching my arm before dropping his hand. "I—"

My voice comes out on a sharp growl. "I'm fine."

Damn it. I have to stop saying that.

I keep my eyes on my feet, partly to keep from stumbling, but mostly to keep from looking at him. He inhales, and I know he's about to say something because I feel his guilt and sadness, but I hold up a hand. "Don't."

His sorrow deepens, and spots dance before my vision as my throat closes with the threat of tears born from Rydel's emotions. I swallow around the lump in my throat, satisfaction coursing through me at his despair. A whimper actually passes through his lips, and when I glance over, tears glitter in his eyes. One tumbles down his cheek.

Shit. I pull back on the magic, releasing Ry from the sorrow I forced on him. I hadn't realized I was using my power on him. He quickly wipes the tear from his face, continuing on without a word.

The eastern gate comes into view, and Casin jogs over, saluting.

Rydel nods, and Casin turns, keeping pace with us as we pass through the gate. "The rebels still haven't engaged, your Majesty, but their numbers have grown. Last count there were over forty."

The blood drains from my face. I don't know that I can control that many with my magic.

Ry turns to me, placing his warm hand on my shoulder. I flinch as our eyes meet, and for a moment, it's just the two of us. I can't seem to catch my breath. He nods at me, and I'm hit with his determination and under that ... love. It's so painful, my legs almost give out, but I lock my knees. His voice is soft, meant only for me. "Do what you can. I've got the rest."

Before I can respond, he turns, striding away from the gate, toward the city's edge where black and green clad rebels mill about. They snap to attention when a few notice our group, and they scurry around like ants in a panic. Rydel's name floats across the clearing as the rebels recognize him, and their alarm and fear shoots higher. The tremor in my arms and legs spreads to my entire body, and little sparkling black dots once again swim at the edges of my vision.

Shaking my head, I will myself to keep going. Our people need me. And, reluctantly, I admit a small part of me is doing this for Ry. He needs me too.

Damn it.

A hit of smug confidence rolls though my chest, and I can't keep my lips from pulling into a smile even though the emotion isn't mine—it belongs to a lone man who breaks from the rebel group, walking calmly toward us. He's too sure of himself, and I open my mouth to warm Rydel, but I snap my lips closed. He knows. Better than anyone, Ry knows what this man is thinking, what his intentions are, and most importantly, what deepest fears haunt his dreams.

As the man, obviously the leader of this group, continues forward, he spreads his arms, a sword glinting in his right hand. I catch Ry's smile. This time, my grin is my own, and I let my chuckle slide from my lips.

The rebel practically saunters toward us, calling out, "Rydel Wescaryn." I scowl at his informal greeting. I want to rip his tongue from his mouth and watch him choke on his blood. But Ry just laughs. The rebel doesn't pause, his confidence unwavering. "The false king. How far you have fallen." The man drops his arms at his sides, tilting his head.

"You look tired, Rydel. Adastra wants to string you out until there's nothing left of your black soul before he kills you."

Ry palms his dagger, spinning his favorite blade in his left hand, angling his head to the side. The leader's smirk falters, and Rydel tsks. "You haven't actually met the famous Adastra."

The man's eyes widen, and his hand clutches his sword. Ah. I smirk. There's the fear.

The leader's voice is strong despite the trembling in his heart. "No, but our orders were clear. Hit the villages, towns, and cities of Lieren hard. Anyone who stands with you is against Adastra ... is against our goddess, Circeon. She has blessed Adastra and will bring natural magic back to us once *your kind* are purged from the land."

The other rebels stay back, their gazes flicking between Rydel and their leader.

Rydel shakes his head. "Bold claims for someone who has never even seen their supposed ruler." Rydel tilts his head, and the leader's face pales as Ry pushes more of his magic into his mind. "I see you were also ordered not to engage with me. I am to be left for Adastra."

Sweat beads along the leader's forehead as Rydel's magic courses through him, picking out his memories and thoughts. The leader's confidence waivers, but his loyalty to Adastra bolsters him. The man shrugs, doing his best to look unaffected. "I saw an opportunity. The two Stones are draining you."

Good. They don't know Rydel and I are now sharing the magic.

The leader goes on, his voice strong with a mocking lilt. "Your greed has rendered your all-mighty magic ineffectual. You took what did not belong to you, and—"

He stumbles back, dropping his weapon to grip the hilt

of Rydel's dagger that's lodged deep in his chest. I grin. Ry loves interrupting a monologue. I didn't even see Rydel move, and I doubt the man did either if his stunned expression is anything to go by.

Rydel laughs. "How's that for ineffectual?"

The rebels behind the leader surge forward, weapons drawn. With a grunt of building agony, I push my magic at them. Agony tears through me as I fight to change their very will. Their rushing steps slow, then stop all together as they lower their weapons. I grit my teeth, letting the pain of the magic wash over me as the rebels bow to Rydel. They are my puppets. The torment of power pulsing from me is inconsequential as I realize the magic could trip them of everything ... their emotions, their hopes, their dreams. I could hollow them out.

This is power.

The rebel leader gasps open mouthed at his group, his voice strained as he tries and fails to pull Ry's dagger from his chest. "Fools! Yo ... you have trained for this. Resist th ... the magic. This false king is not st ... strong enough to hold you. Your loyalty is to Adastra!"

Rydel laughs louder, the sound cruel as he slowly strides forward. As one, the group of rebels under my magic turn toward the leader, raising their weapons, pointing them at him. Rydel looks at me over his shoulder, his grin falling, concerned I'm pushing too hard. I am, but I don't care. These people came into our kingdom leaving death and chaos in their wake. Their lives are mine to do with as I please.

Ry nods at me with a small smirk, his excitement now pulsing off him in crashing waves as he turns back to the group. His emotions batter at me like a hailstorm, threatening to take me down. His voice is like an anvil strike, not only in the space around us, but in the rebels' minds as well. All of them grab their heads as Rydel speaks. "I have been underestimated my entire life. You are just more unfortunate souls added to that list. Your Queen was on that list. Adastra is on that list. There is no limit to what I'll do to hold what is mine. This world is mine to take. I won't be stopped!"

Rydel steps boot-to-boot with the rebel leader whose eyes are wide, blood dripping from around the embedded dagger, pooling between his fingers, trailing down his shirt. The man fumbles for a short sword strapped to his hip, but Rydel grips his dagger, twisting it in the man's chest, pulling a scream from his bloody lips.

I double over, planting a hand on my knee. It's too much. I'm losing control. Rydel's pleasure born from the thrill of wielding his magic causes my cock to twitch. My body throbs with pain to the beat of my heart as Ry's pain joins mine. I gasp at the rebel leader's shock, and tears well in my eyes at his despair. I groan with his agony, and my heart races with his desperation to live.

All the rebels clutch their heads, and I follow suit as their suffering slams into me. I need to kill them all. Right now. I need to cut off this flood of emotions.

A whisper of calm flutters through my chest, and Ry's voice floats across my mind. 'Done, my friend.'

In one swift move, Rydel rips the blade from the leader's chest and slices it across his throat, saying, "See you in hell." The rebel falls, clutching his neck, blood soaking him, his eyes wide with pain and panic. His death is painful. His body goes cold, pinpricks stabbing his skin. I feel it all.

And then it's compounded forty times over as the rebels scream, their minds being torn apart by Rydel's magic. His power sends the message that the electrical pulses in their minds are fading. Confusion washes over me as some of the rebels forget why they're here. Some open and close their mouths, having forgotten how to speak. Others look around, blinking blankly as they forget who they are. It's beautiful to watch Rydel work. It's excruciating.

I'm hit with pulse after pulse of agony, panic, terror, and as the rebels forget how to breathe, their deaths slide through my magic, and the world around me spins. The pain in my knee is the only indication that I've fallen, as my vision blurs. I wish I could block the emotions as easily as I can project them, but the magic is cruel. It demands a price. A price I will pay ... for the power ... for Rydel.

Damn it.

Ry's voice sounds far away. "Keep one alive."

I'm vaguely aware of our soldiers working their way through the fallen rebels, and I press a hand to the snowy ground. Staring at my fingers buried in the snow, I wonder why it doesn't feel cold. I try to push myself back to standing, but the world flips, and the next thing I know I'm on my side, the snow seeping through my pants and wool cloak.

I've done all I can. The weeks I spent starving and locked in my mind are still affecting my body. That, combined with the magic pulsing through me weighs me down, making my limbs impossible to move. My eyes close, and my heart skips at Ry's sharp, fearful inhale. His hand presses to my cheek, his touch cool and so familiar. I want to pull away, to hold onto my anger, but Ry is home to me, and I allow myself to take his comfort as his voice drifts down to me. "I'm sorry, Luc. You did well. Rest."

His touch leaves me, and he shouts something, but I'm falling into the shadowy darkness of unconsciousness.

6

RYDEL

It's been a little over two weeks since we took care of the rebels gathered at our gates. My strength has returned, and I'm beginning to fill out my clothes again thanks to Asha. I adjust my cloak, smiling as the weight of wrapped apple tarts thuds against my side. The royal cook is always slipping her famous treats into my pockets, trying to fatten me up.

I love that woman.

My gloved hands grip the edges of my cloak, pulling it tighter against the sleet falling from the gray sky, the icy pellets stinging against my exposed skin. To my right, Casin shakes back his short hair before brushing his fingers through the blond strands, his marriage tattoos on proud display across the back of his hand, disappearing under the sleeve of his jacket.

A small pang of jealousy sours my stomach as I picture

Lucaryn and me with matching scrolling tattoos on our hands. My teeth grind together in an attempt to expel that thought.

Luc is recovering quickly. After he passed out at the eastern gate, he remained unconscious for a full day before waking with a grimace, his stomach growling across the silence in his room. He's been able to eat more and more each day and has added light training with the Sagas to his daily routine—when we're not hunting rebels in our city as we're doing today.

Casin and I pause in the shadow of a building, four soldiers crowding the wall behind us. With a deep breath, I push the magic of the Mind Stone outward, searching for the thoughts of any rebels in the area. Casin grips his sword, keeping his gaze on his boots. The soldiers behind me hold themselves still, their quiet breaths the only sound in this dark corner of the street, their thoughts a low hum of noise as I focus beyond.

'It's much colder today. The height of winter is almost here. My walkway back home is going to be covered in ice' ... *'This weather is miserable. I should have moved to the south when I had the chance'* ... *'I'm hungry'* ... *'I'm cold'* ... *'I need to replace my shoes, but that hole in my roof needs fixing first'* ... *'Does he really like me'* ...

I take each thought, throwing them aside as they come. And then I hear it.

'Patrols are still out. I need to get to the Old Stan–the place, the place, right foot, left foot, right foot. This sleet is awful. What if the King finds us? So many dead. I want to go home. I'm doing this for my home, for Adastra. Natural magic will return. The goddess Circeon will bless us. Right foot, left foot, right ...'

Casin chuckles, and I bring my awareness back to the

shadowy street. Glancing at the tall beast of a man next to me, he grins, nodding at my left hand. "You found them."

At some point while using my magic, I must have grabbed my dagger, the blade now playing through my fingers. I nod at Casin before jerking my head over my shoulder. "The Old Standard."

Our group backs up, making our way back the way we came. The streets get narrower the farther south-west we move through the city, and I hug the frozen walls of the houses and stores we pass, shuffling my boots over the ice-covered cobblestones. The buildings are so close now, they block the relentless prick of sleet, but the freezing wind still blasts down the narrow passages.

"Shit!" One of the soldiers behind me bites back the curse as his boots slide and scrape on the ice. I glance back just as his shoulder slams against a wall, and the soldier to his left grabs his arm to keep him from falling on his ass. Pressing his hand to the building, the man rights himself, lips pressed in a tight line, his thoughts growing louder with his embarrassment.

'Of course, I would be the one to nearly fall in front of the king. Great. Just great.'

I keep moving, ignoring the flustered soldier. Anticipation tickles down my arms, my dagger still playing in my left hand as the Old Standard Pub comes into view. Icicles cling to the bottom of the wood sign, and though it's just past midday, the flicker of torches is visible through the grimy windows.

We pause in the shadows of another dark street corner with a decent view of the pub. Casin notices the direction of my stare and nudges my boot with his. When I glance at him, he raises an eyebrow, his thoughts sharpening in my mind.

'Go in now, or wait?'

Halting the movement of my spinning blade, I grip the soft leather hilt tightly. I don't need the blade to subdue or kill these rebels, but my trusty blade calms me.

I whisper, "Wait."

The pub's door opens with a screech of sticky hinges, and a woman's loud bark of laughter proceeds her as she stumbles outside, her feet skidding. Her arms windmill, her eyes wide, as she tries to keep from falling, and a chuckle floats out of the pub before another woman rushes out, grabbing the flailing woman around the waist, holding her up. They smile at each other, giggling as their lips press together. Their thoughts shove into me, and my cock stands to attention.

'What would she do if I took her to that dark alley and shoved my hand down her pants?' ... *'I want her so much* ... *'Her lips are so soft'* ... *'gods, I'm wet'* ... *'fuck me'* ... *'take me'* ...

They finally break their kiss and thankfully move away from the dark street where we are hiding, arms wrapped around each other as they walk away, taking their delicious thoughts with them.

Casin leans over. "I can only imagine their thoughts ..."

I blow out a breath on a smile, adjusting myself. "Yeah."

Casin chuckles, and the soldiers behind us snort and chuckle with him.

I sheath my dagger, rolling my shoulders, keeping my voice low. "Okay. We give them enough time to arrive. I didn't get how many are supposed to be here, but the rebel's thoughts made it sound like at least a small group is meeting here."

I shrug my cloak behind my shoulders, exposing my fur-lined leather vest with my broken crown emblem branded into the right breast. The soldiers do the same as I turn to them. "When it's time, you four go to the front. Two flank the door. Two move inside. Casin and I will enter through the back. Hopefully, the rebels will panic at seeing you four and attempt to rush out the back." I crack my neck side-to-side. "If they try to rush past you, or if they engage, just take them out. No prisoners."

Everyone nods before shifting to keep an eye on the pub. Casin slinks off, keeping to the shadows, his thoughts telling me he's going to keep an eye on the back door. The soldiers and I press a little deeper into the shadows, waiting.

I can't keep my thoughts from wandering to Luc. He's out on patrol with another small group of soldiers in a different part of the city. Has he had any luck in finding more rebels? Is the Heart Stone weighing on him? Is he okay? Will he ever forgive me? Do I deserve it? He's fine. I'm sure he's fine.

After a few minutes, a nervous staccato of thoughts dissolves my internal litany and brings a smile to my face.

'Left foot, right foot, pub, there's the pub. I haven't been followed. Stupid soldiers, stupid Rydel. How dare he. My queen. Adastra will avenge her, he will avenge us. Be careful. Right foot, left foot, right' …

I nod in the direction of the man walking slowly toward the pub. His shoulders are hunched, his hands shoved in his pockets, the tips of his shaggy brown hair frosted over. He glances side-to-side, eyes passing right over our hiding place before he grasps the door's handle and wrenches it open. Soft conversation and the click of plates and cups escapes into the street before the door closes with a thud behind the man.

After another minute, a woman comes from a side street, absently fiddling with something in the pocket of her coat, but her thoughts are nervous, and I nod toward her, the soldiers taking note.

A few minutes pass before a pair of men approach the pub from opposite directions, each making eye contact before reaching for the door handle. I nod at them as well. And not a full minute later, two more men head toward the pub, and just as one reaches for the door, a woman rounds the corner of the pub, and the man holds the door open for her. She smiles, giving him her thanks, but then she leans in, her smile falling as she whispers something. I may not be able to hear her words, but her thoughts are mine.

'I think we're being watched. Dark form behind the pub. Maybe I was imagining things.'

The three enter the pub, and I nod, stepping closer to my soldiers. "They are jumpy. That last woman might have seen Casin, but she's not sure. Expect violence once they spot you."

They all nod, their faces pressed into serious lines, their thoughts humming with anticipation. I feel that anticipation as well. It's coursing through my blood, and my erection from earlier has yet to abate. This is the fun part. The chase. The fear. The fighting. The hope. The defeat. The death.

We wait another handful of minutes, watching as a man and women enter, hand-in-hand, and I shake my head. Then a lone woman enters, and my nod confirms her as a rebel. Two more no's and a yes enter the now bustling pub. We stay in the shadows for another long moment before I nod at the soldiers. Turning, I angle down the side ally that will take me to the back door. My soldiers stride across the street toward the pub. As I round the corner, Casin moves out of the shadows, coming to my side.

"I think one of the women might have seen me."

I shrug. "She did, but she wasn't sure what she saw. However, they are on edge. Be ready."

Casin's hand wraps around the frozen over iron door handle, opening it slowly before peering inside. The noise of the kitchen clamors out of the open door, pots and pans clanking, steam billowing around Casin's boots. He enters on silent feet, and I follow. Casin presses a finger to his lips as several of the cooks and servers stop mid task, all eyes on us.

I curl my fingers into fists to keep from rubbing at the pain that's starting to pound in my temples, and I push my thoughts into the minds of the staff.

'Go about your work. We are not here for you. Stay out of our way.'

Another moment of silence passes before the kitchen slides back into chaotic movement, two servers grabbing plates as they rush out to the main room of the pub.

Casin stations himself behind the door leading out of the kitchen, his sword drawn.

We wait.

I know the moment our soldiers enter the pub. There's a sharp scraping of wood against wood as chairs are shoved back. Footfalls scatter in the room beyond, and someone calls out, "Henrik, don't!" At the same time, another, louder voice rings out. "You won't take us alive! For Adastra!" Several voices ring out, "For Trislen!"

The Stone grows hot under my skin, my shoulder blade feels like my skin is melting off my bones, but I welcome the pain. The pain means magic. The pain means power.

I push through the door, Casin on my heels. A woman slides across the floor, trying to stop her sprint for the back door. Her eyes go wide as she nearly skids right into my arms, but instead of grabbing her, I slam the magic into her mind, finding those bright lights of thoughts, of her consciousness, and I snuff them out. Her mind goes dark, and her body crumples to the floor in an awkward heap.

Someone screams, and the mental noise mixes with the panicked rush in the pub until my head feels scraped raw from the inside. But I face the room, a manic grin exposing my teeth, and the room goes quiet for a heartbeat.

I growl into the silence. "Adastra's fools. You can't hide from me."

A man runs for the front door, a short sword in his hand. He makes a clumsy swing at one of my soldiers but is quickly struck down, his neck sliced open to the bone.

The servers and a few patrons hug the walls, crouching low. The woman behind the bar ducks down, her thoughts nearly bringing a chuckle from my lips.

'Just duck and cover. The king will make short work of this. But damn, if I had known they were rebels, I would have kicked them out, or reported them, or something. I need the coin. Maybe the king and his soldiers will stay for a drink after ...'

Maybe we will.

I bite my tongue to keep from groaning in pain as I shove the magic into the rebels' minds. I tell their brains that their throats have closed. The clatter of a few weapons hitting the sticky wood floor rings out as the rebels gasp for breath. They claw at their throats, their eyes going wide as they try and fail to suck in air.

The mind tells the body what is happening and how to react, and their minds are telling their bodies they're suffocating.

One man collapses, his boots flailing and scraping, kicking over a chair. Two more fall. Then another, and another until over a dozen bodies are writhing on the floor, their lips turning blue, their necks scratched and bloody as they continue to claw at their own skin.

I hold the magic until the twitching stops, and every rebel's mind is silent and dark. Dead.

Reining in the magic, I take a deep breath, giving in for just a moment to rub at my temples before pressing my fingers between my eyes, trying to dispel some of the pain. What I wouldn't give for a small taste of street drug to dull the pain.

Dropping my hand, I step over a body and lean against the counter just as the woman behind the bar stands up slowly, eyeing the mess of the room before bowing her head to me.

"Your Majesty. I didn't—"

I hold up a hand, the silver coin between my fingers catching her attention. "I know you didn't know." I press the coin onto the bar and slide it across to her. "Drinks."

She pockets the silver with a smile and a nod before turning and reaching up to grab a couple of clean glasses, or what passes for clean anyway. I admire her ass and the sliver of pale skin that peeks out along the waistline of her skirt every time she reaches up for more cups.

I need a good fuck. I want Luc. Beatuis, I want Luc, but ... maybe I'll go visit Asha in the kitchens. I begin to stiffen at the thought, but at the same time, it feels wrong. Besides, last time I was with Asha, all I could think about was Luc. Shit. I think he's ruined me for anyone else.

Casin folds his forearms on the bar next to me, and I turn, pressing my back into the bar, surveying the room. Most of the patrons have left, but a few go back to their tables, trying to avoid looking at the dead rebels, but their eyes keep flicking to the bodies littering the floor.

My soldiers sit around one of the larger tables near the

front door, one propping his foot up in a vacant chair. They all relax around the table, but their eyes are still alert.

Glass slides over wood as the barkeep pushes my ale next to my elbow before crossing the room, dropping off several glasses at the soldier's table.

Still next to me, Casin raises his glass, taking a deep drink, his throat working with each swallow. Not for the first time, I admire him. He's strong, well built, and loyal. My eyes snag on his tattoos. And married. And not Lucaryn.

I grab my glass, the cold surface cooling my hand as I bring it to my lips. The alcohol burns down my throat, spreading warmth through my stomach.

Casin's glass dangles from his fingers as he swirls the ale. "Two solid weeks of hunting these rebels. You'd think they would have all run back to Trislen by now."

I take another drink. "I dug through the mind of the one we took captive yesterday. There aren't any reinforcements coming. At least, that is what she was told." The woman's mind had unfurled under my magic, and her utter defeat was like the sweetest dessert on my tongue. "She believed Adastra wants me to come to him."

Casin hums into his ale. "Adastra's magic, if it is indeed real, doesn't seem able to reach us here."

Indeed, when I was in Trislen, every move I tried to make to take back the capital was met by a counter move by Adastra's troops. Over and over, he thwarted my every move until I had to concede he very well might have the natural magic of visions and foresight. But like Casin said, his rebels aren't outmaneuvering me here, so we must be out of his reach. Adastra can't see what I'm up to way up here in the north. Which means that even though his 'magic' is natural born, there's limitations. Just like mine. Good.

The cool ale slides down my throat as I take another big

gulp. Grinning, I slam the empty glass on the bartop. "Get these bodies out of here. Burn them, then report back to the barracks."

The four soldiers hastily finish their drinks, one spilling a bit down his beard in his haste to gulp it down. They push away from the table, each grabbing a body and hoisting it over their shoulders before pressing out into the freezing street.

I turn to the woman behind the bar, sliding another silver coin across the surface. "For the trouble. My soldiers will have all the bodies removed shortly."

She nods, ready to give me her thanks, but I spin and quickly stride to the door, Casin on my heels. The sleet hits me in the face, and I once again pull my cloak around my shoulders, resisting the urge to bury my face in the warm folds to see if it still smells like Luc. I know it won't, but the urge is still there.

Casin and I make our way back toward the castle, walking the more open streets, this time staying away from the freezing shadows, trying to remain in the weak sunlight. The dark gray stone turrets of the castle come into view, and as we round another corner, a soldier spies us, and jogs over, saluting.

"Your Majesty." She looks at Casin, saluting. "Capt—sorry." She stumbles over her words, forgetting Casin is no longer acting captain now that Lucaryn is back. Casin waves her off, and she turns back to me. "Your Majesty. The—"

I hear her thoughts before she says them, and I hold up a hand, silencing her.

"When did he arrive?'

She snaps her mouth shut before swallowing. "A few hours ago."

I stride forward, just short of a jog. "Be specific."

65

"Just over two hours ago."

Casin's long strides keep pace, but the female soldier breaks into a jog to keep up. Casin's shoulders bunch up with tension as my pace picks up. "Who?"

The three of us turn a corner, and I force myself to slow down, changing my pace to a casual walk. The eastern gates come into view, and as we pass through, I glance at Casin. "Find the captain. Mica Kafir is here."

Time to see what the Shadow Lord knows.

7

LUCARYN

I'm tempted to roll up the sleeves of my dark shirt to stave off the heat radiating from my body. The air is cold, the five soldiers walking behind me huddle into their cloaks, but even without my cloak, I'm sweating.

I feel so much stronger, muscle definition once again filling out my clothes, and I don't tremble every time I stand up, but the strain of hunting down rebels has been taxing. Today, we tracked down two more rebel groups. I used the magic of the Heart Stone to lull them into a state of calm serenity while my soldiers apprehended them. We have twenty-seven new guests in the castle dungeons, though I'm sure Rydel will weed that number down once he interrogates them. These days, it seems Ry has no patience for keeping his prisoners in suspended torture like he used to enjoy. Once their usefulness has passed, Rydel kills them and moves on.

Our shift done for the day, the soldiers and I pass through the castle gates, and I roll my neck doing my best to release the pain and tension from the barrage of feelings I've dealt with all day. I'm slowly getting used to the power, but the magic still hurts. It will always hurt. Not only does it burn where the Stone is sewn into the flesh of my chest, but the magic slamming everyone's emotions and feelings into me feels like a hole growing deeper and deeper in my chest.

How did Rydel do this? How has he lived with this for ten years? It has to get better, right? It's going to get easier, or at the very least, I'm going to gain better control. I have to.

The long, low building of the barracks comes into view, snow capping the wide roof, and I spot Carelle leaning against the fence post of one of the training rings. Changing my direction to go speak with her, she scowls, knowing I'm going to ask her how she's doing after being bedridden for so long. I understand since I still cringe every time one of my soldiers looks at me with concern or worse, pity. But my name rings out behind me, saving Carelle from my questions.

Casin strides up to me. "Captain, the king requests your presence in the throne room." He pauses, waiting until he's by my side and we're both heading toward the castle. "Mica Kafir is here."

Casin's unease mixes with mine, and I fist my hands to keep from rubbing my chest. I haven't met the famed Shadow Lord of the south, but I don't trust him. Rydel seems to, though—to a point. Which is surprising, because Ry doesn't trust anyone, including me now.

Jealousy and longing spear through me before I reach for the anger. The anger feels good. It doesn't hurt or confuse or drag me into the depths of my sorrow. Rage is cleansing. It feels as if my blood is tingling. I can't feel the pain or sadness or ... anything. Just anger—it gives me purpose. It keeps me going.

Casin growls, and when I glance over, his hands are balled into tight fists, and his jaw flexes with his clenched teeth. Oops. I draw back on the magic. I didn't realize my anger was leaking out with the power.

Stepping into the castle, I give in and roll up my sleeves and undo the top two buttons of my shirt. Casin rolls his shoulders, shaking out his hands. His concern washes over me, but he keeps his eyes trained straight ahead.

Keeping my eyes focused ahead, I mumble, "I'm fine."

Gods. Damn. It. I have to stop saying that. I don't know why I feel the need to reassure everyone, but I find myself doing it over and over. Maybe if I say it enough times, it'll be true. Maybe, at some point, I actually will be fine.

The large wood doors of the throne room loom before us, and Casin presses his large hand against the carved surface, pushing one open, but remains outside. The door whispers shut behind me, and as I cross the room, I avoid looking at my king. Instead, I take the time to observe our guest.

Mica Kafir is on the shorter side. Under his black-on-black clothing, he's lean with cut muscle. His black skin melds with his clothing, and a tie holds back his shoulder-length locs. I slow my pace as I walk past him, meeting his light brown eyes with a stare of my own. He smiles and dips his head in a small bow. The magic of the Heart Stone slithers out of me reaching for him like a heated trail of invisible smoke. He is calm, confident, curious.

At my core, I know the magic would alert me to any nefarious emotions, but I can't help but think I'm missing something, so, I dig deeper.

Nothing.

I glance at Rydel as I climb the dais steps and barely contain the catch in my breath. I haven't seen much of him these past weeks, purposefully so, but he's already almost back to his old self. Broad chest and shoulder muscles nicely fill out his embroidered shirt. His chest harness is buckled in place, holding several sharp throwing knives, and his dagger remains sheathed on his left thigh, for now, and the sheath hugs the muscles of his leg. I swallow, recalling when he knelt on those powerful legs in my room, taking my cock into his mouth. Gods, he was glorious.

Rydel crosses his ankle over his knee, and I lift my attention to his face. A small smile lights his green eyes, and his amused and aroused emotions slam into me. Damn it. He caught me, again.

Fine. Your magic is invading my thoughts? My magic will amplify your feelings.

I slide my magic toward him. Ramping up his arousal, growing desire unfurls inside him with every push of my power. His smile falls, and his lashes flutter as he tries to keep from groaning. His hand grips his dagger so tightly, the leather hilt creaks. Narrowed eyes filled with anger turn on me, and with a little smile, I release the magic.

Rydel shifts, turning his attention back to Mica as I chuckle softly, taking up my position slightly behind Rydel and to his right. His voice is a little strained as he addresses me, but I doubt anyone would notice but me. "Thank you for joining us, captain. I was just welcoming the Shadow Lord to Farden."

Mica smiles, simple delight seemingly his only emotion. "Indeed. The north in winter is more beautiful than I imagined."

I frown at his words. Southerners rarely find the frigid, blustery winters of the north beautiful. I don't like this guy.

But Rydel chuckles. "Our winters are not for the faint of heart, but I'm glad you get to experience the majesty of the north."

Mica returns Rydel's smile, and Ry leans forward in his throne, propping his forearms on his knees. "I think we should retire to a room where we can talk in a little more privacy."

My brows want to climb my forehead at his suggestion. Rydel loves the intimidation of his cavernous throne room, so why is he being so casual with this man who we know so very little about?

Mica nods, bowing his head. "Whatever you wish, your Majesty."

Rydel slaps his thighs and stands, turning and striding past me. I follow, heading toward the door on our left. Mica draws up behind us, and we push into the small side room, leaving the throne room guards behind.

Mica closes the door with a quiet click, and the hair on the back of my neck rises. There's no reason for me to be so on edge, but tension itches down my spine. Rydel takes the seat at the head of the rectangular wood table, a fire crackling in the hearth behind him. A bead of sweat sticks my shirt to my back just looking at the flames, so I take the chair at the far end of the table. My chair scrapes loudly across the stone floor, and I sit ramrod straight in the too-small chair.

Mica takes a chair to my right, exactly halfway between Rydel and me. A ripple of boredom and curiosity thrums through me from the guards out in the throne room, but all I'm getting from the two occupants in this room is confidence and interest. I can't help but wonder what kind of thoughts Rydel is picking up from the mysterious Shadow Lord.

'Nothing of note, yet.' I meet Rydel's eyes. *'Don't think I'm going to forget about that little display back there.'* My cock goes hard. Let him try to punish me.

I feel the pain that spears through Rydel as he projects his thoughts into my mind, but there's not even a hint of discomfort on his face, even as he glances at my crotch. I feel his desire to smirk, but he just leans back, flicking his dagger into his left hand. The blade dances around his palm and between his fingers in the self-soothing habit he's had since he was a child. Inwardly, I smile as I remember the day Rydel swiped that dagger off a soldier, determined to sell it for food for us, but I insisted he keep it.

The blade stills, and his fingers tighten around the hilt as he catches the memory in my thoughts. This time, a small knowing smile lifts his lips, and longing that matches my own swells through my heart. The heat of the Heart Stone intensifies, and I can't seem to rip my eyes from his gaze. I can't tell whose desire I'm feeling, mine or his, or both.

Mica clears his throat, and I snap my eyes to my lap. Rydel doesn't move, though, as Mica says, "I feel like I missed something."

Rydel waves his dagger before sheathing it. "Nothing. Just the familiarity of old friends."

Ry is oversharing, and I can't for the life of me figure out why. Mica's gold eyes pass between us before landing back on Rydel. "You two grew up together."

It's not a question, and neither of us respond. Instead, Rydel props himself on his elbow. "What news from the south?"

Mica sits a little straighter, and I feel his resolve as he organizes his thoughts. "Things have ... settled somewhat since your ... departure, your Majesty."

"You mean, since I ran away with my tail between my legs."

I hold myself still at Ry's angry words, even though there is a small self-deprecating smile on his face. Mica shrugs, continuing, "Word on the street is that Adastra is pulling his fighters out of your kingdom, back to Trislen. The prevailing theory is that our new ... ruler is testing you—to see if you will remain satisfied with your slice of Imoria here in the north, or if you will push back and try to take back the south."

With practiced ease, I keep my face blank as I look at Rydel. I'd love to know the answer to that question myself. He doesn't comment though, and his determination becomes a solid press in my stomach.

Ry asks, "Have you met with Adastra?"

Mica doesn't respond right away, and a flicker of fear skitters across my lower back, but just as quickly as I register it, the feeling is gone. Interesting. Is Mica afraid of Adastra or Rydel—or something else?

The Shadow Lord interlaces his fingers, leaning forward and resting his arms on the table. "I have not." The truth of his words settles in me, but I can't shake off my unease. "Adastra has been sending out messages to arrange meetings with ... well, your southern council, town and city leaders, and other big players in Trislen."

"And Adastra doesn't consider you a significant player?"

Mica shrugs, "It doesn't seem so."

I can tell Rydel is not satisfied. Neither am I. Before either of us can ask another question, Mica looks between us again. "Are the rumors true?" He pins his gaze to Rydel, raising an eyebrow. Rydel's face remains impassive, but he waivers for a moment before answering the question he must have heard in Mica's mind.

"I have both Stones."

I sit back, willing my body to mirror Rydel's relaxed posture. Technically, his statement is true. He does have both Stones, in that he can use me to use the Heart Stone for his purposes.

Rydel's brows furrow, and his displeasure is like a slap to the face. I keep my expression blank, stony. He may not like the direction of my thoughts, but they're the truth. He can deal with it however he wants.

Mica, unaware of our internal exchange, nods. "So Erathan's stone is a fake. Poor fella."

I almost smirk, and Rydel's lips curl up in a small smile before pulling down into a frown. "Reliable messages have been hard to come by of late. Any word on King Erathan's condition? Were they able to save his leg?"

Mica leans back. "From what I've heard, his leg was saved. The spider bite rotted two of his toes, but his healers were able to stop the spread of poison."

I internally cringe at the thought. Erathan and Rydel had an alliance formed on a promise Rydel had no intention of fulfilling. But when Adastra moved to take back Trislen, Erathan came to our aid. And because of his involvement, an attempt was made on his life—one that almost succeeded. The king's guards found Erathan unconscious in his tent. His lips were blue and sweat slicked his skin. A tiny spider, native to the kingdom of Eshina across the sea, was found in his boot. Adastra's message was clear—if you side with Rydel, you're my enemy.

And it worked. With their king on his deathbed, the army of Adren withdrew, leaving Rydel to fend for himself.

And here we are.

Mica taps his finger to his chin. "The last I heard,

Erathan is awake. He's reported as 'quickly recovering and is determined to be strong for his people'."

Well, that could mean anything. No one ever tells the truth when it comes to ailing kings.

The room remains silent for a handful of moments before Mica takes a deep breath, resting his hands on the arms of his chair. "Your Majesty, would it be possible to speak privately?"

Hell no! My eyes jump to Rydel, but I'm not getting anything from him but curiosity. Damn it! I know ... I know he can take care of himself, but this doesn't feel right. Rydel raises an eyebrow at me in question, and I swallow a sigh. I can't lie. What's the point in trying? *'No, I'm not getting anything suspicious from Mica. But isn't that suspicious in itself?'*

Mica waits us out with his seemingly endless patience, apparently content to sit in silence, observing the room like it's the most fascinating space he's ever been in.

Rydel nods, and my heart sinks. Damn him.

"My library is just as private as this room, but a bit more comfortable. Captain Lucaryn, I will send for you once Mica and I have concluded our meeting."

Send for me. I hate him at this moment as he dismisses me like a servant and not his best friend since birth, not his lov—no, I won't say it, I won't even think it. Right now, Rydel feels so far removed from the boy I grew up with. But he's not that person anymore. He's the man who brought me to my knees with his magic and tossed me aside.

The slightest frown pulls at Rydel's lips, and his guilt slams into me followed by annoyance at my hesitation to leave him. His emotions pinch my shoulder blades together. Fed up, I nod, shoving my chair back a little too forcefully. I bow to Rydel, and without meeting his gaze, I spin and leave the room, even though every muscle is pulled tight and begging me to stay, to keep Ry safe. But I've been dismissed.

I hear the scrape of their chairs as Mica and Rydel stand, and their footfalls fade as they walk in the opposite direction.

I lean toward the guards standing a discrete distance from the doors. "Post up outside of the king's library." They both nod, but their apprehension slithers across my shoulder blades. Rydel is known for slipping his guards and going off on his own. "And send for a third to post discreetly outside the doors to the gardens. I want the king protected and Mica watched the entire time he's here."

With a sharp salute of their fists over their hearts, the two guards stride away.

My short nails dig into my palms, and instead of going to my rooms for a shower, I march out of the castle, my heavy strides carrying me to the soldiers' barracks.

Carelle is watching a sparring match and turns as she hears me approach. Her eyes sweep down my body, catching on my clenched hands before meeting my gaze. "You need to spar?"

"Not with you."

Her lips press tight, and her shoulders hitch, but I hold up a hand. "You're still recovering from your wound and infection. Don't push, Carelle." I pause, taking a breath to try and calm myself. "I know. Better than anyone, I know."

She relaxes slightly at my words and reluctantly nods. Looking over her shoulder, she calls out, "Baret, you're up."

The pale woman pushes off the rail she was leaning on, a smile spreading across her wide face. "Oh good, the captain is in a mood." She grabs a sword from the weapons' rack as she crosses the training ring.

My fingers wrap around the hilt of a sword as well, and I swing it in a circle a few times. "Your attitude isn't helping."

Baret chuckles. Not bothering with a fighting stance, she just charges. Good. I need a good fight.

Baret and I clash again and again, each getting in our hits. As a member of the coveted Sagas unit, she is well disciplined and deadly. But her emotions betray her moves; a quick flash of excitement when she thinks she's found an opening, a hint of anger when she misses a strike. Before long, she begins to grow tired, and her fatigue stacks on top of mine. When my right arm grows tired, I switch to my left, and a few minutes later, she does the same.

Time passes in a blur of straining muscles, and the occasional slice of pain when Baret gets in a strike. She is bleeding from several shallow cuts as well. Her next parry falters, and she curses, rolling out of the way of my strike. Quickly standing, she shakes out her arm, her frustration and fatigue almost becoming my own, but I push her emotions back. With a scowl, she tosses her sword to the ground, and I do the same, grinning.

We charge, fists flying and connecting. The faint sound of wages being made reaches my ears, and I vaguely notice a small crowd of soldiers standing and leaning around the training ring fence. Their amusement and revelry press into me, and my chest burns with the unwanted emotions. My stomach roils. I have to swallow several times before I'm able to sort out which emotions are mine and which are coming at me from the growing crowd of soldiers.

Another half-hour passes until Baret and I are both too exhausted to go on. We fall in a heap of tangled legs on the hard-packed ground, the dirt-smeared snow a muddy mess. We're both gasping for breath, and the crowd grumbles at the draw, slowly dispersing to go back to their own training and duties.

Baret spits into the dirt. "Good match, captain."

I clap her on the shoulder. "Good match."

She shrugs. "You would have had me a dozen times if you were at full strength." Realizing what she said, she jerks back stiffly. "I mean ... sorry. It's just ... you were ... you've recovered so quickly ... I ..."

I laugh, rolling to my knees before pushing myself to my feet. She stands as well, and I grab my sword. "It's okay. I know what you meant. Rematch once I'm a bit stronger?"

She picks up her sword and holds out her hand for mine. If it were my personal sword, I would refuse, preferring to clean and care for my own weapons, but this training sword goes back to the barracks, and I let her take it.

She smiles. "Of course, captain. Anytime."

I spend the next hour checking in with my unit leaders, then go through the stables, sneaking Kahar and Yara some extra treats. Kahar pins his ears against his head, snatching the treat from my palm, and I laugh at my angry horse. Though, I suspect he's more Rydel's at this point.

My muscles are loose and a bit sore, and I feel much better having worked off some of my annoyance at Rydel. A quiet chuckle escapes my lips as I mount the castle stairs and head toward the library. Being annoyed with him is familiar. It feels almost normal, like our relationship before ...

The thick stone walls, the lavish tapestries, the old paintings, the largely unused rooms open to the dim winter sunlight all pass unseen as my thoughts turn inward. How do Ry and I get back to that place? How do we forgive? I doubt either of us can forget, but can we move on? Can we get to a place of trust again?

I don't know.

I want it so bad. Can I use the magic to make him love me again, like before? Yes. I know I can. But I also know it wouldn't be real.

My palm rubs my chest, the ache in my heart all my own. I love him. Still.

I nod at the two guards standing several paces down either side of the hall and frown at the closed library door, raising my hand to knock but stalling before my knuckles meet wood. Rydel said he'd send for me. The faint mumble of low voices reaches me from beyond the doors, and I drop my hand.

Calm focus washes over me from the guard to my left, but a spark of amusement hits me from the guard to my right, and I have to fight from snickering at the emotion that's not mine. Instead, my anger overrides the foreign feelings as I turn to the guard on my right, noticing the Prioi unit patch on his jacket. "Something funny, soldier?"

His stony face pulls back in surprise, his eyes going wide for a second. His surprise fades, and amusement rises. "No, sir."

He stands tall and rigid, but his delight morphs into an oily feeling bordering on disdain. I lean into his space and grin as I finally feel a thread of fear from him. "With me."

Outwardly, he doesn't react, just moves to follow me, but inwardly I feel the equivalent of a mental eyeroll. My smile pulls up into a full grin. This should give me an outlet for the last of my pent-up frustration.

We make our way through the castle, pushing back out into the cold late afternoon. I blink several times to keep the falling snow out of my eyes, the heavy wet flakes quickly wetting my dark hair, the curls hanging wet over my forehead. We approach the barracks, several soldiers stalling for a moment to watch us pass, questions in their eyes, curiosity in their hearts. But they are quick to go about their business, knowing the look on my face means I'm not to be messed with.

"Captain?"

I don't respond to the man's question as he follows me to the training rings. I find it interesting that the longer we walk, the angrier he gets. Let's see if I can uncover the reason behind his rage.

I nudge open the wooden door to one of the sheds dotting the work and training areas for the soldiers. He stands in the doorway, his eyes following me as his annoyance mixes with his growing anger. I'm trying to place how long this soldier has been with us, but I'm coming up blank. I know he's been a member of our army for a few years, at least.

I grab the metal handle of a small bucket, and the dull thud and clink of tools sounds around the small space as I throw a few items into it. Shoving past the soldier, I stop at the closest post of the nearest training ring. A heavy metallic clatter rings out as I toss the bucket at his feet. He looks down then up at me, not moving to grab it.

I nod down at the bucket. "The training rings need repair." His indignation and surprise flash through me, and I smile. We usually work on repairs in the spring, dividing work amongst the ranks, but this soldier needs to learn his place. "Sand down each post and rail. Repair or replace any popped nails. Tar over worm holes and replace any rotted sections."

His anger ramps up the longer the list gets, and I have to unclench my own fists as my body reacts to his anger. More than a few soldiers are loitering, trying to look busy, but straining to overhear what's going on.

I continue, "When this ring is done, start on ring two."

He glances to his right, taking in the large training rings before looking back at me. "Captain, that would take days, maybe even weeks in this weather. I have other duties to—"

"Your only duty is these posts and rails until you finish."

He crosses his arms, doing his best to tamp down his anger while holding on to his bravado. "Why?"

I place my hands on my hips, feet planted wide as I feel his resistance. He's a big guy, but I'm bigger. "Because I'm your captain. I gave you an order. You want me to add the horse pens?" I take a single step toward him, and he puffs out his chest, standing firm as I lean into his space, staring him down.

His jaw flexes with his rage, and I wiggle the fingers of my right hand, the simple ring with the plain pink stone glimmering on my middle finger—the fake ring that is a match to Rydel's. As his eyes catch on the ring, believing it's the real Stone, his anger dissolves like sugar in hot tea. In its place is a smug confidence.

I step back just as he grips and unsheathes his sword with one swift movement.

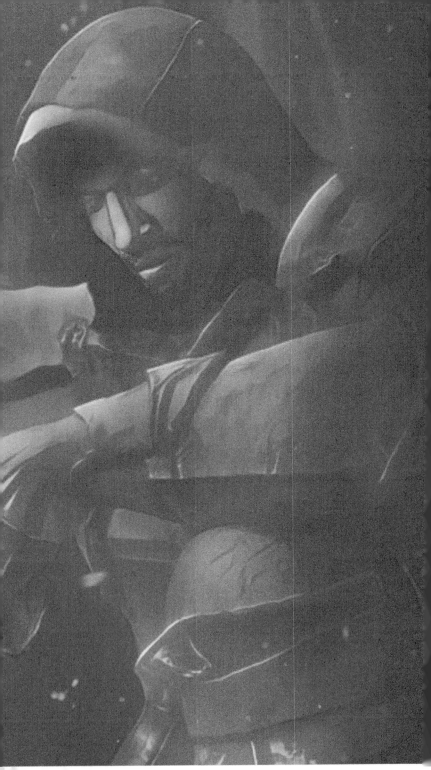

8

LUCARYN

I leap back out of range of his swing, and the surrounding soldiers go deathly still. A few grip their own weapons, ready to defend me but are confused as to why one of their own is attacking their captain.

The man before me snarls, pointing his sword at me before waving it around at the other soldiers. "Aren't you all tired of being at the whim of the king and his lover?"

I raise an eyebrow. It wasn't common knowledge that Rydel and I slept together, but rumors become truth when passed around enough.

The soldiers begin inching forward, and desperation born from the man before me quickens my heart. "Adastra had the right to the Trislenian throne. He has natural magic. He will save Imoria! Our king plunged us into a war all for the sake of his whore!"

Anger and shock pelt at me from the surrounding

soldiers, but my own anger swallows them down. I palm a throwing knife, hurling at his chest with one swift movement. Amazingly, he deflects it, but it's enough to distract him, and I charge. Ducking under his sword, I wrap my arms around his waist, taking him to the ground. We both land with a heavy umph. I grab his wrist and forearm, snapping the bone. His scream echoes with the clang of his sword falling to the ground.

He bucks, trying to unseat me, but even though I'm not at full strength, I have the necessary leverage to hold him down. "Are there others that have defected?"

He spits at me. "Many." The pang of fear and disappointment rolling off him tells me he's lying. There may be others, but not the 'many' he's claimed.

My knuckles split as I punch his face, my blood mixing with his dribbling from his lips. He attempts to hook a leg over mine to flip us, but again, I hold him down. Gritting my teeth in a feral grin, I lean down, pressing another of my throwing knives to his throat. "What was your aim, here? Undermine me to my soldiers? Undermine the king to his people? You were going to single-handedly unravel us from the inside?"

He spits again, and I don't flinch as his saliva and blood drip down my face. His eyes narrow, and his disgust sours my stomach before I can push it away. He sneers. "You're enjoying this, holding me down, aren't you, whore?"

Someone tsks to my right. "Orik has a death wish."

I laugh. "Indeed, he does." I look down into Orik's eyes, letting him see his death in my stare. Finally, his anger gives way to a wave of fear. "I shall oblige you. But first ..." I gather the magic that's been spooling in my chest, scraping everyone's emotions against the underside of my skin.

Rydel has always been the feared one. He makes a grand

show of his power. He likes to flaunt the magic and make examples of those who oppose him. He displays his darkness without question, without pause. I'm the one always in control. Ry reacts, and that works for him. I think, plan, scheme ... we really are a good team.

I smirk down at Orik as I shove the magic into him. My smirk turns to laughter as my power floods his body, overwhelming him with the last thing he'd expect—lust.

His pupils dilate and his skin sensitizes with gooseflesh. "No."

I push up to my feet, grinning down at him. I sweep my hand between us. "From one whore to another."

I flood him with unrelenting desire, and I begin to get hard at the sheer pleasure and pain of the magic. I get it. I understand how Rydel feels when he wields his power. Now, I understand the sheer satisfaction that hits with the pain— that zing along your skin that says you're in control, that you are untouchable. That the pain you're feeling is a mere tickle compared to what you can do to others with a single thought.

Orik groans, thrusting his hips into the air. "No, please." His cock is straining against the thick fabric of his pants, and his breaths fog in the air as his inhales become shallow. The soldiers around us slowly back away, some sneering with satisfaction, others wide-eyed and uncomfortable with what I'm doing.

I don't care.

I cover his every nerve ending with intense sexual hunger, and he moans again, his hand involuntarily grabbing his crotch, rubbing hard to try and relieve the pressure. I want to adjust myself as the desire of the magic mixes with my own emotions, but I stand still, watching Orik as he sits up. His scowl shoots hatred at me, even as he shuffles backward on his ass, his broken wrist hugged close to his body as his other hand fumbles at the fastening of his pants.

"Fuck you, Lucaryn."

I laugh. "I'm sure you want to." I *do* grab myself now. "Unfortunately, this cock isn't for you."

I shove another wave of arousal at him, and his hand dives down his pants, his eyes rolling back even as he bites his lip so hard, more blood drips down his chin. He pumps himself, and even under his pants I can tell his tugs are hard and brutal. It must hurt without any lubrication. Good.

Stepping forward, I follow him as he once again tries to shuffle backward. I chuckle. "You're my whore now."

The magic builds, bringing him to the edge of an orgasm. I feel the pleasure building in his lower abdomen, and his breath hisses between his teeth. So, I pull back ever so slightly, denying him release. He groans, jerking himself even harder. "Fuck. No. No, Fuck. Fuck. Fuck!"

He's so busy trying to reach orgasm, he's stopped moving away from me, so I kneel between his thighs, bracing my hands on either side of his chest. "You chose poorly."

Moving back, giving him space to suffer, I shove pleasure at him, and he bellows through his clenched teeth, his hips bucking under me, and just as he reaches the crest of his pleasure, I pull back again. Over and over, I ramp him up until tears fall down his face. It's glorious to watch—this man crumbling under my magic. His pain, his humiliation is like a drug. I'm nearly dizzy with the high of watching him struggle helplessly.

He squeezes his eyes closed as he works his pants down over his hips, desperate for relief. He moves his other arm like he's going to cup his balls, but a shout of pain rips from his throat as his broken wrist flops against his thigh. His boots scrape at the ground, trying to get purchase, and his hips jerk as pulse after pulse of magic invades his body.

"Please. Stop. Fuck!" He manages to drag his hand off his abused cock and rolls onto his side.

My chest feels like it's on fire where the Stone sits under my skin. I'm sweating, but not just from the magic. The rush of using the power, of so fully dominating someone, heats my body and tingles across my skin.

I lick my lips, delighting in my power, but then I'm forced to grit my teeth against my wavering vision. I don't let up, though. Sending another wave of lust at him, his cock jumps, and for a moment, Orik resists before grabbing a handful of snow and wrapping his fingers back around his throbbing cock. If he thought the cold would give him relief, he was wrong. The snow quickly melts, allowing him to thrust more smoothly into his tight grip. Moans and curses bubble from his lips as he flops onto his back once again.

He's close, right at the edge, his pleasure spearing through me. It feels so good. All of it. The magic, the pain, the lust, his fear, his loathing ... The urge to grab my own cock is so strong, I grip my dagger to give my hand something to do, and as I watch him stroke himself harder and harder, I wait.

Again, he climbs toward his climax, and a moment before he tips over the edge, I move, sliding my dagger between his ribs, robbing him of his orgasm and his life.

As I pull the bloody dagger free of his body, the magic pulls back, and the lingering pleasure swirls with my nausea. I almost tumble sideways as the exhaustion of using the magic crashes over me, but I manage to stay standing, shuffling back as a couple of soldiers step forward. One bends down, grabbing the dead man's arms, two others grabbing his legs. The man at the head smirks at me. "That was ... creative."

The other soldiers chuckle, but I feel their discomfort. Under that, though, there's loyalty to Lieren, to me, to Rydel. I raise an eyebrow, and everyone pauses for a moment as I say, "A threat to one is a threat to all. I'll never allow that to stand."

And with those few words, all traces of discomfort vanish, and my soldiers' pride fills me. With a nod, they carry Orik off. As I turn, everyone jumps to action, scattering like rodents. A female soldier from the Annarr unit approaches from the main barracks, glancing behind me. "Captain, do you still want the post and rails worked on?"

I rub my hand over my face, grounding myself with the abrasive scrape of my beard over my palm. "No. They're fine."

"Yes, sir. I'm on my way to relieve the king's guards."

"Is he still in the library?"

She nods. "That's where I was told to report."

"Then I won't keep you. If their meeting concludes while you're still on guard, come find me."

"Yes, sir." She walks off, and after a deep breath, I follow, peeling away once I pass through the towering doors, heading toward Rydel's and my wing of the castle. As soon as my door clicks shut behind me, I let my shoulders droop, doing my best to release as much tension as possible. It's tempting to go to the library and 'listen' with my magic. But I'm tired, physically and emotionally. I want Rydel to want me in the room. I just want ... Ry.

I reach up and over my head, grabbing the collar of my sweaty shirt, dragging it over my head and dropping it to the floor. In the past few weeks, I have quickly cluttered up my rooms, feeling much more comfortable in the organized chaos. Toeing off my boots, I kick one, and it tumbles under a chair, the other thudding into a pile of clothes and clinking against a long-discarded plate. I undo my pants on the way to my washroom, kicking them free as well, my semi-erect cock springing free.

I'd prefer to take a long soak, but a quick glance reveals the empty tub and the cool coals in the trench that runs under it. So, I cross to the corner of the washroom and turn the faucet that draws up the heated water from down in the room off the kitchens. As soon as steam starts to crawl along the stone floor, I step under the water, sighing as it soaks my hair and runs down my back, over my shoulders, and down my chest.

The flat of my palm presses to the stone wall, my next exhale spraying water from my lips. Since first taking the Heart Stone a few months ago, I've grown to appreciate Rydel's strength even more. This magic is powerful, draining, painful, and addictive. I like it. No. I love it. We may be broken, but we are powerful. Together we could …

Ugh. Together.

I want to talk with him about this, about the magic, about … us. I ache with wanting him to come into my rooms, to undress and slip under the water with me. I want him to kiss his way down my back while telling me how turned on he gets watching me use the magic. I want him to reassure me that everything will be okay.

And I'm angry that I want him.

I recall the memories of panic and pain when Rydel used his magic against me. The rage is not as sharp, but it's still there. And I'm sure my betrayal ran even deeper through him. But he's had over a month to process and deal with it. I don't want to process it. I don't want to let go of the anger, because that would mean I would have to acknowl-edge all my other feelings.

I fist my cock, biting back a groan with my first pump. Anger and arousal mixes. Behind my closed lids, I picture Ry's face, imagining his body trembling under mine, his wrists bound to the corners of my bed. My fist works over my shaft as I imagine oiling my hand and easing a finger into his tight entrance, then adding a second finger. He would squirm under me as I add a third, stretching him.

My entire body trembles, pleasure collecting in my lower stomach and between my thighs.

Thinking about sliding my cock teasingly slowly into Ry's ass sends me over the edge, and strong spurts of cum coat the wall of the shower. My fist squeezes a few times, mimicking the aftershocks of Ry's ass shuttering around me, then I quickly clean up, slowing my panting breaths.

I jerk when, as if summoned by my thoughts, Rydel's deep voice carries into the washroom from my sitting area, cutting through the heavy steam. "Lucaryn, I've brought dinner."

My cock twitches, and I slam my hands against the wall to keep from fisting myself again. Did he hear any of my thoughts? I'm so wound up; I have to work for a moment to breathe past the flood of fresh arousal pulsing low in my belly. The water flows over me for a few more minutes before I turn the shower off and reach for a towel.

I wrap it around my waist, and the second I pass into the main living room of my quarters, our eyes clash, heat flares, and desire snaps between us. He licks his lips, and I fight back a groan, ripping my eyes from his.

He clears his throat, setting the heavily laden tray on the low table, flopping onto the cushion on the far side with the quickly darkening window at his back. The snow is still falling, and the winter scene frames his pale outline, his blond hair shining in the low light.

The muscles of his arms flex as he scoops fragrant roasted vegetables onto my plate, then onto his. He continues to dish out our dinner in silence while I pull a thin sweater from my dresser. Pulling the top over my wet hair, I drop the towel, feeling Ry's eyes on my exposed ass before I pull on a pair of soft, loose pants.

Settling on the cushion across from him, my chest tightens at how familiar—at how normal this feels.

Ry takes a drink of ale, but I reach for the water. Before I take my first bite of what smells like rabbit, Ry clears his throat again. A small smile pulls at the corners of his lips. "I heard what you did, out at the barracks."

My eyebrow rises. "Word travels fast."

"That was a juicy bit of gossip." I chuckle, and he grins. "A very clever bit of punishment, I must say. Death by edging. I wish I had thought of that." I shrug, and he changes the subject, but not before a wave of his desire washes over me. "I'd like to catch you up on what Mica and I discussed. I'd like your opinion on what our next move should be."

His calm washes over me, but under it, there's a hint of uncertainty. We've always been partners. We've been through ... everything together. But Rydel has never, in all the years I've known him, been one to ask for help. He has more of a 'do it and see what happens' personality.

But here he is, asking. This feels like a move forward for us.

His knife scraps against his plate, and he sets it down, a frown on his face.

I mirror his expression, shrugging. "Sorry. I keep forgetting you can hear everything." I tap my temple, and he smiles, but it doesn't reach his eyes.

He sighs, "I'm trying, Luc. I don't know how to go about fixing ... things. But I'm trying."

His sincerity eases a bit more of my tension, and I fully relax into my cushion. I take a bite of rabbit, the earthy taste rich and salty. Stuffing a thick slice of bread into my mouth, I chew, and crumbs fly from between my lips as I say, "I know, Ry." I swallow, smiling. "I think we're both trying. Unfortunately, I think it's just going to take time." His impatience jitters through me, causing me to tap my fingers against the table. I grit my teeth, stilling my fingers. "Rydel, you're going to have to give me time."

He leans forward, his green eyes flicking between mine. "I want to undo what was done. I want ..." His gaze flicks to my lips before snapping back to my eyes. "I want ..."

His frustration and desire mix with mine, settling over the stubborn layer of anger that feels like it's pinned to my heart with the blade of his beloved dagger. I can't deny I want him. I've tried to ignore the love I feel for him. How is it possible to hate and love someone at the same time?

His voice is quiet but sharp. "You're still angry. Rightfully so. And I'd be lying if I said there aren't moments when I feel gutted thinking about the truth you hid from me for twenty-seven years." I open my mouth, but he hears my thoughts before I can voice them. "I know, Luc. I understand. I think I understand anyway."

I scowl. He says he understands, but he's still refusing to let me speak, to explain. He may be able to hear my thoughts, but he doesn't seem to understand my need to actually talk to him. My jaw grinds as he presses his hand to his chest, our meals forgotten for the moment.

He continues, "Feel my sincerity. Feel the truth. More

than anything, I want you to know that I'm sorry. I'm sorry you felt you had to keep that from me. I'm sorry I reacted so poorly. And I'm sorry I reacted exactly how you expected me to."

His longing coats my aching heart, and my body moves without me telling it to. My hands press to the table, and I lean forward. I pause, clenching the table in anger at my body's betrayal, but the damage is done.

His cup of ale tips over, the golden liquid spilling over the table and dripping onto the floor as he vaults over the low table, shoving me back, straddling my lap. I gasp as his hands frame my face, his fingers digging through my beard.

Letting my eyes travel over his strong face, I stare at the small scar along his left cheek before my eyes travel to the deeper, longer scar above his left temple, partially hidden by his hair—the scar he got the night his father nearly beat him to death—the night I killed Rydel's family.

I've always loved Ry, maybe too much. And despite the low hum of anger, I crave him. In fact, I think my anger is driving my need for him even higher.

My eyes snap back to his as his whispered words carry the scent of ale to my nose. "I hear your thoughts, but—"

"I *know* you can hear my thoughts!" I shake my head. My desire bleeds and blends into rage. I shove him, and his back thuds into the table. "You steal my words before I say them! You assume my thoughts are my truth. Have you never worked through something, thinking through options, considering and discarding until you find your own truth? Not every thought I have reflects how I actually feel, you bastard. I HATE you!"

A loud crack sounds through the room as my fist meets his jaw. His head snaps to the side, and when he turns back to me, blood drips from the corner of his lips, and the beginning of a bruise already marks his pale skin.

His eyes narrow as he braces a hand on the table behind him. "One free punch, Lucaryn. That's all you get."

"Fine!"

I bend my legs under me, launching at him. I land another punch, but he grips my wrist, twisting. He yanks my arm up behind my back, and I'm forced to turn to keep my shoulder from popping out of the socket.

Holding my back against his front, his words whisper across my ear. "If it's a fight you want, then let's fight."

I hate the shiver that steals down my spine. My cock jumps, but I grit my teeth, holding onto my rage like a comforting melody. The anger sings through my blood. Planting my right foot onto the floor, I spin into his hold, shoving my shoulder into his stomach. We tumble onto the table, the wood creaking, the food scattering and tumbling to the floor.

His legs wrap around my waist, and my cock grows stiffer. Bucking his hips against me, his erection presses into mine, his voice deep with arousal. "Heady, isn't it? The rage and desire and pain?"

I rear back, punching him again, and his head snaps back into the table. Shoving off him, I try to move away, but his leg hooks around mine, and he pushes off the table, slamming into me. My head hits the floor, buffeted by the thick rug, but I still see white dots for a moment. Ry straddles my stomach, and as he reaches for my arms with the intent to restrain me, I grab his hand, yanking his thumb down into his wrist. He grunts in pain, and it's enough of an opening for me to throw him up and over my left shoulder.

Flipping over, I press to my hands-and-knees as he rolls, spinning on his knees to face me. I launch at him. Wrapping my arms around his waist, tumbling us both to the floor. Now I'm straddling him, but instead of trying to restrain him, my fists fly. Pain flares from my knuckles up my wrists all the way to my shoulders as I strike his jaw, his cheek, his eye, his chest ...

"You used your magic on ME!"

Snap. Crunch.

He lands a punch to my side, and I grunt before screaming, "You tortured ME!"

Thud. Thud.

"You said you LOVED me!"

My rage is like the mythical tales of dragons. Talons of anger tearing apart my heart. Breaths of fire searing my blood. I'm trembling. I'm wound so tight I'm afraid I might shatter.

"You threw me away! You tossed me aside! You LEFT me!"

Wet splashes hit Rydel's face, and horror stutters my breath as I realize I'm crying. Throwing my head back, I scream, fisting my hands in my hair.

His palms slam into my chest, shoving me off him. Falling to the side, I crawl to my knees, staring at him. My breaths are ragged, and I pant, taking in his swollen face. His eyes travel over my face, his own labored breaths matching mine, and when his gaze meets mine, desire slams into me.

"Fuck!"

I shuffle forward, grabbing his neck and crashing my lips to his. Our teeth scrape in our desperation to taste each other. I bite his lower lip, tasting blood. My cock pulses in time with my heartbeat, pre-cum wetting the front of my pants. Ry's desire sweeps over me again, mixing with my anger until all I am is throbbing need and fury. I reach for his shirt, fisting it and tearing it over his head.

His hungry eyes snap back to mine as soon as his shirt lands on the floor. He grips the waist of my pants, yanking them down my hips before shoving me back. I allow myself to fall, catching myself on a forearm. I lift my hips as he tugs my pants all the way off.

"Suck me, Rydel."

Hard lines of anger still pull at my face, but my words come out on a deep growl of desire. Leaning down, his breath feathers over my cock, and it jerks, more pre-cum dripping down over my balls. My eyes threaten to roll back in my head as his lips close over my straining length, and the warm heat of his mouth sucks me down. I force my gaze to remain on him, though. I watch his cheeks hollow out as he sucks hard, and I fist the rug.

"Fuck!"

A shiver trembles down my spine as he slowly draws his mouth up my cock until his lips pull free with a quiet pop. "I will, Luc." He holds my gaze as he strokes my shaft while single-handedly undoing his pants. I buck into his hand as his cock springs free, and he grins. "I will fuck you. Uh zuhss uhe'a uss a iyai, Luc." *I will have all of you, Luc.* And he lowers his head once again.

9

RYDEL

Lightly, I scrape my teeth along his solid length, and his thighs tense. His taste coats my tongue, and I groan, letting the vibration hum over his cock. My jaw is sore, and my left eye is swelling shut, but I don't care. I easily ignore the pain as I pull back slowly, sucking hard, but before I'm even halfway off him, he fists my hair. Grabbing tightly, close to my scalp, he bucks his hips into my mouth as he shoves my head down. I have just enough time to relax my throat before my nose presses to the flesh of his lower abdomen, and the head of his cock slams down the back of my throat.

"Take it. Take all of me, Ry."

It appears he's not done punishing me. That's fine.

My fingers dig into his thighs as he pulls on my hair before shoving me back down again. I relax into his grip, letting go. A languid sensation washes through me, like free-

T. B. WIESE

falling, but gentler. I submit to Luc, and my entire body hums with the freedom of surrendering to him. I never thought I'd love being dominated as much as I do, but I suspect it has nothing to do with being controlled and everything to do with the fact that it's Lucaryn. Letting go with him is easy. I want him to use me, to rage at me with his body.

Spit leaks from the corners of my lips, and I simply concentrate on the feel of his hard shaft sliding along my tongue as his hips and hand work in tandem to work me over his cock. I feel like an object he's using to get off. It's driving me insane. I could come just from the feel of him forcing his cock down my throat over and over.

I release one hand from his thigh and coat my fingers in my saliva that's running down his shaft and over his balls before I circle his entrance. He hisses, his grip in my hair tightening even more as I slide the tip of my finger into him, and my groan matches his as I recall the feeling of sliding my cock into his ass.

Luc thrusts his shaft deep into my mouth, groaning, "Your arousal is overwhelming, Ry. Fuck. So much. Too much." A stab of jealousy courses through me that I never had the chance to use the Heart Stone magic like this. Having Luc's desire mix with mine as we fuck would be ...

For a moment, he's lost to the desire, and I'm able to lift my head. Saliva runs down my chin as I grin at him. He's panting, his pupils so large and dark, I barely see the brilliant blue of his irises.

"Get back on my cock, Rydel."

Obliging, I suck him down as I slide my finger deeper into his ass until I'm knuckle deep. His head thumps back, and while he's momentarily distracted, I draw my finger out of him and grip his shirt. My lips pop off his cock, and I pull his shirt over his head. Throwing it aside, I smile as it lands among a pile of clothes. Dirty or clean? I don't know, but his rooms are once again comfortably messy.

He shoves my head back down, brutally slamming his hips up to drive his cock deep. I gag, spit pooling between his thighs and dripping between his ass cheeks. Breathing heavily through my nose, I take his punishment until his fingers yank on my hair, lifting me off his cock. Deep inhales suck down into my lungs, but my breath catches when I meet his gaze. Desire flares through his eyes even as they pinch at the corners with his still simmering anger.

The muscles in my lower abdomen clench at the promise of pain and pleasure in his look.

"Turn around." His deep voice thrums through me, making my cock even harder. "Hands on the table."

When I hesitate, he uses his grip in my hair to spin me around, shoving forward so I have to slap my palms on the table to keep from slamming my face into the scattered plates and smashed food. My thighs tremble, and my stomach clenches with anticipation as he leans over, his hand reaching over my shoulder. He grabs the bottle of oil meant for our bread, and I groan. I'm never going to be able to eat bread without getting hard again.

The soft pop of the cork coming out of the bottle causes my muscles to clench, and I push back toward him as a cold stream of oil slides down my lower back and between my ass. I try to turn my head so I can see him, but his grip tightens, pushing me farther forward until I'm forced to drop to my forearms. A roasted carrot squishes under my left arm, and the fatty juices of the cooked rabbit slick between my fingers.

My cock is pulsing with anticipation. I bite my bottom lip as his free hand grips my shoulder, and without warning, the head of his cock presses to my entrance and thrusts deep.

"Fuck! Lucaryn!"

Pain sparks up my spine, and I struggle against his hold, trying to create some space between us. His grip clamps tighter as he shoves himself all the way inside, then holds his hips against my ass. The pain turns to a delicious burn. Luc's breaths come out in harsh growls. He slowly withdraws before slamming deep once again. It's so forceful, a burst of air passes my lips with a grunt. His hips drive forward again and again, slapping against my ass, his balls pushing into the backs of my thighs.

"Shut your mouth and take it, Rydel."

Pleasure and pain spiral together, challenging for dominance. His hand in my hair pulls me back into his thrusts, and a few strands rip free. I hiss at the flare of pain, but as his cock slams into me, pleasure winds around my core. His hand on my shoulder is bruising, yanking me back into his pounding rhythm. He fills me completely. I am consumed by him.

His next thrust is so violent, my hips collapse into the table, pinching my cock between the hard wood and my trembling body. I grunt in pain, but his body holds me pinned as he slams into me over and over.

I shift, sliding my hand under my body to fist my cock and hopefully find some relief from the increasing agony of being slammed into the table, as well as the building pleasure of having Luc deep inside me. But before I reach my goal, Luc snarls, grabbing my arm and pinning it to the table. His nails dig into the flesh of the back of my hand, drawing blood, and the pain morphs into pleasure. My cock jerks painfully against the press of the table, and I struggle under him.

I fight to get my other hand to my aching shaft, but his thoughts batter against my skull. There are no words, just a dark, roiling anger, like storm clouds rumbling with thunder. When he leans over me to keep me from fisting my cock, I throw my elbow back, and it snaps against his cheek. His hips never stop pounding into me as he swears, shaking his head, the new cut on his face already dripping blood into his bread. Grabbing me around the throat, he yanks me back into his chest. Our sweat-slicked skin slides together, and we fall back.

Luc's cock drives into me as he lands on his back with a thud. I wrap my leg around his, trying to find leverage to flip our positions, but he rolls, pressing the front of my body flat into the floor, wrenching my arm behind my back, pinning the other near my head.

His whispered words brush against my ear, "You will find release when I let you."

Fuck. I've never been so turned on in my life. Every pump of his hips radiates pleasure up my spine, all the way down to my toes. Having him fight me like this—hearing his grunts and growls as he punishes me—it's the perfect mix of pain and blinding pleasure. The two sensations snap and swirl inside me until the pain is pleasurable and the pleasure is painful.

Sweat slicks my skin, and the rug fibers scratch and burn against my too-sensitive flesh.

His pace is unrelenting.

I struggle harder. The burning pain forces little grunts from my lips with every thrust of his cock in my ass. Over and over, his cock slams deep, and I try to shove against him again, but I have no leverage. I know if I told him to stop, he would, and if I really wanted to get out of his hold, I could— but I don't, and Luc doesn't stop.

"Luc."

He doesn't respond, so I flex my thighs, the movement allowing me to inch forward slightly along the abrasive rug.

"I don't think so, Rydel."

He wrenches my arm higher up my back until I stop moving. If I were to resist at all, my shoulder would snap. The pain is intense. My entrance is raw even with the oil slicking down my thighs, and my cock is burning where it's been rubbing against the rug with Luc's thrusts. Desire and anger lick along my skin, and I thrash and buck as my body pulls tighter and tighter toward orgasm.

He just fucks me harder.

"Ahhhh!" Pain shoots down the right side of my body as my shoulder pops out of the socket. Luc releases my arm, and it thumps painfully to the floor at my side. I ignore the pain—I'm good at that. I've grown up with pain.

I'm agonizingly hard and in desperate need of release. Just as I gather my strength to roll over my busted arm to get Luc off me, a cold stream of oil slides between us.

"Fuuuck!"

I go limp under him, the new layer of lubrication easing the burning pain around my entrance. Pleasure streaks through my body, and my cock jerks against the rug. The wet slaps of his hips driving into me echo around the room, and the only other sounds are his grunts and the snap and crackle of the fire in the hearth.

Luc's punishing thrusts send pulse after pulse of plea-sure through my body, collecting low in my belly. And that's what this is—punishment. And it's delicious.

I'm on the edge of orgasm again, and as the warm rush of buzzing bliss sharpens in my lower back he stills, holding himself deep inside me, robbing me of my climax.

I groan as he pushes his thoughts at me. '*Your orgasm is mine.*'

I don't have a chance to completely register his thought before a pulse of his magic hits me. Desire floods my body; unlike anything I've ever felt. It's like every nerve ending is coated in ecstasy. I'm floating. I'm falling over the edge of a waterfall.

'*Come for me, Rydel.*'

The pressure finally snaps, and my vision goes white as I come—hard. Waves of his magic crash through my cock, spearing up my stomach until my entire body trembles with my release. I'm so lost, I barely notice Luc's erratic thrusts shoving my body into the floor, his growls echoing around the room with his own release.

I fight to get my breathing under control as Luc pulls out of me, oil and cum dripping to the floor between my thighs. My head falls forward, and I pant into the rug, breathing in the earthy scent of the fibers, the nutty scent of the oil, and the sharp scent of our cum.

With a deep breath, I ignore the stab of pain in my shoulder and take a chance, letting a smile lighten my words. "We ruined dinner."

The muscles in my back relax slightly when Luc chuckles.

I angle my head to look over my shoulder at him, but as I do, my shirt hits me in the face. I grab it with my good arm, pulling it away from my eyes and catch Luc striding away toward his bedroom. A minute later, I hear the splash of water.

I take a deep breath, pushing to my knees before sitting back. Gripping my shoulder, I inhale, hold it, and rotate it up and in. The bones grate against each other, but it doesn't snap back into place. With a groan, I push to my feet, glancing down at the floor. For some reason, I'm turned on at the sight of my sticky cum all over the expensive rug, and the ruined mess of the table brings a grin to my face.

I think this might have been just what we needed.

I gather my clothes, shaking my head with a small smile, and turn toward the door with the intention of going to my rooms to shower.

Awkwardly, I reach for the handle, but Luc's sharp voice stops me.

"Wait."

I turn. Luc is dressed again, this time in a tight short-sleeve shirt and loose pants. His black hair is wet once again and curling around his face. I bite my bottom lip with the need to kiss him, but I force my feet to hold their ground as he crosses to me. His large hand presses to my back between my shoulder blades.

"Brace."

I clench my teeth as he gently grabs my shoulder and with one sharp move, pops my shoulder in its socket.

"Thanks."

He's avoiding my gaze, so I turn, reaching for the door handle again, but his voice stops me once more.

"Just use mine. I'll send for more food. We still need to talk."

The tension in my neck pulls at my temples, threatening a migraine. As I move to pass him, his hand snaps out, gripping me around my bicep. He pulls me into his chest. Slowly, eyes on mine, his lips lower to mine in a soft, caressing kiss. A knot in my stomach unfurls, and as he pulls away, he sighs, pressing his forehead to mine.

With a shallow breath, he says, "I'm ... I don't know what to say."

And just like that, the pit in my stomach returns. His

thoughts tumble over each other, scrambling for purchase, so I take control. My hand gently wraps around his throat, and I lean into him.

"You have the right to work out your feelings. But know this, Lucaryn." My fingers press into his pulse until I see his eyes start to roll back, and I release the pressure just slightly. "Next time, *you* are submitting to *me*." His nostrils flare, and a small frown tugs at his lips. "You will kneel before your king, and you will take *my* cock." Leaning in close, I brush my lips over the edge of his ear, satisfied when he shivers. "And yes. There will be a next time. And many times after that." I inhale, drawing in his petrichor scent. "You are mine, Lucaryn, and I won't ever let you go again." I pull back, looking into his bright blue eyes. "Never."

I pad across the room, hoping my words did something to alleviate his pain and uncertainty.

His earlier shouted words of betrayal and abandonment echo through my mind, and I wince, passing through Luc's bedroom into his washroom. He was right, I did leave him. It was a mistake; one I'll gladly pay for until he forgives me.

I don't wait for the hot water, simply step under the spray, washing quickly before drying and returning to where Luc has tidied the table, fresh food already plated. I gather my clothes, dressing quickly then flop back on my cushion. I nibble at the bread, unable to look at the bottle of oil without thinking of what we just did, and I grin, meeting Luc's smiling eyes.

His cheeks are flushed, and his pupils are still too large. The magic use on top of the sex is causing his body to run hot. He spears a roasted carrot and stuffs it into his mouth.

I shift on the cushion, grinning and letting a deep chuckle slide from my lips. "I'm going to be sitting funny for days." Luc's head snaps up, and when he sees my smile, his lips turn up. I raise an eyebrow at him prodding my tongue along my teeth. "And I think you knocked a tooth loose."

I laugh again, and this time he laughs with me. Thank the gods. I've missed that laugh. I've missed us.

Pulling my wet hair back at my nape, I shake my head. "But damn, Lucaryn. That was ..." My eyes travel down his body suggestively, a smirk keeping my smile in place.

He throws back his head, his laughter ringing around the tall ceilings. For the first time in months, I feel ... content.

Luc's laughter dies off, and he takes a sip of ale. "Of course you would take a beating and get fucked nearly raw and come out the other side satisfied and still aroused."

I drain my mug of ale. "You pulled your punches."

He shrugs in answer, his lips still curved up in a smile as he takes a big bite of roasted rabbit. "So?" The mouthful of food muffles his words, and I smile as he asks, "What did the Shadow Lord need to talk to you about in private?"

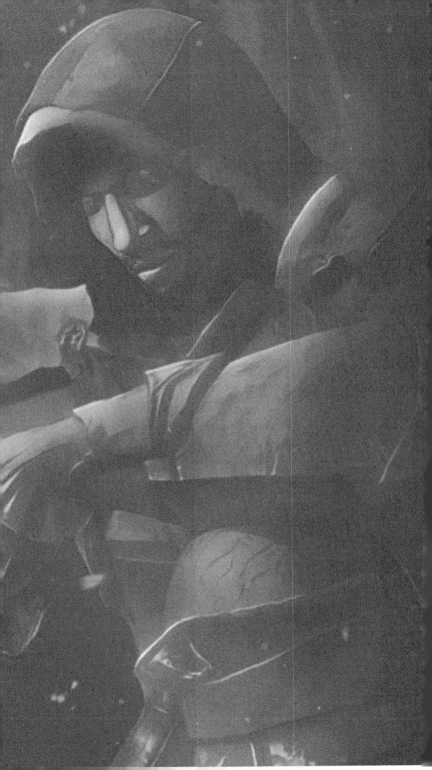

10

LUCARYN

Rydel raises an eyebrow at me.

Thoughts tumble from my mind into his. *'Nope. No, we are not going to talk about what just happened. It happened. It was great. Tell me what you and Mica talked about.'*

Ry chuckles again, shaking his head, spearing a few roasted vegetables onto his fork. "Adastra, mostly."

"Surely he knew you'd tell me everything."

"He suspected as much. He just wanted to see how far he could push me, and how much you'd allow."

I tap my fork on my plate. "He likes his games." Rydel nods. "But there was no ill will or fear or suspicion coming from him. It was almost like he was bored."

"Content actually. His mind was calm. He's more curious than anything."

"About what?"

Rydel cracks his neck. "About how this whole mess will turn out."

"Honestly, I'm surprised he has stayed loyal to you."

"He's not. Not really. He's an opportunistic bastard. Which is why I like him. He would be feeding Adastra information, but he can't seem to get any closer to Trislen's new ruler than I could."

I rip a piece of bread off between my teeth. "I thought the Shadow Lord had people everywhere?"

"He does. But apparently, the southern palace is on lock down. Since Adastra took the capital, no one has gone into the palace, and no one has come out."

The bread sits heavy on my tongue, and I have to swallow twice to get it to go down. "Are there any first-hand accounts of seeing Adastra actually enter the palace?"

Ry shakes his head. "Not that I've heard, and not that Mica has heard either. It's all rumor."

I laugh. "So, the person in the palace could be anyone. Adastra could be anywhere. He could still be sailing the seas. He could still be in Eshena. He could be working behind the scenes until he gets here."

Ry nods. "He could even be a fabrication, but I think we have to move forward with the assumption that he is indeed here in Imoria and has taken the palace."

I nod. "So, if he's barricaded himself in, how is he getting orders out to his army?"

Rydel sets his fork down and absently grabs his dagger. The sharp blade flashes in the low light as it spins around his fingers. "That, Mica did know. Birds."

My left brow climbs up my forehead. "He's sending messenger birds from the palace into the city? That's risky, isn't it?"

"Is it? He ran us off. Those left in the city are loyal to

house Lurona. Mica has gotten his hands on a few messages, but they were all defensive orders to protect the border and the capital. Mica hasn't seen or heard anything about what Adastra wants with me. But I assume he wants me dead."

I shrug, refilling my mug with ale, the dark amber liquid frothing over the lip. I hold up the jug, and Rydel nods, so I refill his mug as well.

"So, what do we do?"

He takes a sip, the foam sticking to his beard over his upper lip. "What are your thoughts?" Before I can make a sarcastic response about him already knowing, he says, "I want to hear them from your lips. I ... want you to be open with me ... if you can."

I take a slow breath, considering. This *is* what I wanted. I can do this. I need to do this. He's trying. I should too. It's not where we were, but it's something.

I finish off the last of the food on my plate, thinking through different options, setting some aside to consider more, discarding others. I shove my plate toward the center of the table and lean back into my cushion.

Rydel just watches me. Between organizing my thoughts, I get little flutters of his emotions. Amusement, curiosity, contentment, a low hum of arousal, and under it all, his least favorite emotion to feel and the emotion he most loves to exploit—hope. He's hopeful.

I suck at my teeth, and when that doesn't dislodge the piece of food, I use the tip of my knife to dig it out. "Do you still want Trislen?"

Rydel takes a deep breath. "I didn't intend to take Trislen this early in my reign."

"You wanted both Stones."

He nods. "And I wanted the time to figure out the magic." His eyes dart to my chest before coming back to meet my gaze. "I always planned on asking you to take the Heart Stone, Luc."

I press my lips together in a tight line before rolling my shoulder. "I figured as much."

"Then why didn't yo—never mind. It doesn't matter. I knew killing Ravaxina would move up my timeline ... *our* timeline." Ry runs his hand over his face, and my fingers burn with the desire to feel his beard scratch against my palms. He sets his dagger on the table with a gentle clink. "And to be honest, I was a little relieved when I was forced out of Trislen and back home." His eyes hold mine. "Back to you."

I clench the cushion to hide the shiver that skates down my spine. His emotions wash over me again before I'm able to press them away.

"But we can't look weak. We can't let Adastra win."

Ry nods, his gaze going distant as he considers.

I continue, "Do you think Adastra would make a move on either Adren or Lieren in the future, or will he be content with his piece of Imoria?"

He chuckles. "Have you ever known a ruler to 'be content' with what they have?"

I shrug. "Erathan seemed content enough."

"He was just waiting to see who would come out on top, Rava or me. He planned to let us fight it out, leaving him only one foe to go up against. He would have made a move eventually."

"Only because he knew you or Ravaxina would make a move on him." I tilt my head. "Do we involve Erathan again? Do we invoke his treaty?"

Rydel shakes his head. "No. He knows we have the Heart Stone. He knows I deceived him. We are going to have to deal with him eventually—if he does survive."

"Was Mica lying about Erathan's condition?"

"No, at least he wasn't lying about what he's been told. But Erathan's not out of the woods yet. The Leaf-Tailed spider poison is lethal. His healers may have stopped the spread, but it can still take its toll. Time will tell."

Crossing my ankles, I smile. "And we will be ready to pounce should he fall?"

"Not necessarily. If the timing works out, yes. But we can take Adren whenever we want."

I think Ry is under-playing our neighbor to the south ... but then again, he did take Trislen in a day ... by himself.

Ry chuckles. "Yes, I did. And now we have both Stones. But first, Adastra."

Absently, I rub my chest as his anticipation hits me. "So, we move on Trislen." Rydel remains silent, watching me, waiting, letting me think. After a few minutes, I sigh, scratching my beard. "I hate to say it, but I think we go small."

"How small?"

I crack my neck, hating this plan, but knowing it might be the only way.

"You, me, Carelle, and Mica."

Ry's brows shoot up toward his hairline. "I thought you'd recommend a small group, but that's ... I'm not sure Carelle is strong enough yet."

Nodding, my hand drops from my beard to my chest, rubbing in small circles. "I'll assess her tomorrow. If necessary, Casin can come, and Carelle can stay as acting captain."

"You know I prefer to move small and fast, but I'm surprised, Luc."

"Well, you said he countered every move you made against him. I think we have to operate under the assumption that Adastra does have natural magic. Moving on the capital with our army would alert him well before we even make it to the border. And the problem with a large force is we *have* to plan; we have to move with intention—all things Adastra will be able to 'see.' I think our only chance is to go in with stealth. See if we can slip in undetected."

"That's assuming he has to focus on someone to use his supposed magic of foresight. What if his magic alerts him to all threats?"

My head quirks to the side, and I frown. "Then, we're fucked."

Ry laughs. "Okay. So, we go small. We sneak into the capital."

"We sneak all the way into the castle. We use our magic to keep the alarm from going out, and we take him out." I hold Rydel's gaze, letting him see the seriousness of my next words. "We take him out fast, and quiet. No big show of power, no torture, no dragging it out, no interrogation ... no *playing*. If the opportunity presents itself, we kill him."

A flicker of disappointment streams from Ry and sinks through my chest before he calms with resolve. "Agreed."

"Is there any way—"

Ry holds up a hand, shaking his head. "No. I won't stay behind. I know I could send any number of people to attempt to infiltrate Adastra's stronghold, but I'm going. I will be there when the light leaves his eyes. He will know you and I were his end."

Taking a deep breath, I sit up straighter. "When do we leave?"

He glances out the dark window behind him. It's pitch-black outside, but the sharp ping of ice hitting the window sounds in the silence.

"This storm will be bad. It's been blowing in from the

west for days now. The worst of it should be hitting us in a day or two."

"So, we leave in two days."

He nods. "Everyone will be sheltering, and those that brave the storm will be easy enough to evade. We can slip from Lieren with only Casin aware of our departure. With any luck, the storm's reach will drive south and aid in hiding our progress."

"And when the weather fails to hide us, our magic will take over."

He smiles. "Exactly. Like ghosts, we'll slip into the Trislenian palace, kill Adastra, take back Trislen, and celebrate with drink until we pass out."

"Easy."

"Easy."

We both laugh, knowing full well it's going to be anything but. Ry smacks his palms to the table. "I'm tired ... and sore." I bite the inside of my cheek, but he smiles, and my anxiety melts. "I'm going to soak in my tub, and if I manage to keep from falling asleep in the water, I'm going to pass out in bed."

We stand in unison, and as he rounds the table, I grab Ry's arm. A wince crosses his face as his sore shoulder tugs, and a matching wince pulls at my face as I feel his pain. "Should I come with you to make sure you don't drown?" His eyes flare, and his arousal washes over me, but I also feel his exhaustion, so I shake my head, smiling. "I'm sure you'll be fine."

We stand there for a moment, neither of us willing to pull away first. Eventually, with a sigh, I lean into him, and he meets me. Our bodies press together, and my hands slide around his waist as his lips press to mine. Our breaths mingle. Ry's fingers comb through my beard, cupping my face, and we pull closer together.

The kiss is soft, slow, lingering, and ... sweet. There's no groping, no desperation. We simply hold each other as our lips caress gently. His scent surrounds me—hay and cedar— and I breathe him in. He is home to me. No matter my anger, no matter my frustration, no matter what we go through, Rydel will always, always be a source of comfort. Fuck.

With a final press of lips, I step back. His hands stay on my face, and I tilt my head back slightly to look up at him. He pulls me in for another quick kiss, then pulls back, his hands squeezing my face. His green eyes blaze, and his sincerity coats my insides as the magic flows through me.

"Lucaryn." I can't stop from trembling under his intense stare. "I won't lose you. Never again. You're mine."

My body freezes, my thoughts stall. Before my brain catches up to what he said, Ry turns and slips from my rooms.

Shit. I'm exhausted, but after that declaration, I doubt I'll get much sleep tonight.

11

LUCARYN

The past two days have blurred by. Ry and I have seen little of each other, both busy with our preparations to leave while maintaining our normal schedules.

Mica was a little surprised that both Rydel and I were planning on leaving Lieren, but it's not as if we are leaving it undefended. Our army is disciplined and ready. The Shadow Lord put in a half-hearted effort to convince us to take a few more soldiers, but in the end, he agreed to our plan.

Honestly, I expected Mica to turn us down and head out on his own. The rumors of the Shadow Lord indicate he prefers to work alone, running his small empire of thieves, spies, and crooks. The faint flare of emotions coming off him told me he consented mainly out of curiosity. He wants to see who wins—ready to shift allegiance when necessary. I certainly don't trust Mica and plan to keep a sharp eye on him.

If we can manage it, our small group plans to slip out of the city tonight without anyone knowing other than Casin. The official story—if anyone asks—is, the King is busy. Simple. Believable. No one will push back.

My story will be a little harder to pull off. I'm seen around the castle grounds much more often than Rydel, so to account for my disappearance I am 'going to Adren to speak to the captain of Erathan's army to discuss them rejoining the fight against Adastra.' It's an easy enough lie to pull apart, but luckily, my soldiers don't ask questions, most of the time—especially after my show of power with Orik.

The soft thump of my boots on the wood floor of the soldiers' barracks keep time as I walk through the quarters checking that beds are made, and the quarters are clean. I turn a corner, and the glint of weapons reflects the light of the flickering torches. Pressing my thumb to the edge of an arrowhead, I pull it back to see a tiny bead of blood well up. The sharp metallic taste coats my tongue as I suck the blood from my finger.

Very good.

I know this is the calm before the storm, and I find comfort in my routine as I inspect the long swords, short swords, daggers, throwing knives, axes, spears, and bows. But then, my back twinges slightly as fatigue threatens to slow me down—a reminder that I'm still not completely recovered from ...

I pause at the barracks threshold, looking out over the snow-blanketed expanse of the yard. Taking a big breath in, I let it out slowly. The anger that usually spikes when I think about what Rydel did to me is absent. Instead, there's a small ache in the pit of my stomach that feels more like hurt than anger. I must admit, hate-fucking Rydel released something in me.

Gusting wind pushes the fall of the icy snow at a slant. Dark clouds churn overhead making the day much darker. Snow crunches and squeaks under my boots as I step into the quickly-fading day. The clouds hang heavy and low, like I could reach up and run the tips of my fingers through them. A stinging wet combination of sleet and snow batters my face, sticks to my cloak, and clings to my hair.

The bay of excited hounds calls across the clearing as I near the kennels. The master of the hounds stands in the yard, a wide smile spread over her face as the large wolfhounds bound around her legs. There is a surprising grace to the dogs' movements for beasts so large.

The gate squeaks softly as I push it open, and I have to grab it quickly to keep it from slamming against the post as the wind catches it. I pull it shut behind me as a few hounds break from the group to circle my legs. Absently reaching down to scratch one on his wiry head, I cross toward the Master.

"Getting ready for a hunt?"

She flicks her fiery-red braid over her shoulder. "Captain. Not today. This storm will make catching a scent near impossible, and we're not desperate for a catch right now, so I'm just taking them for a quick run through the northern woods to calm them before dinner and bed."

A wolfhound rears back, bringing his head nearly level with my chin, and I chuckle as I gently push him down. He lands with a thud, shaking his coat sending a spray of droplets against my legs. "They seem ready to go."

She smiles, looking around the pack, her love for the animals obvious in her eyes, and I smile as I feel her happiness at being around the dogs. "They've been cooped up for almost two days. I was trying to wait out this storm, but it doesn't look like it's going to let up."

"The joys of living in the North."

"Wouldn't trade it for anything, captain."

With a nod, she presses her fingers between her teeth, and a shrill whistle calls the dogs to her. Passing through the gate, she walks off, the dogs sticking close as she moves through the castle grounds toward the north gate.

I skirt the kennels, leaving through the back. I walk the grounds, checking that everything's in its place and my soldiers are doing their duties. An hour passes before I finally find myself on the small, shoveled path leading toward the stables. By the time I get there, the light of the day has faded from a steel-blue to a shadowy grey, telling me the sun has set behind the thick clouds. Kicking my boots against the side of the barn, packed snow drops to the cobbled floor, and I shake the ice crystals from my cloak and hair.

The clop of hooves against stone draws my attention to the end of the aisle where Mica leads a grey mare from her stall toward the back doors. A thick pack is tied down to the back of his saddle, and leather bags hang heavy over the pommel. Mica pauses at the end of the aisle, drawing his hand down the mare's nose, waiting. He's a little nervous, but mostly dreading going out in the brutal weather. These winter storms are not something he's used to, and I grin as his distress kicks up when a strong gust of wind batters the stable walls.

A voice calls out behind me, "Ready, captain?" I turn as Carelle leads a bay mare from her stall.

I glance over her shoulder, looking out the front doors. "Riding through this storm at night is going to be hell, but yes, I'm ready."

She smiles, her left hand with its two missing fingers stroking down the mare's strong neck. "We're northerners. We can handle it."

I return her grin with a nod. "Indeed. Doesn't mean I like it." I jerk my head toward Mica. "And he's none too thrilled."

She chuckles, tucking her blond hair into the hood of her thick cloak, her usual braids keeping the strands out of her face.

"Are you guys already grumbling?"

Rydel's voice pulls at me like a thread drawn tight between us. Kahar, the giant black war horse, stands at Ry's side. The muscles of the horse's chest quiver, and he shakes his head in impatience, tossing his long mane. I do miss riding the crazy horse, but him and Ry are a better match. Besides, I've been working on a new gelding, and he has the makings of a magnificent mount.

I press my hand to my horse's stall. "I don't grumble."

Ry chuckles, the deep sound curling through my stomach. I flick open the latch, and Phoenix moves back. The gelding is tall, almost as tall as Kahar, but where Kahar is broad and thick with muscle, Phoenix is lean. His red coat shines, proof that Shana—the young stable hand—pays special attention to the care of the horses in our stable. Phoenix dips his head as I approach, his quiet acceptance like warm sunlight to Kahar's dark demeanor. I rest my hand on his white forelock before combing it down his face. "Ready for an adventure?"

Phoenix huffs a breath into my hand, and I give his lips a little tickle like he likes. For a moment, I wish the magic worked on animals, but then I cringe. That would be too much. That would kill me for sure. Scooping up my saddle, I swing it onto Phoenix, cinching it tight. I lean down, heaving my pack up, securing it tightly before I slip the bridle over his head. His teeth clench as I work my thumb into the back of his mouth. He fights taking the bit, tossing his head before I apply more pressure, prying his jaw apart enough to slip the bit in place.

"Are you going to fight that every time?"

He just looks at me, and I pat his neck before grabbing the reins and leading him out. Kahar snorts, pinning his ears back. I leap to the side as Phoenix attempts to dance out of the way, but Kahar manages to land a bite to his flank. Phoenix's back leg snaps out, but cracks against the stall walls, missing Kahar.

I scowl at the giant war horse. "Damn it, Kahar."

Rydel pulls back on the reins, forcing the black horse to take a few steps back. "I told you it was annoying."

"It's funnier when you're the one riding Kahar."

Rydel chuckles, gripping a handful of Kahar's mane, shaking him affectionately.

Carelle's quiet voice breaks our banter. "The dinner rush is under way. This is the best time to leave, your Majesty."

Ry and I nod, turning our horses toward the back of the stable. Mica presses his palm against the door, sliding it open just enough to poke his head out. I rub my chest as his trepidation turns to despair. The Shadow Lord really doesn't want to go out in this storm. When he ducks back in, snow and ice crystals cover his hood. "It's dark and quiet."

Hmm. I have to admit, I respect the man for hiding his feelings and putting forward a brave face. He certainly doesn't need to be here.

With a nod from Rydel, Mica pushes the door open enough to walk his mare through. A blast of freezing air tunnels through the stables, pulling at the edges of my cloak. Phoenix ducks his head against the wind, and as

Carelle moves forward, Rydel follows, and I bring up the rear.

The loud clop of hooves dies as soon as we step outside, the cobblestone floor changing to hard-packed dirt covered in snow. The tracks where the paths were shoveled clear earlier today are already almost filled again, and puffs of snow kick to the side as we make our way as silently as possible to the edge of the castle grounds. Luckily, the late hour and the weather has driven everyone inside.

The western gate is closer, but we want to avoid the guards, so we head north as planned. The forest presses against the northern gate, and the thick trees border the unforgiving Imorian Mountains. This gate is nearly impassable for outsiders, but just to be safe, we keep a staggered rotation of guards on the northern wall.

Our perfectly timed arrival brings the gate into view. According to the set schedule, the next sweep of guards won't be by for another twenty minutes.

Our group slips through unseen, and once we take a few steps into the dark forest, we mount up. Kahar skips and dances to the side, tossing his head, but Ry keeps his seat, actually smiling at the crazy stallion, and his amusement flutters through me. They really are a good fit.

I fan my cloak around my back and down Phoenix's sides to give him a little extra protection from the elements, as well as to trap some of his heat. With a gentle squeeze of my legs, Phoenix moves forward, and our group weaves single-file through the trees.

The forest shields us from the worst of the wind, and only the occasional drip of ice pelts against my hood. But I know this small reprieve won't last. As we skirt the edge of the kingdom, the trees are going to thin, then break. It'll be then that the unrelenting winds coming from the western sea will whip around us, and we'll be forced to move unprotected through the storm.

It's going to be a long few days until we're able to escape the unrelenting winter weather.

Rydel turns in his saddle, shooting me a smile that warms me from the inside out. I grin back, catching his excitement. Ry has always been a man of action. I shift as I begin to grow hard, recalling our 'action' the other night. Ry's grin turns to a smirk as he catches my thoughts. My blood goes molten at the look in his eyes, and I shiver as he turns back around, shifting in his saddle, his arousal floating back to me, the magic warming in my chest. There's also a hint of pain from him as he shifts again, trying to find a comfortable position in the saddle.

A smile tugs up one corner of my mouth. I guess his ass is still sore.

I groan on a quiet chuckle, ideas and plans forming, discarding, and solidifying. I can't very well spend this entire trip, traipsing across Imoria fighting an erection. At some point, I'll find a quiet place to lure Rydel away from our camp.

Ry's back stiffens, and he rolls his shoulders. His quiet laugh floats back to me on the wind, and with a press of his magic, his thoughts flick into my mind.

'We're not an hour away from the castle, and you're already plotting on how to get me alone.'

I send my thoughts back to him, catching his small flare of pain as the magic takes its toll from Rydel.

'It's been two days. Two long days. And I recall the promise of making me submit.'

Ry shivers, the move fluttering his cloak. The soft buzz of the emotions coming from our small group is overpowered by Rydel's arousal as it slams into me. The magic tears at my chest, the pain of the power slicing at me like knives against my skin. The pain does nothing to dampen my desire, though.

With a few deep breaths, I'm able to calm the magic. To keep my thoughts off Rydel's cock, I go over the plan for when we reach the Trislenian capital city. Ice pelts against my cloak, the tiny thunk of the sleet drumming a random rhythm. I've thought through the plan countless times, but I do it again, working through any sticking points, trying to calculate anything that might tilt the results in our favor. It's a solid plan, yet there are so many unknowns. But where I thrive on plans or order, Rydel thrives off chaos. When the plan goes to shit, Ry will be there to do something crazy to get us out of trouble.

I hope so, anyway.

Thunder rumbles, and a second later a flash of lighting sparks behind the clouds, lighting up the forest around us, freezing the snow and ice in midair for a moment. Then the world goes dark again. The wind snaps and pulls at my cloak, so I grip it tighter, tucking myself deeper into its folds. I allow Phoenix to follow Kahar, and I go over the plan again.

12

RYDEL

Four days of fighting the storm made our progress slow. We're only halfway to Adren, when we should be crossing the border tomorrow. But the storm broke yesterday, so we should be able to make up time.

I run a hand down my face, scratching at my beard as the flames of the fire flicker. I shift on the horse blanket, moving my weight to my hip, bending up a knee as I brace on my hand. My ass is still sore.

A smile tempts my lips, but I press my mouth tight. I would have healed by now, but long days in the saddle have done me no favors. Every step of Kahar's hooves sends a reminder up my spine of what Luc and I did. I've been semi-hard since we left.

And Luc's thoughts tell me he's been in much the same condition. I open my mouth to excuse myself into the woods, hoping Luc might follow me, but Mica snaps his teeth around a length of dried meat. The loud sound of his chewing crosses the small space we chose to camp, and around the grinding of his teeth, he says, "I must admit, I'm happy to see the tail end of that storm. Are all winters like that here?"

Carelle laughs, her fingers combing through her long hair, separating it into sections that she starts to braid. "Some are worse than others, but yeah, our winter storms are pretty intense."

Mica runs a hand through his locs. "Well, I really appreciate the south now."

Luc pokes the fire with a long stick, and embers float into the sky, dancing around each other like will-o-the-wisps. "Now, all we have to do is kill Adastra and take back Trislen, and you can have your shadow empire back."

Mica smiles, his teeth stark against his black skin. "I never lost *my* empire."

I raise an eyebrow. "It has been curbed, though."

Mica shrugs. "Slightly."

Carelle wipes her hands down her thighs before standing. "I'm going to patrol."

We're in the middle of nowhere. The threat level is near to zero, but Luc nods to her, his thoughts floating through my mind. '*A patrol may not be necessary, but it's good to keep the habit. Plus ... you never know.*'

His thoughts drift off as he thinks over the watch schedule for tonight. I turn back to Mica. His mind is quiet —content in the moment. The only other person I've met who was so in control of their mind was Erathan. It's ... disconcerting.

I shift to my other hip, hiding a wince as I brace my forearm on my other knee. "Mica, you had people in the palace." It's not a question, but he shrugs. "Are they still there?"

"I'm not sure. I assume so. I only had three people in place ... keeping an eye on things once you left back for the north."

I nod, a smirk playing across my face. "I expected as much. Runic was keeping an eye on your 'eyes,' but I don't know that we identified them all."

"Your man was very thorough, but you can't find a spy who doesn't know they're spying."

A wave of concern flutters through my stomach. I have no idea of Runic's fate. My hand falls to my thigh sheath, but I just rest it there instead of drawing my dagger. Fuck Adastra.

Luc absently draws little designs in the dirt with his stick. "You had spies who didn't know they were spies?"

Mica nods, his thoughts kicking up as he weighs the pros and cons of revealing his players, concluding that at this point he's thrown his lot in with us—until it's more advantageous to switch sides.

The Shadow Lord's finger taps his thigh, looking at me with a shrug, knowing I'm listening in on his every thought. "My second in command was fucking one of the cooks, and she loved pillow talk. One of the royal gardeners was a frequent visitor to one of my gambling dens. He was a bad player and a talkative drunk. He never questioned my continued extension of credits. He wasn't aware he was paying me back with secrets."

He pauses, his eyes going distant. Luc raises an eyebrow. I wonder what he's feeling from Mica? I hear the Shadow Lord's thoughts, but I'm enjoying pulling the information from him. "And the third?"

Mica lifts his head, his eyes focusing on me. "Hm?"

"You said you had three in the palace."

He smiles, his gaze darting between Luc and me. "You two are quite the pair. If your magic can rival what I expect Adastra has, you might just rule all of Imoria."

Luc glances at me. '*He's evading.*'

Despite the cold, crisp night, sweat is starting to stick my shirt to my skin as my magic heats under my skin and pain flares across my temples. "We just might. But, your third on the inside?"

Mica shakes his head with a knowing smile. "The healer."

My brows climb my forehead. Now that does surprise me. The royal healer was a no-nonsense woman who spoke her mind and had a crush on my South Lieren captain, Runic.

Mica registers my surprise and nods. "I paid her good money to stitch up my fighters. She's the best in Trislen, and if my fighters can't fight, or if they're too damaged to win, that means I'm losing money. She is worth every coin."

"She talked about what was going on in the palace?"

All I want to do is fling my cloak off my shoulders to escape the heat of my magic, and I watch as Mica's fingers grip the edge of his cloak, pulling the edges tighter around him, saying,

"No. She wouldn't be so unprofessional. It took time to pull her secrets from her. My people kept watch on her supplies. We tracked when she was running low on certain medicines. Occasionally, she would request ... certain illegals."

Luc looks up from his dirt drawings. "And since you run the drug game in Trislen, it was easy to track where they were going."

Mica smiles. "It pays to have your fingers in a lot of pies."

I nod, rolling my shoulders where the Stone burns in my back. "But you haven't heard from any of them since Adastra closed up the palace?"

A frown pulls at Mica's handsome face. "No. Nothing."

"And you haven't been successful in getting anyone in?"

He takes a deep breath. "I've tried. But Adastra's guards are vigilant. No one has gotten into the palace, that I know of anyway."

Luc clicks his tongue. "And I guess if anyone were to know, it would be you."

Mica's face is serious as he meets Luc's gaze. "Yes. If I can't get anyone in the palace, no one is getting in."

I laugh at Luc's skeptical expression, and his lips relax as I smile, saying, "The Shadow Lord has a confidence that rivals mine."

Luc rolls his eyes. "He fits right in."

Mica sighs, but there's a slight twitch to his lips like he's holding back a smile. He drops down onto his side, pulling his blankets up to his neck and his hood down low over his face. His voice comes out muffled as he curls his knees into his chest. "Good night, your Majesty. Captain."

The space around the fire goes quiet, broken only by the occasional crack of splintering wood. A large log collapses, and sparks twirl into the sky before going dark, and the wind pulls the ash away. If I listen hard enough, I imagine I can hear the crash of waves to the west where the freezing sea churns. But we are too far inland.

Luc eyes the fire, then stands with a grunt. "I'm going to get more wood for the fire to make sure we make it through the night."

I glance at the pile of sticks and logs over where we have the horses tethered. We have more than enough. Luc's broad back stalks into the darkness, and his low voice carries to me as he finds Carelle and speaks to her.

The fire dances before me, its heat unnaturally warm, like the flames are actually licking my face. But this isn't the heat of fire or pain of the magic, this is my body wanting Luc's. I was unable to catch Luc's thoughts before he left camp, but if I were a gambling man, and I am, I can guess that he's trying to draw me away from the fire.

My cock twitches in anticipation as I quietly push to my feet. As I step away from the clearing we made for camp, my boots sink into snow. I slow my pace, trekking lightly, heel to toe. Carelle moved off to the west after Luc spoke with her, so I skirt to the east, tracking Luc's boot prints.

Like magic, the clouds break for just a moment, and moonlight spills between the trees, highlighting Luc's broad form. Gods, I'm beyond lucky. The poisoned arrow, the secrets, the anger ... he's still with me.

His back is to me, his hand pressed to the rough bark of a tree. His other arm is wrapped around his waist, and when I silently move closer, I notice the subtle up and down motion of his shoulder.

I go rock hard, and his back flexes with the next pump of his hand.

"You can't sneak up on the owner of the Heart Stone, Ry."

I close the space between us, pressing my front to his back. He's so warm, I unclasp my cloak and let it fall to the ground. Leaning over his shoulder, I whisper against his ear. "You need help with that?"

His head turns, bringing his lips a breath from mine. "You offering?"

My face darts forward, and I bite his lower lip. He sucks

in a sharp breath, his hand never stopping his slow strokes. "Yes, but I'm going to get mine first."

Luc groans, and blood pools in my cock. My breaths are shallow as I remove his cloak, hanging it on a low branch before my fingers grip the waist of his pants. They're already loose where he undid them to free his aching cock, so I tug them down his thighs. I run my fingers over the muscular swell of his ass, and he shivers.

"Your hands are cold, Ry."

My palms caress his back as I work my way up his spine. "They'll warm up."

He shivers again, his fist moving faster. "Inner left pocket of my cloak."

I grin, biting his shoulder before fumbling around the heavy folds of his cloak. Wrapping my fingers around a small bottle, I remove it, noticing a pale substance inside. When I tilt the bottle, whatever is inside moves too slow for a liquid.

Before I ask, Luc says, "Clara at The Broken Mountain has this made for her whores. I haven't tried it yet, but she claims it glides like a woman's wet pussy and warms the flesh."

The pop of the cork whispers between us as I yank the top out with my teeth. I dip a finger into the bottle and rub the substance between my thumb and finger.

"Oh fuck, Luc." It does indeed feel like a woman's cunt, and my fingers start to warm and tingle slightly. "When did you find the time to go to the Broken Mountain?"

The pleasure house in the center of our capital city, Farden, is seedy, dangerous, and the place to go for any vice you might want to indulge in.

"The day before we left. Now shut up and—"

I slide my finger between his cheeks and into his tight

ass. The lubrication helps my finger press deep with little resistance. Luc's groan shoots lust through my stomach, and his fist grips his cock tight before he resumes his slow pumping.

"Do it, Ry. I need you."

His voice is strained, and there's such longing in his words, I immediately pull my finger free, coating my cock with the lubrication, then fisting myself. I pump once, twice, then spread the warm substance down his crack, circling his hole. I'm so tense, pleasure winding me tight. Gripping my cock, I press it to his ass. My teeth bite down hard on my lower lip as I slowly slide into him.

The pulsing head of my cock has barely breached his entrance when he grunts and shoves himself back on me. I slide all the way to the hilt, my balls pressing against the back of his thighs. Our combined moans are like the sweetest music as I just hold myself deep within Luc. This is where I want to spend the rest of my life.

Reaching around Luc, I yank his hand off his cock, and wrap my lubricated hand around his shaft. It throbs under my grip, and I pump him a few times. His breath pants out in little clouds around his lips. "Fuck, Clara is a genius."

My hips slowly pull back before I slide back into Luc even slower. "Indeed. I'm buying as much of this as she has when we get back."

Luc's chuckle is cut off as I cup his balls and slam my cock deep in him at the same time. Pleasure curls across my lower back, through my stomach, down my thighs, all the way to my toes. The reminder of how Luc used his magic to make me come, gives me an idea. If I can use the Mind Stone to convince the body that it's experiencing real pain, surely, I can do so with pleasure.

Luc's muscles stiffen. He rips my hand from his cock and

grips himself, stroking fast and hard. "I feel your anticipation, Ry. What are you—"

Before he can finish his question, and before I can experiment with my magic, we both go still—his hand tight around his cock, my shaft deep inside him. I press my thoughts into his mind.

'Do you feel it?'

He nods. 'Doesn't feel like Carelle or Mica. How many do you hear?'

'One. Maybe two.'

Luc nods again, shoving his cock into his pants. More reluctantly than I've ever done anything in my life, I pull out of him, putting myself away. Silently, we gather our cloaks. I make sure I have the little bottle of magic lubrication, tucking it into my pocket.

Someone is close. Friend or foe? I'm not sure, but I always assume foe. I feel the soft buzz of thoughts but can't make out the words yet. My dagger is in my hand with my next breath, and my magic is at the ready.

Luc rubs his chest, the magic pushing emotions on him. Slowly, he bends down, and my cock weeps pre-cum. He reaches into his boot, and when he stands, a small knife is in his hand.

We stand close under the shadow of the tree and wait for our foe to come to us.

13

RYDEL

A handful of moments pass in silence, and once the mental voices get close enough, I sigh, relaxing my shoulders down my back. Luc slides his knife back into his boot before standing.

My heart skips a beat, and I hold my breath as he leans back, resting against my chest. His head turns slightly, and my gaze snags on his profile, watching his lips move with his whispered words. "They're not after us. Hunters?"

I can't help myself, leaning forward, nibbling on his ear. "Yes. A pair of hunters out checking traps. They will move on soon."

Kissing the warm flesh behind his ear, I move down his neck as he tilts his head to the side. I grip his hair, holding him as I bite the thick muscle where his shoulder meets his neck. His salty taste is delicious. He is perfection. His breath puffs out on a silent gasp before he rubs his ass against my cock. "You are a distraction, your Majesty."

I love the tinge of playfulness in his voice. He is always so serious, but with me, he allows his mischievous side out. It sparks happiness that blooms in my chest like a shot of really good whiskey. Smirking against his neck, I lick my teeth marks in his skin and wrap my hand around his waist, quickly undoing his pants once again. "As are you, Captain."

Luc shoves his pants over his hips.

I free my cock, groaning, "I need you."

Reaching back, he finds the bottle in my pants pocket, pulling it free, asking, "The hunters?"

"Already moved on."

"And Carelle?" He smears a small amount of the lubrication on his hand before pumping himself slow and strong.

I work my hand under his, collecting the lube before stroking myself. "She suspects we are doing this so she's keeping her distance."

Luc's chuckle cuts off as I slide back into his tight entrance. "Fuck, Luc. So tight. So perfect."

My hand snakes around his waist, and I grip his shirt at his chest, holding him against me in a tight embrace. I want to feel him. I want to experience him. I need his closeness right now. His scent, his moans, his brown skin against mine, his panting breaths ... I need it all. He's like a drug, and I'm not quitting this one.

My other hand wraps around his pumping fist. With a groan, he lets go of his cock so I can grip him, then he closes his fingers around mine, saying, "Look at your pale fingers stroking my cock, Ry." I look down over his shoulder, my cock aching at the sight. Luc turns his head, lightly biting my ear before staring back down at my hand pumping his cock. "I could come just from watching your large hands touch me."

"Not yet, Luc. I need more." My hips thrust in time with my pumping fist. My arm around his chest crawls up his body until I have a soft grip on his throat. As he tilts his head back, I'm left speechless at his beauty. He is all hard angles tempered by soft brown skin, silky black hair, and startling blue eyes.

He swallows, his throat flexing against my palm. My fingers squeeze the edges of his neck, and his eyes roll back as his body bucks back into mine. His thoughts get hazy as I restrict the blood flow. His hands slap against the tree trunk, giving him leverage to meet me thrust for thrust.

Just when I feel his muscles start to quiver and his thoughts float away, I release my grip on his neck. His head lolls to the side as one hand grips mine away from his throat, bringing my fingers to his mouth. He sucks two of my fingers between his lips, rolling his tongue around my sensitive flesh.

Fuck me. This man will be my undoing.

My hand on his cock grips tighter, and then I'm stroking him in time to his sucking motion, and my cock slams into him with every pull of his tongue on my fingers.

I am dangerously consumed by Luc. I know this. I don't care. I would let an enemy come up behind me and stab me in the back right now. My need for him burns away everything else. I would die for him, but more importantly, I would burn the entire country, the entire world to keep him safe. He needs to know. There can be no doubt.

With my next thrust, I stop. My knees nearly buckle with the effort it takes to keep myself still while buried deep in Luc's ass. I run my thumb over the slit along the head of his cock, and he slides my fingers from his mouth, swearing as he tries to grind against me.

My hand climbs back up his throat, and I gently grip his jaw. Turning him, my lips hover over his. Luc's breath pants against my face as I say the words for him. Only for him. "Lucaryn. You are my everything. It will always be you and me. My life is yours. My body is yours. My ... heart is yours. Forever. Uh sahe'a iyai. *I love you.*"

His body goes still, his gaze bouncing between my eyes, looking for the sarcasm or the lie. He won't find it. The brilliance of his blue eyes sparkles with his desire. I'd like to believe his eyes are shining with love, but I can't know that for sure.

Wait. What?

I look at Luc, really look at him. A smile spreads across my lips with my joy, and it quickly morphs into a full grin.

Luc licks his lips, tilting his head in confusion. Before he can say anything, I press a kiss to his mouth, sliding my tongue between his lips. Luc melts into me, kissing me back, and as one, our bodies move. His hand joins mine again, and we stroke him together with a firm grip. My cock slides in and out of his tight entrance, and when I feel his abs flex and his hips lose the pace, I deepen our kiss, swallowing his shout as he comes. I follow a moment later, my body bursting with pleasure as my skin tingles and white stars dance behind my eyelids. Sagging against his back, his tongue continues to stroke mine.

I stay seated in him for another moment before pulling out, hissing as the freezing air hits my wet, spent cock. We clean ourselves up as best we can, and with a quick kiss to his cheek, his beard tickling my lips, I turn to head back to the camp, but Luc grips my arm.

"Ry, wait."

I raise an eyebrow, taking in every shift of his face, every movement of his eyes, waiting.

"I ... I feel the same way." My heart stalls before kicking up into a fast gallop. He steps back into my space, wrapping his arms around my waist, hugging me tight. He kisses me before he rests his forehead against mine. My arms hold him tight, reveling in the muscle that's built back up across his back. His eyes are closed as he shakes his head, his hair tickling my face.

I swallow, hoping I'm making the right choice by saying, "What are you thinking?"

Luc snorts, but keeps his eyes closed. "Very funny, Ry."

I take a deep breath, whispering, "I mean it, Luc."

His eyes pop open as he pulls away, but I hold him tight. His gaze bores into mine, and I shrug. "I can't hear you, Luc. The magic is quiet."

Wide eyes search my face as his mouth drops open. We stare at each other, and though I wish I knew what he was thinking, I'm eternally grateful that I can't hear his thoughts. Thank Beatuis.

Luc bites his lip. "Just like that?"

I chuckle. "Don't make it sound so simple. But yes. I realized my love for you trumps everything else, Luc. Nothing else matters if I don't have you. No matter what, I trust you. You have gotten me this far. I trust you to get us to the finish line ... whatever that looks like."

His eyes pass over mine once more before he takes a deep breath, nodding. "Okay. Okay. I ... Fuck, Ry. What do I say to that?"

Pulling him back, inhaling his petrichor scent, I kiss him before saying, "You don't need to say anything. I just wanted you to know."

Leaning back slightly, he brushes a strand of hair out of

my face. "Well, one thing I can say is that I love you. Iyai use'a niy zasss, saa. *You are my world, too."*

"Thank fuck." He laughs as I crash my lips to his, our tongues dancing and licking, and when we pull apart, we're both breathing hard again. "Luc, I'm so so sorry. You know that, right? I just—"

"It's okay, Rydel. I've had time to be angry. I've processed the hurt. I've worked through the sadness and guilt. I forgive you. I want to move forward."

My next breath leaves me on a slow exhale as all my tension unfurls, draining from my body, seemingly through my toes. "Me too."

We take a step away from each other as Carelle's voice calls quietly through the woods. "Sire? Captain? I'm headed back to camp. You should too."

I shove Luc in the camp's direction. "She's right. We need rest."

"You first. I'll watch."

"We can make Mica watch."

Luc glances at me over his shoulder. "You trust him like that?"

My lips tick up in a small smile. "No. Alright. You watch first. Wake me in an hour."

He tilts his head back as we break from the tree line into the small camp clearing. "Make it two hours. You need the sleep, Rydel."

Mica snorts in his sleep before rolling onto his other side, his dreaming mind floating through my head. The specifics of dreams have always been closed off to the magic, but there's a distinct feel to a person's sleeping mind. It's like the feeling of running your hand over blades of grass—both sharp and soft.

Carelle rolls her eyes as she curls up under her blankets.

"The King can sleep through the rest of the night. Captain, give me two hours, then I'll take watch. I'm well rested after being on bed rest for so long. Okay?"

I barely hold back a chuckle. I'd forgotten how much I like Carelle. Smart and pragmatic. And I am tired. Exhausted, really. "Sounds like a plan. Captain?"

He sighs. "Fine." Dragging his horse blanket over to me, he sets up his bedroll before moving to the other side of the fire, sitting on a log. Carelle smiles before burrowing into her blankets. I raise an eyebrow at Luc, and he returns the look. I nod in answer, bracing for his thoughts as he pushes them at me.

'You're too distracting. I need to concentrate while on watch, so I'll just be over here or patrolling close by.'

I nod with a smile, snuggling into my blankets, wishing his warm body was pressed against mine.

'Goodnight, Rydel.'

'Goodnight, Lucaryn.'

14

LUCARYN

Ry and I have managed to keep our cocks to ourselves these past few days as we pushed south. Our pace has been grueling, pushing the horses to their limits. The days are cold and the nights are freezing, but we've been so tired, sleep claims us as soon as our shift is over.

One more day.

I'm on edge. I'm itchy with anticipation. Has Adastra foreseen us coming? Are we walking right into a trap? Our plan is solid, but it all hinges on Adastra's second sight staying off us until it's too late.

"That's a deep furrow between those brows." Mica's voice and mild amusement pulls me out of my head, and I shift in the saddle, doing my best to relax my face muscles. The churning discomfort in my gut and scraping pressure in my chest from the Heart Stone is … bearable with just the four of us.

"Just trying to think through possible scenarios."

Mica smiles with a nod. "You seem to be ... the thinker of you two." I raise an eyebrow, and he chuckles, holding up a hand. "That sounded wrong. I'm sure King Rydel has many deep thoughts. He just seems to be a man of action, of impulse, of passion. You, captain, are a man of the mind. You like to consider." I chew on the inside of my cheek as I watch Mica sway with the easy steps of his mare. He nods at me again. "There. See. You're assessing me right now. You have a sharp mind, captain. I'm the same, you see. I like all my options covered, every eventuality thought through. Often, I find myself lost in my thoughts, circling and spiraling into what-if's."

Mica glances forward, aiming his gaze at Rydel who's talking quietly with Carelle.

"It's good to have someone who can get you out of your head. Someone to give you permission to just react. And it's good for him to have someone 'tighten his reins' if you will —when it's needed."

I rest one hand on my thigh, the other on the pommel of my saddle. Mica's emotions are amused, thoughtful, and considerate. For a seedy underground lord of vice, he's a really happy fella. "Is this your way of saying we make a good team?"

Mica laughs, the sound bright and happy. "I guess so. You see?" He points at himself. "Overthinker."

I laugh with him, then we fall into a comfortable silence.

We've moved steadily east, the foothills looming closer, the forests slowly closing in around us. Carelle moves her horse forward, Kahar trying to take a bite out of her horse's flank as she pulls ahead. I shake my head with a smile as Ry pulls back on the reins, admonishing the steed, "Kahar, really? Just once, can you not be an ass?"

Rydel falls in behind Carelle, Mica draws his horse behind Rydel, and I hold Phoenix back to bring up the rear. The clop of hooves softens under the thick brush and rotted leaves. Bare branches brush my legs and pull at my cloak. The press of the woods keeps the chilly winds at bay, and I quickly grow warm under my layers of clothing.

Ry throws his cloak over his shoulders, and Carelle shrugs out of her coat, balling it up and stuffing it in one of her saddle bags. Her mare never misses a step as Carelle twists and turns to get herself situated. Mica seems to be the only one unbothered by the temperature change, keeping his layers and remaining snuggled in his thick cloak. I almost roll my eyes. Southerner.

We travel in silence, each lost in our own thoughts, knowing the capital of Trislen draws near. The longer we travel, the more the Stone burns in my chest as I try to push the magic farther and farther. I want to pick up on anyone that might be out here, lying in wait.

A twig snaps off to my left, and my head whips in that direction. I'm reaching for a blade when a pheasant flutters out of a bush, winging toward the sky.

'*Why are you so tense, Luc?*'

I shake my head. '*Why aren't you* more *tense?*'

His mental chuckle slides through my mind, and my shoulders relax slightly.

'*Your plan is good. We're prepared. We can't account for everything, even though I know you would if you could. Everything is going to be fine. I have you at my side, and we have the Stones. It'll go just as you planned. We get in. We kill Adastra. We clean house. We celebrate.*'

My lips press together, and my cheeks tick up as I try to hold in my chuckle. Classic Rydel.

He cracks his neck, rolling his shoulders, and I know the

mental conversation is hurting him, so I shut it down, but something feels off. I look down our line, gaze halting on each person's back for a moment before moving on. I look side-to-side and even turn in my saddle to check the narrow dirt trail behind us. Everything is quiet.

Why do I feel like something is ... different?

I take a deep breath, dropping my head, closing my eyes, trusting Phoenix to carry along the path. The Stone flares, and I grip the reins to keep from rubbing my chest. There's Mica's contentment. He's a little nervous knowing we will move on the capital tomorrow, but he's mostly curious to see how everything will turn out. Carelle is on guard, tension running through her like silk bands pulled tight. But she's also confident. Or maybe it's a false confidence. Yes, that's it. She's hoping for the best, preparing for the worst.

But Rydel is ...

Nothing. I've got nothing. I screw my eyes tight, searching for anything coming from him.

My eyes snap open, and my head lifts. I stare at the back of Ry's head, his blond hair pulled half-back in a knot. His broad shoulders are relaxed, and his hips move with Kahar's long strides. My hand lifts, rubbing at the scar over the Stone, and as I continue to stare at Ry, the Stone's heat settles, and I have the odd impression of the magic curling up like a cat in the sun.

Is this what Rydel meant when he said the power sleeps around me? Does the magic feel my love for him and ... leave him alone?

Fascinating.

I count out ten slow, deep breaths. Still, nothing from Rydel. Curious, I command the magic to push into him. Immediately, pain flares, my chest muscles spasm, and heat blooms across my body. I get a flash of Rydel's excitement at finally drawing close to Adastra before there's a wave of shock. He shifts, rubbing his chest, and his voice sounds through my mind.

'*What was that for?*'

'*Sorry. Just … never mind. I'll tell you later.*'

'*Well, that's going to drive me insane. Tell me.*'

I chuckle, and he glances at me over his shoulder before shaking his head with a smile and turning back forward.

'*Fine, don't tell me. Make me worry about it all day.*'

'*The day is nearly over.*'

'*You realize you could have told me twice over by now.*'

'*Ry, don't exhaust yourself.*'

I get a mental eyeroll as the connection goes quiet.

Mica turns, looking at me then back at Rydel. "You guys know it's totally obvious you're"—he taps his temple—"doing that magic thing. Right?"

I frown, scratching my beard. Is it really that obvious? We'll need to work on that.

Rydel laughs. "Indeed? It's not like we were *trying* to hide it. If we wanted, we could discuss and execute an entire scheme without you any the wiser."

Mica smirks with a little snort of laughter. "Convenient. That will come in handy if things go squirrelly tomorrow."

Carelle turns in her saddle. "Squirrelly?"

"You know, how those little guys scurry back and forth like they have no idea what they're going to do next? Squirrelly."

I shake my head, an amused smile on my face. "Okay. Yes, we'll use our magic however we need to if things get squirrelly. But, for now, we're drawing closer to the capital. We'll stay in the shelter of the woods tonight, but let's travel in silence from here on out, just in case. Rydel will alert us mentally if he picks up on any outsider thoughts, and I'll alert Rydel if I feel anyone approaching.

"Aye, captain." Carelle settles in her saddle, back straight, free hand resting near her blade.

Mica nods with a sigh. I feel his mirth dissolve under a flutter of distress, and I realize his banter was distracting him from what's looming for us tomorrow.

Rydel cracks his neck again, and I hear, *'You're sexy when you take charge and give orders.'*

'Rydel.'

'Oooh. Say that again.'

'Seriously? Focus, your Majesty.'

'Yes, sir.'

A shiver tingles down my spine, and I shift as my balls tighten painfully against the saddle, and my cock starts to harden.

Ry's voice chuckles in my mind before going silent, and I shake my head, begging my cock to behave.

After an hour, the shadows deepen, and crickets start singing their songs to the stars. There's the occasional screech as night birds-of-prey swoop on small scurrying animals trying to hide in the brush. A sharp bark sounds to the south as a fox calls into the night, and Carelle quietly grabs her coat from her bag, sliding it back on as the air chills.

Another ten minutes pass, and I have to look twice, but I notice the space leaking between the trees ahead of us and slightly to the left is faintly brighter.

Torchlight. It's a little over a mile away, but the collective flames chasing away the darkness within the Trislenian capital create a soft glow along the horizon.

We're here.

15

RYDEL

My dagger spins and flips in my left hand, but my gaze is focused through the trees. The hard ground presses against my right knee where I kneel, cloak draped around me in the darkness.

He's there. Adastra. Are we walking into a trap? Maybe. Probably. But this is the closest I've gotten to the capital since Adastra took the southern kingdom. The leather hilt of my dagger slides along my palm as I flip it again, and my other hand rubs over my thigh with anticipation. I can practically hear his pleas for mercy, his screams of pain, and the very particular silence that wraps around someone the moment I've broken them.

I've sat in that silence—the day I locked Luc away. Never again.

I shake my head, eyes narrowed as if I can see through the city's edge, through the palace walls, and into Adastra's mind. A smile lifts my lips, but a moment later, it falls. Gritting my teeth, I press my right hand to the side of my head, rubbing circles against my temple. My concentration accidentally unleashed my magic, penetrating the edge of the city. Thankfully, my power can't go any further since just that little lick of thoughts and mental images from the heavily populated capital sends spikes of pain through my head.

Closing my eyes, I pull back on the magic. The soft crunch of leaves underfoot draws Carelle to my side, her thoughts sliding into my mind.

'It's almost time. This is crazy. This better work. This is crazy. If we're successful ... wow. But if not, well, what a way to go. Exciting. Almost time.'

I run my fingers through my hair before glancing up at her. "Everyone ready?"

"As ready as we'll ever be."

I smile, standing as I sheathe my dagger and brush dirt from my pants. My eyes travel over the three people standing before me, my magic dipping into their minds for a moment. Carelle is excited. Mica is nervous. And with a purposeful push, Luc is ... worried, anxious, excited, and focused.

Nodding, Mica moves forward, clapping a hand to my shoulder before raising his hood over his head and mounts his mare. He hugs the tree line, moving a little ways off, waiting for me. Carelle nods to Luc, then turns to me, saluting with a fist over her heart. She lifts her hood, passing me on quiet feet as she mounts up and moves to the south to wait for Luc.

Lucaryn and I make eye contact. His bright blue eyes hold mine for a long moment. As one, we cross the distance between us, arms wrapping around each other. He presses his forehead to mine, and I grip the back of his cloak in my clenched fingers, holding him tight.

We need to go, but my hands won't listen to me. I can't release him. I just keep taking deep breaths, soaking him in, memorizing his petrichor scent, his muscular back, his strong arms, his soft hair brushing my face.

This isn't goodbye.

My hand slides up Luc's back, fingers curling over his scalp as I gently grip his hair. I pull him back slightly, a smile pulling at my lips as he grins at me with a deep breath. Holding him still, I look straight into his eyes.

"Uh sahe'a iyai. E'a rue'a. E'a sisse'arr. E'a srarf. Re'ae'a iyai ar se'a ase'as ruhse'a." *I love you. Be safe. Be ruthless. Be strong. See you on the other side.*

Luc leans forward, and I meet him. Our lips brush together, and a warmth spreads from where our lips touch, filling my head, gliding down my throat, coating my chest, filling my belly, and tingling all the way to my toes. I kiss him again. And again. Our lips just lightly brush together, the soft scratch of his beard rubbing against mine. My fingers massage his scalp as his hands grip my waist.

This is so hard—letting go.

With one last lingering kiss, I pull back, and Luc nods, whispering, "Uh sahe'a iyai. Sa zusahe'as uhs suhe'ar sa zanea uzh sa nea." *I love you. Do whatever it takes to come back to me.*

I nod, stepping back, immediately missing his warmth.

Without another word, we turn, facing the capital city. Luc swings on to Phoenix, kicking him south where he passes Carelle who follows him. I run a hand down Kahar's neck, his warmth soaking into my skin. Grabbing a handful of his mane, I swing into the saddle and angle toward where

Mica waits. I fight the urge to look over my shoulder. I have to concentrate. Luc will be fine.

The mother moon is new tonight, and the child moon will not rise for the next three days, so the darkness is complete. Pressure in my head increases until it feels like my brain has swelled and is scraping against my skull. The Stone flares with heat across my back, and I sit taller, letting the magic wash over me in all its painful glory.

Kahar prances in a little side-step, and I easily move with him. He feels my excitement and is ready for action. His long black mane slaps me in the face as he tosses his head, trying to pull the reins from my grip. Laughing, I keep a firm grip on him, my thighs squeezing his sides. "Okay, Kahar. For just a moment. Go ahead."

As soon as I release a fraction of the tension in the reins, he jumps forward into a powerful gallop. The wind whips my hair back, the cool air stinging my face, drawing tears from my eyes. The steady pounding of Mica's horse's hooves keeps pace behind me, but my gaze stays glued to the city and beyond where I know the palace lies in wait—where Adastra will fall.

Reluctantly, I pull back on Kahar, slowing his pace to a canter, then a quick trot, until finally I coax him into a prancing walk. The city gate looms, and my magic pulses around me, enveloping Mica, erasing us from the minds of anyone standing guard, anyone keeping watch, and any passerby.

We cross into the city unseen.

Opening my mouth wide, I crack my jaw, releasing some of the pain from where I was grinding my teeth. The heat from the Mind Stone slicks sweat down my back, and my shoulders are already shaking with the effort to hold the power. Keeping Kahar and myself hidden within the magic is work enough, but adding Mica and his mount is making my teeth ache.

Luckily, the late hour, or I guess the early hour since the first hours of the new day have dawned, presents fairly empty streets. But the few people we pass keep their heads down, their strides unbroken, never realizing the Crown Breaker and the Shadow Lord pass among them.

But the city seems ... normal. The people we pass are concerned with everyday things; money, food, sex ... Torchlight flickers from inns and taverns, and a few shops remain open to those who can only do their shopping after their long day of work or in the hours before their workday starts. Not one thought floats to me of Adastra or me or the conflict between us. If the people are not being asked to give up their coin to fund a war or to give up their lives to fight, they don't seem to care. They go on as they've always done.

Fair enough.

We make quick progress, a grin lighting up my face. So far so good. No traps. No rushing guards. No alerts.

On our next turn, the yellow door of a small, run-down house greets me. I swing to the ground, leading Kahar down the street, keeping my magic wrapped around us as I send it into the building. I'm hit with the thoughts of the woman inside, picturing her moving sleepily around her kitchen as she prepares for her day.

'*Tired. Coffee. No time to eat. Maybe I can grab something at Maggie's on the way. No. I need to save my coin. I still owe the Shadow Lord ...*' numbers float through her mind, and she mentally winces. '*Still so much. I'm never going to get out from under him. This sweater is itchy. I hate winter. I wonder if—*'

Her thoughts stall as she hears our approach. I smile. Mica has picked well. Last night, he told Luc where to go to leave their horses, and this is our stop.

Confusion and a slice of fear ripples from the woman inside as I knock on her door. Brown skin peeks around the door, dark eyes wide as she takes me in. Her eyes flick to Kahar, and she gulps. When her gaze lands on Mica, she actually gasps, stumbling back into her house, bowing her head, wringing her hands.

Angling my head over my shoulder, I raise a brow at Mica. He shrugs with a small smile, and I almost laugh. Man after my own heart.

Mica steps around me, standing in the doorway. "Sibyl."

She doesn't respond, just continues to wring her hands, her knuckles white, her dark hair hiding her face.

Mica clears his throat. "Today is your lucky day. I need you to take care of these horses until one or both of us return."

Her eyes flick up, but her posture remains bowed. Her eyes dance between Mica and me. Chaotic fear and hope swirl through her mind.

Mica steps back. "Do this, and your debts are forgiven."

Sibyl freezes, her impossibly wide eyes going even wider as she whispers, "All of it?"

Mica nods, and I grin at the tears welling in her eyes. The perfect mark. We will use her for our means, and from his thoughts, Mica knows he's not really missing out on much by forgiving her debts. Sure, the amount seemed insurmountable to her, but it is mere change to Mica. Plus, he's fairly confident she will quickly return to the gambling dens to spend her hard-earned coin and dig herself back into his debt in no time.

Sibyl rushes from the house, gathering the reins of Mica's horse, but as she reaches for Kahar's reins, I shove my magic into her head.

'If one hair is harmed on his hide, it will be your life.'

A gasp of pain pants from her parted lips, and she drops the reins. Pressing a hand to her forehead, she moans and takes a step back before her eyes snap to me, drawing another hiss of pain from her lips.

"You ... You're ... t-the Crow ... you're him."

I grin, leaning in, pulling back the magic just slightly. "Yes. Yes I am."

She drops to her knees, the sound of bone striking cobblestone loud in the early morning hush. Her palms slap to the ground, and her head hits the backs of her hands.

"The horses will be safe. I will watch over them as long as needed. On my life."

Her back spasms as I whisper in her mind, *'Yes, on your life.'*

Straightening, I manage to keep myself from cracking my neck. I ignore the little black stars flashing in the edges of my vision. Still, it takes a great amount of will power to release Kahar's reins. He side-steps, flattening his ears, but his muzzle nudges me in the shoulder. I give him a quick pat on the neck, and turn on my heel, pulling my hood up and walking away. Mica's footfalls draw up behind me, and Sibyl's fear and hope fade with every step I take.

Once again, I wrap the magic around Mica and myself as we head southwest. Turning a corner, I shove my hands in my pockets, hunching forward slightly, ducking into the shadows of my hood, even though my magic is wiping us from the minds of the guards walking the perimeter of the palace.

With my gaze on my boots, Mica sticks so close on my heels I feel his cloak brushing against me. I grin as we cross into the palace grounds unseen. My muscles are primed with tension, ready to react to any attack. My left hand slides out of my pocket, hovering over the hilt of my dagger. We travel the familiar grounds, my confidence growing with every crunch of my boots against the gravel. Mica may not have been successful in getting anyone into the palace after Adastra's takeover, but he didn't have me.

The crunch of gravel changes to the snap of marble underfoot, and we quickly climb the narrow steps, skirting the palace walls before slipping through a servant entrance.

The latch clicks quietly behind Mica, and I stand still for a handful of moments. I strain with my ears and magic, listening for anyone walking these back halls. There are a few servants moving to and from the kitchens, readying for the coming day, but overall, the way forward is clear. Mica stays still and silent, nearly pressed against my back. I bristle at his nearness but having him this close is actually helping me keep him within the bubble of my magic.

My thumb rubs against my middle finger and spins my ring around and around.

Excitement courses through me. I'm so close. Honestly, I'm shocked I've made it this far. Have we actually made it past Adastra's magic? I lick my lips, imagining my dagger slamming into his heart.

Right now, Luc should be using his magic to turn people from Carelle's and his presence, getting them both into the palace to find and free any of our captive soldiers who are still alive.

And now that we are inside, I nod over my shoulder, and Mica nods back. We move forward on silent feet, and when the hall splits to the left, the Shadow Lord peels away from me, stepping out of the protection of my magic. But he moves with purpose, head down, strides long. He will find his people here in the palace, learn what he can, get them out if necessary, and meet up with us outside the throne room at the designated time—Once Adastra is dead and Trislen is mine again.

It's tempting to unleash my magic and search the palace for Luc's mind, but I hold back, concentrating on my forward movement, tracking and avoiding people as I catch their thoughts.

As I pass a window, I take a moment to study the sky, finding the rass star, noting its position. Our designated meeting time is not for another half an hour. Perfect. Plenty of time. Though, I promised Luc I wouldn't play with Adastra. What am I going to do with all my time after I kill him? I guess I'll just take a load off and relax.

Despite the pain of my magic, my lips curl up in a smile, my shoulders lightly scraping the wood walls of the narrow hall as I climb the long servant's staircase to the second floor. Fucking Adastra thought he could keep me out. He thought his magic could best mine. My fingers flex with the anticipation of killing him. I want to use my magic to pull apart his mind. I want to bathe in his screams. But, I promised Luc. My finger caresses the hilt of my dagger. Stabbing Adastra in the heart will do.

Pausing at the door that I know leads to the hall where the royal chambers lie, my magic spreads outward as I press my hand to the handle. All I find is the tickle of a sleeping mind and two minds bored but focused.

I grin, hiding in my magic as I step into the hall, my eyes glued to the door several paces down on the right.

Just for a little fun, I push into one of the guard's minds, convincing him that if he doesn't leave right now, he's going to piss himself. Swallowing my chuckle, I watch as he crosses his thighs, dancing in place. He glances at the other guard, a frown creasing his brow. I've already shut his companion's mind down into a deep sleep, so the man looks up and down the hall before rushing off, a hiss of discomfort trailing him as he descends the stairs at the other end.

The soft rug underfoot cushions my footfalls. Before I know it, I'm standing at the door that used to be mine. My dagger slides into my left hand, and I slide it between the sleeping guard's ribs. His mind fades to black, and I wipe my blade on his pants before silently swinging the door open just wide enough for me to slip inside.

The room is dark, the only light coming from the pale starlight streaming through the large windows. My magic buzzes with the activity of a slowly waking mind coming from the bedroom. I smirk as I silently cross the room toward the open doorway to the bedroom, staring at the dark figure curled under the blankets. I barely register the pain throbbing at my temples as anticipation hums through my blood, adrenaline speeding my heart rate.

Time to die, you son of a bitch.

Tilting my head, I realize the figure is smaller than I expected, but my gaze doesn't falter as I approach the bed.

A click sounds under my boot as I cross the threshold, and a puff of air swirls around my face. The cloying scent of rotted roses fills my nose, and the sickly-sweet taste of the street drug coats my lips.

Fuck.

A light laugh sounds from the bed as the soft sound of shifting sheets floats through the room. A clatter erupts loudly at my feet, and glancing down, I realize my fingers have already gone numb and I've dropped my dagger.

Shit.

A soft, vaguely familiar feminine voice calls from the shadows of the bed. "Ah, Rydel. How delightful. There were several possible futures I saw around you. I'm glad this is the one you chose."

Intending to rush the person, I stumble forward. The drug takes hold, and the floor melts as the walls spin. I don't feel any pain as my knees crash to the floor, and I try to crawl forward, fighting the effects of the drug.

The woman slips off the bed, small bare feet coming into view as they stand a few feet from me.

"Poor Rydel."

The drug unlocks something in my mind, and the voice clicks. The healer. The healer? Rannae was her name. What is she doing in the royal chambers? I try to focus past her into the shadows of the rumpled bed. Where is Adastra? Is she fucking him?"

Her laugh slams into me like a physical blow, and my fingers dig into the floor as I fight to keep from toppling onto my side. Rannae takes another step forward. "No, Rydel. I'm not fucking Adastra."

Huh? Did I say that out loud?

She chuckles again. "You're saying everything out loud. The drug has loosened your tongue as well as your mind. But you're all too familiar with the effects of this drug, aren't you, Rydel?"

My skin tingles as pleasure spreads through my body, the mental buzz of my magic fading, and I find myself licking my lips to try and take in more of the drug.

No! Stop! I need ... I need to ... what? Kill. I need to kill ... Adastra.

My head wobbles dizzyingly as I raise my gaze. The warm brown skin of her shins disappears under her green sleeping gown. Her form is hidden behind the shapeless dress, and my eyes travel over her collar bone, up her neck, until I pause on her smiling lips. Slowly, her eyes come into view as she crouches down before me. I command the magic to melt her mind, to bring her pain and death.

She frowns, rolling her head, cracking her neck, but then she smiles. Rage courses through me as she tsks, leaning forward. Her delicate fingers wrap around the ring on my middle finger, sliding it from my hand. I fumble to grab her, to do something, anything ... but I miss. Her form swirls with illusionary trails of light streaming behind her with every move. I'd think she was beautiful if I didn't want to rip her face from her skull so much. She will die for throwing her lot in with Adastra.

She sits back on her heels, chuckling. "All you men are the same. Assuming Adastra is a man, because"—she scoffs with a sharp sound before pinning her eyes back to my face —"the fucking patriarchy. Yet, here I am, the new ruler of Trislen with the great King Rydel at my feet."

Fuck me. *She's* Adastra?

Did Mica know? No. He wouldn't have been able to hide this from me. Right? No.

Kill her!

I lurch forward, the motion clumsy and slow. She laughs as she gracefully stands, moving back a step, and I fall on my face. Still, my arm reaches out determined to strangle her with my bare hands. But the floor feels so good. Mmm. The warm wood pressed against my cheek is nice. There's something wet and hot spreading over my hairline, and I vaguely think I might be bleeding.

Doesn't matter. My back warms as I grit my teeth. I'm not sure if the grunt of pain remains locked inside my throat, or if it's echoing around the room, but I push the magic at her again. And again. And again, until I'm dizzy with the effort and my body feels like it's on fire. Still, I close my eyes and shove the magic at her again.

Satisfaction lifts some of the haze of the drug as she stumbles back a few steps, and a small gasp of pain leaves her lips. She rubs at her temples, cocking her head at me, mouth pressed tight.

"Hmmm." She looks at the ring in her hand, turning it this way and that, the green stone glowing—well, not really. I know the drugs are creating fantastical images in my mind, but it's still pretty as she hums, "Interesting."

She backs away, and I claw the floor, trying to pull myself after her. I feel the pull and rip of a fingernail snapping off, but thanks to the drug, the pain is a mere prick before floating away.

From the corner of my vision I see her pulling a cord. A moment later, or maybe a long time later—I'm not really aware of time right now—boots stomp across the room and hands grab me. The world swirls and tilts as I'm lifted and Rannae or Adastra or whoever the fuck she is stares at me from across the room, then back at the ring in her hand. Her eyes narrow on me as she barks at her soldiers, "Search him."

Hands pat me down, and I groan as my cock stirs, the drug flaring pleasure over my skin with every touch. The hands take away my weapons, and I reach for the one holding my dagger, but my fingers wrap around air as I watch my dagger fly across the room and land with a clatter on the ground against the far wall.

Then the touching stops, and I'm able to take a breath. A deep voice to my right says, "Nothing, sire."

"Strip him."

A laugh bubbles out of me, my head lolling as the room spins again, and I say, "Had I known thasss what you wanted, all you had to do wasss asssk."

Sweat drips from my nose, little splatters landing on the wood floor. The two men holding me up groan, and their grip loosens. My head is heavy, but I manage to look at

Rannae through the fall of my hair over my face. My tongue feels like it's twice its size, but I manage to slur, "Isss thiss what you desssire?"

The man on my right changes his grip to a caress up my arm, while the man on my left licks his lips as his eyes rove over Rannae. The magic pulses from me in chaotic bursts, the drug making it difficult to control. For a second, Rannae's lips part, her cheeks flush, and she takes a step toward us.

Yes, little bird. Come closer. The man on my right rips my shirt over my head before quickly undoing my pants. I'm hard, not with desire for these men, but in anticipation as I watch Rannae lick her lips and take another step closer. My eyes stay on her as the man shoves my pants down, and I kick them free so I'll have freedom of movement when the time is right. The man on my left has his hand down his pants, stroking himself slowly, and Rannae's hand lifts, trailing her nails across the swell of her breasts. The man on my right groans, as he grabs my dick. He shifts back, kneeling before me, licking me once.

With the next pulse of magic, my back spasms and my knees nearly buckle.

It hurts. So much. The magic resists, wanting to fall away with the drug. Desperate, I push, feeling like I'm being ripped apart from the inside, but I feel the magic unraveling, the cloudy buzz of the drug winning out.

The man on my left pauses his strokes, his hand stilling on his cock. Rannae stumbles back, shaking her head. Fuck, I've lost them. Her lips pull back in a snarl as she tosses my ring on the floor. The light clattering of metal against wood heralds my impending doom.

"Snap out of it!" Her shout is sharp and enraged.

Both men look around, the one before me falling back on his ass before scrambling to his feet. I laugh, the sound manic to my ears. The guards snap their rage-filled eyes to me as they straighten their clothes, and the one on the left grips my arm so tight, I imagine my bones grinding to dust. The man previously kneeling before me, ready to suck my cock down his throat, growls at me. My head snaps back as his fist connects with my jaw, and I taste the coppery tinge of blood. I grin at him, spitting at his feet. He kicks the side of my knee. There's a crack, but the pain I should feel is muted by the drug, and I collapse into the other man's arms. He drops me, and I thud to the floor, still laughing. I roll onto my back, cackling at the ceiling.

This is bad. I need to pull it together.

My stomach drops as Rannae says, "Dose him again."

No. No. Yes! More. Please, more. No!

I clench my teeth so hard I can hear the grinding in my ears. They will not get my mouth open. They won't!

But then a dull sting pinches my shoulder, and my head sways as I look over at the grinning soldier. There's a needle in his hand, and the plunger is depressed.

Shiiiit.

I groan as the world floats around me. The ceiling swirls in beautiful patterns, and little drops of light float around my face. My tongue licks the roof of my mouth, the action automatic as I search for the sweet taste of the powder in my mouth, but it's not there.

Oh yeah, the drug is coursing through my blood. Mmm. This is nice. Peaceful. Quiet. I'm adrift in pleasure, my body both tingling and ethereal. I'm no longer flesh and bone, I am light, and mist, and bliss.

Rannae's voice is light and lilting, floating through my mind in a melody of harmonizing bells. I can't understand her, but I want her to keep talking—it's a beautiful sound. One word sneaks through the fog ... scars.

Scars?

There's pressure at my feet, little touches that spark up my legs. The movement works its way up my calves, and someone grabs my leg, lifting it, and the sharp pressure works its way across every inch of my skin from toes to hips. There's a tugging sensation, then another push of pressure.

I groan again as a tinge of pain pierces the pleasure. My legs fall to the floor. I don't feel it, but the thump of flesh hitting wood echoes in my hollowed-out mind. A deep voice pierces the silence, and I frown. Where's the beautiful voice? The grating tone is close, and the words hit my ears. "He's a sick bastard. Look how turned on he is? He's being sliced up, but he's smiling, and his cock is weeping cum." There's a thump against my ribs, and I register the crunch of bones, but I don't feel it. The dose they gave me was ... strong. I've never injected the drug before. It's transcendent. I am on another plain of existence. I think I'll just live here forever.

Wait. Where's Luc? I want him. I need his mouth on my cock. I need to sink into him and release this pleasure. I want to share this pleasure with him. Luc? Something's not right.

But then the beautiful voice comes back, and I strain to make out her words. I want to bathe in the sounds that come from her lips. "Cut him until ... find .... Slice ... every scar and dig ... bone if needed. Don't stop ... you find ..."

Hmmm. I don't think that's good, but the sounds of the words dance with the trails of light streaming around the room.

More pressure continues up my body, pain and pleasure coating every nerve ending. I'm overwhelmed with sensation, so I close my eyes and get lost in the kaleidoscope of colors that bloom and fade and bloom again behind my eyelids. A warmth tingles low in my belly, and starlight fractures inside me as I orgasm, the hot splash of my cum hitting my stomach.

Again. I want that again.

Eventually, the darkness closes in and I sink, down, down, down, like I'm drifting into the waters of a murky lake with no bottom.

As I fall, my struggling mind gets stuck on a panicked thought. '*Luc. Luc. Luc. Please be okay. Luc. I have to ... have to ... Luc. I ... Luc. Luc. Luuuu ...*'

16

RYDEL

My body jerks like I missed the last step on the stairs. While I work to calm my racing heart, I try to sit up, but my limbs are slow to respond. I lick my lips.

Rannae. Adastra. The drug.

Fuck!

With effort, I manage to lift my heavy arms, and I run my fingers through my hair. Tangles catch and snag, but I tug, ripping a few strands from my scalp in my anger. The pain helps clear some of the fog.

Double Fuck!

I slap a hand to the floor—the cold stone floor—and shove to sitting.

"Luc? Lucaryn?"

My voice echoes, and a soft shifting noise carries through the darkness. Looking around, a dark grey stone wall closes in at my back and my left side. A barred partition separates me from the cell on my right, and bars stretch across the front of the small space, a rusted barred door looking across the aisle to more empty cells.

"Luc!" *Please let him not be here.*

"He's not here. Not right now anyway."

I turn toward the voice coming from my right, just now registering I didn't *hear* him first.

My fucking Stone is gone. Again.

I growl, "What do you mean, right now?" I'm surprised my voice barks so strongly since I feel like shit, and my head is pounding from withdrawal. The shifting of someone scooting across the stone floor sounds again, and a dirty form appears from the shadows in the cell next to me. "Runic?"

"Your Majesty."

His voice is raspy, like he hasn't used it in a long time ... or like he's been screaming. His usually trim beard is long, his bald head smudged with dirt and dried blood. Sadness weighs down his brown eyes, and he looks ... resigned. He's given up.

"I'm sorry, Sire. We tried to hold the palace. It was—"

"Runic, don't. It's done. We need to focus on getting out of here."

He snorts, and several sharp chuckles sound from farther down the line of cells. Runic rests his forearm on his knee. His shin is swollen from knee to ankle, and blue, green, and black bruises mark his skin. "I'm sorry to say, your Majesty. I don't think we're getting out of here. Not alive."

Taking a deep breath, I swallow my anger—for once. Runic has been here for weeks. I can forgive him a little fatalism. "Where's the captain? Are Mica or Carelle here?"

From several cells down, there's a wheezing cough, the

sound of flesh hitting stone, then more coughing. Finally, a weak voice calls out. "We're here, your Majesty." Carelle. "Mica is in the cell with me. He's been unconscious since I woke up a few hours ago. Sire, there's ... a lot of blood. He's still breathing, but ..."

Shit.

"And you, Carelle?"

"Okay. I think. Some of my ribs might be broken, and I can't see out of my left eye. But I wasn't going to let them take me without a fight."

I nod, even knowing she can't see me. I look to Runic again. "The captain?"

His head drops, the shadows concealing his expression. "He was here. He seemed to be in rough shape, but conscious. When they threw you in here, he went feral. They stuck him with a dart—a sedative I'd guess from the look on his face—then roughed him up some more and dragged him upstairs about an hour ago."

Fuck. Fucking Fuck!

I lean forward, trying to see down the line of cells, but it's hard to tell how many are here, so I ask, "How many of our soldiers that were taken are still alive?"

"All. We are ... leverage."

I raise an eyebrow, scratching my beard, just now realizing my body is practically covered in clotted and drying blood, some cuts still dripping hot blood down my skin. I vaguely remember the soldiers in the royal chambers stripping me, but I'm dressed once again. I think there were moments of pleasure, and there was some pain. It's all foggy, and I press my fingers into my temples, rubbing little circles. Pausing, I look over my forearms, up my biceps, then pull my shirt away from my body, looking down my chest.

Every scar, every mark on my body has been sliced open.

Shit.

I roll my left shoulder, pain exploding across every inch of skin. The tug of the wound in my back, and the silence in my head closes in on me like a lid slamming down on a coffin. Adastra had her men dig the Stone from my body. I wouldn't be surprised if they kept slicing away even after they found it.

She's smart. I'll give her that.

There's nothing I can do about it right now. Right now, I need information. I turn to Runic again. "Rannae?"

His eyes widen, and a tremor shivers through him. "Don't go against her, Rydel." Fear shimmers in his eyes, and I automatically reach for the magic to see his thoughts. Gritting my teeth, I sit in the deafening silence of my mind. He shifts, a small wince tightening his face. "She likes to play. She knows. She knows what you're going to do before you do it."

Hmmm. I caught her by surprise a few times in her rooms. The drug had a hold on my mind, and I was acting on instinct, on impulse, doing whatever I could to fight the drug and get to her. Maybe the key to beating her is spontaneity. Just let yourself react without thinking.

I almost smile. I can do that. Two can play, I just need to outsmart her.

Holding back my grin, I press my lips in a tight line before licking them. My mouth is dry, and the throbbing in my head is getting worse. My skin is clammy, and I know I won't be able to hold back the shakes for too much longer.

Tilting my head, I say, "Rannae liked you. She wanted you. That wasn't an act. Her thoughts were true when it came to you."

His throat bobs as he swallows. "Aye. She, ah, she came

to me one night before the takeover." He rolls his shoulders. "It would be easier if I could just show you."

I shake my head, clenching my fists. "I've been temporarily relieved of my magic."

There's no shock or surprise in his eyes as he nods. "I figured. I just ..." He sighs. "I had been on near-constant shifts for three days, and I was bone tired. She slipped into my bed, and ..."

He swallows, his eyes haunted as he stares at nothing. For a moment, I think he won't go on and am about to ask someone else what happened, but then Runic's small voice goes on. "She was beautiful. So small and perfect. And she wanted me. I wanted her too. She dropped her shift to the floor, pressing her body against mine. Her skin was like silk, my hands so stark against her beautiful brown skin."

His eyes turn down with sadness as he loses himself in his memory. If I had the magic, I'd climb into his mind to see it and spare him the retelling, but I let him go on. "She kissed me, and I was ready to take her."

His eyes focus, and spit splatters against the stone floor before he wipes at his mouth. "She whispered against my lips, revealing herself as Adastra. I laughed at her—actually laughed as I tried to pull her closer. Before I knew it, I was on my back, my hands full of her, my cock inside her."

Disgust pulls the muscles of his face tight.

"I let her ride me. She insisted she was Adastra, that she wanted me at her side as she took back Trislen. She wanted me as her captain."

Runic runs a shaking hand over his face.

"I swear, the moment I realized she was serious, I threw her across the room, grabbed my sword and pointed it at her. I should have run her through right there. I should have ended it. But she saw. She knew. Her magic warned her I was going to charge, and before I took two steps, I knew she had been playing with me. She knew I was going to refuse her. She knew I would try and kill her. And she came anyway. Two of her soldiers rushed the room. I was able to kill them, but Rannae fled."

He shakes his head, slamming a fist against the bars.

"I should have gone after her right then, but I took the time to put on my pants—my gods damned pants—before sprinting after her. I ..."

Runic's voice trails off, and he drops his head. I have a feeling that was the first time he's talked about what happened, and I think he's done.

From farther down the line of cells, another voice I recognize as Reena's picks up the tale.

"Captain Runic called us to arms, but most of our numbers from the Trislenian army had already defected, Adastra's plan perfectly executed. We were surrounded in the courtyard. We fought. We lost many. Those of us who survived were brought down here. Adastra came down day after day, asking the captain to join her, and every day he refused. Captain Runic never wavered, not even when ... when she ... ordered the guard to ..."

Reena's voice fades, and I sit in silence.

A full minute passes, then another, and another before another voice swears from the shadows of another cell. "That bitch sent one of her soldiers into the captain's cell to beat him bloody. When the captain refused Adastra again, she had the soldier ... he ..."

Runic grunts, his shoulders pinched, his back muscles quivering. From the pain on his face, and the way he sits angled on one hip or the other, gives me an idea what the guard did to him.

I'm going to burn this place to the ground.

Runic shifts again, his wince of pain deepening as he tries to find a semi-comfortable position to sit, saying, "It doesn't matter. It happened. It might happen again." A tear rolls down his face, and I sit on my hands to keep from punching the bars as he continues, "She knew. All along, her magic knew I wouldn't turn—that I will never join her. I was a message, a lesson to everyone down here. Join her or suffer. Death is a reward too sweet for the likes of Rannae Adastra Lurona."

Runic's back slides across the bars. Landing on his side, he curls into the fetal position and goes silent.

Rage courses through me. FUCK Adastra.

I open my mouth, but before I get a single word out, there's a click and thud, then the sound of boots thudding down the stairs, but I can't see past the solid wall on my left. There's an odd slide-thunk sound that doesn't keep time with the steps descending toward us.

I find out why when two soldiers come into view, dragging an unconscious Luc between them. I don't react. My body is frozen with fury. He's shirtless, and scores of cuts mark his beautiful skin. There's not an inch of his body that's not covered in his blood, and I know. Adastra has dug the Heart Stone out of him.

The toes of his boots drag behind him, his dark curls hang over his limp head. At least his face is intact. Not a cut or bruise marks his features. In fact, my face feels fine as well. Odd.

The soldiers throw Luc into the empty cell across from me, slamming and locking the door shut. They turn to me, wicked smiles on their faces.

Oh, my turn again?

I growl, adrenaline lending me speed as I shoot my arm through the bars, grabbing the closest soldier. But he grins, yanking my wrist to the side. Glancing down, I struggle as the needle pierces my skin. Everything starts to go fuzzy.

Gods. Damn. It.

The soldier chuckles at me, his grin splitting his face in a disgusting pull of flesh and teeth as he says, "Adastra saw that coming, Crown Breaker. She'll always see."

My eyes find Luc's prone body, and I slam my head into the metal bars, trying to stay conscious, trying to hold back the drug. But the world goes soft, the light around me sparkling as I imagine Luc's phantom voice floating through my mind.

'*I love you. Be strong.*'

Blinking several times, I clear my vision enough to look back at Luc. My body trembles with the rush of the drug, but I bite the inside of my cheek, forcing myself to focus. Lucaryn is unmoving. I hold my breath as I stare at him. My breath leaves in a rush of relief as his chest rises shallowly. He's still breathing. He's still alive.

I will do whatever I must to get us out of here. I will endure. I will burn it all down if I have to.

The stone walls close in, and I realize this dose is different. The darkness takes me quickly this time, but I'm calm. Let's see where I wake up next time. Hopefully, Adastra will be there.

I'm going to fucking kill her.

17

LUCARYN

It has been at least a few hours since I woke up. It's hard to tell the passage of time down here in the dark. There's not a single window to reveal the waning of daylight, but the torch has burned down slowly, giving me some guess on the time I've spent breathing through the pain.

My body burns with every breath, every small twitch of muscle. Even thinking hurts. Cuts flay my skin, shallow and deep and everything in between. I haven't moved much since consciousness ripped me from the foggy mists back into the reality of pain and suffering and anger.

Taking a deep breath, I brace myself as I roll from my side onto my back. My entire body erupts in pain, every nerve ending screaming, and I can't keep a sharp shout from passing my lips. But I breathe through it, and after a few moments, I settle into my new position staring at the dark stone ceiling.

My hand moves, creeping up my stomach before brushing over the left side of my chest. Blood slicks under my fingers, and the deep hole in my skin mocks me with a sharp stab of pain.

The past few hours or days—I'm not sure—I've been in a hazy cycle of darkness. I've floated through the mists of unconsciousness with the occasional pull towards reality, only to feel the prick of a needle before sliding back into the fog.

Then—and I'm not sure how long ago this was—I was allowed to fully crawl back to consciousness, my body twitching as feeling slowly came back to my limbs. A woman stood before me, and soldiers lined the small, sunlit room. Before my mind righted itself, a soldier hauled me to my knees, and ripped my ring from my finger.

I wasn't going to let it be that easy, though. My chest burned as my magic flared. The female soldier's face relaxed. My magic swirled through her, filling her with guilt for taking what was not hers. She held the ring back out to me.

A small woman laughed from across the large room, and I realized I should have aimed my magic at her and not the soldier. Whoever that was, I knew I needed to take her down. But before I could hurl the magic at her, a needle pricked my skin yet again. My vision immediately started to fade as the woman sauntered toward me, her bright yellow skirt rustling, her bare toes peeking out from the hem. Before I blacked out, she ordered the soldiers to tear me apart until they found the real Stone. I tried to hold on. My mind scrambled with options as the magic dissolved under the sedative. But I passed out with a curse on my lips.

The next time I woke, my body was indeed torn apart, and the Stone was gone. I was tied to a chair, the ropes digging into my raw flesh, but hatred narrowed my eyes as I stared daggers at the same small woman who was sitting in a large green velvet chair across from me. Her cream dress, decorated with pearls, contrasted beautifully with her dark skin and the deep color of the chair. Tiny bare toes peeked from the hem of her dress as she lazily kicked her crossed leg. Her eyes danced with amusement as she returned my stare.

She asked me one question.

Would I abandon Rydel and join her? She promised to give the Stone back in exchange for my allegiance. And it was then I knew. This woman had tricked us all. I was staring at Adastra.

Bitch.

Thinking back, I should have accepted, taken the Stone and killed her. But I imagine she would have seen it coming. Instead, I laughed, coughing around the pain, then laughed some more.

She nodded, knowing that would be my reaction, but said she wanted to ask anyway. Her exact words were, "It's boring knowing everything that's coming. I'm waiting for a surprise. Will you surprise me, Lucaryn? Will you join me?"

My increased laughter was my answer, and after another quick beating, I passed out and woke here in my cell.

I have yet to see Rydel, but from what Carelle told me, I imagine he's with that sadistic bitch right now. I'd respect Adastra for her cunning and cruelty if I wasn't on the receiving end.

I feel useless. I can't just lay here and wait. But I can't move. I might pass out if I try. Yet I must. Yes, maybe being unconscious would be better than living in this state of pulsing, throbbing agony, but I'm not going to give up now.

I'm dizzy just laying here, the blood loss making my

mind feel floaty. Gritting my teeth, I count my breaths, and on three, I roll back to my side with a muffled shout.

Runic calls out from the cell across the way. "Don't move, captain. Rest. It's no use hurting yourself more by—"

"Fuck off, Runic. I may be down, but I'm not out."

In the few hours I've been conscious in this cold cell, I've grown tired, then down-right angry at Runic's fatalism. If one more negative word passes his down-turned lips, I'm going to kill him myself.

As I press a hand to the floor, pushing myself to my hands and knees, bile shoots up my throat, and vomit splatters between my hands. I spit several times before shoving back onto my ass, swaying before settling.

There. See. I did it. I sat up all on my own.

I snort a laugh at my absurd thoughts as I look at Runic, trying once more to get some information. "Tell me about the guards. Rotations. Numbers. Descriptions."

Runic shakes his head, gaze glued to the floor where he sits propped on one hip, his hand holding him up. When he stays silent, another voice calls out from his cell. I look beyond Runic into the shadows as a figure peels away from the back wall. I hadn't realized another person was in the cell with him.

I recognize the female as one of ours. She is with the Annarr unit, and her name is ... Zinnia. That's right. Her long blond hair hangs in dirty strands around her face, her blue eyes sunken. She walks forward, a slight limp catching along her right leg. She leans against the bars, glancing at Runic before looking my way.

"Don't blame him, captain. He's had it the worst of us. And we've all had it pretty bad."

I take as deep a breath as my battered body will allow,

trying to banish my impatience. "Okay, then, Zinnia. You tell me about the guards and the situation down here."

Her fingernail scrapes little flecks of rust on the bars of her cell, the amber bits falling to the floor at her feet.

"We're fed once a day. Can't tell you if it's morning, afternoon, or night."

A voice sounds from two cells down on my left. "Pretty sure it's night."

Zinnia continues. "One guard shoves our plates under the bars while another stands watch. We're instructed to stay at the back of our cells or they won't give us the food."

I shift, wincing. "Same guards or different?"

"Same ones."

"Do they come down any other time?"

She shrugs, her gaze intent on the rust she's still scraping. "Used to. Used to come down at least three times between feedings, dragging one of us out of here to torture."

"Where did they take you?"

Her finger pauses before scratching at the bars again. "I was brought one level up into a small room with one door and no windows." She swallows. "After, I was brought right back."

I'm curious, but I don't ask what they did to her.

The person down to my left speaks up again. "The first time I was brought up, I think it was that same room. Sounds the same. Next time I was taken down two flights of stairs and outside. They stripped me and staked me over an ant hill for an entire day."

A faint chuckle floats from his direction, and I wonder how close my soldiers are to crossing into madness, or if some of them are already there.

He goes on. "The fresh air was nice, but those ants were not happy with my presence."

Reena calls out. "I was taken to the same room upstairs all three times."

My tongue clicks against the roof of my mouth. "What did they want?"

Zinnia snorts. "For us to defect."

The man on my right chuckles. "And when we refused, they wanted information. On you, captain. On the King. On your magic."

I nod to myself. "What does Adastra know?"

Zinnia answers. "Nothing more than what the rest of the country knows or suspects. The King has the Mind Stone and wields it without remorse or restraint. That you have the Heart Stone, and that while the magic is new to you, you command the magic well."

Leaning forward, I narrow my gaze. "How did you all hear that I have the Heart Stone?"

The dungeon falls deathly silent before Runic snarls. "When Rydel tucked tail and ran, I knew the magic of both Stones was the cause. When Adastra started asking about you and your power, I assumed Rydel gave the Stone to his —" He cuts himself off from saying whatever he was about to say before continuing. "To you, captain."

Zinnia nods. "You're the only one the King would trust enough to take the Heart Stone."

I shake my head, the movement sending spikes of pain down my neck. "Did you ever think Adastra was asking about my magic as a bluff? To see if you would confirm her suspicions?"

Runic shrugs, his voice dripping with sarcasm. "We couldn't really confirm for her one way or the other. We've been down here. How were we to know what the truth was?"

Zinnia frowns down at Runic, but nods. "And that's all

we could say. But it was never enough to make the pain stop."

There are grunts of agreement from several of the cells, and my fingers curl into a fist. "Okay. Do you know when, or about when the next food delivery will be brought?"

Zinnia nods, but before she can say anything, Runic barks, "You can't do anything, Lucaryn. Don't try. It'll only bring you more pain."

"Listen, Runic. I'm not asking you to do anything. But I'm getting out of here. I'm getting you all out. And I'll kill Adastra and her entire army if I have to."

Runic snickers, shifting to give me his back, his thin shoulders pressing against the bars of his cell. "You will die."

Zinnia watches him for a moment before looking back at me. "Food should be arriving in a few hours." She nods toward the burning torch. "When that's about a finger's length from the base. That's when the food usually arrives."

I nod, breathing deep again, shoving the pain down. Muscle by muscle, joint by joint, I move. I flex and wiggle and stretch. I force my body to loosen up.

Keeping an eye on the flames eating away at the torch, I work out a few plans in my head, discarding a few, modifying one, adding another. Scenario after scenario scrolls through my mind, and I work through each eventuality. There are some outcomes I won't be able to fight against. But I'll just try again next time. And the next. And the next. Until I'm free or I'm dead.

18

RYDEL

Adrenaline sparks over my skin as I jerk awake, yet again. I'm getting sick of this.

When I try to move, something restricts me. I'm bound. Of course I'm bound—to a chair it seems. I take a shallow breath, testing my body, pinpointing the areas where the worst of the pain flares; left knee, right side of my ribs, left side of my upper back.

My teeth grind as the silence in my head swallows me. The magic. My magic. Gone. No. Stolen. I'll get it back.

A faint chuckle comes from in front of me, but I don't move. My head hangs over my chest, my eyes still closed. Fucking Adastra. Her voice mocks me from ... I'd guess ten paces away.

"I know you're awake, Rydel. Be a good boy and talk to me. I have a proposition."

I don't think so. Let her stew in my silence. Maybe if I piss her off enough, she'll make a mistake.

She tsks, and a wet smacking of lips and soft chewing follows. Enjoy your meal, bitch. If I have my way, it'll be your last one.

A question burns, and my curiosity eats at me as slowly as Rannae eats her meal.

I miss my magic. Its absence is like a grave dug deep in my soul. I shake away my thoughts, not willing to dwell on what I can't fix right now. Right now, I want to know something. Keeping my head bowed and my eyes closed, I say, "You're a healer."

"Mmm. That I am."

"You treated me."

There's silence, then more chewing before she says, "I did."

Sarcasm drips from my voice. "Isn't there some kind of healer's code?"

She snorts, and I almost look up at her, but I relax my neck and let my head continue to hang heavy as she says, "No. Well, I'm sure some healers live by some moral code. I, however, prefer to use my knowledge of the human body to my advantage. I can heal ... but I also know how and where to inflict the most pain, to draw out the agony, to prolong death or make it quick. It's a beautiful art form."

Well, fuck. I wish there was a way I could convince her to work for me. But alas, I'd never be able to trust her, plus she's had a taste of power now, and I know there's no going back from that. Oh, and I despise her with every fiber of my being and have fantasized over a dozen ways I'd like to kill her. Soooo.

"Why didn't you kill me then? We were alone."

A soft chuckle floats across the room, but I refuse to look

up as she says, "While you were easily distracted by my lust-filled thoughts of your man, Runic, if I had allowed myself to even consider causing you harm, I'm sure you would have caught me easily. So, I promised myself I wouldn't even let the thought cross my mind while you were here."

There's clinking, like utensils settling on a plate, then a scraping sound as she continues, "Besides, had I killed you then, all your people would have rallied in your name. I wasn't about to make you a martyr. It wasn't the right time. This game is all about timing, wouldn't you agree, captain?"

There's a groan to my left. Pain spears through my temples as my eyes snap open, and I whip my head around.

Luc.

His black hair hangs over his face, and his breathing is shallow. But he's breathing, and he's here. He groans again, his muscles tensing then relaxing as he realizes he's bound. I ache to call out to him. My body is trembling with the desire to touch him. But I just stare for a long moment before slowly turning my head toward Adastra.

"What do you want? Why aren't we dead? You have what you want, correct?"

Her pretty brown eyes crinkle as she tilts her head. "I have your Stones, if that's what you're referring to. But before you get any ideas, I don't have them on me. I have others holding the magic for me. Now's not the time to experiment with new magics. I don't want them ... yet."

Interesting.

"As to why you're alive? I'm bored, and you amuse me, Rydel. You're ... unpredictable." Her red lips close around a piece of melon, the juices coating her mouth. She chews slowly as she smiles at me.

I keep my mouth shut. Let her talk.

The silence draws out between us as she continues to eat

her breakfast. The occasional clink of her fork hitting the plate, the only sound breaking the quiet.

Luc's groan draws my attention, and his head lifts. His eyes are pinched in pain, his jaw flexes. "Rydel?"

"I'm here."

I keep my eyes on Luc. He blinks a few times before a smile lifts his cheeks. "Ze'ass, sus suhs ras fa sa sur, i?" *Well, that didn't go to plan, huh?*

Loopy Luc is funny. I chuckle, shaking my head. "Ar sa zur e'a." *On to plan E.*

He laughs, but it's cut off by a pained cough, and my heart constricts as a fresh wave of anger at Adastra surges through me. Then he laughs again. "Rise'a. Zur e'a." *Sure, Plan E.*

Adastra claps her hands like a child who was just given a toy. "How sweet. You have your own secret made-up language."

She stands, and I turn to her, my lips pressed tight, but Luc spits, the glob slapping wetly on the floor. "It's not made up, sizuhs zanur." *Stupid woman.*

She takes two steps forward, perching her hand on her hip. "Whatever, I don't care. I need you boys to focus."

Luc snorts, but I keep my eyes on the woman before me. Raising an eyebrow, I shrug against the ropes. "What, Rannae? What do you want?" I sound like a father scolding a petulant child, and she scowls at my tone.

Her arm flicks out, and gold glints in the morning sun. Two rings clatter on the floor as they tumble at my feet. It's our fake rings. My brow climbs even higher up my forehead as I lift my gaze back to Adastra. I stay silent, waiting. I'm not going to give her anything. She's going to have to spell it out.

Her middle finger taps her thumb nail. "Only I and two of my most trusted guards know these aren't real."

Her eyes flick to the rings before meeting my gaze again. I want to roll my eyes as she tries to outlast my silence, but my face remains blank, and the tapping of her nails becomes louder.

Hmm. She can't read my mind. So she really doesn't have the Mind or Heart Stones on her. She has indeed given the power away—for now. Excellent. I wonder how quick her visions of the future happen?

Luc sighs, rolling his head before looking around the room, seemingly bored. I love that man.

Adastra pauses the clicking of her nails before taking another step toward us. "I'll give those back, plus the real ones"—she glances at the rings—"but you need to do something for me."

I adopt the same bored look as Luc, keeping my mouth shut. Why the fuck would she give them back? No. She's trying to play me.

The clicking of her nails picks back up. "Shall I go on?"

I don't move. My eyes stay glued to her face, and I feel Lucaryn continue his 'bored' perusal of the room. Her middle finger slides down her thumb, the nail picking at the skin along her thumbnail. Interesting. She's nervous.

After a long moment, she sighs at our silence, and I barely keep my smile from my face as she says, "I'll give the Stones back if you finish off Erathan."

It's a struggle to keep my face blank. I know Luc is as shocked as I am, but his posture doesn't change as he looks at a portrait hanging on the western wall.

I hold my tongue for several long moments before saying, "No. Do it yourself. You almost succeeded with that spider. Surely you have someone, or several someone's in place that can finish what you failed to do the first time."

She stares at me, and I know she's trying to hold back

her temper due to her fingers curling in the folds of her skirt, the muscles of her forearms flexing slightly.

I smile. "You can see the future, can't you Rannae? It should be easy for you."

She sighs, her nail scraping her skin raw. Turning, she heads back to the table where her half-eaten breakfast sits. She slides into her chair, her red skirt flowing along the floor, her bare toes peeking out. "There are many lines that lead to the future."

A litany chants in my head; stay quiet, let her talk, let her unravel what she knows.

Her lips purse as she looks at me. "It is true that Circeon has blessed me with the natural magic of the sight, but ... I cannot look into my own future."

Go on little bird, keep singing.

"Erathan is"—she rubs her temples—"too far for me to see his paths."

Ah, just as I suspected.

She goes on. "But there are at least four, no six possible futures for you, Rydel, if you take me up on my offer."

Delicious. Keep talking, woman.

She smiles. "Now, that may change tomorrow when I look again, and then your usefulness will have expired, so I'd take my offer now while it's still good."

I shrug again, the ropes pulling against my cuts, but I relish the pain; it keeps me alert. "I think I'll take my chances on a future where I don't lift a finger to help you."

We fall into a stare off, and I settle in. I'm not going anywhere. I'm a patient man when I need to be. She turns to Lucaryn who looks at her with a bored expression on his face. I almost laugh.

She asks, "And you, captain?"

He smacks his lips but remains silent.

Adastra's eyes narrow, her anger coming to the surface. I do smile at that, and she glares at me before closing her eyes and leaning back in her chair. From the corner of my eye, I see Luc turn to me, and I glance at him. He raises an eyebrow, and I shrug, turning back to Adastra.

Sweat beads across her forehead, and there's a slight tremble in her fingers. A moment later, her hands clench the fabric of her skirts, and her shoulders bunch up around her neck. Her lips open with panting breaths.

Is she looking into the future right now?

Luc and I sit in silence for several long moments, watching as Adastra's face gets paler, her short hair actually slick with sweat, her entire body shivering with her magic.

I wonder if I tip the chair back, will it break? Can I get free and kill her while she's lost to her magic?

With annoyingly perfect timing, she moans in pain, the sound delightful to my ears. Her voice croaks out. "Don't try it, Rydel. Those chairs have a metal core." Her eyes slowly peel open.

I shrug.

Luc and I wait her out for another long span of time. She presses her palms to her chair, and standing on wobbly legs, she crosses the room. She cracks the door open, speaks quietly—I presume to a guard—and comes back in, sitting back in her chair.

We wait.

Adastra pokes a piece of bread with her finger, but her face turns a shade of green, and she shoves the plate away.

Seems natural magic rides you just as hard as object magic. I bite the inside of my cheek to keep from smiling. I'm learning so many delightful things today.

A soft knock turns Adastra's head, and she's not fast enough to hide the wince of pain that movement causes her.

"Enter."

Two people shuffle into the room. A woman, dressed in the soldier's green and black uniform, staggers in, sweat beading on her face. Her eyes dart around the room, and her fists clench and unclench at her sides. The male next to her, dressed in light linen pants and a tight-fitting long sleeve shirt, rubs at his chest, his shoulders hunched as he crosses the room.

It takes everything inside me to keep still. I fight to keep my face blank, my gaze bored as I pretend to ignore the newcomers. Instead, I watch Adastra. I have no idea what her play is here, but she's brought these two people right to me.

There stand the people with our Stones.

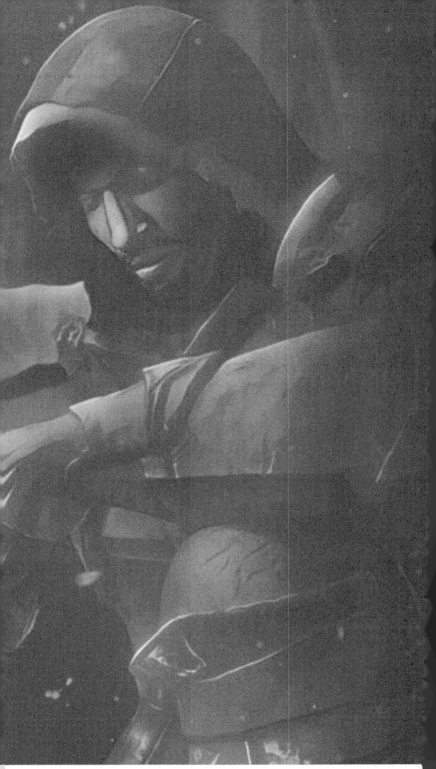

19

LUCARYN

Seeing Rydel, even tied up, bleeding, and bruised, releases a knot from my chest. My soldiers in the dungeon told me he was alive, but hearing and seeing are completely different things. I want to drink him in, memorize every inch of him right now. And if I'm being honest, seeing him tied up is giving me ideas ... for after. After we're free of all ... this.

This is quite the game Rydel and I have found ourselves playing. Sure, our plans didn't work out, but that was always an option. And I think, where Adastra is concerned, Rydel's approach might be best—wing it.

The idea grates my nerves, but I have to admit that all my meticulous planning will be wasted on someone who can see the future ... or my possible futures from the sound of it.

Our Stones stand before us—the two people merely

holding places for Ry's and my magic. I keep my features clear of emotion while I dredge up the pain from the beatings, the anger at being caught, the rage at seeing Rydel hurt ...

From the corner of my eye, I notice the man's fingers flex on his chest, and a moment later he grunts as he stumbles back a step.

Yes, take it all little man. I soak in my satisfaction at his pain. Amusement flutters through my chest. Determination floods my limbs. Love and pride for Rydel coats my heart, and rage at Adastra spears through my every nerve. I let myself experience every emotion, amplifying the feelings until the man lurches forward. Vomit splatters on the floor at his feet. He reaches a hand out to the woman beside him to steady himself, but she falls back, her hip crashing into a small table along the side wall. Her hands slap to her head, her palms pressing against her ears as she shakes her head back and forth. I grin, assuming Rydel is mentally screaming in her head.

Adastra tsks at them before looking between Rydel and me. I aim my grin at her. She takes a deep breath, and besides the retching of the man and the moaning of the female soldier, the room is silent once again.

When neither Ry nor I say anything, Adastra clicks her nails. "As you can see, the Stones are here. I'll keep them safe for you, and once Erathan is dead and I have proof, I will give you your *magic* back."

She says the word magic like a slur, like object magic is beneath her. That's fine. Rydel and I haven't lost yet. Our magic will be her undoing. Somehow.

Rydel shifts in his chair, the wood creaking as the ropes pull. "Fuck you. There's no way you'd give up that power. Especially to us."

She's quick to answer. "It's simple. The Stones are lever-age. They are the only thing you truly want, Crown Break-er." She glances at me with a smirk. "Well, almost, but I've seen first-hand what happens when someone messes with your—"

Rydel's bark snaps out. "I'd be careful how you finish that sentence."

I shiver at the command and possession in his voice, and Adastra shrugs. "See? And besides, the most favorable future is one where you two work together for me with the Stones as payment. I trust Circeon's visions. I go where she leads. And she's leading me to the future where I give you back the Stones."

It's an effort not to roll my eyes. The gods don't exist. She's lying. She must be. But her eyes sparkle with that certain glint that only the blindly faithful have. Whatever, let her rely on her goddess. I'll rely on my sharp mind and ... him. I glance at Rydel, his form large and powerful despite the cuts and bruises marring his body. But I'm sure she won't give them back. She must know doing so would mean her death.

That doesn't mean we can't play her game, though. I wonder how far we can push her?

For the first time, I focus fully on Adastra. "Release our soldiers."

"No."

Rydel grins. "Then, no deal."

Her chest lifts with her slow inhale, her nails clicking before they start to dig into her flesh again. A small bead of blood wells along her thumbnail, but she doesn't even flinch as her nail continues to dig into her flesh. Her eyes drop to her lap, and her hands start to shake. She must be using the magic to try and see the trails of our future and where they lead if she gives us what we want.

She lifts her head, her eyes blinking quickly before landing on me. "Fine. If you agree, once I have proof that Erathan is dead, I will have your people delivered to your border."

My voice is even as I deadpan, "You will not kill or harm any of them in the meantime, and you will make sure they receive three meals a day."

She nods. "Done."

Rydel adds, "I want Carelle with us."

"No."

Rydel and I stare at Adastra, and she stares back. We hold our silence for several minutes before Rydel says, "Then, you'll release half of our people, the ones the worst off, once Luc and I leave for Adren. And you will release the other half as promised upon completion of our ... task."

Adastra quickly nods. "Done."

She must have already seen a future with that scenario. Or maybe not. Maybe this is all one gigantic bluff.

I play along though, adding, "And ..." She raises her eyebrow at me, and I get the impression she doesn't know what I'm going to ask. I smile, my interest in her magic and how this game will play out shoving the pain of my injuries to the background. "We get half of Adren."

Ry twitches, the movement so slight, I don't think Adastra noticed, but I know he's amused by my ask. The male by the door throws up again and slumps against the wall, sliding down it until he lands unconscious in a heap on the floor. Poor fella.

I smirk as Adastra shakes her head. "Half?"

I nod. "We will be doing all the work, after all. And without magic, so ..."

"I will give you a five mile expansion beyond your current border."

I press my lips together while shaking my head. "Not good enough. In fact, now make it half of Erathan's territory and every port city."

Her eyes narrow at me, her teeth grinding, and Rydel finally lets out a barking laugh. Her head whips to him. "You think this funny? You think this is a game?"

His laughter falls into a wide grin. "Isn't it? You heard my captain's terms. Take 'em or leave 'em. We're content enough in our rooms downstairs. You can take your chances with Erathan on your own."

She looks between us, her anger evident in her glittering eyes.

The female soldier in possession of the Mind Stone grunts, then falls to the floor, landing on top of the male as she too falls unconscious to the pain of the magic.

Adastra ignores them both, keeping her gaze trained on Rydel and me. "Half his territory including the four most northern ports."

Rydel lets the silence hang, and I sit quietly with him. Eventually he shrugs. "Deal. How would you like your proof?"

"His head or his ax. Have a messenger bring whichever you choose, and instruct them to tell the gate guards, 'the payment is here.' They'll know to bring them to me."

Ry nods, and I know, if we actually do this, he'll send Erathan's head. Rydel has always admired Erathan's double sided ax. That will be coming home with us, along with our people and our magic. But there's a lot between us and that end.

Rydel flexes against his bonds, his shoulders straining. "And the Stones?"

"I will send them via messenger bird to whomever you want as soon as I have the proof that you have done all I've asked. They will be waiting for you once you leave Adren and return to your frozen northern kingdom."

Awww. Does someone not like the cold? Poor baby. Ironic, since when this is all done, her body will lie cold and lifeless at our feet. But sending the Stones via bird is risky. What if they fall into someone else's hands? What does it matter? She's not going to give them up. We're going to have to find a way to take them back by force.

Rydel's thoughts must mirror my own because he shakes his head. "No birds. Send them back with Carelle." Adastra stares back at him, and Ry says, "The prisoner with the two missing fingers on her left hand."

Smart. Out of everyone down in those dungeons, she's the one I'd pick.

Adastra's fingers switch their picking so her thumb now scrapes at her middle finger. Her eyes flick between us before she nods, standing and going back to the door, swinging it open. Soldiers file in, two slinging the unconscious Stone holders over their shoulders, carrying them from the room. Two others peel away from the group, approaching us. The early afternoon sun glints off the sharp needles in each of their hands. I sigh, and Rydel aims an angry look at Adastra.

She shrugs with a smile. "I still hold all the cards, Rydel. This is how it must be. To win, you must trust that I will stick to my end of our bargain. There's no other way. You did say this was a game. It's your move."

Rydel chuckles, the sound deep and dangerous. My cock inappropriately begins to stiffen as he says, "And I wager you'll spend many sleepless nights haunted by all the bloody futures your goddess will show you if you don't deliver on every single promise." He leans as far forward in his chair as he can, the back legs even lifting off the floor. "I'll come for you, Rannae."

His chair thunks back to the floor, and I nearly chuckle at her wide eyes and pale face. But she recovers quickly, trying to shrug off Rydel's threat. "I'll deliver as long as you do as you're told. We can both come out of this on top."

There's not enough room at the top for all three of us.

I don't even feel the needle slide into my shoulder, but then the slight burn of the sedative spreads from the injection site, flooding my bloodstream. The room starts to go dark, and I look toward Rydel.

Shit. I don't think they have been giving him the same thing they've been using to knock me out. His eyes are already glassy, and he licks his lips as his fingers flex and relax. I know that look. I saw it on his mother's face often enough. I've seen it on his face too, whenever the magic rode him too hard.

Shit. Has Adastra been pumping that drug into Rydel this entire time? If so, I'm surprised he was as lucid as he was today. I'm going to have to watch him.

I'll always watch out for Rydel. We can do this. We're deep in Adastra's game, but no matter what, Ry and I will come out the winners, or we'll die trying.

Rydel's hair falls over his face as his head droops toward his chest. His even breaths lifting his shoulders is the last thing I see before my vision goes dark, and the sedative pulls me under ... yet again.

20

LUCARYN

Attempting to shake off the last of the sedative, I roll my head, breathing deeply. The edges of my vision are still a little hazy, but I'm not going to sit here and wait it out. I need to move.

Flexing, the sharp pull of the ropes binding my wrists and ankles restricts my movement. My gaze lands on Rydel's still sleeping form. His inhales are even, but there's a flush to his skin that tells me he's still riding the drug pretty hard. His hair drapes over his face where he's lying on his side. Dead leaves litter his blond strands and beard.

With a grunt, I ignore the sting of the cuts covering my skin and roll until I'm sitting. There are trees shielding us from the late morning sun, and wherever we are, we must have been dropped here a while ago because my clothes are slightly damp with mist and dew. Two birds chirp loudly at each other in the branches over my head. Looking up, I catch the flash of wings and feathers as the small brown birds flit from branch to branch, one chasing the other before it's chased back.

Smirking at their loud argument, I say, "Hey, it's not our fault. We didn't mean to invade your tree. We were dumped here. I'll get us out of your hair as soon as I—"

A glint to my right snags my attention. Turning, I see the dagger—Ry's dagger—sticking out of the trunk of a tree about fifteen paces away. There's a paper pinned by the sharp blade, but I can't read it from here.

A smile curves my lips as I look at the base of the tree where all our weapons lie in a heap. Okay then.

Rydel groans, curling in a little tighter on himself, the movement restricted by his ties. But his eyes remain closed.

I look back up at the birds, now quiet, perched on their branches cocking their heads at me. "You wouldn't want to go fetch that dagger for me, would you? No? Okay. Well, this isn't going to be graceful."

My toes wiggle, and I flex the muscles of my legs. I twist side to side before rolling my shoulders, then my neck. Not too bad. The pain is bearable. Other than the cuts and what I suspect is a bruised rib, I'm relatively intact.

Flopping onto my side, I roll over my shoulder, my arms stretching against the ropes holding my hands tight against my back. I roll again, and again. Dirt coats my tongue, and I spit as much of it out as I can before correcting my course and roll again. I hold back a wince as a small rock wedges into one of the deeper cuts along my right bicep, and several of the smaller cuts reopen, leaving a smear of blood behind me.

But I've made it to our weapons.

Heaving myself up to sitting again, I scoot backwards, digging the heels of my boots into the dirt until I feel the scabbard of Rydel's sword. I wrap my hands around it and work my fingers until I'm gripping the hilt. Inch by inch, I work the scabbard down the blade.

"Shit. Ouch!"

The sharp edge catches along my palm, but I keep going until the sword is free. I look across the disturbed trail I made, checking on Ry. His breathing is picking up, and there's a slight tremor in his muscles. He's coming out of his drug haze. But it might still be a while, and while this would be ten times easier with his help, I'm not going to sit here and wait.

Shifting, I carefully sit on the hilt and work my wrists over to the edge of the blade. The position forces me to lean slightly to my left and twist around to get the right angle, but the rope immediately frays, then unravels, then snaps.

Ahhh. That's better.

I roll my wrists, rubbing at the raw skin before shaking out my arms, trying to dispel the prickles crawling along my skin. I pause, noticing the ring on my middle finger. The fake stone mocks me as I turn the ring around my finger with my thumb. Glancing at Rydel, I can't see his hand with it tied behind his back, but I assume his ring is in its place on his middle finger as well. I guess they'll come in handy moving forward. If people assume we still possess the power of the Stones, they should be less likely to go up against us.

Spinning, I grab the sword, slicing through the ropes around my ankles.

With a hand pressed to the tree trunk, I stand. My vision starts to close in and a ringing presses in on my ears, so I hold still, breathing slowly until the world rights itself. A snarl leaves my lips as I grab the dagger, yanking it from the tree, pinching the note between my fingers.

You have five days before the remaining half
    of your people die, I destroy the Stones,
    and come for your heads.
Your horses are at The Charging Boar in the
    town five miles west.
Good luck.

And Lucaryn, when the time comes—if it
    comes, depending on your decisions—go
    down, not up.

RAL

My hand flexes with the desire to crush the letter in my
fist, but I resist, folding it before shoving it in my pocket. I
strap my sword to my back, my short sword to my hip, and
secure my throwing knives in my boot and along my chest
harness.

Gathering up Ry's weapons, I cross back to where he's
still lying in the dirt and leaves. I unload my arms and kneel
next to him. My fingers brush his hair back from his face,
my hand stalling on his cheek as I rub my thumb over his
skin. He's alive. We're both still alive. We have each other.
We can get through this. Together.

For an indulgent moment, I press my lips to his forehead. He's warmer than he should be, but I smile against his
skin as a moan slides from his lips. "Luc."

"Zanea uzh sa nea." *Come back to me, Ry.*

He groans, trying to roll toward me. I pull away, quickly
cutting his bonds. The second his arms are free; he curls
into a ball. The withdrawal is going to be bad this time.

My hands stroke his arms as I roll him onto his back, my
eyes catching on the green stone of his ring. "I know it's

hard, Ry, but you need to wake up. You need to get yourself out of that haze."

His lashes flutter but remain closed. "Luc."

"Yes, Rydel. Wake up."

His jaw goes slack, and his lips part as his breathing evens back out.

Oh no you don't.

Gripping his shoulders, I yank him to sitting, holding his weight, giving him a little shake. "Wake up, you bastard."

He mumbles something before his head lolls back.

My palm stings as the sound of my slap reverberates through the woods. The birds take flight, their angry chirping fading into the thick press of trees.

"Fuck, that hurt."

I smile, keeping my grip on him as Rydel rubs his face.

"Well, you can't sleep all the damn day. We have things to do. People to kill. Kingdoms to conquer."

He chuckles but it turns into a round of coughing, and he wraps an arm around his waist. "Well, at least one rib is bruised, if not broken."

"Same."

His eyes lift to mine, the green depths still a little dazed by the drug, but there's fire and anger there too. He asks, "You okay?"

I nod, scooting closer, my hand curving around the back of his neck. "You?"

He nods, gripping my shirt, pulling me closer. "I've got you. That's all that matters."

I smile, shaking my head. "Not all. There are people counting on us. We need to—"

His lips press to mine, and I close my eyes, drinking down his taste, breathing in his scent. There's the sharp smell of his sweat, the tangy scent of blood, the earthy scent of the dead leaves still clinging to his hair, but under all that is ... him—fresh cut hay and cedar.

He presses little kisses to my lips before pressing his forehead to mine. "You. Are. All. That. Matters."

My fingers tighten around his neck. I love his man.

Pushing back, I press a quick kiss to his temple before handing him his weapons. With shaking hands, he secures his weapons, then I pass over the note. His brows crinkle between his eyes as he reads it. He does crush the paper in his fist before shoving it into his pocket.

I dust the dirt and leaves from my clothes, and Ry does the same. He pulls his hair back, combing his fingers through the mess as best he can. The muscles in his arms flex with the movement, and I swallow with the desire for those strong arms to hold me, to touch me, to ...

Ry laughs, rolling the top half of his hair into a knot and securing it with a leather strip he unfastens from his chest harness. "I know that look. I don't need the Mind Stone to tell me what you're thinking." He holds his arms out at his sides, a devilish smile on his lips. "I'm filthy but I'm game, Lucaryn." He raises an eyebrow, and my cock twitches. "I'm always game for you, Luc."

Gods. This man.

I take a step forward before forcing my feet to stop. Shaking my head, I laugh. "You are a distraction, Rydel. We need to get moving. Our soldiers—"

He sighs. "Yes, yes. Five days. Do you know where we are? I don't know this Charging Boar place, do you?"

I shake my head. "No, but I figure if we head west, we'll find it."

Ry turns. "Unless she's fucking with us."

I rest my hand on his shoulder, his muscles flexing under my palm. "She probably is, but let's go anyway."

He nods and starts walking. I keep pace, watching him closely. His strides are even, but his shoulders are hunched ever so slightly, and the fingers of his left hand tap his thigh in a quick rhythm.

Eventually, we come to a dirt road, and a glance east then west reveals the way is empty of travelers. We turn west, little dust clouds kicking up behind us. The sun is warm, but the breeze is cool. Snow blankets the mountains in the far distance, and I realize back home, the city is probably settled in under deep snow drifts, and thick icicles will be glittering from roof eaves.

There's no snow here, though.

Ry's face drips with sweat, and I know it's not from the sun. The fingers of his left hand now tap against his dagger, and his tongue keeps swiping at his lips. I need to get him some water, fast.

Ry sighs, palming his dagger in a well-practiced move, spinning the blade between his fingers. His voice is gruff. "I can practically hear your worried thoughts. I'm fine, just ..."

"How much were you given?"

He pauses, and I stop next to him, searching his eyes. His right hand scratches at his left arm. "I'll get through it. I'm fine."

"How much?"

"A lot! Okay! A fucking lot. I never injected the drug before." His head falls back. "Fuck, the rush hit my blood stream so fast. There was no build up. It was immediate bliss, Luc. Over and over." He drops his hand, aiming his determined eyes at me. "I'll be fine, but ...." He lifts his dagger in front of him. It trembles, and Rydel's right hand snaps out, grabbing his wrist to try and steady his hand. It doesn't work, and he swears, lowering his arms, but the flash of his spinning blade picks back up. "Luc, don't let me near it again." His fingers fumble around his dagger, and he almost drops it. My eyes go wide as he sighs, sheathing his favorite blade. "It was ... I want it, Luc. I want the high, the ecstasy, the nothingness." His eyes land on mine. "Don't let me take it again."

I clasp his shoulder. "I promise. We haven't made it this far for me to lose you to some street drug."

He nods and takes a deep breath. We continue west, the sun traveling over our heads, casting small shadows at our feet. There's no one else on this road, and as a small house comes into view, a pen of sheep bleats at us as we pass. After another ten minutes we pass another house, then three closer together.

Ry's face is pale, and as I watch, a drip of sweat clings to the tip of his nose before falling to the ground. I grip his shoulder, and he pauses. His body trembles under my touch, then he folds at the waist, vomiting into the dirt between his boots. He spits, wiping the back of his hand over his mouth before patting my hand. "Okay. I'm okay."

He's not, but I nod, and we move on.

Finally, a town spreads before us, and we pick up our pace.

Ry glances around, his head whipping at every sound, his muscles bunched and ready for action. It must be excruciating not having the magic of the Mind Stone after ten years of hearing every thought. Plus, the paranoia must be compounded by the withdrawal crawling under his skin. I only had the Heart Stone for a few short months, and I'm finding myself seeking the feelings of those hidden within their homes and shops.

As our boots clomp onto cobblestones, I fall back, whispering, "I've got your back."

His shoulders drop a fraction, and my own tension

lessens slightly. We spent our entire childhood and early adult lives looking out for each other long before we had the Mind Stone. We'll do the same now.

We pass into what I presume is the center of this town, several people pausing and shooting side-eyed looks our way. A little boy with strawberry blond hair tugs on a woman's skirt. "Mommy, those men are hurt. What happened?" She tucks the boy into her side, pulling him around a corner.

We are a bloody, dirty mess. We definitely stand out.

Rydel, never one to miss an opportunity to take charge, points across the small square at a man sweeping the entrance to what I assume is his shop. "You there, what town is this?"

The man's arms pause, his broom halted a few inches from the stone steps. "Um, Gepata."

"Is there a place called The Charging Boar here?"

He nods, his wide eyes fighting to stay on our faces, but they stray to our many wounds and dirty clothes. "Um, yeah." He points to our right. "Follow that street. You'll see a shop with a red door. Turn left there. When you see the mermaid fountain, turn left again, and the Charging Boar'll be on your right."

Rydel turns, crossing the square with long strides, and I follow, eyes scanning every doorway, every street, every shadow. Ry does the same, occasionally jumping at the sound of doors opening or closing, or footsteps sounding from down a side street.

We follow the man's directions, and before long, we're approaching a wood building with a sign hanging over its door with a boar's head roaring across its surface. Rydel doesn't break stride as he pushes through the door. I blink a few times, adjusting to the darker interior. Dark wood tables and chairs dot the darker wood floors. A wood bar spans down the back wall, and dark wood ceilings hang low, so low, I could brush my fingers against the beams without stretching. The overall effect is oppressive, closed in.

A deep voice calls from a room in the back corner. "Ah, finally!"

We're the only ones in here right now, and I'm thankful I don't have to worry about keeping an eye out on a tavern filled with patrons. Though, why this place is empty during the lunch hour is …

A short man pushes through a swinging door, his stomach bumping it, a scowl on his face. "You the fellas?"

I angle myself so my right side faces him, and my left side faces the front door—just in case.

Rydel calls out, "I don't know. Are we?"

The man puts his hands on his hips, his scowl deepening. "Look, I was paid to keep my place closed until two men came to collect their horses. But the lunch hour is upon us, and if I don't open, I'll lose more than I was paid to close up, so?"

I hold back a chuckle at the man's annoyance. If only he knew who he was berating. There's a twitch along Ry's left shoulder, and I can tell Rydel's tension is climbing, so I answer, "Yes. We're here for the horses."

The man spins with surprising grace, bumping back through the swinging door, his voice trailing after him. "Well, come on then. Quickly now."

Ry grips his dagger, his knuckles turning white. We follow the portly man through a back door, the sunlight tempered by the shadows of a barn. The man stops, turning toward us, jerking his thumb over his shoulder, seemingly not at all concerned with Rydel's hold on his blade. "They're in there. They've been fed and watered as instructed. That black one is the devil himself. Get him outta here."

I press my lips together, and I catch a ghost of a smile on Rydel's lips as the man shoves past us, the door to the tavern slamming shut behind his mumbled curses.

We step into the barn, the only two stalls occupied by our horses. Phoenix's ears perk up, his head lifting high, a soft whinny greeting me. Kahar pins his ears back as Rydel approaches, the giant war horse barely fitting within his stall. Kahar's neck stretches as he snaps his teeth, but Ry just shakes his head, thumping Kahar on his muzzle before stroking his face.

"E'assa, Kahar. Use'a iyai ahuiy? Se'ausiy sa fe'as ais a e'ase?" *Hello, Kahar. Are you okay? Ready to get out of here?"*

Kahar stomps with impatience as I lead Phoenix out, quickly saddling him. Ry does the same with Kahar. Once our horses are ready, we tether them to the post outside, and I follow Ry to the pump sitting to the side of the barn. His arms flex, and the pump squeaks with every downward thrust of the handle. There's a gurgle, then a gush of water.

Rydel nods. "Go ahead."

The cool water hits my hands, and I nearly groan as I rub them clean before cupping the water and splashing over the dirtiest parts of my body. The water runs brown and red around my boots, but I feel so much better now that most of the grime is washed away. I spend a little extra time scooping the water and holding my shirt away from my chest as I clean the deepest wound where the Heart Stone used to hide. It burns with each pass of my hand, and the twinge of pain reminds me of my failure.

I shake my head, switching places with Rydel, and he leans down, slurping at the water, his throat bobbing. With a final gulp, he goes about cleaning himself as he says, "We'll get the Stones back. We'll get our people back."

My arm pauses, the rush of water slowing slightly before I pump again. "What if we can't?"

Rydel stands, running his wet hands through his hair, his fingers only trembling slightly. He takes a deep breath. "We will. Lucaryn"—he grabs my shoulders, his wet palms soaking through my shirt—"I will burn all of Imoria for us. For you. Magic or no magic, no one in this world is safe from me. We've fought too hard. We've come too far. But ..." —I hold my breath during the long silence as his eyes bore into mine—"if it comes to it, if all really does seem lost. We run. We leave Imoria. We go somewhere far away. You and me, Luc. We start over."

My eyes go round, and I know I'm gawking. Rydel smiles, stepping into my space until we're toe-to-toe. "I told you, Luc. Without you, all this means nothing. If I can't win with you, I'll leave it all behind—as long as you're with me." He grins, and my body responds. "But don't worry. It won't come to that. Imoria is ours."

I have no idea how to respond to that, so I press my lips to his, pulling him tight. Between little licks and kisses, I mumble against his mouth. "Iyai urs nea." *You and me.*

My hand scrapes his scalp, and his arms wrap around me, his broad palm splayed across my back. Our tongues flick together, and he pulls me even tighter, his hard cock pressing against mine. I groan into his mouth, and he nips my bottom lip before pulling back just enough to say, "You and me."

21

RYDEL

Luc and I mount up, Kahar standing still for once as I swing my leg over his back. A little shake of his head is his only indication he's ready to be on our way.

My back itches with the unknown all around me. It's quiet in my mind, and I don't like it. At least this time, I've got Luc with me. My blood still itches with the need for more of the drug, but I ignore the crawling sensation along my skin as best I can. With a press of my heels, Kahar jumps into a fast canter, and Phoenix keeps pace. It takes little time to clear the small town, and when we're about a mile out, Luc pulls back on Phoenix, turning north.

I stop next to him, eyeing him before aiming my gaze north as well. "We can't, Luc."

He smirks, but I can tell he's annoyed by the white-knuckled grip he has on the pommel.

"We could get reinforcements. We could make sure

Adastra did indeed release half our people. We could return with our army and wipe her off the face of this country."

I shake my head, but a grin pulls up at my lips. "I like where your head is, but we can't. I've tried brute force." I scratch the back of my neck, forcing away the memories of pain and death. "We need to do this differently. We have five days. It would take longer than that just to get home."

His fingers relax as he sighs. "So, what's the plan?"

I laugh, my head falling back. Kahar hops to the side, arching his neck against the pull of the reins. "Easy. Kill Erathan. Get our Stones back. Kill Adastra. Rule all of Imoria."

Luc's laugh joins mine. "Sure. Easy. Because all of our previous plans went so well."

"That's why this time, there's no plan. We just go with our gut. Trust our instincts. And do whatever it takes to win." I press my left leg into Kahar, and he side-steps toward Phoenix. Leaning over, I slap Luc on his back. He winces around a smile.

I frown. "Shit. Sorry."

"It's okay. We're both pretty roughed up."

His hand snaps out, grabbing my forearm before I pull away. He tugs a little, and I lean farther into him as he says, "I don't care what you have to do. Promise me you'll come out of this alive."

A smile starts to spread across my face, but it falls as I notice the serious glint to his bright blue eyes. I nod. "I promise." With a little chuckle, I add, "You know me. I'm not one to sacrifice myself for some greater good."

Luc's grip on my arm tightens. "You would for ..." His eyes drop.

"For you?"

He shrugs, and I place my hand on his thigh, ignoring

the slight shaking of my fingers. Instead, I focus on his warmth seeping through the skin of my palm.

"Lucaryn. I promise. We'll both come out of this alive. I'll sacrifice everything and everyone but you or myself. I'm a selfish bastard, and I'm not about to change that about myself."

A small smile melts away the lines pulling at Luc's face as he leans in. "I know."

I lick my lips, my eyes stuck on his mouth. A moment before our lips press together, Kahar jerks his head, hopping away from Phoenix with a violent swish of his tail. My body pitches to the side, and my core clenches to keep my seat. Righting myself, I playfully smack Kahar on the neck as Luc chuckles.

"Se'ahuhs asre'a." *Devil horse.*

Luc looks around, the afternoon sun glinting off his black hair, cutting shadows across the perfect plains of his face as he asks, "So. Do you know where we are?"

I nod. "I think so. I'm pretty sure we are still on Trislenian land. Which makes sense. If we head northwest, we should come to the border wall before nightfall." I pat Kahar. "These guys can easily handle the jump, which means we can avoid the official border crossing. Then, it's a straight shot west through the night and a little stretch south to Adren's capital."

Luc takes a deep breath, squaring his shoulders before nudging Phoenix into an easy canter. Kahar shakes his head, his long black mane smacking me in the face, but he waits for me to press my heels into his side before he moves to keep pace with Luc.

We ride in silence until the stacked rocks of the border wall come into view. Standing, it would come up to just above my shoulder. Luc leans over Phoenix's neck, the red steed taking the jump with muscular grace. I check Kahar's pace and stride, lining him up for the jump. Leaning forward, his earthy scent climbs down my nose as the war horse's front legs push off the ground. I'm weightless for a moment, my thighs hugging my body to the saddle. As we hit the apex, my body moves, tilting back slightly to take the weight of Kahar's landing. The beast of a horse under me doesn't even break stride as he continues his steady pace trailing Phoenix.

Luc mutters over his shoulder. "Maybe we should add more patrols and stations along our border."

"I was thinking the same thing. Or at the very least, maybe we employ some tradespeople to heighten our wall and add shards of glass, ceramic, and metal along the top to discourage climbing or jumping. But if this all works out, we may not need border walls, so ... We'll put it on the list of things to do if needed."

"You mean the list that includes killing both monarchs, reclaiming our magic, and saving our people?"

I chuckle, the sound whipping away on the wind. "Yup. All that, then a good night's sleep, a solid meal, and a full day of celebratory fucking. Maybe two. *Then* we assess our border needs."

Luc's hands clench on his reigns, his back muscles bunching as his eyes slam to my face. Heat and desire shoot from his hooded gaze, and his teeth scrape over his bottom lip.

"Yes. After that."

Fuck, he's distracting.

I shift in the saddle, trying to find a somewhat comfortable position to ride with my now stiff cock. I notice Luc doing the same, and I chuckle with a shake of my head. "We are worse than love-struck boys fresh into their manhood."

Luc smirks, shaking his head, shifting in his saddle again.

After a few hours, we stop, resting the horses at a small creek that's fed from the river that flows from the snow-covered Imorian mountains. Luc and I strip down, fully cleaning every inch of our bodies. I grit my teeth as I take in his bruised and sliced up skin. How dare that woman abuse and hurt what is mine!

Luc cups the rushing water, splashing his face, running his fingers through his hair. "I know that look."

"What?"

"You have murder in your eyes."

I lift a hand toward him. "Look at you. Look what she did."

He shrugs. "You're not looking much better, Ry."

My eyes narrow, and my muscles bunch as my anger builds, but Lucaryn turns, giving me a glorious view of his ass. The water flows around his thighs as he scoops water over his body. He smiles over his shoulder. "Reminds me of the old days."

Indeed. How many times did Luc and I bathe in the freezing river outside our small village?

"Back then, the sight of you didn't do this to me." I grab my cock, stroking it once. His gaze snaps to my hand, and I catch the jerk of his own swelling cock. I pump myself again, pleasure pooling between my thighs. "Lucaryn."

His hands fist at his sides as he watches my hand slick up and down my cock. His voice is raspy with desire. "We don't have time, Ry. Five days."

I wade closer to him.

"We have a few moments for this. I've been aching for you." I squeeze my cock, barely holding back a groan. "I *will* have this."

Luc takes a step toward me, and I move with him. He stops, gripping his length, matching my pumps, his eyes never leaving my stroking hand. "I want to watch you, Ry. Show me."

Fuck.

"Yes, sir." His lips part and his eyes dilate. His dominance rivals mine, but I enjoy the pleasure I gift him with my submission. My thumb rubs over the head of my cock in a slow circle, and he copies the move. My hand slides down my length, and my pace picks up. Our breathing comes out in dual sharp pants as we watch each other stroke ourselves. Every pass of his tight fist over his beautiful cock has my mouth watering and my body tightening with need. I wish my mouth was where his hand is, or my own hand, or my ass.

Luc takes another step, the water splashing against my thighs and lower stomach with his movement.

"So good, Ry. I love how your stomach muscles flex with your thrusts. Look at the way the water slicks your giant cock. I could get lost in watching your arm muscles stretch and bunch with your effort to find your release." His voice is a growled whisper, and my toes nearly curl. "I miss your taste on my tongue. I miss the sight of you kneeling before me with my cock shoved down your throat."

"Fuck!"

My balls draw up as my fist punishes my cock.

"Rydel." My eyes reluctantly leave Luc's hand pumping his length to climb to his face. "You're mine." His jaw flexes, then the slick wetness of his spit hits my dick. He does it again before spitting on his own cock.

Starlight unfurls through my center, shooting to my toes and bouncing around my skull. Ropes of cum spurt from my cock, covering Luc's hand and dick. My spend runs down his thigh as my cum glistens on his length and between his fingers.

With a shout, he comes. I step closer, letting his hot release coat my stomach. With the last few jerks of his hips, my fingers reach out, gathering the dripping cum from the tip of his cock. I bring my fingers to my lips, licking and sucking them clean.

His face is relaxed, his breathing deep and heavy as he watches my tongue lap up his release.

My finger pulls out of my mouth with a pop. "That'll hold me over for a little while."

He smiles, stepping back so he has enough room to bend over and splash water over his skin to clean away the mess we just made. I do the same and we both wade out of the water to where the horses stand where we left them.

Dressing quickly, we mount under the fading light of the day. As we push west, I smirk at Luc. "See? That didn't eat up too much of our time. Though, I wish I had been inside you."

Luc laughs. "Yes. We found our release in a matter of minutes like a couple of adolescents."

"What can I say? You do it for me, captain."

He shakes his head, his bright smile lighting up his face.

I love him. So much.

"Luc?" His head swivels, his blue eyes dancing with amusement. "I love you."

His face smooths into serious lines, then his brows pinch together. "Don't say that like a goodbye."

"I'm not. I'm just trying to be more ... open with my feelings—with you anyway."

Some of the tension leaks from his face. "Well, it's strange. I don't think I like sappy Rydel." He grins at me. "But, I do like hearing those words." His face angles forward, eyes on the empty path before us. "I love you too, Rydel."

My insides go warm at his quiet words. How can such a simple phrase have such a profound impact?

An hour passes in silence before the path we're following changes into a wide dirt road. We pass the occasional traveler, most of whom barely give us a glance, but some do nod before dropping their gazes to the ground, continuing on their way.

The hours slide by, the child moon moving swiftly across the sky as the mother moon hugs the horizon. Farms dot the landscape, miles separating the sprawling properties. A dog barks from a small house well set off the road. The scent of ash coats my throat, and I notice the grey smoke curling up from the chimney. I chuckle to myself. A fire? Sure, it's the dead of winter, but this far south there's no snow on the ground, and while there's a bite to the wind, the air is temperate.

Southerners.

I look at Luc, his arms bare, showing off his muscles, but also his many injuries. My own sleeveless shirt keeps me cool, holding back the persistent fever flushing my body with the desire for more of the drug. I feel a bit better after the quick wash in the creek, but my skin still feels too tight, and the occasional wash of nausea attempts to bring the water I drank earlier back up my throat.

Glancing at my exposed arms, I take stock of the bruises and cuts along my skin. I nudge Kahar closer to Luc, and we both slow our horses to a walk.

"We need to find different clothes. I'd like to hide"—I lift my arms then point to Luc's—"as much of this as we can. We need to look ... normal. Strong." I hold up my hand, the ring glinting in the moonlight. "Like we still have our magic."

Luc nods without a word.

The mother moon slips below the horizon, its fading light enhanced by the first pale light of the approaching morning. The edge of the capital city of Adren comes into view. We crest a small rise, the city spreading below us, crawling all the way to the edge of the sea. The silver light of the child moon shimmers on the waves as they crash toward the capital.

We hold our steeds still, gazing at the castle spearing up along the coastline.

Luc's voice is quiet, barely a whisper. "Are we really going to kill him?"

"Yes."

22

RYDEL

The familiar press of the city rises before us, and we dismount, leading the horses through the quiet streets. I try to keep from jumping at every sound, but the shadows are deep, and my mind is empty of the buzz that used to tell me the location of every mind that drew close to me.

I nearly jerk in the saddle as my head snaps to the left at the sound of a woman stepping through a doorway, smacking her hands together, a cloud of flour floating up around her before she flips a sign to open. The scents of sugar, fruit, and fresh bread waft across the street, and my mouth waters as we move past the bakery.

Luc whispers from behind me, "Too bad Adastra didn't leave a few coins with us."

I nod, taking turn after turn, winding our way slowly on a roundabout path toward the castle. I pause at the edge of a small square, the cobblestones clean and gleaming with the morning mist. Dropping Kahar's reins, I say, "Stay here. I'll be right back."

There's a shifting of Luc's boots over stone, and I know he's about to protest, but I hurry away, keeping to the shadows as I hug the edge of the square. I slip down a narrow side street, the walls skimming my shoulders. As I round the building on my left, a small patch of yard opens behind the small house. A thigh-high wood fence contains a small garden, and the entire length leans inward as I grip the edge and step over it. Keeping my footsteps light, I grip the clothes hanging from the line, satisfied that my hands barely tremble with the task.

My head swivels side-to-side as I pull two long-sleeve shirts from the line, the thick fabric heavy. These will be too warm, but they'll hide our wounds. Glancing down, I take in the dirt smudges on my pants. Good enough. Nothing here will fit me or Luc. I wrap my hands around a hooded cloak before sneaking back the way I came.

Handing Luc one of the shirts and the cloak, we shrug into our new garments. Luc pulls the long sleeves down to his wrists. "It is much too warm for these thick sweaters. Southerners really are weaklings when it comes to the cold."

I chuckle, nodding as my body already starts to heat. I'll be sweating in no time.

We continue making our way west, the shadows growing longer as the sun threatens to break over the horizon. The spires of Erathan's castle come into view, and I tilt my head back, looking over the tight press of buildings to the cream limestone of our target.

Luc's voice draws my attention. "I think we should split up."

"No."

"Ry, it's just the two of us. If we run into trouble, there's no one to come to our aid. That's it. Game over. I think you should go in alone. Feign your visit as a concerned ally checking up on Erathan's health."

"I may not be granted an audience. By now, he knows we have … had the Heart Stone, that his is a fake. That I lied to him. I wouldn't allow him into my castle if the tables were turned."

Luc smirks. "Wouldn't you?"

I pause. Maybe I would. I do like my games. I'd be interested in the real motive behind his visit. Maybe Erathan will be as well. Maybe he'll think he can lure me in and take me unawares. Maybe he'll ask for a real alliance since he knows he can't best me with both Stones in my possession. There's no way for him to know Adastra took the Stones, unless she has told him in a move to have Erathan take me out for her.

There are too many variables. Too many unknowns. I have too many enemies.

"And while I'm doing a song and dance for Erathan, where will you be?"

"Casing the castle. Talking with the servants." He gestures at himself. "I blend in here. My darker skin will get me into places without suspect." His eyes travel up to the soaring castle. "Give me a time and place. I'll be there to either back you up or get you out." His weight shifts to his left foot, his fingers tapping his waist. "Should I send word to Farden for reinforcements? A bird can make it to Casin in a day, two at most."

It's tempting, but what if Rannae saw a movement against her while she looked into my possible futures? She will be prepared. I can't lose more of my army to her.

"Send word that we are okay—that we need more time to complete our mission, but for Casin to hold our castle, our capital, our kingdom. Protect and defend. Watch the borders. We need to make sure there's a home to go to once this is over."

Luc nods, and I turn to face him. Cupping his face, my palms scrape against his beard. "I hate the idea of us separating. But you're right. It's the smart move." I brush my lips against his, craving more, but pulling back. "Be careful."

His hand snakes around the back of my neck, pulling me back to his lips. We kiss with passion, with fear, with longing. His fingers squeeze my neck, and my hands press into his jaw. He pulls back, my lips raw from his beard, his breath fanning over my face as he says, "You too. I'd prefer not to have to come rescue you."

Leaning in, I nip his bottom lip. "Yes, sir."

His eyes flare, and his lips pull back in a smirk.

We arrange a time and place to meet, then he shoves me away with a smile that doesn't quite cover the worry in his eyes.

I grip Kahar's reins. Without a glance back, I lead the black steed down the street, the soft thud of my boots and the sharp clop of Kahar's hooves taking us away from Luc. My body winds tighter and tighter. I slow my breaths. He'll be fine. We'll be fine. Nothing has worked quite how we wanted so far, but here is where we turn the tables. We have to.

I blink against the shot of sunlight that hits my eyes as I round a corner. The morning rays shimmer over the sea, illuminating Erathan's castle so that it practically glows with a hint of pink.

Squaring my shoulders, I grip Kahar's reins tighter as I approach the open gates. I'm still at least twenty strides away when a voice calls out, "Halt. What's your business here?"

I pause, the silence broken by Kahar's hoof stomping against the cobblestones, little sparks flying up around his metal shoes.

"I am King Rydel Wescaryn. I've come to speak with your King."

I stride forward before permission is granted, and I catch the wide-eyed stares of two of the three guards before they school their expressions. The one out front steps forward, his broad shoulders filling out his armor, the metal gleaming in the early morning sun.

Full armor. They weren't in full armor on my last visit. Maybe Erathan isn't as recovered from the spider bite as is rumored.

The guard eyes me with a smirk on his lips as I approach. "Yeah, you're King Rydel. And I'm the fairy king of the northern wood. Stop right there."

A grin lifts my lips, and the two soldiers behind the arrogant man move their hands to the hilts of their swords. I remain relaxed, knowing I can have my dagger in my hand in the blink of an eye.

One of the men clears his throat, his eyes flicking to my hand, landing on the ring on my middle finger, and I fight back a chuckle as he says, "Um, sir. That *is* King Rydel. I recognize him from his last visit." His eyes skirt to Kahar, and his hand flexes on his sword. "And I definitely remember that, um steed of his."

The warmth of Kahar's hair presses into my palm as I stroke his neck with a wicked smile on my face. The lead soldier snaps his gaze over his shoulder, aiming a harsh look at the man behind him before he turns back to me. I raise an eyebrow, and he eyes me up and down before holding out his hand.

I stop. Kahar throws back his head, and the man steps

back, saying, "I'll request that you wait here ... your Majesty. I'll alert our king to your presence and your request." His eyes fall to my ring before leaping back to my face.

My teeth grind together at the silence in my head. They're worried. They're hiding something. I nod, reminding myself to be civil.

"Of course."

I watch the man stride away, the other two shifting with nervous energy.

I wait.

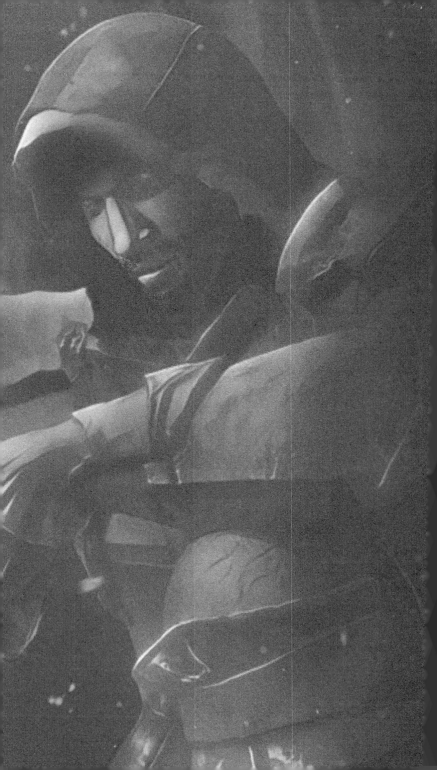

23

LUCARYN

I skirt the city, sticking to the long shadows of the early morning.

I left Phoenix in the barn of a small quiet tavern with no patrons. I picked the place due to its rundown appearance and lack of customers. The woman whose black dyed hair showed exposed dirty-blond roots, eyed my sword as I handed it over for collateral, promising her payment in coin upon my return. I could tell she wanted to refuse, but the promise of payment was too much for her to resist, as I knew it would be. I made sure Phoenix had fresh water and tossed two flakes of hay into his stall before leaving him behind.

Now, steam rises from the cobblestones, dancing around my shins as I leave the small bird house. My message to Casin is on its way with Ry's instructions.

After a short walk, I pause in the shadows of a building

to assess the open stretch of road leading to the northern gate to the castle grounds. As I watch, a woman and a young girl approach the gates. The two guards stop them, exchange a few words and allow the women to pass. The guards, in full armor, shift from foot to foot as they keep a lazy eye on the road leading from the castle into the city.

They both plant their feet, standing tall as a man approaches. The man is dressed similarly to the two women who passed through before—clothing of varying shades of grey with a cream apron looped over his neck and tied around his waist. The guards nod to him as he passes through the gates without a word. But, I notice the guard on the left keeps his eyes trained on the man for a few seconds, his gaze falling to the man's ass before he snaps his eyes forward once again. A smile ghosts across my face.

I prop my shoulder against the wall of the building to my right, the sun slashing a sharp line of light across the stone wall about two feet above my head. A group of five soldiers, all also in full armor stride from the castle grounds, a few slapping the gate guards on the back with words of farewell as they head into the city—for patrols I assume.

The block of sunlight creeps ever closer to my head as I watch people come and go through the gates, but then hushed voices behind me grab my attention. I don't turn, but I listen in as they draw closer, their pace slow, granting me plenty of time to eavesdrop.

"Do you think the king—"

"Hush, Heath. We are not paid to think. We are paid to clean. And you will thank the gods you have such a prestigious position within the castle."

There's a pause before the first voice grumbles, "Yes, ma'am."

The light click of their shoes comes up behind me,

246

passing along my left, and I see an older woman with grey hair tied in a knot at the base of her head. A young man walks at her side, his dark hair brushed away from the sharp angles of his face. His eyes catch mine, and he nods, mumbling a 'good morning' before they pass by without breaking stride. I nod back with a small smile, and the woman nudges the young man.

"Heath, pay attention. Now today, we are starting in the west wing with the guest chambers and bathing rooms. We'll have to work fast to get through them all before noon ..." Her voice fades as they continue down the road toward the castle.

The beam of morning light caresses the top of my head, its warmth startling on my scalp. I've been waiting for a large enough group of servants to approach the gates where I could slip in amongst them, but that opportunity hasn't presented itself yet.

The kitchens. The kitchens or the laundry. That's where I was hoping to infiltrate. That's where the gossip spreads. Whispered words shared like tasty morsels. But as I glance at the gate guards again, the glint of their armor gives me an idea that I begin to mull over.

There's a lull in foot traffic, and my mind wanders to Rydel. Did Erathan grant him an audience? To refuse a fellow king would be problematic. But Rydel has shown up without announcement, so ...

I rub my hands down my thighs, wiping away the sweat on my palms.

Squaring my shoulders, I push off the wall and turn away from the castle gates. I'm not going to be able to slip in with the castle servants. Or, at least I'm not willing to wait all day for an opportunity that may never present itself. I need another way in.

I wind down the streets, keeping track of my path, until I see what I'm looking for. Two men come stumbling out of a small brothel, the low pitch of the roof hiding them in shadow before they burst into the morning light. In tandem, they squint, holding their hands above their eyes, groaning. They shuffle down the street, their steps uneven and heavy.

The scarred wood of the door scrapes against my hand as I push it open. I have to blink several times until my eyes adjust to the dim interior. Stale beer and too-sweet perfume permeates the air. There's no one behind the bar, and a man slumped over a table snores loudly as I work my way through the near-empty space. My boots stick slightly to the dark wood floor. I almost startle as a form moves from the drunk man's lap, and a woman sits up. She spares me a passing glance as she tucks her left breast back into her dress. Her hair is tangled around her head, and the stench of beer and sex wafts from them both as I pass, my eyes on the stairs.

With every step, the wood creaks as I climb to the second story. I have to duck under the heading as the low roof closes in at the top of the stairs. There are five doors down the right side of a long hall, and five more down the left. Some are open. Most are closed.

This brothel is close enough to the castle to be convenient for soldiers coming off shift, but if I strike out here, I'll continue my search deeper into the city. The first door on my right is open, and a quick glance reveals the room is empty. The door on my left is open as well, but only a crack. With a gentle push, it swings inward a few inches, and I spy a tangle of naked limbs covering the single bed. Both women's bodies are flushed, clothes scattered around the floor, their breathing deep and even.

I continue down the hall, checking each room before

coming to the fourth door on the left. It's closed, but as I quietly turn the knob, the door opens on a soft groan. My right hand hovers over my sheathed dagger as I peer into the room, but there's no movement. No one calls out in outrage.

A grin lights up my face as I catch the glint of armor stacked in the far corner of the room. Soft snoring comes from the bed, and the large man grumbles as he turns on his side, pulling the sleeping woman with him, a hand grabbing her breast. She moans but remains asleep.

I cross the room on silent feet, assessing. He's a little larger than me, but his armor should fit. The steel of my dagger's hilt cools my palm as I grip my blade. I stalk to the edge of the bed, pressing the sharp tip to the soldier's neck as I wrap my hand around the whore's upper arm. The man grumbles again, and the stench of sour ale fills the space between us as he belches in his sleep. My nose wrinkles as I pull the woman out of his arms. Her eyes flutter, and her tongue licks at her dry lips as she blinks up at me. She glances down at the man in the bed, not even registering my dagger pressed to his flesh before looking up at me. She raises the arm I'm not gripping, palm up.

"Three coppers'll get you a room and an hour of my time." Her breath reeks of ale as well, dried cum sticks to the corners of her mouth, and her eyes are bloodshot. She swallows, swaying slightly, obviously still drunk.

I shove her toward the door, her ass jiggling, her breasts swaying.

"Leave. And close the door behind you." My whispered words come out on a growl, and she frowns at me before glancing at a pile of clothes on the floor. I kick them toward her, and she bends down, hugging them to her chest before slipping from the room on shaking legs, the door clicking shut behind her.

She might remember me, but then again, she's still unsteady with drink, and she looks ... well used. Picking me out of a lineup of men would be hard for her. And the word of a whore only goes so far.

I turn my attention back to the man still snoring away on the bed.

This soldier, however ... I can't have him stumble back to the castle to report his armor stolen. Now maybe, his shame and embarrassment might lead him to try and cover up his misfortune, but I'm not about to risk it.

My left hand presses over his mouth until I feel the cut of his teeth against my palm. I slide my dagger into his neck. The hilt slams against his skin, the tip of my blade punching out the other side. His eyes fly open, the dark brown ringed by burst blood vessels. His mouth works against my hand, his saliva coating my palm, but I press down harder. Blood leaks from the wound, soaking into the dirty pillow and staining the sheets. His legs kick out, his dick flopping against his thigh. I twist the blade, and his chest arches off the bed, and his muffled cry floats between my fingers. Another twist of the blade, and he goes still, his wide eyes staring through the ceiling.

I pull my hand away from his mouth, wiping my palm off on a semi-clean part of the bed sheets. As I slip my dagger from his neck, a strong gush of blood flows from the wound before slowing to a crawl, then a drip. Wiping my dagger on the sheets, I slip it into the sheath and cross the room, hefting the armor from the floor. With practiced moves, I buckle and secure the armor of the Kingdom of Adren onto my body. It rubs uncomfortably at a few of my joints where the fit is imperfect, but overall, it'll pass.

Leaning down, I search his crumpled pants and find a few coins. Slipping them into my pocket, I grab his sword, carelessly propped against the wall, the tip digging into the soft wood floor. I tsk as I slide it into the sheath at my hip. That's a good way to dull your blade.

I slip from the room, closing the door behind me and slowly make my way back down the stairs. The main room is still empty, and the woman is gone from the man's lap. He now snores alone, cheek pressed to the table, drool sliding down his face.

Stepping back outside, I take a deep breath, trying to expunge the stale scent of beer and sex from my nose. With another quick adjustment of the armor, I head back in the direction of the castle.

I haven't even traveled a block, when a man steps from the shadows of a narrow street. His short black hair is oily and slicked back from his face. His dark skin stretches over a thin frame that's struggling to hold on to some muscle. His eyes gleam as he takes in my armor then flicks to the brothel I just came from before landing back on me with a greedy look.

He steps in front of me, his hand pressed to my chest. "A single copper and I'll suck ya off. Take off some of tha tension before ya head back ta work."

I step around him without a word, but he follows, grabbing my arm with surprising strength. "I'm good. I know how ta work a cock."

Against my will, my dick stirs, not because I want this whore on my cock, but because his words have elicited an image of Ry beneath me, his muscles flexing, his skin slick with sweat.

I grab the man's wrist, pulling him off me. "No."

I continue down the street, but he trots behind me. "I'm

better than any whore ya had back there in that place. Just one copper. I'll let ya have my ass if that's what ya want."

I wish I had my magic to silence this whore, but instead, I spin. The man freezes then backs up at the look on my face. My hand wraps around his neck, but as I squeeze, his eyes roll back and his mouth falls open on a groan. Fuck. I squeeze tighter as I growl, "I said no. Now get lost. Find another cock to suck."

I release him, and he staggers forward a step, his hand rubbing his throat. "Oh, so you're too good for tha likes of me, huh?"

I don't respond as I turn away and aim back for the castle. He curses at me, then the soft sound of his footsteps carries him in the opposite direction before I hear his voice. "Hello, fine sir. One copper and I'll let ya do ta me all the things ya wished you'd been able ta do ta her last night."

He's already found another mark, and I smile as the castle comes back into view.

The same two guards stand at the gates, and I gamble on the large size of Erathan's army and the hope that these two men can't possibly know every soldier in the Adren ranks.

I keep my stride even as I pass them, nodding. They nod back, their bored expressions quickly turning back toward the road, and I smile as I pass onto the castle grounds.

I'm in.

I look at the castle. The faint sound of the crashing waves blends with the sharp cry of seabirds. I've only been here a handful of times, mostly for the harvest festival, but while all castles are sprawling, winding spaces, for some reason, there's a similar layout that threads between each towering castle or palace I've visited. So, it's easy to find an appropriate entrance, keeping my head down as I wind through the narrow halls.

Turning a corner, a sharp voice stops me. "You're late. You were supposed to relieve the guard upstairs ten minutes ago." The female soldier grips my shoulder, and I turn with her as she leads me back down the hall as she says, "If you wanted to sneak some breakfast from the kitchens before your shift, you should have woken up earlier." She pats my shoulder, and I return her smile. "Gods know, the food down there is better than what we get in the mess hall, but I'm afraid you're going to have to go hungry today."

I have no idea who she thinks I am, but I play along and shrug. "My own fault."

We turn two corners then come to a winding stone staircase, the occasional narrow window spilling light onto the pale stones. She nods upwards. "Up you go. It's a long, boring day, but someone has to do it."

Fuck, it seems whomever I'm impersonating has some kind of guard duty today. I roll my eyes with a smile. "And I'm that somebody."

She laughs, slapping me on the back, the metallic sound bouncing off the walls. She turns, her braid swinging down her back as she strides away. I glance up the stairs, wondering if I can get away with sneaking off, but I sigh, my thighs bunching as I climb the steps. Might as well see this through, for now at least.

I hit the last step, and a long hall greets me. I could stretch out my arms and not touch the walls. Large windows crawl down the left side, exposing the view of the sea. Gigantic oil paintings decorate the right side of the hall. There are two guards standing on either side of a door about halfway down. As I approach, I glance at the paintings, and my pulse picks up. They're all portraits of the royal family.

Have I really stumbled into such luck?

I stop in front of the closed double doors, and the man on the left scowls at me. "Finally."

I shrug, switching places with him. "Sorry. Thought I had time to sneak a bite from the kitchens."

The guard on the right smirks, and the man I replaced clasps my shoulder. "Ah. I get it. In fact, I think I'll head down there now. Lorell likes me." He winks, and I assume he's talking about one of the cooks as he turns with a laugh. "I'll convince her to give me a nibble of her sweet bread, and then maybe she'll give me a nibble of her sweet cunt."

The man on my left laughs, and I join in, calling after the retreating man's back. "Good luck."

He waves a hand over his shoulder as he disappears down the stairs I just climbed.

I settle into my post, the silence stretching.

My posture is relaxed, my feet planted slightly wider than my hips, a soft bend in my knees. My gaze is trained on the white limestone of the wall that stretches between two windows. But despite my body language, my skin itches with anticipation. My fingers ache to grab the door handles and peek inside what I suspect are the royal chambers.

If Rydel was granted an audience, I assume Erathan would meet him in the throne room, but maybe he opted for a more informal meeting, and they are inside this room right now? Or maybe there's no one inside, and we're simply here to keep anyone out. And maybe I'm completely wrong, and this isn't Erathan's room.

Time passes slowly, and other than the occasional clink of our armor as we shift, there's no other noise in this long hall. When the sun hits its apex, the waves glittering as they crash into the rocks along the shore, footsteps sound from the stairs.

A blond head appears, then a heart-shaped face, then a

skinny body draped in grey servants' clothes. Her small hands clutch the handle of a pail, and as she starts down the hallway, her gate is awkward as she walks around the weight of the bucket hanging heavily between her legs.

She stops in front of the door, and the guard next to me grips the knob, his eyes drinking in the servant with an all-too familiar look. He smiles down at her, and she returns it with a blush as he says, "Hello, Marcy."

The guard swings the door inward on silent hinges, and I hold my breath as Marcy crosses the threshold, saying, "Hello, Willen."

Willen's hand drops over hers that's gripping the pail. "You need help with that?"

She shakes her head. "No, thank you. I've got it."

His fingers caress the back of her hand, and I smile as she shivers. Willen leans down. "You sure? The king's quarters are your first stop of the day. You have many more buckets of coal to haul today. Let me help."

Holy shit!

The servant blushes, stepping away from Willen's touch. "Thank you. But I'm fine. You'd get in trouble if you left your post."

I smile down at her. "I'll keep watch. He's not technically leaving his post if he's inside the King's room. I'll leave the door cracked and whistle a warning should anyone come this way."

Willen looks at me with gratitude in his eyes, and Marcy's blush deepens. "Well ...?"

Willen grabs the pail, easily hoisting the heavy bucket filled with black lumps of coal. His other hand presses to her lower back, gently guiding her inside, but she hesitates, chewing on her lip.

I whisper, "Go on. It's fine."

She glances at Willen, then into the dark interior of the room. "I ... what if he ...?"

Willen applies a little more pressure to her back, and she takes a step into the room. "Don't worry, swee—Marcy. The healers are keeping him in a deep sleep. He won't wake."

A frown crosses her face, but my heart is pounding so hard, I'm surprised they can't hear it as Marcy says, "Still no change then?"

Willen shakes his head.

Holy fuck. I can't believe this. Can I be this lucky?

Marcy squares her shoulders. "I'm sure they'll find a way to heal him. The king is strong."

Willen nods, and I do the same as the two disappear into the shadowy interior of Erathan's room. I keep the door cracked as promised, my gaze piercing the darkness.

The darkness of Erathan's room.

I press my lips together, swallowing the laughter that wants to burst from my chest. I don't know what Rydel is up to right now, but luck has landed me here, and I'm not going to waste this opportunity.

I can just imagine Ry's smile, his laughter filling my soul when he learns of how I ended up right at the king's door. I can hardly believe it myself. Did Rannae foresee this? If she did, I'm sure she had a good chuckle over it.

The bitch. She's next on my list.

My mind churns with ideas, plans unfurling, options spilling through my thoughts as I force myself to wait for the perfect moment to strike. Getting in will be easy. Getting out once Erathan is dead ... that's another matter.

I'm not Rydel. I can't run into this on a whim and a prayer.

Relaxing my shoulders, I work through possible scenarios, noting the position of the sun, calculating how much time I have before I am supposed to meet Rydel. I suppose he's trying to work his way into the castle somehow, since Erathan obviously isn't accepting guests right now.

I smile.

The muffled whispered voices of Marcy and Willen float through the crack in the door, then there's a sweet little gasp. Hmm. Seems the two are taking a moment for themselves in the forbidden shadows of the king's chambers. Naughty.

A deep moan comes from Willen, and my smile spreads to a full-on grin. Good for them. They should take this moment. Their kingdom is about to be shattered and reformed.

This is ... perfect.

A plan snaps into place as Marcy's whispers flit through the crack in the door. "Willen, not here."

I gather my thoughts, ready to put my plan into action, and as Willen slips from the room, I give him a wink, and he smiles with a nod of thanks. A few moments later, Marcy slips through the door, avoiding my gaze, a deep blush staining her cheeks.

Here we go. These two pawns primed and ready to dance to my will.

24

RYDEL

Kahar stands next to me as we wait. The flicking of his tail and the twitching of his muscles to dislodge the occasional buzzing bug are the only movements breaking his unnatural stillness. His ears are perked, aimed at the two guards doing their best to keep from shifting under the war horse's intensity. I allow a smirk to cross my face as the guard on the right takes the smallest step back, eyes trained on Kahar.

Silence pulses in my ears. The absence of their thoughts is deafening. My skin itches with the desire to feel the heat of the magic light up my back—and I admit some of the crawling sensation is also due to my body craving another hit of the drug. Just one more taste. Just a few minutes more in the floating void of bliss.

No.

My chest expands with my slow inhale, my ribs pulling

with a twinge of pain. I focus on that pain to remind myself I'm alive, I survived, I'm strong.

The snap of boots on limestone has the two guards straightening as the third man returns. I'm sure he thinks his face is impassive, but I'm exceptional at reading people, and I know I'm not going to be pleased with what he's come to tell me. And the small twitch of his forefinger tells me he's nervous to deliver the news.

The soldier's eyes flick to the ring on my middle finger before he meets and holds my gaze. "I'm sorry, your Majesty. King Bryrel is not receiving guests at this time." I raise a brow, and to his credit, he maintains eye contact. "Not even a guest of your ... standing."

I run a hand down Kahar's neck, and he snorts with a little shake of his head. The pause in conversation lengthens, and I flex my hand then run my thumb over the ring. The men before me shift but hold their ground. I can practically smell their fear, and I'm sure they're sweating under that heavy armor. They are hiding something, something I would know if I had my damn Stone.

I smile, meeting each of their gazes while saying, "Relax, boys." The main guard doesn't quite manage to hide his sneer, but I continue. "I'm not going to shoot the messenger ... this time. I will simply see to my horse while you have a room prepared for me. I will stay a few days, and surely in that time Erathan's schedule will open up to allow me a bit of time with him."

The soldier on the left actually slumps slightly in relief, but crease lines furrow between the head guard's brows. "Your Majesty—"

I hold up a hand, my other gripping Kahar's reins. "Have someone fetch me when my guest quarters are ready. I'll be" —I wave my hand—"around the castle grounds."

My cheeks twitch as I fight to keep the smile from my face. I lead Kahar through the gates, the head guard's low voice sounds behind me. "Stillan, see that a room is prepared for King Rydel."

Smart man. He could have tried to stop me, but, well ... few go against the Crown Breaker and live to tell the tale.

Rannae's face flashes in my mind. Fucking gods damned woman.

As I pass the soldiers, Kahar dances to the right, his flank slamming into one of the guards, his armor rattling as he tries to stay on his feet. My chuckle floats on the sea breeze as Kahar and I leave the guards behind, Stillan moving with fast strides toward the castle to see to my needs.

I know the stables are to the north, but I circle the castle to the southwest. The clap of limestone underfoot changes to the crunch of gravel, and the roar of the sea grows louder. Movement on my right slows my pace. A woman rises to her toes, arms stretched overhead as she plucks fruit from a tree in a small orchard.

Fruit? This time of year?

The bright red berries fill her small hand before she drops them in a basket at her feet. She repeats the process over and over without a look in my direction. Kahar and I move on.

Following the sound of crashing waves, I find a narrow path that seems like it might lead toward the shore. Thorns grab and pull at my pants and scrape at the leather of the saddle. I'll have to check Kahar for scratches and thorns stuck in his hide.

The brush gets higher and tighter as I weave down a small rise, Kahar forced to walk behind me. With a final push through the brambles, the sea opens out before me.

My boots sink into the sand, and a small pink crab scuttles sideways and shoots under a rock. The sharp cry of a bird precedes its shadow as it zips overhead. My hair whips around my face, and I take a deep inhale of the salty air.

Stopping at the edge of the wet sand, the waves desperately reach for me before being pulled back to the sea. Kahar shakes his head as I move around him, my hand running along his hide, searching for stuck thorns. Finding none, I lean into the giant steed, and his muscles twitch as the breeze tickles his skin. As the sun paints the sparking water a soft blend of pink and orange, I sigh. It really is beautiful here. Different from my mountains. But if this goes according to Adastra's vision, this capital city will belong to the bitch of the south.

My eyes travel up the coast. There are several port cities between here and the border of my kingdom that will belong to me. I smile, my hand absently stroking Kahar. Maybe I'll set up a seaside vacation residence for Luc and me to get away to once in a while.

A slow, burning ache spreads through my chest, temporarily overshadowing my bruised ribs.

Lucaryn.

Shifting, I look over my shoulder toward the castle. Where is he? Has he had any better luck infiltrating Erathan's fortress? I run my hands through Kahar's mane, and though he pins his ears back and swats his head at me, I keep up the combing motion.

"Don't be so contrary, Kahar. Look at where we are. Does the sea not calm you?"

As if in answer, he paws at the sand, the grains flying up around him. I close my eyes with a chuckle. Once he stands still again, I peel my eyes open, making sure the air is clear of sand before turning back toward the castle.

"Luc uhr fauhr sa e'a ahuiy." *Luc is going to be okay.*

Kahar snorts, and I take that as his agreement. I lead him up a different path that opens to a small garden. The bushes are sculpted, and a small fountain bubbles in the center. Kahar yanks on his reins, and I let him pull me toward the splashing water. His nose dips in the basin, his lashes catching little droplets that splash from the tiers of the stone fountain.

"Excuse me, sir. The stables are on the north side of the grounds where your horse can drink from the troughs. This is the fountain King Bryrel the third commissioned for his wife and is not meant for—"

I turn, facing the tall woman, releasing Kahar's reins to allow him to continue drinking his full. "He was thirsty and chose this lovely spot for a bit of respite. If you want to deny him"—I take a step away from Kahar and hold out my hand—"be my guest."

The woman's face turns to stone, her grimace pulling her deep-set eyes downward. She storms forward, scowling at me when she should have been concentrating on Kahar. The second she steps into his space; the giant black steed snaps out his hind leg never lifting his head from the water. The crack of his hoof slamming against her hip echoes through the air. She gasps, stumbling back, rubbing her side. Tears rim her eyes, and she takes another step back, her leg nearly buckling as pain shoots through her eyes. But behind the pain, there's anger on her face as she turns back to me.

"Get your beast out of the Lily fountain! I will have the guards escort you from the castle grounds."

When I just raise an eyebrow, making no move to gather Kahar's reins, she actually bares her teeth at me.

"I don't know who you think you are, but this disrespect

will not stand." She whips her head to the left, calling out, "Guards!"

She waits a beat, and when she opens her mouth to call out again, I almost laugh out loud as Stillan comes jogging down the path. The woman crosses her arms, aiming a pleased look at me, but I just smile at her, and her amusement falls as Stillan stops before us.

"There you are, your Majesty."

The woman's head snaps between Stillan and me, her mouth falling open in obvious indignation as Stillan raises his arm, indicating the path leading north out of the garden.

"If you will follow me, we can get your steed settled, and I will show you to your quarters."

Not bothering to grab Kahar's reins, I head up the path Stillan indicated, throwing a smile at the woman, her mouth still hanging open in shock. Kahar follows, and I swear he flicks his tail in her direction.

The clink of Stillan's armor follows along as we round the castle. Scents of horses and hay greet me as the stables come into view. A middle-aged woman comes jogging out, lead in hand, ready to take her next charge, but she skids to a stop, her boots leaving lines in the dirt behind her. Her eyes go wide as she backs up, shaking her head.

"No."

I can't hold back my laugh as I walk past her, crossing into the stables. "Don't worry. I'll get him set up."

Kahar follows me like a puppy—an angry puppy with his ears pinned back and his head lowered. As I get him settled in a stall, making sure to choose one at the end of the aisle and without a horse in the neighboring stall, I let my amusement chase away the tension in my back. Kahar is such a delight.

With a final playful smack on his neck, I leave Kahar,

following Stillan toward the eastern entrance to the castle. The bright light of the sun is tempered as we cross the threshold, but the large windows along the western wall help brighten the stone interior.

I map our path as Stillan leads me down hallways and up several stairs. I've been here a handful of times, and I'm pretty sure Erathan's quarters are in the north wing, so I'm not surprised when I'm led to the southern wing.

The bright white limestone that glimmers and reflects the sunlight on the exterior of the castle is carried throughout the interior making it feel open despite the heavy stone walls. Our footsteps echo loudly without rugs or drapery to dampen the sound. It's just stark white stone, everywhere.

It feels like my eyes are burning, and tension creeps back into my shoulder blades as the absence of my magic claws at my mind. I scowl at a closed door on my right, not knowing how many people are within that room or what they're thinking. It's infuriating.

Stillan stops, wrapping his hand around the handle of a door on our left, and I flex my jaw, releasing the hard clench I had on my teeth. The door swings inward, and Stillan stands to the side, gesturing into the room.

"Hopefully, this will suffice. With no notice—"

"It's fine."

I stride past him, blinking at the white stone floor and walls. The ceiling is plaster but is painted white as well. A large bed made of pale wood is positioned to face the windows giving me a view of the lower levels of the castle and the sea beyond. The bedding is white, and I want to rub my eyes just to create little stars of color behind my lids. This stark castle is already driving me mad.

Turning to Stillan, I wave a hand. "I'll take lunch in the mess, but I'll take dinner in my room."

Stillan nods, glancing at my ring before bowing slightly. "Warren tends this wing. The cord next to the bed will call him. He will do his best to accommodate your needs."

I turn on my heel, giving Stillan my back and his dismissal. A second later, the door clicks shut behind me. My fingers press to my temples as I try to rub away the growing headache. It seems my head is determined to pain me with or without the magic.

Now alone, I give into the trembling of my muscles. I fan my shirt away from my body, trying to stifle the heat my body is pumping out with the craving for more of the drug. I need a distraction.

Where is Luc? Where is Erathan? I suspect the guard's excuses are lies, and the lack of heat in my back and whispers in my head is maddening.

Well, one thing's for sure, I'm not going to sit around in these rooms and wait.

Silk caresses my hand as I wrap my fingers around the cord hanging from the ceiling to the left of the bed. I give it a sharp tug, then head through the door on my right. The bathing room is small but pristine with more white floors, walls, and ceilings. The tub is white limestone, and a window over the tub lets in the sea breeze. I'm sure some would find this peaceful, but the lack of color stabs at my eyes.

Running my hands through the water in the white stone basin, I splash my face with a shaking hand, combing my fingers through my beard before heading back into the main room. I watch the glittering waves in the distance until a sharp rap of knuckles on wood draws my attention. A soft voice calls out as the door cracks open. "Your Majesty?"

I straighten, forcing the trembling to a minimum. "Enter."

A young man enters, his reddish-blond hair curling around his face, framing his brown eyes. He bows, his lean frame built with muscle born of constant manual labor. As he rises, he says, "I'm Warren, your Majesty. How can I help?" His eyes flick to my ring before landing on the floor and staying there.

"Where's the mess hall? I plan to take my lunch there later this afternoon."

Warren keeps his gaze downcast. "There's no need for you to eat in the mess, your Majesty. There is a dining hall reserved for honored guests. I can—"

"The mess hall is fine."

Warren swallows. "It is outside the eastern wing. The building with the low roof. There's a large pink shell nailed to the wall next to the double doors. I can take you there now if you'd like, so you know where it is."

"That's not necessary. I'll find it."

I let the implication hang that I intend to wander the castle, and I catch the slight flex of Warren's hands. The idea of me roaming the halls distresses him. Damn it. Something is going on beyond people simply being uncomfortable with my presence. I'm used to people being afraid of me, of them watching their words, of them avoiding my gaze. This is different. I strain to hear what he's not saying, and the emptiness of my magic echoes in my mind.

"I need new clothes."

His eyes flick up, his gaze taking me in from head to toe. He nods.

"I will take dinner in my rooms."

He nods, keeping his eyes on the floor. "I'll have some

clothing brought immediately, and I'll deliver dinner at your summons."

"Leave the clothes here." I wave a hand at a nearby chair, and he nods again.

"That is all for now, Warren."

Without another word, he turns and hurries from the room.

Reaching up, my cuts burn slightly, and my ribs twinge with pain as I pull the tie from my hair. My fingers comb through my hair again, snagging on tangles. I quickly shed my weapons and discard my clothes, leaving them in a heap on the bathing room floor. Slipping into the tub, the warm water slides over my skin. My cuts burn slightly, but I ignore the pain as I quickly wash and work to get the rest of the tangles out of my hair. I slide under the water, waiting for the burn in my lungs, the dancing stars behind my eyes.

Water sloshes as I shove back to the surface, and I gasp. I grip the edge of the tub, hauling myself out, puddles forming under my feet as I lurch toward the latrine. My empty stomach clenches and bile splatters in the bowl.

Damn it.

I spit a few times, before rising on shaking legs. I towel off, rinse out my mouth and chew on some mint before padding naked into the bedroom. A neat pile of clothes sits on the chair, and I'm unsurprised by the cream, grey, and white fabric of the pants and sweater.

For the moment, I feel a little more stable, so I dress quickly, securing my weapons and pull half of my hair back, tying it up in a knot.

I swing the door open striding into the white hall. I look right, left. Deciding on left, I run my hand along the limestone wall with a smile on my face. Let's see what trouble I can find. I have my suspicions about Erathan, and I'm eager to find the answers to the questions spilling through my mind.

Not knowing—it's unfamiliar and enraging.

Maybe I'll run into Luc while I'm snooping. My smile grows. Mmm. Hopefully, I'll run into Luc.

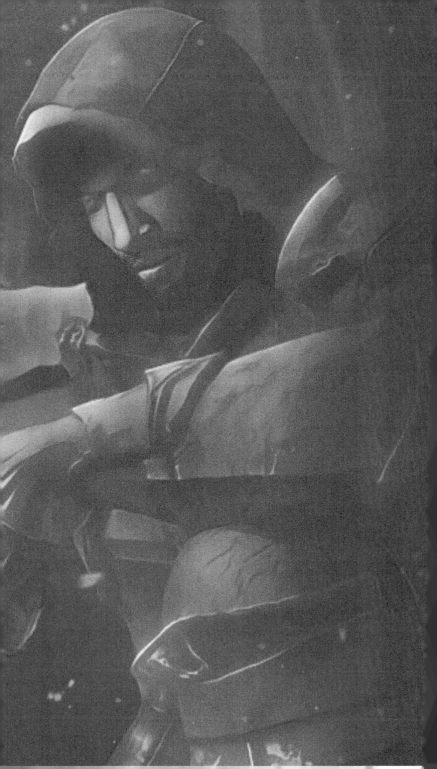

25

LUCARYN

I'm sure my eyes are shining as I look between Marcy and Willen, and hopefully they interpret it as sharing in their mischief and not the absolute excitement that's threatening to tremble through my body.

Marcy pats her hair with a blush before hoisting her pail, now about a quarter emptier than it was before. She glances at Willen before ducking her head and heading down the hall. Before Willen can take up his post at the door, I take a step and nudge his shoulder with mine, our armor clinking lightly. I nod toward Marcy's retreating back.

"I'm sure she could use some help hauling that heavy bucket to the next few rooms."

I raise an eyebrow, and he looks after Marcy. A moment of longing crosses his face before he wipes it away, but I know I've got him. He starts to shake his head, but I nudge him again, a small smile crawling across my face, but not for the reason he thinks.

Taking a guess, I say, "Those rooms are empty." I tick my brow up in suggestion, and he glances down the hall again, his lips pressing together as Marcy pushes through a door on the right.

My head jerks toward the doors behind us. "I've got this. The king is secure. This hall is empty. And Marcy looks like she needs—"

"Alright, alright." Willen grins as he claps a hand to my shoulder, and I chuckle as anticipation thrums through my blood. "If you're sure?"

His eyes flick up and down the hall, and I lean into his space. "If anyone comes while you're seeing to Marcy's"—he shoves me, and I let myself fall into the wall at my back. I raise a hand with a wide grin on my face. "No offense. I just mean I'll explain your absence. I've got you. Go."

A small smirk lifts one side of his mouth as he rubs the back of his neck. Then, with a quick nod, he turns. "Thanks. I'll be quick."

Yes!

I chuckle. "Not too quick, I hope."

He tosses a smile over his shoulder before rushing down the hall. He disappears into the room Marcy went into a few moments ago, and the door clicks shut behind him.

Holy fucking gods. I cannot believe this. Maybe all those little laments and prayers Ry made to Beatuis have paid off.

Not wasting the opportunity, I check the hall one last time, making sure it's empty and quiet. Reaching behind me, my palm presses into the iron of the handle, and the door slides open on silent hinges. As soon as it's open enough to fit through, I slip into the dark room and quietly close the door.

I hold my ground, breathing through my nose as I give my eyes time to adjust. My fingers are trembling with nervous energy. Gods damned, I wish Rydel was here. To be able to see the look on his face.

I flex my hands, trying to stop the shaking. No. I think being able to tell him this story will be even more satisfying.

The shadows begin to reveal the corners and far sides of the room as my sight adjusts. Heel-toe, I cross the room toward a door that's cracked a few inches open. A flickering orange light peeks from the opening. My ears strain to pick up any sound, but the room is utterly silent, and there's still no noise coming from out in the hall.

My palm presses to the door, and it slides open. The soft glow of a single candle spreads light from a bedside table casting a small circle around the large bed. Out of reflex, I scan the room, checking for hidden figures and means of escape. There are three windows along the west wall facing the sea. A glass door leads to a stone balcony, and green vines scrape against the glass as they sway in the breeze. The sun attempts to add its warmth to the lone candle, but the drawn drapes keep most of the room in shadow.

My gaze returns to the bed.

Erathan's face is pale, his bald head shiny with sweat, his red beard stark like flames against his gaunt skin. Dark circles cup his closed eyes, and through the thin sheet that covers him from toes to chin, I notice the way the sheet lays flat against the mattress where the lower half of his left leg should be.

I draw my dagger, my hand slightly clammy but steady.

Erathan's eyelids flutter, and I pause as his dazed gaze lands on me.

If Ry were here, he'd slam his dagger into Erathan's heart without hesitation, but I wait. My dagger is poised, ready to strike, and his gaze flicks to it before he looks back at my face. His brows draw together, and his tongue darts out to lick his cracked lips. His voice is weak. "Soldier, what are you doi ..."

His eyes go wide as his words trail off. I almost take a step back in shock when a small smile lifts the corners of his mouth. His pale, dry tongue darts out again, trying to wet his lips. A weak cough punches from his chest, and he squeezes his eyes shut, breathing through his obvious pain. Once he catches his breath, his eyes find mine again, and he whispers, "I expected it to be Rydel."

I tilt my head, and he smiles wider, licking his lips again. "I thought I'd come to my end by Rydel's hand. But here you stand, Lucaryn."

My hand flexes around the hilt of my dagger. I'm at a loss for words, and Erathan chuckles, which means I'm not doing a good job at keeping my emotions from my face.

He whispers, "I'm glad. I'm in pain. I'm dying, and no one in this entire castle will do me the favor of making my end quick and painless." He shifts, the sheet balling around the stub of his leg under his knee. "I can't take it anymore. My body is wasting, but my people are clinging to some scrap of hope that's doomed me to this never-ending agony."

I step closer, my thighs pressing against the edge of the bed.

His eyes slide closed on a slow exhale. His weak voice cracks, but he swallows and manages to say, "You and Rydel have won, though I suspect Rydel will be unsatisfied with this end. It lacks the drama he so loves."

I can't help the small smile that curves my lips as I raise the dagger and press the tip to the space between his ribs. Erathan's head falls to the side, face turned toward me, but his eyes remain closed. "You had it, didn't you? Since the caves. You had the real Heart Stone."

"I did."

My dagger slides between his ribs with little resistance. A small grunt of pain puffs from his lips, and then he sinks into the bed, lifeless. As I pull the dagger free, blood begins to pool on the sheets. Turning, I sheath my dagger and slide the sword from the belt at my hip. Its weight is foreign and unfamiliar, but a sword is a sword, and it's not like I'm about to face off in battle. I just need one good swing.

Pressing my thumb to the edge, a line of blood immediately wells up, and I nod. I focus on Erathan's neck as I lift the sword with two hands. My arms flex and my core tightens as I swing the blade down. The sharp edge slices through skin and muscle. Bone crunches, and then there's a thud as the blade sinks into the mattress. I pull the sword back, carefully wiping it clean on the sheet before securing it to my hip.

On quiet feet, I keep alert as I cross the room, opening the standing wardrobe in the corner. I shake my head in disbelief as my luck continues to hold. There, lying on the floor of the wardrobe, under the folds of hanging cloaks and pants, shoved behind a pair of polished boots, is a leather bag. I grin as I reach in, grabbing it, stuffing a few shirts in the bottom to soak up the blood, and cross back to bed.

I know from experience that the body will pump most of its blood from his neck and will probably be dripping through the mattress and pooling on the floor in a matter of minutes. But the head actually has very little blood in it—less than would fill a mug, so the few shirts in the bottom of the bag will be more than sufficient.

Without pausing, knowing my time may be running out,

I fist Erathan's beard and stuff his head into the bag, tying the opening, and slinging the strap over my shoulder.

I turn and grab a blanket that's draped over a chair by the fireplace, Marcy's coals glowing hot in the hearth. Fluffing a pillow where Erathan's head used to be, I arrange the blanket over his body and around the pillow. It definitely won't hold up to any sort of inspection, but it'll buy me a little time.

Quickly, I search the room, opening and closing drawers, finding a small bag of coins in one and stuffing them in a pocket of the bag holding Erathan's head. I pocket a jeweled knife that would work as payment for any number of things we might need in the near future, and then I turn to leave. My hand trembles as I reach for the door handle, sliding back into the hall after I check to make sure the way is clear.

Willen must still be with Marcy. It feels like I was in there with Erathan for hours, but I'm sure it was only a few moments. Flexing and clenching my hands, I walk down the hall, grinning wildly as the sounds of flesh slapping against flesh comes from the room on my right. That might be the last moment of joy Willen experiences in a long while.

I come to the end of the hall, and a different staircase greets me. The steps climb and turn to the right, faint light spilling down toward me. Glancing down, the treads disappear into darkness. I recall Rannae's words, and I'm not sure if this is the moment she was referring to, but I take a chance and start descending.

The stairs widen as I go, and the sound of my boots clicking on the limestone joins with the clang of my armor. I feel like I'm making a ridiculous amount of noise.

Finally, I hit the bottom step and cross an open space. An empty room that looks like some type of solarium stands to my left, and as I continue forward, the sound of approaching footsteps echoes across the room. I square my shoulders, determined to look like I belong here.

A shadow enters the room followed by ...

"Rydel?"

26

RYDEL

"Lucaryn?"

I know my mouth is hanging open, but as much as I longed to run into Luc, I didn't actually think I'd literally run into him. That armor looks uncomfortable, but he doesn't break stride as he crosses to me, grabbing my upper arm, guiding me back the way I just came.

"Luc, what—"

"We need to leave."

"What?"

He yanks on my arm, picking up his pace. "We need to go. Now."

With a little pull back, Luc releases me, but I keep pace. I open my mouth to ask a question—which one of the million questions streaming through my mind, I'm not sure—but I press my lips together as a servant comes toward us with head down, gaze on his feet.

We pass in silence, the man never even looking up.

I jog two paces to come up alongside Luc, leaning in, whispering, "Nice armor."

He smirks, but the crinkle at the edges of his eyes tells me he's anxious. His voice is teasing, though as he says, "It worked better than you know."

I raise an eyebrow. This is a wonderful distraction, taking me out of my head and away from the thoughts that scream for more of the drug.

Rolling my shoulders, I say, "I requested an audience with Erathan but was told he is 'too busy' to see me right now. I have been appointed a guest room while I wait for a meeting I don't think will ever happen. I was on my way to hunt down some gossip or Erathan himself when I ran into you."

Luc's eyes cover every inch of the halls we travel, searching every room we pass, watching every servant who scurries by. A hall branches off to our right, and I move to turn down it, but Luc grabs me again, growling, "No. This way."

He continues straight, and I'm dragged along with him.

I point behind us. "My room is that way. It's private. We can—"

"Your Majesty."

Luc's hand drops like a lead weight as Warren approaches. His gaze lands on Luc, but quickly dismisses him as just another of Erathan's soldiers. Turning to me, Warren bows. "The lunch hour has begun in the mess hall, if you're hungry. I can escort you there if you'd like."

I wave at Luc. "I ran into this soldier earlier, and he offered to show me the way."

Luc's face remains impassive, but I can practically feel his impatience. Warren glances at Luc before nodding, bowing, and backing against the wall. What a good little servant.

I stride past him, aiming down the hall Luc was so eager to go earlier. He falls into step behind me, and the second we round a corner, he picks up his pace again, placing himself in front of me, like he's ready to cut down anyone that approaches.

My trust in Luc is complete, so I follow, though my mind is spinning with questions at his behavior. Every room we pass, Luc snaps his head, searching before continuing on. The hall we're in opens into a large space, and he grunts a single word on an exhaled breath. "Finally."

A few people hug the edges of the room, and from their dress, I recognize them as members of high families or court members waiting for an audience. Their gazes flick to us with anticipation that their wait is over, but frowns fall over their faces as Luc and I cross the room with long, determined strides, not sparing them a second glance.

My shoulders pinch as a whispered voice carries across the room, "Is that King Rydel?"

Luc's pace picks up so he's nearly jogging. His hands slam into the door on the right of a double set. It groans open, and the courtyard opens before us. Luc skips down the steps, but slows, realizing I'm falling behind. I refuse to run from this place, no matter the urgency.

I ache to rip my dagger from its sheath, but I tap my finger against the hilt instead. The silence stretches between Luc and me, and the dull pain behind my temples sharpens to a stabbing pain that scrapes at the back of my right eye. Nausea cramps my stomach, but I swallow and force my back to remain straight.

Luc keeps his gaze forward as he asks, "Is Kahar in the stables?"

"Yes."

He nods, moving in front of me again. I curse the clap of limestone underfoot as the sound of our strides emphasizes the words not being spoken right now.

The same female stable hand sees us coming, and steps aside without a word, not even offering to tack Kahar for me. Luc gathers Kahar's blanket and saddle as I slide the bridle over the steed's large head. Luc rounds Kahar, throwing the blanket then the saddle on his back. As he leans down, passing the girth to me under Kahar's belly, he whispers, "Phoenix is at a small rundown tavern on the northern edge of the city."

I nod as Luc secures his new bag to the back of Kahar's saddle, and the steed skitters slightly, his nostrils flaring. Glancing at the bag, my eyes cut back to Luc as the loud clang of a bell rings through the air.

Luc smiles. He rushes into a nearby stall, yanking a bridle over the horse's head. Luc steps onto a stool, swinging onto the horse with grace, even in bulky armor. I mount up and we move out of the stalls, trot down the wide stretch of the stables, and as soon as we're clear, Luc picks up into a canter and I follow suit.

Glancing around at the clamoring soldiers rushing around the castle grounds, I look at Luc, then at the bag bouncing against Kahar's flank.

Excitement courses through me. Did Luc do it?

The temptation of the drug doesn't hold a candle to this!

I laugh as a guard steps in front of the gates as two more stand at attention. Luc pulls back on his horse's reins, barking orders like he's the commander of this army.

"Secure the gates. We are going to gather those currently on patrol in the city. Be on guard. No one in or out without proper documentation."

The guard steps out of our way, saluting, calling over his shoulder, "Let them through!"

I duck my head to hide my smile as Luc kicks back into a fast canter, and we burst through the gates, the metal screeching and clanging shut behind us.

In a matter of moments, Luc aims for a crumbling building, and before Kahar has come to a stop, Luc swings his leg over his horse's neck, leaping to the ground. He sprints around the back of the building, emerging a few moments later without the armor and astride Phoenix. A red-faced man comes running through the doors, waving his arms, screaming, "You promised me payment! Hey!"

Luc and I turn, aiming our horses to the north, to the quickest way out of the city. The bells sounding from the castle fade as we break from the capital and hit open country. I glance behind us, making sure we're not being pursued.

My head whips around at Luc's chuckled words, "Long live the king."

I glance back at the bag. When I turn to face Luc, his smile spreads to a grin, and I throw back my head and laugh, ignoring the painful pull of my ribs. "I can't wait to hear this story."

Luc's laugh joins mine, and damn if my cock doesn't go hard.

27

RYDEL

We aim east, riding hard for hours, heading for the cover of the forests. I manage to keep from throwing up, and the sweats seem to be tempering off. I keep my ears tuned for any sounds of us being chased down, and the way Luc's head twists and turns at every sound tells me he's on high alert as well. We skirt small towns and cities, pushing our horses until their bellies are lathered around their girths.

I start to breathe easier as the trees begin to close in, and once we are forced to slow to a walk and then dismount, I let myself relax ... a little.

The leaves crunch with every step as I follow Phoenix's ass, Kahar trailing behind me, his breathing slowly returning to normal, his nostrils puffing white clouds of mist against my back. The sun set a little over an hour ago, and the chill in the air has turned into a biting wind.

Looking up through the tight-knit branches, the low clouds hang heavy and dark.

There might actually be some snow flurries tonight. I smile. That's good for Luc and me. The southerners are terrified of ice and snow—they rarely have to deal with it. Everyone will close up shop and bolt into their homes at the first sign of winter weather.

I turn my face into the wind, breathing deeply of the pre-snow air. After the long day of hard riding, the cold feels nice. But we can't let the horses cool down too fast. Luc passes up several decent spots where we could set up camp, and I know he's keeping the horses walking. I don't mind, the farther we are from the capital of Adren, the better.

Glancing back, I watch the leather bag bump against Kahar's flank. Shaking my head with a smile, I almost run right into Phoenix's tail as Luc comes to a stop.

Interlacing my fingers behind my back, I extend my arms, flexing and stretching before reaching into one of my saddlebags. Luc goes about removing Phoenix's tack as I grip the coarse length of rope in my hand. Bending down, the scent of dry earth climbs down my nose, the scent so similar to Luc's natural scent. Rummaging through the leaves, I find a decent rock, tie the end of the rope round it, and toss it into the air. It arcs over a high branch before lightly crashing down at my feet. Unstrapping the leather bag from Kahar's saddle, my nose wrinkles as the smell of blood and decay wafts from the interior. I quickly secure it to the rope and haul it up the tree, tying it off.

When I turn, Luc has unsaddled Kahar, and both horses are nibbling on a small patch of grass under a nearby tree. Luc flops to the ground, leaning against a tree trunk, and I take a seat across from him, bending one leg under me and propping my forearm on my other knee.

"Soooooo?"

Luc smiles, shaking his head. "You're not going to believe this."

As he tells me what happened, I laugh with him at the sheer ridiculousness of Luc's luck. I lean back, bracing myself on my hand.

"I was prepared to stay there for a few days until we figured out how to get to him, and then how to kill him." I laugh again, the pull of my healing cuts barely noticeable. "And you go in and are practically invited into Erathan's chambers. Ha!"

Luc rubs the back of his neck with a wide grin.

"I know. I've never had to try so hard to keep from laughing my entire life." He gestures to the hanging bag. "So, what nex—"

His eyes snap to me as I crawl toward him. This is what I need right now. Not that damned drug. Luc. Luc is all I need.

The delicious bite of rocks and twigs dig into my hands and shins. Reaching out, I grab his leg, flexing my fingers into the muscles of his thigh.

"I wish I had been there to see you swing that sword down on Erathan's neck."

He lunges forward, his hand wrapping around my throat, squeezing. His slightly sour breath flutters against my face.

"With Erathan's head in my hands, and the guard and the maid fucking down the hall, it was like a fever dream, Ry." His lips brush against mine, and my entire body lights up from my toes to my scalp. "You should have been there."

Crawling forward, I deepen the kiss, pushing him back until I have him flat on the ground. His cock presses against mine through our clothes, and I work my way down his body. My fingers unfasten his pants, and when I glance up, Luc is propped on his forearm, his bright blue eyes watching me with a fierce hunger.

Licking my lips, I work his pants over his hips, and he lifts his ass so I can pull them all the way off. Rage courses through me as I take in the dozens of cuts along his abdomen and down his legs. Fuck Rannae.

I expel her from my mind as I bite the inside of his thigh, and his groan nearly has me coming. Gods, this man. No one understands me like Luc. No one accepts me like he does. And if I would burn the country down for him, he would lay waste to the world for me.

His musky earth scent is stronger since he didn't have the luxury of a bath today. I dip my head, and his cock jerks, precum slicking down the head. Wrapping my hand around his base, I squeeze.

"You did well, sir."

"Yes, I did, your Majesty. I'll take my reward now."

His hand snaps down, gripping my hair and shoving me onto his cock. His hips buck, and I do my best to relax my throat, but I still nearly gag. I don't care. I take more, sucking him hard, pumping him with my fist.

I desperately miss the warming lubrication that we lost during our captivity, but when my fingers are coated in my saliva, I slide them down, circling his entrance once before pressing a finger into him.

Fuck, I want him inside me. I want to be inside him. I want to consume him, and him me.

I add a second finger, and his grip tightens in my hair as he growls, "More."

Oh, fuck yes.

I pop off his cock, delighting in the gooseflesh pebbling his thighs as a gust of cold wind whips by.

"Turn over. Hand-and-knees, Lucaryn."

Leaves crackle as he quickly obeys. Undoing my pants, I free my dick, gripping it hard. I lick my lips, gathering saliva, but Luc sits back, turning on his knees. His spit splatters on my cock, and my eyes nearly roll back in my head. I stroke myself, pleasure already tight between my thighs. Luc spits again, and again before gripping my neck and pulling me in for a crushing kiss.

Our teeth clack in our desperation, and when he bites my lip, I taste blood.

Pulling back, I pant, "Gods, Luc. Fuck."

His hand wraps around mine on my cock, pumping with me.

"More, Ry. Give me more."

I shove him around, and he braces his hands on the trunk of the tree, bark flaking off under his palms. Leaning over him, my wet dick slicks between his cheeks, and he rubs against me. I grip his chin, turning his head and pressing my fingers to his mouth.

"Suck. Get them nice and wet for you."

His tongue flicks out, and my cock jumps against his ass as he sucks three of my fingers into his mouth. He works them, licking between the seams, coating them, drenching them. I pull them out, and a string of saliva drips from his lips.

Two of my fingers glide into his entrance, and we both groan. I pump once, twice, and add a third. His hips jerk back, and his hands flex against the tree, more bark crumbling from its surface.

Luc's head drops as he uses the tree to push into me. I rip my fingers from him, grab my cock, line up, and shove inside him. He growls, and I throw back my head.

"Lucaryn. You are mine."

My thrusts pick up speed, his ass gripping me every time my hips slap against his skin.

"Yes. Yours."

I can feel my heartbeat pulsing through my cock. Starlight gathers behind my eyes, and I know I'm about to shatter. Falling forward, I press my chest to his back, and he reaches around, gripping my neck with one hand as he whispers, "Come, Ry. Give me your pleasure. Give me all of you."

I explode. The stars behind my eyes black out. My skin tingles with bliss as I come, my hips pounding against him, cum leaking down his thighs. Wave after wave crashes through me until I fall limp against him.

Quick as a lightning strike, Luc shifts, and I fall to the ground as he rolls out from under me. My body is still sluggish from my mind-blowing orgasm, so I don't react as he presses my chest into the ground, straddling my legs. I muster the energy to turn my head, smiling back at him. His cock bobs as he shifts. He's like a god kneeling over me.

Licking my lips, I keep my eyes on him as he uses his knees to spread my legs. The hard ground scrapes against my skin, but the bite of pain pulls a groan from my lips, and I watch as Luc fists himself.

"Are you going to stroke yourself until you come all over me, captain?"

"No." He pumps his fist, lining himself up. "I'm going to fuck you, my king."

Without any prep, he slams into me, and I swear he's split me in two. Pain radiates up my spine, and a rock under my body cuts into my chest with the force of his thrust. I fist the forest floor, leaves and dirt crunching between my fingers.

"Again, Luc."

He leans into his arm pressing me down, and his other hand grips my shoulder. His next thrust creates pleasure that cuts through the pain. Again and again, he drives into me while holding me down. My body floats away with the release of letting go, of submitting. It's a headspace I've only found with Lucaryn. Only him.

Luc owns me right now. I trust him with my body, my heart, and my very black soul.

As if he's reading my thoughts, he growls, "You're mine, Rydel."

My mind drifts in a state of bliss as I sink further into the submissive state of mind, barely managing a whisper. "Yes. Yours, sir."

He pulls out of me, and we both groan. The world spins, and I find myself on my back looking up at Luc's face—a face that I know better than my own. A face I cannot and will not live without. He leans down, cupping my face with one hand, running his fingers through my beard. His own beard tickles my lips as he takes his time with a languid kiss.

The head of his cock presses against me, and I bend my knees, planting my feet to give him better access. Slowly, with love and lust shining in his eyes, he slides back into me, and we share a sigh. He holds himself deep as we kiss. When he pulls back, I press my hands to his chest.

"I can only let go with you, Luc. Only you."

He kisses me again, his fingers flexing on my jaw before saying, "Then let go, Ry. I've got you. I only ever want to give you what you need." He rocks his hips, and my cock starts to get hard again. "I've always wanted you, Ry." Another roll of his hips brings a gasp from both our lips. "Whether it's in your bed in the castle, in a rowdy tavern room, or here in the dirt. I'll never get enough of you."

I grip my cock, stroking it in time with Luc's slow thrusts.

His hand pushes my shirt up my torso, exposing my skin to the cold air. My nipples tighten as his fingers caress my stomach. His muscles bunch and flex as he rolls his hips. He's so beautiful, so strong. He flexes his jaw, and his saliva spits onto the head of my cock, gliding with my next stroke. My eyes threaten to roll back, but I keep my gaze on him.

"Fuck! You are a distraction, Luc. The best kind. And I won't lose you. Ever." With my free hand, I pull him down, pressing my lips to his. Breathing against his mouth, I whisper, "I love you, Lucaryn."

His hips roll again, and my head tilts back slightly, my hair tangling in the leaves and twigs as he says, "And I love you, Rydel. Always. My king."

He slides to the hilt, and his body shudders. My hand grips my cock, and I watch his orgasm. His muscles flex, his eyes hold mine, and his lips part on a silent scream. Pleasure floods my body, and my cum paints my chest as I hold Luc's gaze, watching him ride his orgasm as I shatter into a million pieces.

Falling forward, his weight lands on me, his lips pressing light kisses along my shoulder and neck, mumbling, "I don't need anything else in this world as long as I have you."

I'd be lying if I said I felt the same, so I remain silent. I do love Luc, above all else. But I do need more. I need my magic. And I need vengeance.

Luc shivers, and I chuckle, slapping his ass. My skin pebbles as he rolls off me, and we both sit up. I'm sticky, and I try to brush the dirt and debris from my shirt, but it's a lost cause. Luc runs his hands down his thighs, smirking.

"We're a mess."

I shrug, standing up to relieve myself before pulling my pants back on, and Luc does the same. My stomach grumbles loudly, and Luc looks around.

"I could go out and see if there's any small game in the area. Maybe a rabbit or squirrel."

I shake my head.

"We are close to a border village in Trislen. We can clean up, change, and find something to eat there. For now, let's get some rest. We have a head to deliver."

Luc looks up before cocking his head at me.

"Aren't we going home? Rannae was pretty clear she didn't want to see us again."

"Well, tough shit. I don't trust that bitch. I want my Stone."

"*And* our people."

I raise a brow with a small nod of my head. It's not that I don't care about those we left behind. Of course I want to free them and bring them home. But every nerve in my body is screaming for me to reclaim my magic. It's nearly all consuming. I glance at Luc. Nearly.

He shakes his head with a chuckle.

"You're never one to leave well enough alone. But I'm with you. Always. Till the end."

"You say that like we're not going to survive."

His shoulder hitches up, and a small frown pulls at his lips.

I shift. "Hey. Talk to me. We c—"

He holds up a hand. "I'll follow your lead." A slow exhale deflates his posture. "Besides, I finally got you gushing your feelings to me. I'm not about to die now."

I snap my teeth at him with a wicked grin on my face. "And I'm not about to die without your marriage ink on my hand."

His eyes go wide, and his mouth drops open. I throw my head back and laugh, pointing at his dumb-founded expression. "Look at your face! Ha!"

He scowls at me, but there's a smile in his eyes, and as my laughter dies off, I hold up my hand, pleased that it's fairly steady, turning it over, staring at my skin. "Seriously, Luc. I don't want anyone but you."

"Are you seriously asking me to marry you right now? Here, in the woods with a severed head hanging from the tree, our bodies dirty, cut up, and sticky with cum?"

"I mean, not right now." I wave a hand at the dark forest around us. "There's no one here to marry us." He tsks, and I chuckle. "Besides, I learned a while ago what a needy lover you are. I'll have a whole grand celebration planned once we return home." My smile slides from my face as I look him dead in the eye. "But yes. I want to marry you."

He stares at me for a long moment. And keeps staring. I stare back. The silence stretches between us, but our love speaks for us. His eyes soften, and there's a tiny nod of his head—so slight I barely catch it.

I take a deep breath, determination flooding my body.

Luc shifts, crossing his arms. "So, how do you plan to work around Rannae's visions?"

I grin.

"We don't. No plan. No schemes. We're going to walk right up to her fucking palace and drop Erathan's rotting head at her tiny, evil bare feet."

"And after that?"

I shrug. "Whatever comes to mind."

He laughs, pulling his horse blanket under him and rolling onto his side.

"You know I'm a planner, Ry. It makes me itchy and sweaty to go in blind."

I shake out my own blanket, spreading it next to him, but remain sitting.

"Maybe you'll grow to like it. I mean, I never thought I'd love submitting to you so much ..."

"Yeah, no."

I laugh. "Well, then, just think of this as a challenge."

"I know I can't out-crazy *you*, but I'll try."

I slap my thigh. "That's the spirit. We've come this far."

"Yeah, by the skin of our teeth."

I hold out my arms with a smile.

"Amazing, right?"

He snorts, closing his eyes.

"Wake me in two hours, and I'll take watch."

I nod, even though he can't see it, listening to the occasional wing flap of a night bird, the rustling of leaves, and the buzz of persistent insects. A gust of wind sends the tree branches scraping together, and a single snowflake lands on my knee, melting so quickly I'm not sure it was even there. But then another floats down between the trees, landing on my upturned face, and I smile.

I feel like I'm bringing the north with me to Rannae's house. I wonder if she saw a possible future where I return on the back of a bitter winter wind? Probably. I'm excited to see how it plays out.

28

RYDEL

The whinny of horses, and the light clinking of armor reaches my ears ... again. Luc draws Phoenix to a halt meeting my gaze with a raised brow. I shake my head with a small shrug. This is the third time we've drawn close to the border only to run into a contingent of Trislenian soldiers. We've ended up much farther east than planned, climbing through the base of the foothills to avoid Adastra's troops.

Though, this latest group is a smaller one than the last. I count off eleven soldiers as I watch their movements through the trees.

With a gentle pull on the reins, I back Kahar up a few paces, turn him, and head back the way we just came. The crunch of the near-frozen leaves underfoot sound abnormally loud, but the soldiers are making much more noise, and we're able to pass unseen.

Ten minutes later, when we hit a small break in the trees, Luc pulls up next to me and we both draw to a stop. He rubs the back of his neck, white vapor puffing out with his breaths, his annoyance coming through in his tight voice. "There's too many Trislenian soldiers this side of the border to be a coincidence."

I nod. "It seems Rannae is already pushing her boundaries."

"Do you think she already knows Erathan's dead?"

Without realizing it, my dagger flashes in my left hand, and I tap the blade on the pommel in thought.

"Perhaps."

"We have the ... payment. Surely we can—"

I shake my head. "No. Let's avoid them." Luc cracks his neck before nodding. I jerk my head to the southeast. "Let's continue on and see if we can find a way into Trislen deeper in the foothills."

Luc's bright blue eyes turn upward.

"That takes us further from the Trislenian capital. It's been three days, Ry."

I don't respond. I know as well as him how long we have. And yes, I know it would be easier to hire someone to deliver our payment as Rannae demanded, but I don't want to do *anything* for that woman.

Pressing my heels into Kahar's sides, I move us forward, Luc on my tail. We travel in silence for another few hours before we find and follow a dirt trail snaking to the east with a gradual curve south. The thump/swish of the bag tied to the back of my saddle keeps time with the quickly dying day.

The scrape of branches against my legs and shoulders lessens as the path widens. Sitting taller, my back tense, I scan the play of light and shadows in the forest.

Without warning, bile shoots up my throat, and I pitch to the side, vomiting violently. My stomach cramps and sweat coats my body. Heat prickles my skin, and my face feels like it's on fire. I spit the sour taste from my mouth, wiping my lips with a shaking hand.

Gods damn it. I thought I was through this!

I shake my head, grinding my teeth. I'm stronger than this. I don't need it. I want it. Fuck. Okay. I do. I want just one more hit. But I know, it won't be just one more. I drop my head, gripping the pommel until the leather creaks.

Kahar snorts, swinging his head to snap at Phoenix as Luc forces his way next to me on the too-narrow path. Branches scrape and pull at my clothes and skin as Kahar tries to move away from Phoenix, but there's nowhere to go but into the thick press of the trees. Luc's hand falls to my shoulder, gripping me with his solid strength, and I take a deep breath. He doesn't ask if I'm okay. He doesn't offer to help. He just lets me know he's here.

One-by-one, I peel my fingers from the pommel before raising my hand, resting it atop his. I give him a little squeeze. His fingers tighten then slip from under mine, falling away. He lets Kahar pull back in front.

The heat subsides, and the trembling fades, but the churning in my gut remains. So, I focus on the way forward. The fading sunlight drapes the foothills in contrasts of deep shadows and golden light. We wind around a heavy copse, and as soon as we clear it, rocky soil and large boulders hold back the forest from climbing any farther into the foothills, while keeping the blowing sands from the Varyen Desert from encroaching into the forests. We pick our way between the giant boulders. The chilly winds and stubborn sands, even this far west, batter my face as they're funneled through the tight pathways.

Eventually the trail opens to more of a dirt road. I'm shocked when the road clears even more, obviously maintained, and a post-and-rail fence leads the way south.

I lean over, Luc now able to ride at my side. "Did you know there was a village out here?"

His gaze follows the fence line, creases pulling at the edges of his eyes. "I've never seen anything this far east on our maps."

I haven't either.

The scent of smoke tickles my nose, and a dog's bark echoes in the distance.

Luc lowers his voice. "Could be a single homestead. Someone, or maybe a family trying to live beyond the reach of the capital."

"Possibly, but this seems like ... more."

I don't have to tell Luc to be on guard. That's his natural state. Every snap of a twig, every crunch of leaves, every scurry of an animal in the brush pulls his attention, and my stress winds tighter with every clop of our horse's hooves.

Kahar tosses his head, and Phoenix snorts as we move alongside a cleared field. The barking dog sprints across the field, a flash of black and white through the tall grasses. A woman strolls along the far fence line, her hand raised, shielding her eyes as she looks our way. But she doesn't pause, continuing her walk as the dog races back and forth across the field and back to her. Houses dot the open space before us, nestled along the gentle slope of the foothills, a stream running along the edge of the small village.

My head swivels back and forth, waiting for an ambush, but nothing happens as we pass the first house, then two more, until we find ourselves in the center of a collection of buildings. Low, thatched roofs hide the wavy-glass windows of a tavern, a general store, a blacksmith's shop, and a heal-er's hut.

Instinctively, I search for the thoughts of everyone in this village, waiting for the sparks of each mind to map out their locations and tell me how many live here. Silence grates at me, and now my skin itches for an entirely new reason.

Fuck! I'm going to get our magic back!

With a deep breath, I glance south, noticing a path leading from this village toward the border of Trislen. Luc notices and leans over.

"Keep going?"

A man steps from the tavern, propping his shoulder against the door jam, crossing his arms, watching us—not frowning, not smiling, just watching. A young girl ducks under his elbow, a large glass bottle in each hand. She tsks at the man as she passes, holding the bottles up.

"I'm going to bring these to Salle. I'll be back in a bit."

When she turns, she skids to a stop, eyes going wide as she takes us in. Her arms drop to her sides, and she tilts her head with a smile.

"Strangers! You're a long way from any city ... any town for that matter. Where ya headed?"

The man in the door doesn't move, but he grunts in a deep voice. "Bellrain, off with ya."

She rolls her eyes, and I smile, swinging down to the ground, and Luc does the same ... without the smile. I stride forward a few paces, Kahar following without me having to hold his reins. The woman, Bellrain, looks Kahar up and down, saying, "That's some steed. Don't think I've ever seen anythin' like him. Not even the soldiers ride somethin' that fine."

I pat Kahar's neck, stopping a few paces from Bellrain. "He's ... unique. Have there been soldiers here of late?"

She shakes her head, her braid of brown hair swinging over her shoulder. "Not here. Not yet anyway. They've been moving all along the border the last few days though. There are rumors of them pushin' deeper into Adren. But ya can't trust tavern gossip." She looks past me, toward the west, a frown pulling at her lips. "Just a matter of time before they come here though."

The man still standing back at the tavern snorts, arms still crossed, but his hands tighten on his biceps.

"They won't be comin' here. There's nothin' here for 'em. Nothin' to keep out. Nothin' to keep in. Nothin' to take."

Bellrain shifts both bottles to her left hand, the glass tinkling together. She wipes her hand on her skirt before holding it out toward me with a bright smile on her face.

"I'm Bellrain. That's my father, Killock. Welcome to Hillsound. This is our tavern. You're welcome to grab somethin' to eat. There's a pump out back if you wanna wash up, or the creek is quite refreshing—cold, but it'll get the job done faster than our leaky pump."

I take her hand, shaking it once before dropping it and backing up a step. She seems nice enough, but without her thoughts to confirm her intentions, I'm keeping my distance.

Luc shuffles behind me. "I'm afraid we're a bit low on coin at the moment, so I think we'll just keep mo—"

Bellrain pfts a huff of breath, waving her free hand. "Nonsense. You're here. Just pay what you can. From the looks of ya, ya both could use a bit a rest. There's no room to rent, but our barn out back is clean and warm. Y're welcome to stay there the night."

Bellrain's father rolls his eyes, but turns, disappearing into the dark shadows of his tavern. She nods her head after him.

"Go on in. I'll grab ya some drinks and a bowl a stew."

I nod at the bottles in her hand.

"And what of Salle's delivery?"

She glances down, then shrugs. She turns, nearly skipping across the threshold of the tavern, her voice trailing after her. "You've saved me the trip. Once word gets out we got visitors, the tavern'll be packed. Salle'll come for sure."

Leaving the horses, we follow. Luc presses in close, watching my back, asking her, "You don't get many strangers coming through, I guess?"

"Through Hillsound?" She snorts, skirting around the bar, setting the bottles on a low shelf before standing and wiping her hands on her skirt again. "Nah. I don't think we're even on most maps of Imoria."

Killock pushes backward through a door, turning with a tray in his hands holding two steaming bowls and a large loaf of bread. He jerks his head at a small table to the right, and Luc and I meet him there. The scrape of the chairs over wood is loud as Luc sits to face the door, and I sit to his left, keeping my left side open ... just in case.

Killock sets a bowl before each of us and tosses the bread on the table while grumbling, "And I hope we stay off the maps. We're simple folk out here. These soldiers traipsing across the land, following some order or another from a king or queen far away have nothing to do with us. We're proud Adrens, but whoever is on the throne makes no lick of difference to us. Let 'em fight it out. Just a bunch of crazy people fightin' over imaginary lines drawn on a map."

Luc almost snorts his stew up his nose. The reddish-brown broth splatters across the table, and he slaps his chest as he coughs. I smile, tearing off a hunk of bread. The crust crackles, and steam rises from the pillowy center. Dipping it in the stew, I take a bite, letting the sour bread and the earthy stew warm me from the inside before saying, "Fair enough. Though, don't you find it strange that Trislenian soldiers are patrolling this side of the border, and in such large numbers?"

Luc wipes his lips with the back of his hand before shoveling another mouthful of stew into his mouth. Shifting slightly, he keeps an eye on the open door as the woman from the field steps inside, her dog laying in the dirt outside, his tongue lolling out of his mouth in a happy pant of exhaustion. She crosses the room, feigning non-interest in us, but I catch her discrete glances. Luc tracks her every move.

She nods at Killock, propping her elbows on the bar. "Afternoon, Killock, Bellrain. Got some visitors, I see."

I raise my spoon with a smile, but Luc keeps eating and watching, his scowl back in place. Killock comes back around the bar, two mugs in hand, thunking them on the table before us, froth spills over the lips, blending with the other stains and scars of the wood surface.

He grumbles again as he settles behind the bar, smirking at the woman. "You've got a good pair of eyes on ya, Gird."

She rolls her eyes. "Don't be such a grump, Killock."

Bellrain smiles, wiping glass after glass with a rag which isn't doing much cleaning—mostly just spreading the smudges around. The thump of boots announces more villagers, and Luc sets his spoon down, pushing his empty bowl back. He grabs his mug of ale and sits back in his chair, legs spread, feet planted. He looks relaxed, but I know he's ready to jump up at the slightest sign of trouble. As the small tavern begins to fill, Luc's leg starts bouncing, and I feel his unease mirrored in my own bunched muscles.

There are too many strangers in this cramped space, and I have no idea what any of their true intentions are. But, I keep the smile on my face as people grab seats, pulling up along the other two tables. They line the bar, curious glances shooting our way while they try to carry on seemingly mundane conversation—as if the entire village normally gathers in this tavern every afternoon.

Bellrain shoves through the bodies, setting another pair of mugs on our table. "You're good for business."

I raise my mug in salute with a warm smile, but Luc leaves his new beverage untouched and his scowl in place.

A man standing at the bar turns, leaning his back against the smooth wood, elbows hooked behind him.

"So, you two runnin' from somethin'?"

I shake my head, and Luc remains silent, eyes tracking every villager. I fight to keep my chuckle from surfacing as I notice people avoiding making eye contact with Luc.

Crossing my arms, I rest the mug in the crook of my elbow. "Not running. No. Just trying to get into Trislen ... mmm ... quietly."

An older woman from farther down the bar raises her voice. "Those horses out there aren't no commoner's horses. You two high lords or somethin'?"

I shake my head again. "No."

Bellrain reaches up, sliding a glass onto a shelf. "Well, the nearest border crossing is about twenty miles west, and I imagine if you're wantin' to cross 'quietly' you're avoiding tha crossing stations?" Neither Luc nor I respond, but she nods her head. "The border is bein' patrolled as well. It's gonna' be hard gettin' across."

Leaning forward, I brace my arms on the table, thinking through our options. There will be a way. They can't cover the entire length of the border. We'll find a spot to slip through. But if we have to, we'll approach the smallest contingent we can find. We'll get them to let us pass. And if they give us trouble ... we'll kill them. But that's what I'm trying to avoid. I don't know what Rannae is up to, but our usefulness to her expired with Erathan, and I don't trust my former soldiers turned hers.

I'm pulled from my thoughts as a small boy skirts around the legs of the villagers, ducking under arms until he stops a pace from our table. His eyes are wide, his brown hair curling around his flushed face. He wipes a finger across his nose, smearing dirt over his brown skin.

The boy looks us over, and I stare back. His eyes flare with a flash of fear as he looks at Luc for a second too long, and I know my captain is trying to scare him off. The lad stays, eyes finding mine, his feet shifting from one to the other. His hand grips the hem of his shirt as he says, "Ya can go east. 'Bout six miles. Then cut south. Tha sharp terrain kept 'em from finishin' the border wall all tha way, so if ya know tha way, ya can slip across no problem."

I grin at him, and his eyes widen as Luc slides two coppers across the table, keeping his finger pressed to the stacked coins. I look between the coins and the boy's eager face, asking, "And you know the way?"

His head bobs. "Of course."

A woman with black hair and dark skin pushes through the crowd, wrapping her arm around the boy's thin arm, pulling him away from the table. "Quinn, come on. Leave 'em alone."

He struggles against her grip, his little boots digging into the wood floor. "But ma, I know tha way!"

I'm about to call out, trying to find a way to get the little one to spill his secrets, but the dog barks, leaping to his feet, ruff up, growls and snarls lifting his lips. Luc and I both stand at the same time, our chairs falling backward. As one, we spin toward the door. The room goes silent, and the press of bodies part as we stride outside.

The food and drink have actually settled my stomach some, and I feel sturdier even as I realize Killock's wish to stay off the map has just been shattered.

The late afternoon sun glints off Trislenian armor, eight soldiers spread in a semi-circle around the tavern.

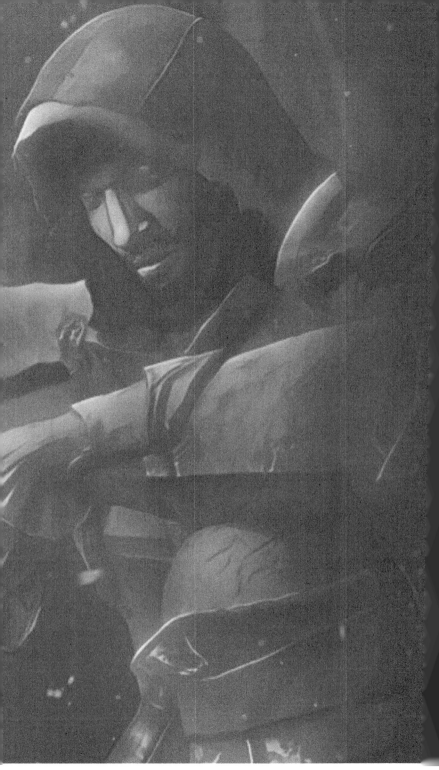

29

LUCARYN

Shuffling feet file out after us, but the villagers hug the building, not willing to get any closer to the soldiers. A female in the center of the group steps forward, pointing at Kahar and Phoenix.

"Those yours?"

Rydel nods, his hand relaxed near his dagger. I stand to his right, keeping my eyes on the spread of soldiers, tracking each twitch and shift of movement.

In a calm voice, Ry says, "Kahar, Zanea." *Kahar, come.* The warhorse moves forward, stopping at his side. His front hoof paws the ground with earth-shaking strikes. I repeat the command, and Phoenix comes to my side, standing still as a statue. His coat is warm under my hand as I run it down his neck. He's such a good steed, and still so young. It's a shame he was gelded before I bought him. He'd make a great stud.

I press my lips together, fighting to keep my scowl in place as the boy, Quinn, whispers behind us, "Woah. So cool! Did you see that? The horses listened, like dogs."

The female soldier eyes Kahar for a moment then draws her sword, pointing it at Rydel. I see red, ready to strike her head from her shoulders, but I hold back as the rest of the soldiers do the same. The villagers shuffle back, and I hear a few of them rushing back into the tavern, trying to get away from whatever is about to happen.

Ry raises his arms, his left hand stroking Kahar, his right held out at his side as the female soldier takes a step forward, saying, "This village is now part of Trislen. As such, you will need to pay the necessary taxes." She glances around, a condescending smirk on her face. "We realize this is sudden, and you obviously have ... very little."

The other soldiers chuckle, and Bellrain shouts behind us. "How dare ya'!"

There's a scuffle of noise, but someone must hold her back.

The female soldier ignores Bellrain, gaze focused on our horses. "We are not so cruel to take your harvest in the middle of winter, so we'll take those horses as your first payment."

She takes another step forward, and Rydel smiles, knowing what's about to happen. I step to the side, and Phoenix follows. The soldier reaches out, fingers brushing Kahar's reins. Rydel leaps backward as Kahar spins, slamming his flank into her chest. She stumbles back, and before she's even registered what's happened, Kahar snaps both his hind legs out. She's in the perfect position for him to reach full extension, and his giant hooves make contact with her chest and face. The crack and crunch of bone echoes through the stunned silence as the soldier slumps to the ground, dead.

Quinn whispers behind us, "Whoaaaaa."

The other soldiers look from the dead woman to us, eyes wide, some of their mouths gaping open. Then, two scowl, gripping their swords tighter, charging us, the rest following with a war cry.

Rydel's voice is calm but clear as he says, "Kahar, ussuzh." *Kahar, attack.*

The war horse spins again then rears back, his hooves cracking against the chest plate of the nearest soldier. The man falls flat on his back, his armor crushed, his breaths wheezing around his broken ribs. My sword is in my right hand, and I give it a little swing. Rydel has his sword, as well as his dagger in his left hand. With a smile on his face, he yells at the fast-approaching soldiers, "I missed out on a bit of fun earlier, so I'm infinitely grateful for the opportunity to wet my blade on your blood."

I bark a laugh as I charge two soldiers. Steel crashes and whines as I cover Ry's back. We're quickly surrounded, but I easily cut down one, then two. Rydel takes out another.

There's a loud scream as Kahar spins, his hind legs snapping out again, grazing one soldier, but nailing another who crumples to the ground, skull crushed.

Phoenix's red mane blurs as he turns, using his smaller size and speed to snap his teeth at anyone who comes close, his tail flicking in excitement. I block a downward swing of a blade while tucking into Phoenix's side, moving with the horse, using him as both shield and weapon.

I barely notice the sting of a slice along my bicep as I kick my attacker at the knee joint. Her leg crumbles, and her armor jolts as she falls to her side. Fast as a snake strike, I sink my dagger into her neck, killing her with a twist and slice of my blade. Rydel stumbles and his back slams into mine. I brace myself so he can push himself upright, his muscles flexing as he swings his sword.

A soldier slips past my right side, the arc of her swing heading straight for my shoulder. I don't have time or space to move, but before the blade can bite into my skin, a large rock smashes into the soldier's face. She stumbles, dropping her sword as blood drips from her temple.

I glance over to see Bellrain hefting another rock in her palm. Without looking, I throw my dagger, hearing it sink into the flesh of the stunned soldier as I nod at Bellrain.

Rydel laughs, calling at Bellrain over his shoulder, "Good shot."

She smiles, pitching her new rock at another soldier.

From the corner of my eye, I catch movement. With a burst of speed, I race toward the tavern, chasing a soldier who has decided the villagers are fair game as well. Several screams ring out as the people try to back away, too frightened to run.

Rydel growls behind me, "Damn it, Luc."

A knife sails over my shoulder, thudding into the back of the neck of a soldier to my right, and I notice the glint of a blade in his hand as he falls to the ground.

Without breaking stride or turning around, I call out, "Thanks."

With two fluid strikes, I cut down the soldier before he reaches the tavern, his body falling at the feet of the wide-eyed villagers.

Spinning, I sprint back toward Ry, watching as he drops to the ground, a sword whistling over his head. He grips the hilt of his dagger, yanking it from the forehead of a dead soldier at his feet. Spinning on his knees, he hops up, slicing his sword across the hip joint of a soldier's armor as he slams his dagger into his neck. The man slides from Ry's blades, and he turns, ready to meet the next.

With a grunt, I slash my sword across the neck of the last soldier, and stand panting, holding my blade out at arm's length as the woman falls.

Silence presses in on the small village.

I take a moment to assess Rydel, and I only see one shallow cut and the beginning of a bruise on his left forearm. With a deep breath, I feel a tightness on my cheek that means I'll have a bruise of my own. I have no idea when I got hit in the face. The cut on my bicep isn't too bad, and there's also a slice along my right shoulder, but it's not too deep. I rotate my arm, wincing slightly, but I've got full range of movement. That's all that matters.

Sheathing my weapons, Rydel does the same and we look around. It's always oddly deafening after a fight. The adrenaline still pumps through my blood, roaring through my ears. The sudden absence of the clash of metal, the grunts of pain, and the quick shuffling of feet, rings with silence. Phoenix puffs at my side, his hide slick with sweat. His muscles twitch as he too attempts to come down from the high of battle.

The shocked villagers stare wide-eyed, their silence adding to the stillness.

My breaths slowly even out, and I pat down Phoenix, checking for wounds.

Rydel does the same with Kahar, whispering, "Iyai ahuiy, Kahar?" *You okay, Kahar?* The black war horse paws the ground, tossing his head. Soldier's blood splatters three of his hooves, and I grin as Rydel pats him on the neck practically cooing, "Saas-suhssiy zus asre'a. Ze'ass sare'a." *Blood-thirsty war horse. Well done.*

I walk over, rolling my shoulder again, unable to keep

the wince from my face. Rydel frowns at me, but I grip Phoenix's girth, giving it a tug, making sure it's tight, saying, "I think we should move on."

He nods. Without another word, I reach into my saddle bag, retrieving a few more of the meager coins we have. They clink in Rydel's palm as I drop them in his outstretched hand. Ry turns toward the tavern, but before he takes two steps, Quinn's mother steps forward. The boy hugs her skirt, his knuckles white, his eyes wide, lips trembling. His mother plants her hands on her hips, and Rydel's back muscles bunch. I know what he's thinking. We're about to be run out of this village for bringing trouble to their doorstep.

I'm ready to leap on Phoenix, but Quinn's mother's voice stops me. "Let's get your horses in the barn, out a sight. You two get some rest. We've got your backs for tha night."

Rydel's shaking his head, and I continue to check our tack, readying to ride on. But Bellrain steps forward, standing next to Quinn's mother, resting a hand on her shoulder. Her other hand brushes through Quinn's hair, easing him with her touch. Bellrain looks at us, saying, "Stay. We may not be fightin' folk, but we know this land better than anyone. We can watch the woods and the paths ... now we know to be lookin'."

I shift, resting a hand on Phoenix's shoulder. "There will be more. When these fail to report back, more will come."

Killock comes to stand next to his daughter, his arms crossed. "You didn't have ta fight. We coulda paid. Our harvest was better than most years." His eyes fall to the female soldier who made the first move. "She didn't give us a chance ta pay." Killock's eyes climb back to my face. "Ya fought. Though ya were defending your property, ya defended us too."

My voice drops, my face hardening to stone as I say, "We're not good men."

Rydel's brows pinch at my words, and I want to shake my head at him. I'm not ashamed of who we are, though I think my tone came out a bit too harsh. I keep my eyes on Killock, continuing, "You've just seen what we are capable of. And trust me"—my voice drops again, the gravely sound rumbling through my chest—"we are capable of much, much worse."

Rydel's lips quirk up in a small smile before he turns back to the villagers, holding out his hand. "Take what coin we have ... for the trouble."

Killock shakes his head.

Quinn starts tugging on his mother's skirt so hard she has to grab the waist to keep him from pulling it over her hips. She looks down, snapping, "What, child?"

Quinn's large eyes are locked on Rydel's ring, and Ry drops his hand, fingers wrapped around the coins. Quinn whispers, "Mom, I think that's—"

I press my finger to my lips, and the boy's eyes snap to mine. He claps his mouth shut, eyes going impossibly wider as he nods.

His mother looks down at him, asking, "What, Quinn?"

He shakes his head back and forth, his dark curls brushing his face. "Nothin' ma."

He grins as I wink at him, saying, "Now, about that secret way across the border ..."

Quinn glances up at his mother, and she strokes a hand down his wild hair. There's such love and caring in her eyes, a pang shoots through my chest. My parents died when I was young. I don't really remember my mother. But I remember Rydel's mother. Never did I see her look at her son that way, not even once.

I step up behind Ry, pressing my warmth against his back. His exhale comes out a little shaky as he leans into me for a moment.

Quinn's mother's voice draws our attention as she says, "Aye, my boy knows the way, better than anyone." She flicks his ear with affection, and he yelps with a laugh as she shakes her head. "This one likes ta roam, ta find trouble. But he's had quite tha afternoon. He'll help ya in the mornin'. So, ya might as well rest up in tha barn ... while ya can."

Quinn shifts back and forth, eager to spill his secrets, but I notice the adrenaline seeping from him as his shoulders slump, and his eyes blink a little slower.

I squeeze Rydel's shoulder, feeling him relax a bit more as I say, "We thank you."

The small crowd slowly disperses, hushed words passing between them as they set up rotations to watch the borders of their village. My eyes narrow slightly as I watch them move about, dragging the bodies of the soldiers to a cart that's quickly hitched to a mule and pulled to a far field. Before long, grey smoke curls into the air, and I know it will carry the stench of burning flesh and hair on the wind.

I roll my head, cracking my neck. Stepping away from Rydel, I cross the space. A woman looks up, her arms flexed where she pauses from running her rake over the hard-packed dirt, spreading the pools of blood as another villager tosses sawdust behind her.

I nod in the direction of the thickening smoke. "The smell might alert any patrols nearby. If you have any late-season herbs, or even boughs of evergreens to throw on the pyre, that will help mask the smell.

Her eyes follow the trail of smoke, her lips pressed tight. After a moment, she nods, turning, but pauses, swiveling back, eyes finding Rydel where he talks to another villager off to our right. She whispers, "He's *him*, isn't he?" Her gaze flicks to my ring, not lifting again to look at me. "You're his captain, and he's the Crown Bre—"

"It doesn't matter who we are. You all have shown us kindness today. You didn't have to. So, regardless of who we might be, we will extend your offer back to you—you have our protection this night. And if the village of Hillsound ever has need, send word to Farden."

Her eyes flick up to my face, a small knowing smile on her lips. "So, you are—"

I raise an eyebrow. "The fires."

She snaps her mouth shut, turning again then jumping into a quick jog. A moment later, thundering hooves sound, and she races off, riding a grey mare bareback along the edge of the fields.

Some people walk down paths toward their homes, but several stay in the village center, collecting blankets and baskets of food, bringing everything around to the small barn. The wind picks up, and almost as one, the villagers pause whatever they're doing, a collective shiver running through them before they go back to work. The sight almost makes me laugh.

Rydel chuckles, coming up behind me, leaning in, whispering, "I don't understand this."

I glance at him over my shoulder before following his gaze, watching the villagers. I shrug. "True. They don't know us. They just witnessed us kill eight soldiers. Yet, here they are, giving us what they have. Offering us protection from a threat they don't really understand and are not a part of."

He shakes his head. "Why?"

I shrug again. "Don't know. But I'm glad there are people out here like them. They balance people like us."

He grips my shoulder, turning me. His brows are

furrowed with anger, but I shake my head. "Don't misunderstand Ry. The world needs people like us. And I would much rather be us than them."

He smiles, nodding, the tension leaking from his face.

I smirk. "I wouldn't have you any other way, your Majesty. I love every bit of you from the top of your wicked head to your evil toes."

He laughs, shoving me, but I hope he knows I mean every word. I started us on this journey all those years ago when I killed his family. I've never looked back. As long as Ry is with me, I don't really care what else happens.

We turn, heading toward the barn, our horses trailing behind us, Kahar calm for once. We get them fresh water, remove their tack, and brush them down, before drinking our fill of water then switching to ale that Killock left for us in the barn.

Rydel turns, arranging a stack of blankets to shield him from the itchy hay. I lean over, resting a hand on his broad back. He goes still, his muscles expanding under my touch. My lips graze his ear, and he shivers as I whisper, "You and me, Rydel. I don't care about anything else. It's just you and me."

He growls, the deep sound shooting straight to my cock as he spins on his knees, gripping my shirt, pulling me into him. "You and me, Lucaryn."

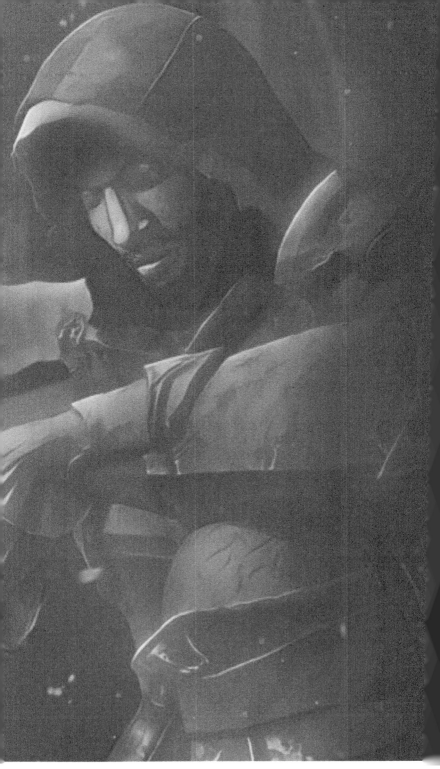

30

LUCARYN

While I should have slept well last night, tucked next to Rydel between us taking shifts to walk the village ... I don't think I slept at all. My mind circled and spun with options and plans, schemes, scenarios, and possible outcomes. I'd think through a few ideas, change them, adjust them, discard them, only to come back to them an hour later to rethink everything. At one point, Rydel nudged me in the back with his elbow, telling me to quit fidgeting or go outside, so I walked the village for an hour before returning to the barn, standing in the stillness, watching Ry's slow, even breaths, marveling at the fact that we are both still alive.

In the morning, Rydel woke with a groan, his skin coated in sweat, his knees pulled to his chest. I filled a cup with water from the pump, my hands shaking with rage at what Rannae did to him. Rydel took a few small sips before gulping it all down. My fingers massaged his tense neck as he breathed through the nausea. Minutes passed, and his trembling lessened. Sitting slowly, his desperate eyes met mine, and I brushed my fingers through his beard, holding his gaze. "You're going to make it through this. You'll be okay."

He nodded, swallowing, eye closing for a long moment before he opened them again. Helping him stand, he found his balance, and after another long drink direct from the pump, seemed much steadier. Still, I felt like I was hovering like a mother hen as I followed him into the tavern, sitting at a table with him where Killock and Quinn were waiting.

With a serious set to his face, Quinn described the route we needed to take, Killock carefully sketching a map from the boy's words. Once done, I ruffled the boy's hair, handing him my smallest throwing knife. His eyes were round as he wrapped his small fingers around the shining metal, and I knew if his mother had been there, she would have refused. But Killock only smiled, nodding at the young boy as I said, "Now, that's a weapon, not a toy. I better not come back through here and find you missing any fingers or toes."

Quinn bobbed his head, barely looking up from the blade in his hand.

I plucked it from his fingers, twirling it around my hand twice before flicking it to the side. The blade thunked into the wall, shaking back and forth from the impact before going still. Quinn's mouth dropped open, and I smiled. "Wielding a weapon as special as that takes practice and discipline but should only be practiced once your normal chores are completed. Understand?"

Quinn nodded again, his face earnest and determined. Killock chuckled, yanking the blade from the wall, spinning it around his fingers with surprising dexterity, saying, "I'll teach the lad. It'll be good for him to focus on something. Work on that hand-eye coordination."

I nodded, turning to leave the tavern, but before I reached the door, little hands tugged at my pants, and I paused, looking down at Quinn as he whispered, "One day, I'm gonna come all the way to Farden. I'm gonna be your soldier." His voice lowered even more, and I had to kneel down to hear him. "I'm going to be the King's best soldier."

I smiled, clapping his shoulder, my hand nearly engulfing him. "I'll be waiting."

Quinn straightened at my words, shoulders squaring, lips pressed tight as he nodded.

As I packed my saddle bags, I was surprised at the reluctance I felt to leave little Hillsound. My bags were near bursting, but villagers kept handing Ry and me things; food, ale, water, clothes, blankets, weapons ... until finally Rydel laughed, holding up his hands, proclaiming we couldn't possibly take any more.

With a final nod to Quinn, I mounted Phoenix and left him behind, hoping I would one day see the young boy again. Ry's eyes tracked me as I approached where he was waiting atop Kahar, his gaze going between me and the boy vigorously waving goodbye from the tavern doorway. Rydel raised an eyebrow, and I nodded in response, letting him know I was ready to go. He glanced at Quinn again, but I didn't look back, pointing Phoenix east.

Rydel and I made it across the border unseen, and oddly, didn't see one single patrol, not a single soldier or traveler. And, once we were in Trislen, the way was clear and easy.

Too easy.

Now, as the Trislenian palace comes into view over the lower pitch of the city buildings, I catch myself wiping my sweaty palms along my pants for the third time since we crossed into the capital. My ears strain to pick up any sounds that indicate an attack. A shadow shifts between the buildings on our right, and I whip my head around, trying to see into the dark corners of the alley. Nothing moves.

My jaw cracks as I yawn from my restless night, even as anticipation flutters through my stomach. Rydel's shoulders are rolled back, posture tall, but he keeps cracking his neck side to side, and I know the nerves are getting to him as well.

If I'm being honest, I'm shocked we've made it this far into the capital city.

Phoenix tosses his head, the afternoon sunlight highlighting his red mane, seeming to set it on fire. The coarse strands comb through my fingers as I give him a pat. My eyes stall on my hand, and my heart skips a beat. For a moment, it's hard to breathe as I recall Rydel's words the other night. He wants us to get married. I flex my fingers, imagining the scrolling marriage ink flowing over my skin. A small smile lifts my lips as I rest my hand on my thigh, feeling lighter than I did a moment ago.

The light dusting of snow that fell the other night did not stick, and it hasn't snowed again, but the ground is wet and slick. The few people out are huddled in their cloaks as if the fiercest winter storm had plowed through their city.

We stop a few blocks from the palace. As we dismount, I look around, disconcerted at the lack of soldiers we've seen in the city.

Rydel turns to me, whispering, "There's an inn one block over." He jerks his head to my right. "We can leave Phoenix there."

I cock my head at him in question, my stomach roiling, knowing I'm not going to like what he says next.

He smiles.

Uh oh.

"Just like in Adren, I'm going in the front door. You're going to find our Stones while I keep Rannae busy." I feel the scowl on my face deepening, but he barrels on. "Once you have the Stones, it'll be child's play to get our people out of the dungeons." He flicks his wrist, his dagger flashing. "Then, you'll come to my rescue … if needed, and we'll ride into the sunset."

I shake my head. There are so many objections running through my mind, but I say, "This sounds an awful lot like a *plan*, Rydel."

He shrugs. "Can't be helped. At least I have no plan for what I'm going to do once I'm in front of Rannae again."

I raise an eyebrow. I can guess … *if* he can catch her by surprise.

I take a slow breath. "I don't like separating."

He chuckles. "But it worked so well with Erathan."

He thumps the bag tethered to Kahar's saddle, and a whiff of rot climbs down my nose.

"But it went horribly wrong last time we tried to get to Rannae."

He shrugs, waiting for me to come up with a better solution. I have three at the ready, but I have to admit, the divide and conquer might just work.

He sees the moment I give in, and quickly describes the layout of the palace, giving me the best routes between the wings and different levels. Neither of us know where Rannae is keeping the Stones, and we're betting that she has kept them close to her. He also gives me several ways to get to the dungeons … just in case.

I hate this.

Once he's done, I sigh. "If we end up dead this time, I'm going to make hell a living hell for you."

He steps into my space, his cedar scent stronger, his

breath fresh with a hint of mint. I groan as he fists my shirt, yanking me into his chest, his lips brushing against mine as he smiles. "See you in hell, Lucaryn. But not for many years yet."

His lips crash against mine, and our teeth scrape together in our rush to get closer. I lick his lips, and he opens for me so I can dive deep, stroking his tongue like I'd like to lick his cock. My hips roll against his, his hard length pressing to mine, and my cock jumps at the contact.

Rydel groans, bucking into me again, and I grip his hair, yanking his head back, exposing his neck. My teeth scrape along his skin before I bite him, hard. A whoosh of air leaves his open mouth, his eyes staring at the sky through the break in the buildings, his cheeks flushed.

He is glorious. So strong. So powerful, even without the magic. He's mine.

I release my bite, licking up the column of his neck before whispering against his skin, "See you on the other side, Ry."

Letting him go, I take a step back, both our chests rising quickly as we struggle to catch our breath. He grabs his cock, adjusting himself with a laugh. "You expect me to be able to concentrate after that?"

I smirk, grabbing my own aching length. "Incentive to stay alive and come back to me."

He licks his lips, and I almost come in my pants from the heated look of desire he aims at me. "Oh, I'll stay alive. I'll come back to you, then I'll come inside you."

I groan, my hand tightening around my cock. "Fuck."

He chuckles, and I manage to peel my hand from my pants, grinning at him. But my smile fades as the teasing light dims in his eyes. He nods, mounting Kahar, and heads toward the palace at a quick trot without another glance back.

I pat Phoenix, leading him down the cobbled street toward the inn. It seems all I've been doing these days is sneaking in and out of other people's castles. I miss my castle. I miss my home.

Forcing myself to focus, I whisper to Phoenix, "Time to find our Stones. Wish me luck."

The steed snorts, tossing his head gently, nudging my arm, and I smile around the nerves dancing in my gut, trying to shut out the list running through my head of all the ways this could go wrong.

31

RYDEL

Two soldiers step into my path, blocking the way through the gates to the palace grounds. The sun shines off the bald head of the black woman on the right, the sharp planes of her face pressed into a harsh frown. Trails of mist float around her face with every exhale into the chilly afternoon. The pale-skinned man on the left grips the hilt of his sword, but keeps it sheathed.

The woman steps her feet a little wider. "State your business."

I swing from Kahar's back, untying the leather bag from my saddle, holding it out. "I have a delivery of payment for your Queen. She's expecting it."

A flex of her jaw is the only acknowledgement by the female soldier. The male nods. "I'll let her Majesty know you are here."

He turns and walks away, but the female soldier draws her sword with a metallic whine. Assessing her, I notice her stance is a bit too wide, but her grip on her blade is confident. A glance at her free hand reveals the lack of calluses. She's right-handed and hasn't bothered to train with her left —sloppy.

Silence stretches between us, and every now and then I catch the guard's gaze snapping to my ring before flitting away. She's nervous and unsure. Good.

A fly buzzes past my face, and I swat at it. The insect slaps against the back of my hand, its flight sluggish due to the cold weather. It's amazing there are flies still out at all.

The male soldier returns, his eyes on the bag dangling from my hand. "Come with me."

The female spins, foolishly giving me her back as she says, "Don't you know who he is? Is the Queen really allowing him entry?"

"Shut your mouth, Ninia. The Queen has given the order. Just watch the gate."

I smirk at the man's annoyed tone. The female points her sword at me, and I'm ready to cut her down as her voice rises. "But, he's—"

"I'd watch where you point that thing, *Ninia*." My voice is calm, but my eyes bore into her with the promise of death. Her grip doesn't falter, but she visibly swallows as I continue, "Have you already forgotten how I took Trislen from Ravaxina?"

Ninia's sword dips as her eyes land on my ring again.

I step closer to her, ready. The male soldier barks, "Fuck, stand down woman! I won't keep the Queen waiting."

Ninia frowns, lowering her sword, slowly stepping to the side. I cross my hand in front of my chest, twirling my ring around my finger while staring her down. She swallows again, but her grip shifts on her blade and sneers at me. A slight shift of her feet warns me she's about to attack, but I don't give her the chance.

In one fluid movement, I take two long strides while drawing my dagger, and slice it across her neck. The metallic clatter of her sword hitting the cobblestones rings out as she presses both hands to her throat. I'd like to kill every soldier here for turning against me to side with fucking Adastra ... and after I allowed them to live after I took the Trislenian throne. Ungrateful.

The male soldier gasps, his own sword now in his hand, but he makes the mistake of faltering. I tsk, pointing my dripping dagger at his face. "Time's wasting. Let's not keep Rannae waiting for her prize. It won't keep forever."

The man drops his gaze to the bag still in my hand, He lowers his sword, sparing a glance at the female crumpled on the ground, her boots scraping the ground as the last of her life leaks from the deep slash in her neck.

With his eyes still on her, the male sheaths his sword, backs away from me, and turns, bravely giving me his back again. I clean my dagger on the female's shirt and sheathe it. Following along, the soldier leads me up the polished marble steps, through the front doors, and down the main hall toward the throne room. One of the soldiers flanking the doors steps to the side, gripping the handle, pulling it open. The man who escorted me stops, saying, "The Queen will see you now."

No shit.

I'm shocked and a bit worried when I step into the throne room, and none of Rannae's soldiers follow me. My fingers flex as I resist the urge to grip my sword as the door thuds shut behind me. Striding down the center of the long room, I count ten soldiers, five lining each side, eyes tracking my progress.

And there she is. The queen bitch.

Her face is impassive as I approach.

My back aches as I search for the thoughts of the soldiers and the queen but get nothing. My boots clip-clip in a steady rhythm, mocking the lack of noise in my head. I'm waiting for the trap to spring. I'm waiting for the pain, the barked order to kill me, the snap of a crossbow, or the slice of a steel blade hissing through the air.

But nothing happens as I draw closer to the dais.

The sound of my blood rushing past my ears is loud, like a raging river, but I feel steady, excited. My mind is clear, and the misery of the withdrawal is gone.

Rannae sits on her throne, her legs crossed, her top leg bouncing slightly. Her cream tunic beautifully contrasts her dark brown skin, and her green wide-legged pants flow around her legs. Her bare toes peek from the long hem, and I wonder at her aversion to wearing shoes.

Whatever, not my concern.

As my gaze lands back on her face, the look in her eyes surprises me, but I keep my face blank. I don't think she knew I was going to come here. My chest flutters with the desire to laugh, but I swallow it down. Doing the unexpected might just win us the day.

I'm still more than twenty paces away from the dais when I swing the bag up to my chest. My eyes water as the smell hits me. Flipping it open, I reach in, fingers brushing clammy skin. Grabbing a fist full of beard, I tug the head free, all while keeping my pace steady and slow.

There are now ten paces to go, and I drop the bag, swinging my arm, letting Erathan's head fly. The hollow thud of skin hitting marble pulls a scowl of disgust from Rannae's lips. The head thunk-thwap, thunk-thwaps as it rolls, settling with a final squelch against the bottom step of the dais. Erathan's eyes stare up at Rannae perfectly.

Her gaze darts between Erathan's head and me. The silence stretches, broken only by the quiet hum of the soldiers drawing their swords, but they keep them lowered at their sides.

I cross one arm over my chest, the other bent, my finger picking blood from under my thumb nail.

After a few more moments of silence, I tsk, sweeping my hand toward Erathan's head. "There is your payment." I drop my arms, and my face ices over. My voice drops, and the words practically growl from my chest. "Now, give me the Stones."

Rannae's eyes are fixed on Erathan. Her mouth opens, then closes, opens, and closes again. What the fuck is wrong with her? Why is she acting ... so shocked?

Without looking at me, she whispers, "You actually killed him?"

Seriously?

My laugh rings out in the vaulted space. "Why so surprised, Rannae? Is your magic"—I wiggle my fingers at my temple, mocking her—"not working?"

Her breaths come a little shallower, and her eyes are a bit wider. Her focus is still on the severed head, and her hands fist the folds of her pants. "You were ... you were supposed to go home. You were going to leave Erathan for another time and come at me with your army." Her gaze snaps up, her eyes wild and unfocused. "The probability of you coming here was nonexistent! My army was going to cut you down in a bloody field along the border!" Well, that explains her soldiers crossing into Adren. She was moving into place.

Her hands press into her temples, and though she's looking my way, it's as if she's seeing through me. "You were going to die! It was all going to be mine!"

Hmm. Interesting.

Rannae's fingers tug her black curls piled atop her head.

Keeping my footfalls light, I step over Erathan's head, hitting the second step. My thighs flex, the pain of the few slices and cuts and bruises fade to the background with the rush of adrenaline sparking through my body. Shuffling sounds tell me the soldiers have moved, but Rannae's eyes focus, and she holds up her hand. The room goes quiet again.

Rannae watches me climb the steps, but she doesn't move. I narrow my eyes. What's her play? Surely, she's not going to let me near her? She's not that stupid.

But, I stride right up to her, a smile on my face as I snap out my arm, wrapping my hand around her throat. Armor clinks as the soldiers rush forward, but again, Rannae lifts her hand, and they stop.

Rannae's skin is hot, and she watches me with a blank expression as I lean into her space, my teeth snapping in her face. "The. Stones."

We're pressed together, so I feel her move. I shift, angling my body away from her, but not fast enough. Pain shoots up my side, and my muscles spasm as her knife sinks into my flesh. She smiles, the panic and confusion gone from her features. If I hadn't moved when I did, she would have pierced my heart, and I would be dead right now.

Her head falls back so she can look up into my eyes. "You arrogant man."

I grit my teeth against the pain. I've been stabbed before. I'll live.

Raising my brows, I snarl. "So, all that ... an act?"

She laughs again. "No. I am surprised ... shocked if I'm telling the truth. This was such a small thread of your future; I almost dismissed it completely. But"—she twists the blade, but I keep the grimace from my face—"here you are, Rydel." With another twist of her wrist, her blade scrapes against one of my ribs, and my left leg spasms, nearly buckling. I grit my teeth as the wound begins to burn and sweat slicks my forehead.

Gods damn it. What is with this family and poisoned weapons? Doesn't matter. I have time ... not much, but I'll worry about it later. A wide grin pulls her lips back, baring her teeth as she laughs, the sound giddy, almost like a little girl.

This. Fucking. Woman.

My hand tightens on her throat as the edges of my vision start to close in. Hot blood slicks down my side, and I grunt as she twists the blade again, smirking. "I *saw* this, Rydel. I may have missed your heart"—she rips the blade from my flesh, and my knees nearly buckle—"but when at first you don't succeed ..."

I lean into her, using my grip on her neck to lift her off her feet. Her eyes go wide as I drop her, my hands snapping to her head. I growl down at her. "Did you see this?"

My arms flex, and the sweet sound of her neck snapping reverberates through the throne room. It's not the tortured death I fantasized for her, but her limp body in my hands is oh so satisfying.

I drop her, her small body folding in on itself at my feet. Pressing a hand to my side, my palm comes away covered in bright red blood. My heart flutters, and I can feel it struggling to beat. I force my muscles to work. I have to move. I have to survive—for Luc.

Turning on shaking legs, I brace, gripping my dagger and pulling Rannae's blade from my side. I turn, ignoring the agony and dizzying double vision, ready to confront the soldiers rushing the dais.

32

RYDEL

A roar rips from my throat.

I lean back as a sword slashes at my chest, barely missing my neck. Kicking out, my boot slams into the soldier's chest, his armor clanking with a dull thud as he tumbles down the steps. I unleash Rannae's blade, and it slams into the eye of one of the rushing soldiers. He falls, but the rest keep coming—and I'm sure reinforcements will arrive soon.

My boot squeaks and slides on the marble. My blood coating my entire left side, pooling at my feet.

Shit.

I swallow, fixing an image of Luc in my mind to keep me going. My hand tightens on my dagger, and I flex my thighs, ready to leap from the dais into the throng.

They stop.

I look at them, my brows furrowed in confusion.

"Rydel."

Luc's panting voice draws my attention like a starving man to a dinner bell. His hand is pressed to the doorway, and he's folded over, trying to catch his breath. He's wearing a servant's uniform, and it hugs every inch of him. As I drink him in, a knot unfurls from my chest when I see there's not a scratch on him ... not any new ones anyway.

I blink a few times, clearing my vision of sparkling white stars of pain, looking back at the soldiers swaying in place at the base of the dais. My eyes snap back to Luc, and he smiles. My heart stutters—maybe from the poison, and my cock stirs—definitely due to the man grinning at me from the far end of the throne room. He lifts his hand, palm up, and there they sit, two small Stones, one green, one pink and black.

I grin, then throw back my head, laughing to the ceiling. When I look back at Luc, he shoves away from the door. When he moves toward me, I see the dead guards outside the throne.

Shaking my head with another chuckle, I descend the first step, eyes on the love of my life. Fire erupts up my side, and it feels like my heart is trying to punch its way out of my chest. My knee buckles, and the room spins as I tumble down the steps. The soldiers don't move a muscle, held within Luc's magic, and I crash into the dead body at the bottom of the steps with a grunt. I blink a few times trying to clear my swirling vision. I can't catch my breath.

"Rydel! Rydel!"

Luc's hands are on me. He's putting pressure on my wound. I want to look at him. I try to say his name. I try to tell him I love him, but nothing comes out. I bellow in rage, but it stays locked in my throat as my body gives out.

Not like this.

Please.

Luc lifts my hand, and his fingers press into my palm, his voice laced with panic. "Ry. I got them. Here. You have your Stone. You have your magic. Open your eyes." *When did I close them?* He curls my fingers around the Stone, and heat spreads through my body. The tingle of the soldier's minds hits me, but their thoughts are vacant as Luc holds them in a complacent stupor.

He rests my closed fist on my chest, and I hear his tears. "We're going to get you fixed up." My struggling heart breaks at the fear in his voice. He wraps his hands under my arms, and a scream of agony rips up my throat, but doesn't pass my lips.

I'm being dragged.

Nothing. Sweet darkness.

I'm being lifted.

Pain. So much pain.

Where's Lucaryn?

Darkness comes again, but I'm scared. What if I don't surface again? No. No.

Nothingness.

I'm cold and hot. My brain feels like it's pressing against my skull and leaking out my ears. My limbs are heavy—too heavy to move. There's a scratching at my mind. Magic.

I'm dragged back toward the darkness, but I claw and kick and fight the entire way until the void closes in over my head once more.

E nergy courses through my blood, like a lightning strike. With a scream, I sit up, panting, rubbing my chest. The room is dark, and a large hand presses to my back. I relax into Luc's touch as he says, "Take it easy, Ry."

His voice is hoarse, and when I turn my head, I notice the pinch of his eyes and the hard set to his jaw. His hands are covered in blood, almost up to his elbows. He must see the worry in my eyes, because he shakes his head. "All yours."

I lick my lips, pressing a hand to my side, feeling the thick bandages wrapped around my waist. Everything hurts. It's beyond pain, it's agony, it's my body trying not to rip apart, but I let it wash over me. Licking my lips again, I smile. "Hey, look at that. I'm alive."

Luc chokes out a stuttered laugh, and though it hurts like hell, I laugh with him. I look around the room, but before I can ask, Luc says, "We're in Rannae's old healing chambers. I used my magic to get some of the soldiers to help me carry you down here, then I killed them."

Blinking my eyes against the darkness, I just now notice the three dead bodies slumped against the wall.

I press my hand back to the bandages. "I was poisoned."

Luc nods, his hand rubbing his chest. "After my own close call with the poisoned arrow, I had that healer teach me what he used to purge my body. He also taught me several different remedies for different poisons."

I shake my head, my hair tickling my neck. "Of course you did."

Luc shrugs. "I got you patched up as best I could. It was close, Ry. Too fucking close. I think I've countered the poison, but I don't know what she used exactly, so I had to improvise."

I gasp. "You ... *improvised*?"

He chuckles, shoving me gently. "I've injected you with a stimulant to get you up and moving." Well, that explains the jittery energy I feel. "I know you feel good right now, but you're still injured Ry, and the poison probably did some damage, so as much as you can, take it slow."

I take a deep breath, testing my body. "I wouldn't call my current state 'good' but I'm alive and I'm awake. Help me up."

His brows furrow, and he's silent for a moment. With my next breath, the pain eases ... a lot.

"What did you just do?"

He rubs his chest. "I used the Heart Stone to convince your body it's healed. Well, mostly." He grips my arm, steadying me as I slowly stand. "You're not though, you just feel like you are, so"—his voice cracks, and he clears his throat—"take it slow."

His touch grounds me, and I lean into him, pressing my lips to his. Wetness trickles down my beard, and I open my eyes to find Lucaryn crying silently. I wrap one arm around his waist and the other comes up to cup the back of his head. I pour my love for him into the kiss. His tears continue to fall as he shivers in my embrace, taking care not to touch my wound or hold me too tightly.

I love him so much. My heart is near bursting, which I'm not sure is a good thing right now. With a smile, I pull away, pressing my forehead to his, breathing in his petrichor scent. He is home to me. He always will be.

Luc trembles, his tears gone, but his back muscles are still tense. I shift back enough to see his face, and the strain I see there brings a frown to my face. He shakes his head, saying, "I've got us protected right now, but I'll be honest, it's getting hard to hold the magic, Ry."

He swallows, and I search for my magic. It flares immediately. Thoughts and images crash through my mind, and for a long moment, it feels like I can hear every thought of every person in the world. Black spots dance in the edges of my vision, but when I screw my eyes closed, the dots turn white and sparkling. I feel the room spinning, and just when I think I'm going to fall, Luc's broad hands grab me, holding me up. I breathe deep into his touch until I'm able to rein in the magic, pulling it back inch by inch until finally, there's only the buzzing hum of nearby soldiers and servants held under Luc's magic.

I grin.

Hello sweet power. How I've missed you. I let the scorching pain of the magic meld with the pain from my stab wound. I let my power pulse from me, and when I find the buzz of minds, I extinguish each spark with a single thought. Farther and farther I push, moving my awareness as deep into the palace as I can, snuffing out dozens of consciousnesses.

Luc sighs, and some of the tension leaves his body. "Thanks. I took out as many as I could, but my magic started faltering, and between holding back Rannae's soldiers and trying to keep you alive ..."

I kiss him again, needing his taste. "Lucaryn."

I don't know what else to say.

He smiles, and I melt, the pain fading for a moment. His deep voice rumbles against my chest. "What do you want to do?"

"Let's go home."

My back spasms with muscle memory of the magic, and a new layer of sweat starts to stick my already damp shirt to my body. Slowly, I extricate myself from Luc's arms, moving to the shelves. Bottles clink as I search through them. "Where is the stimulant you used?"

He comes up behind me, and my cock jumps in my pants. Reaching around, he grabs a bottle and sets it in front of me on the table. My finger brushes down the line of amber glass bottles until I find the one I want. I set the opioid on the table next to the stimulant.

Luc grumbles, and I look at him over my shoulder as he says, "You sure about that?"

I nod, doing my best to ignore the spasms shooting down my left side, threatening to buckle my leg. Grabbing a dropper, I add one full depression of the opioid to the stimulant, cap the bottle with a cork, give it a shake, and drop it in a small bag. I find a capped needle and place it in the bag, sliding the package into my pocket.

Turning, I pat the pocket. "In case of emergency."

Luc sighs, turning toward the door, pausing with his hand on the knob. I send out my magic as I know he's doing. The hallway outside is clear, so he yanks open the door, and we make our way through the palace. Only a few minutes later, as we pass through a doorway, I pause at the rush of thoughts, and Luc does the same as emotions barrel into him.

I place a hand on Luc's arm. "You've already pushed yourself. Let me."

He hesitates, a frown pulling at his tempting lips. "Are you strong enough? I can probably—"

I grin, stepping in front of him as soldiers run into the large receiving room we've entered. I pull back my hair, tying it in a knot before spreading my arms wide, saying, "I've been looking forward to this."

Luc snickers behind me, but then the screams start, and

all I hear is the beautiful melody of my enemy's pain and suffering.

33

LUCARYN

Rydel is running on drugs and rage. I'm just waiting for him to collapse, reliving every moment of terror when I thought he was dying in my arms.

But bodies fall before Rydel. Hands grip their heads. Screams ring out.

I add a punch of despair and pain to their suffering, shoving my magic into them, trying to stop their hearts. Their agony reflects back onto me, but I embrace it, swallowing the bile that threatens to climb my throat. Following Rydel, we step over and around the fallen, and I feel the heart of the person closest to me give out. A grunt passes my lips, and my legs nearly give out with my next step, but I keep moving.

Despite the pain, a smile lifts my cheeks. We've won. Somehow, against all odds, we've come out on top ... we just have to make it out of here—and now that we have our magic ...

A side door opens, and more soldiers rush in. I turn, roaring at them with a deep bellow, using my magic to flood their entire beings with terror. The ones in front skid to a stop, eyes wide. Armor clanks as the soldiers behind them crash into their backs. Rydel laughs, head thrown back as they try to scramble from the room, clawing at each other to get back through the door and away from us.

I sneer. "Oh no you don't."

My magic drops a few of them to their knees, effectively blocking the doorway. I sprint on shaky legs, slicing and stabbing until they all lay dead around me. Bending down, I pluck one of my knives from the neck of a soldier, wiping it clean on my pants before sliding it into its place on my harness.

I turn to Rydel. "You ready to move on?"

His arms are crossed, his feet planted with his hip cocked. The smirk on his face sends fire through my body, and his eyes travel down, taking in the carnage. When he looks back up, there's heat in his gaze mixed with the glaze of drugs that's blown his pupils wide.

Stepping over the dead, I almost roll an ankle as I try to wade through the bodies to get to him. I don't know how much longer our luck will hold, but I want every moment I have left to be filled with Rydel. My fingers claw at his shirt, the fabric balling in my fist. His hand comes up, resting over mine, holding me against his chest. Leaning forward, his slightly sour breath tickles my face as he says, "Home."

I nod, falling into him like he has yanked on my heart with a rope. My lips press to his. My free hand curls around his head, not caring about the blood I'm smearing in his hair.

Together, we turn, striding from the room, our long steps taking us down another empty hall and into yet another large open space. And there before us stands the double doors leading outside.

Shrieks echo as people scramble away from us. A woman clutches her chest, the fur wrap around her shoulders pulling tight as she screams, tripping over the long skirts of her dress as she attempts to back away. The man next to her catches her, swinging her behind him, backing them both against the wall. Rydel looks at them for just a moment, but that's all it takes. They crumple to the floor, their eyes wide, and when I search, I find them empty of feelings or emotions, and there's nothing coming from their hearts. Dead.

A group of women scream, the high pitch ringing in my ears. My skin pebbles as I experience their fear, but I wrap it in my magic and send it back at them. They freeze, toppling into one another, then they too fall as their hearts stop from sheer terror.

I roll my shoulders, catching a glance of Rydel swiping a sword from a dead soldier and plunging it into the gut of a servant. Another man yells, running at Ry, but I drop him with a push of my power. Three more men pause, eyes wide and unbelieving as their gazes dance between Rydel and me. Then they all bolt, tearing at each other to get through the closest door. Two grab their heads then drop to their knees, tears streaming down their faces. I wonder what hell Rydel has trapped them in, but from the emotions barreling into me, I know it's painful.

My chest feels like it's going to crack in half, and my back spasms, causing me to falter with my next step. But then the pain lessens, and when I look up, the men have all collapsed, eyes vacant. Rydel strides over, his hand pressing to my shoulder, and just that simple touch eases me.

He squeezes me. "Sorry. I shouldn't play with them. I know you can feel it. I got carried away."

I smile around the nausea. "It's okay. I'm glad to have the magic back as well." I straighten, spitting the sour bile taste from my mouth. "Let's go."

He nods, turning.

Our hands press to the towering doors, and we each shove one open. We are beings of death and vengeance as we stride from the palace. Chaos greets us. Screams ring out. People scatter. Soldiers rush forward.

Rydel grabs my arm, yanking me to the left. An arrow sails over my shoulder from behind, and the next moment I feel Ry's magic blast from him. A body falls from a parapet behind us, splattering on the ground.

Spinning around, I eye the roof lines, picking up each heartbeat, each flutter of fear and anger. I calm their rage, demanding they lower their bows. Then, I flood them with shame and despair. I watch with anticipation as more than ten soldiers step to the edge and fall to their deaths.

Fuck. This power.

I shiver with the rush of it.

When I turn back around, everyone in the courtyard is either writhing on the ground in pain or already dead. Rydel turns to me, and I don't miss the sheen of sweat covering his face and sticking his clothes to this body. His face is pale as well, and there's a pinch between his eyes that hints at the enormous pain I know he's in.

But I also feel his arousal tingling through me, and I can't help but chuckle through my own pain as the agony and deaths happening around me punch through my chest.

Ry smirks at me. "Let's go get our people."

Somehow, I'm able to pick up a slow jog, and Ry does the same as we skirt the palace, gravel crunching under our feet. He presses a hand to his side, and I can't help but wonder how he's even still standing.

A servant rushes by, fear propelling him in a mad rush away from the palace. He doesn't even see us, but our magic slams into him, gravel cutting into the side of his face as he slams to the ground, his heart and mind completely shut down.

We do the same to anyone else we encounter, leaving a trail of death behind us until we reach an iron and wood door. Rydel grabs the handle, his hand shaking slightly as he says, "This leads to a back entrance to the dungeons."

I nod and follow him into the dark, narrow hall—It's very convenient that Rydel knows this palace so well since it was his for a short while. Once inside, Ry pauses, pressing his back to the wall. With a shaking hand, he reaches into his pocket, drawing out the small bag, pulling open the string, and quickly injecting himself with a dose of the drug. He sighs, taking a deep breath, and I keep my mouth closed. It may not be the street drug specifically, but that look in his eyes is all too familiar. I'm worried, but I can't seem to voice my objections because I know this is all that's keeping him going right now.

We make our way down the hall, and within a matter of moments, the sharp smell of unwashed bodies and excrement hits my nose. My eyes water as I fight to keep from vomiting. The smell combined with the pain vibrating through my magic nearly blacks out my vision, but I bite the inside of my cheek, forcing myself to go on.

"Your majesty?" Carelle's weak voice calls out, and I wrap my arm around my waist as the pain of her broken ribs echoes through me. She coughs, and I stumble to a stop, pressing a hand to the slimy stone wall, breathing deep as she says, "Captain?"

The light clink of the key ring reaches my ears, and I manage to stand upright again as Rydel takes the ring from a nail in the wall. He quickly moves down the row of cells, metal whining in protest as he swings each door open. Rydel swears, "That bitch. Of course she didn't release anyone."

Someone calls out from further down the dark dungeon. "Nope. All present and accounted for, your Majesty."

Our people stumble out of their cells, most supporting each other. Zinnia struggles to hold Runic's weight as they emerge from their cell. The rage and pain pulsing from Runic nearly drives me to my knees. His voice is hoarse as he growls at Rydel, "Where is Adastra?"

Ry meets his hard stare. "Dead."

Runic's jaw clenches, his eyes narrow, and his fists tremble. Rydel takes a step back, actually rubbing his temples as he catches some thought or memory from Runic.

Carelle clears her throat, and our attention turns to her as she says, "Mica needs help."

I move forward, careful to avoid bumping into Carelle as I scoot around her and into her cell. Mica shifts, propping himself on his forearm before falling back onto his side with a grunt of pain. I wipe my sweating palms on my pants before grabbing him under his arms, whispering, "Sorry. This is going to hurt."

He nods, screwing his eyes shut. A sharp scream rips from us both as I haul him over my shoulder. I breathe through his pain, experiencing the pulsing agony of his broken leg, his battered ribs, five broken fingers, and a sickening throbbing pain on the back of his head. My vision waivers as he passes out.

Fuck, I'm going to vomit.

I'm about to call out to Ry, but he's already at my side.

"Let me take him."

I shake my head.

"I've got him, just ..."

Rydel nods. "Let me try something."

I focus on breathing and keeping myself standing. The pain starts to fall away, and groans of relief float from our people gathered around us. Rydel tilts his head, whispering, "Interesting."

I shift Mica's weight and follow Ry from the cell as he speaks to everyone. "Take care with your movements. The pain may be gone, but I've only convinced your minds that your injuries are gone. They are still very much there."

My eyes widen at his words. He's taken what I did for him, adapted it to his magic and given it to our people. This might be the first time Rydel has used his magic to take away pain.

I focus my thoughts at him. *"Thank you, Rydel. But don't push. You're still hurt yourself."*

His eyes flick to mine, a small smile on his lickable lips. *"I'm okay. I never thought to use the magic this way."* A soft chuckle sounds through my mind.

I shake my head. Of course he didn't. That's not who he is at his core. He's wickedly delightful.

Following Rydel, he leads us back down the dark hallway. It's hard to maneuver with Mica slung over my shoulder, and I wince as his head scrapes against the stone wall more than once.

Finally, we shove through the heavy door, and I gulp down deep breaths of crisp, clean air, though it's still tinged with the sour scent of Mica's body. Our people shuffle and stumble along behind us as we move forward. Our progress is slow, and when Rydel flicks his dagger into his hand, I absorb his anxious energy and I know he's eager to move on.

I call out, "Rydel. I've got them. Go get the horses."

Rydel turns, his eyes holding mine for a long moment before his voice punches into my mind. *"Don't you dare let anything happen to you. You kill whoever comes along."*

I nod, sending back to him, *"You too."*

He turns, jogging off, and I don't miss the new wetness spreading along the side of his shirt. My crude stitches must have torn open.

Everyone shuffles, gazes snapping around, their restless energy trembling through my chest. Their desire to get away from this place that holds so many horrors for them makes me want to run away from the palace as fast as I can. But I hold my ground, trying to bolster their courage and calm their terror.

The swell of emotions eases slightly, and their nervous movements still.

Before long, the sharp clop of hooves sounds from our right. I heft Mica higher onto my shoulder and move toward the noise, meeting Rydel as he comes around a corner in the path. A string of horses trail behind him. Kahar's ears are pinned back, his giant hooves digging deep grooves in the gravel. I purse my lips. I still have to go retrieve Phoenix. Will this day never end?

I step to the side to avoid Kahar's half-hearted kick in my direction, and I swat at him. "E'ass asre'a." *Hell horse.*

Ry chuckles, and I'm about to heft Mica onto one of the palace horses, but Carelle leads her horse next to me, saying, "Put him with me. We need you and the king free to move and defend us. Some of us can still fight, but not all, and we need you if we're getting out of here alive." Her gaze flicks to Rydel, and she lowers her voice. "Besides, he doesn't look like he's in the best shape. That's a lot of blood on his clothes."

I nod, not responding. If I say it out loud, if I say how close Rydel came to dying, I don't know if I'll be able to hold back my tears. Bracing my feet, flexing my thighs, and tightening my core, I haul Mica up and over Carelle's horse's back, settling him behind her saddle.

As I slide my foot into the stirrup of one of the extra horses, Rydel barks out, "Those of you who are able, help those who need it. Everyone mount up. Pair up if needed. If there are extra horses, tether them and bring them." He swings onto Kahar, turning the war horse in a tight circle. Rydel sits tall, head raised, every inch the king he is in this moment despite his current state. This is the man I've followed my entire life. And I will continue to follow him to the very end and beyond into the fiery pits of hell.

Rydel says, "We ride for Lieren. If we can find a safe place with a healer, I'll make sure you're seen to, but I'll be honest, I don't know that we will find a ... hospitable place to stop until we cross our border." He pauses, looking each of our people in the eyes. "Can you make it?"

Slowly, each nods. I'm not sure if Mica will make it, but we won't leave him. Hillsound comes to mind, and I gently push my thoughts at Ry. He turns to me, pursing his lips in thought for a moment before his voice slides into my mind. *"Perhaps. But it is out of the way. Stopping there will prolong our journey home by a day, maybe two."*

"The way may be longer, but our people need help. You do too, Ry." I pause before adding, *"Please."*

His eyes soften, and he nods.

Thank the gods. We just need to make it to Hillsound. We can do this.

All mounted, we head north, Rydel and I in the lead,

those fit enough to put up some kind of a fight if necessary bringing up the rear.

We only make it a few minutes before thundering hooves sound from the path before us. Without saying a word, Ry pulls Kahar to the right, and I move my horse left. We circle the approaching soldiers, hitting them with wave after wave of our magic. The soldier's horses rear and whinny as some of their riders fall to the ground, and some slump over their mount's necks. In just a few moments, the well-formed Trislenian ranks fall apart, and with a final push of our power, they all die, and the horses scatter.

We still haven't cleared the palace grounds, and I sigh as more soldiers rush us. Rydel hears me, and chuckles. "You're right. This is getting tedious. Let's end this."

His plan flashes through my mind, and I smile. This is going to hurt, and I honestly don't know if we're strong enough to do this, but ...

With a deep breath, I gather the magic, imagining it pulsing away from me like ripples in a lake. Every flutter of a heartbeat I detect, I fill them with the overwhelming desire to follow Rydel's command.

As our small group heads for the gates, Trislenian soldiers drop their weapons, glazed eyes turned toward the palace. A stream of people and soldiers flood from all over the palace grounds, eyes vacant, shuffling feet taking them up the stairs and into the palace.

Silently, we ride through the slow-moving flow of people.

I think my heart is going to give out. It's beating fast and hard against my chest. I'm so hot, it's a wonder my clothes haven't caught on fire. Rydel rubs his chest, feeling my pain, and I close my eyes for a moment to try and block out Ry's own agony hammering at my temples.

As the last few people file into the palace, smoke begins to billow from a few windows. The doors slam shut, and the Trislenians barricade themselves in at Rydel's command and my compulsion. We pass through the gates and away from the palace just as screams start to ring out. Glass shatters, and thick grey smoke curls higher into the sky, melding with the heavy grey clouds. Flames shoot from windows, and the screams get louder.

We ride away from the Trislenian palace as it burns, taking its people with it.

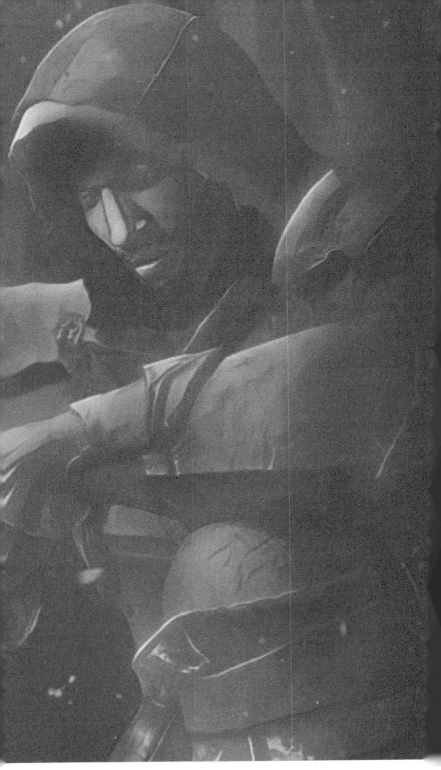

34

LUCARYN

Village by village, town by town, we have made our way through Trislen leaving a trail of smoke and death in our wake. Rydel has injected the drug twice more, and I think the effects are wearing off faster each time. The next time we stop I'll rebandage his wound and bandage up anyone else that needs it.

Phoenix shakes his head, eager to stretch his legs, and I give him a pat. "Not yet. I'm afraid our group won't be able to move much faster than this for a while."

He snorts as if he understands, and I chuckle. It's nice to have my trusty gelding back, and being back in my own clothes, or better fitting clothes at least.

The innkeeper back in the capital was true to her word. My clothes were where I left them, and Phoenix was well cared for. She eagerly tucked the gold coin between her breasts, commenting about the chaos coming from the palace. I told her to get out of the city, but she just tsked, shaking her head.

I tried.

We weren't but a few blocks from the inn when the sounds of rioting and violence reached us. People ran through the city streets, screaming and falling over each other. Some smashed windows, taking what they could hold in their arms. Fights broke out. Rydel and I cleared a path before us but left the city to tear itself apart.

And so it's gone with each city, town, and village.

News, particularly, bad news, travels fast, faster than us.

The smell of smoke clings to my hair and clothes as we move through yet another small city, now a few hours outside of the capital. Phoenix hops to the side as a man sprints past us, his arms full of random cloth and bags. Up ahead, a loud crash sends two people through a window, and they land in the street in a tangle of limbs, fists flying, bodies rolling. A woman leans out the busted window, screaming at the two fighting in the street. "Queen Adastra is dead! This is no way to behave! Stop it! Stop it, now!"

We guide our horses around them, moving on.

One of my men rides up next to me, his comrade riding in front of him, slumped over, breath wheezing from his chest. The man leans toward me, clearing his throat. "Um, captain. Should the king not ... take control? Reclaim the Trislenian throne. Curb some of this violence?"

I open my mouth, but without turning around, Runic's rough voice carries back to us. "Fuck 'em. Let it *all* burn."

His pain slices up my spine, and my gut clenches as his rage slams into me. I shift in my saddle, having no response.

But Rydel chuckles. "Yes. For now ... Fuck 'em. Let them tear themselves apart. Let them burn their own home to the ground. Maybe someone will eventually come out on top.

Right now, I don't care. We need to get home. We're going to make sure Lieren is secure, and once that's done, the rest of Imoria will be waiting. They will come, begging for protection, for help, for law and order."

I cock my head, fighting a smile as I push my amused thoughts at him. "*Look at you.*"

He shifts in his saddle but doesn't turn as his voice reverberates through my mind. "*I can walk away from a fight ... on occasion.*"

Our combined chuckles float through my mind. He's right. We have our magic, and once we regroup and assess, we'll take control.

Silence spreads around our small group, but no one says anything else as we move on.

We're close to the border crossing, and the pressure of multiple people ahead thrums through my magic. Rydel tenses, shifting in his saddle, and he raises a hand in warning. Several of our people, those fit enough to fight, spread out, shifting those weaker to the center of our group in a well-practiced move.

My body shakes, and my head screams with pain as I reach for the hearts of the Trislenian soldiers ahead. Rydel grunts as his magic slams from him, and he slumps in his saddle. I kick Phoenix forward ready to leap down and catch him should he fall, but he manages to right himself with Kahar's help as the great steed shifts his body to keep Ry on his back.

When we round the bend in the road, we come to a group of horses standing in the road, soldiers scattered on the ground at their feet. Rydel took them all out with one massive shove of his magic. He's incredible. With a sigh, I rein in my magic, and we move on.

With every blink of my eyes, it's getting harder to open

them again. Carelle rides up next to me, Mica once again unconscious on the back of her horse, but his heartbeat flutters through my magic, so I know he's still alive. Carelle looks at me, then Rydel. "How much longer to this Hillsound? You two look ready to drop. Maybe we should make camp?"

I shake my head. "We're close. Less than an hour."

She frowns but falls back.

The winter wind cools my skin, and the mother moon shines down on us as a familiar dog bark greets us. Hillsound comes into view just as one of the villagers rides up on a dark brown mule. She nods to Rydel, her eyes skimming our group, growing worry filling her eyes. She turns, leading us into the village, saying over her shoulder, "Wasn't expecting to see you again after ya left, however, news travels faster than wildfire, even all the way out here. Seems you are the only royal left." Rydel smirks with a chuckle, and the woman shakes her head. "I'm sure glad to be so far away from all that trouble."

She aims a look at us, brow raised, and I say, "We weren't followed. Our magic took care of that possibility. We aren't here to bring trouble. We need help, if you'll have us ... again."

She smiles, kicking her mule to a trot. "Come on then. We'll get you settled and rested."

We gather in the small village center, the woman slipping into the dark tavern, returning a few moments later with Killock and Bellrain, both wiping their eyes and straightening their clothes.

Can it only have been a few days since we were here last? It feels like ages.

As we fall and stumble from our horses, Bellrain plants her hands on her hips with a scowl. "Look at the state of ya!

Throwing our country into chaos and showing up here on death's door."

"Yay me." Ry smirks, but he's swaying on his feet. My hand slams to Phoenix's saddle, and I realize I'm about to fall over as well.

Killock tsks. "Stop baggerin' 'em, daughter. They need a healer, and more than old Sam can handle." He waves a hand at us. "Come on, the lot of ya. I'll clear the tables. The floor won't be tha most comfortable, but ya can stretch out, and we'll collect some blankets and pillows for ya all."

Ry clasps his shoulder in thanks, walking with him into the tavern, our people filing in after them. I stay outside, making sure everyone makes it in.

"Captain!"

A smile curves up my exhausted face as Quinn comes sprinting down the dirt road. He skids, slowing down, dust kicking up behind him until he tucks his little body into my side, wrapping a hand around my waist, trying to take some of my weight.

My heart melts, and for the first time in my life, I feel a fierce protectiveness for someone other than Rydel. I let him lead me toward the tavern, but pause when he says, "I'm gonna ride to tha next village. Their healer is really good. Like tha best. She'll be able to fix ya all up."

I shake my head, kneeling to bring myself to his level. Every muscle protests as I drop to one knee. "You can't, Quinn. It's too dangerous right now."

He presses his lips together in a pout. "I'm tha fastest rider. I know secret ways. I can be careful. I'm gonna be your best soldier one day. I can do this."

I want to let him go. I want to feed that determination and fire I see in his eyes, but I fear for him. That's new. I rub my chest, shaking my head again. "Your mother won't—"

365

He smiles. "She told me ta go. Ask her. She knows I'm the best one ta go."

I stand, ruffling his hair. "Fine. I'll ask her."

He nods, and I realize he wasn't bluffing. Shit. He wraps his arm back around my waist, and I let him help me into the tavern.

Our people have spread out on the cleared floor, soft snoring already rising from several lumps snuggled under thick blankets. Rydel is leaning heavily on the bar, tucking the small bag back into his pocket, and I know he just took another dose. Damn it. We need that healer.

Sam, this village's healer kneels at one of our people's side, checking her wounds and sores. His calm voice carries to me as he pats her shoulder. "Your injuries are actually healing quite nicely. It will just take some time. I have a salve you can use to speed up the process. Your biggest need right now is food, water, and rest." On que, Bellrain kneels at Sam's side, holding out a cup of water and a bowl that smells like broth.

Sam moves on, and I cross the room to where Quinn's mother collects more blankets from villagers as they bring them into the tavern. She sees me coming and smiles. "Quinn is the best choice. It'll keep him out from under foot here while we get everyone settled, and he is the best rider."

I open my mouth to object, but she smiles again. "He's good at evading trouble. Sure, that kid can find his fair share of trouble, but he can get around it too." She pats my shoulder in a motherly caress. "He's already left."

My body tenses as I look around the room. Sure enough, Quinn is nowhere to be seen. Shit. Should I ride after him? I catch Quinn's mother shooting a look at Rydel, and before I know it, he crosses the room, taking my arm, dragging me to the bar. "What's got you wound so tight, captain?"

His voice is teasing, but I can't seem to let go of the tension pinching the muscles of my back. "Quinn. He rode for the next village to fetch another healer. It's not safe for him, Ry. He's just a boy."

"We were just boys when we left home and struck out on our own."

I scowl at him, gesturing at us and our current state. "And look at us!"

He laughs, surprising me with a quick kiss. The room goes quiet for a moment before the soft murmur of conversation picks up again. I look at him with a question in my eyes, and he shrugs. "They all suspected. Besides, we're getting married when we get home, so might as well practice kissing in front of people we know."

He waggles his eyes at me, and I can't help but chuckle. The nerves still linger, though, and I know I won't be able to sleep until Quinn returns. Killock slides a mug across the bar to me, and I gulp down the water, setting the empty cup down. He refills it, and I drink that one down as well. With the next refill, I drink it more slowly, feeling the water sloshing in my empty stomach.

The emotions of those awake in the room are calm, relieved, and tired. All except Runic. Even in his sleep, he's angry and in pain. Their collective exhaustion tugs at me, and I take another sip of water, fighting to keep my eyes open.

I jerk awake, sitting bolt upright from my place on the floor. I'm lost in the panic of what happened—until I see Rydel beside me. He's passed out next to me, a slight flush to his face. I brush my fingers over his forehead, and fear claws at me as his clammy skin slicks under my touch. He's not well.

But then I realize what woke me. A shout.

Bellrain is running out the door, and dread lands like a boulder in my stomach. I jump to my feet, but the world spins, and my vision tunnels. I crash to my hands and knees. Crawling forward, I grab a chair that was shoved against the wall. I pull myself to standing, take a few quick breaths, and bolt out the door.

Early morning light paints the clear sky a pale blue, and I sprint across the village square at the sight of a young woman with pale blond hair rushing toward the tavern. She's bleeding from a cut along her hairline, and there's a slight limp to her gait. But it's the boy in her arms that stops my breath.

Quinn.

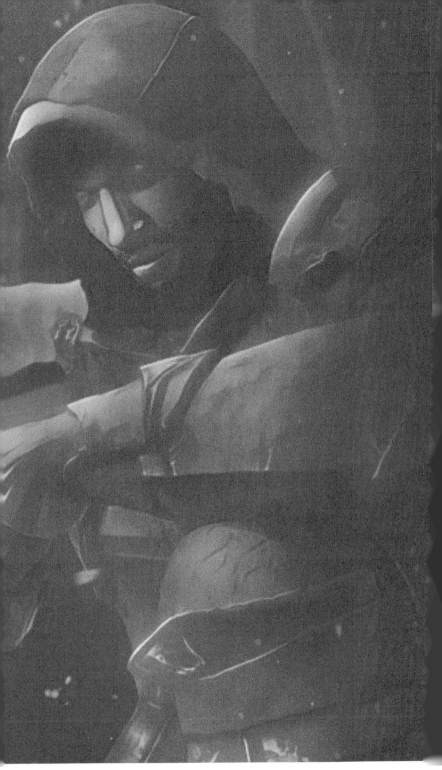

35

LUCARYN

Quinn is cradled in the woman's arms, his mother holding his tiny hand in hers as she jogs at the woman's side. The boy's eyes are open, and when he sees me, tears drip down his cheeks and he drops his gaze. His shame slams into me. He's ashamed of failing at keeping the healer safe. He thinks I'll be mad at him.

I rip Quinn from the blond-haired woman, hugging him to my chest, feeling his shallow breaths and quiet hiccups. "What happened?"

He hiccups again, and the woman wipes sweat from her head, smearing the blood across her face, answering for Quinn. "Trislenian soldiers. If it hadn't been for Quinn's quick thinking, they would have killed us for sure. That kid is smart, and fast. Get him in the tavern."

I rush ahead, Quinn's body so small in my arms. I grab a blanket, throwing it over a table, and gently lay him on it.

The woman comes to my side, shoving me out of the way. "He's going to be fine. Took a blow to the head. I have some herbs to reduce the swelling. His breathing is good as is his coloring." She rests her hand on my forearm. "He'll be fine."

I look at her. "Where?"

She chews her bottom lip, glancing out the door as if expecting the soldiers to come barreling into the tavern. "About ten miles west."

A hand wraps around my arm, pulling me back. Ry whispers in my ear. "Let the healer work, Luc."

I nod, keeping my eyes on the boy as I back up. Pulling from his grip, I grab my sword and storm out of the tavern and jog to the barn. I don't bother saddling Phoenix, I just throw his bridle over his head, and leap onto him bareback. Kicking him into a fast canter, I blast from the barn, Rydel yelling after me, "Luc, wait!"

I ignore him, leaning over Phoenix's neck, his mane brushing my face, the cold early morning air stinging my eyes and cheeks. I hurl my magic before me, searching for my prey.

Hooves thunder behind me, and when I glance over my shoulder, I see Zinnia hot on my trail, her pale skin flushed, her blond hair flying behind her. I slow Phoenix, and when Zinnia pulls up close enough, she shouts over the pounding of hooves and whistling of the wind. "The king sent me."

I figured as much.

I urge Phoenix to pick up the pace, and we race down the narrow road.

Emotions hit me. Anticipation of a hunt. Annoyance at a missed opportunity. Exhaustion from a long night.

I grin, roaring into the quickly brightening morning. The emotions immediately shift ... fear. I tremble with it, recognizing it as theirs and not mine. Still hurts.

Just as the soldiers come into view, my magic slams into them. Zinnia gasps as they all start laughing. Tears stream down their faces, and they wrap their hands around their waists as they try to catch their breath around their laughter.

Joy and amusement—I flood their bodies with it. With my own grin pulling at my lips, I ride right into their group, counting off thirteen beating hearts. I slash my blade across throats, and into stomachs. I stab into chests, scraping ribs with my sword as I yank it free, cleaving a head from its body. One by one, they die, laughing the entire time, never lifting a finger against me. I feel each death, the pain gripping my heart for a moment before the pressure releases with a pop as each person dies.

Breath heaving, I turn Phoenix in a tight circle. He stomps the hard-packed road, flicking his tail. Everyone is dead. All thirteen.

Zinnia is where I left her, farther down the road, her mouth open, her eyes wide, her hands gripping the mane of her horse tightly. She blinks a few times before kicking her horse forward. I raise a brow. "Alright, Zinnia?"

She shakes her head, pulling herself from her stupor. "Yes, captain. I just ... that was ..."

I jerk my head over my shoulder. "Help me get the bodies back on the horses. We'll bring them back to the village. More fodder for the fire."

She nods, leaping from her horse, only wincing slightly as she lands. My leg twitches with her pain, but I push it aside as best I can, sliding from Phoenix's back.

As we work to haul the heavy bodies onto the scattered horses, my arms begin to ache. The body of a large male flops over the back of a skittish horse, and I tug the reins to keep the steed steady. Shaking out my arms, I frown. I shouldn't be this tired already.

But then I glance at Zinnia and catch her rubbing her left forearm. Ah. This fatigue is not my own. She catches me watching her, and she quickly drops her gaze, whispering, "Sorry. It seems my time in the ... the dungeons ate away more muscle than I thought."

I nod, clapping her on the back as I pass, bending to grab another body. "Don't worry about it. There's only three left. I got it." My grip slips on the blood slicked arm of the soldier, but I bunch his shirt in my fist, yanking him over my shoulder. Zinnia holds the next horse steady as the body lands with a thud on its back.

Quickly, I get the final two soldiers loaded, ignoring the tingling in my arms and the disappointment pouring off Zinnia ... in herself for being so weak. I should tell her it's not her fault, but she knows that. I wipe my bloody hands on my pants, and with a nod to Zinnia, I hold out my hand. "Give me your foot." Embarrassment washes over me as her cheeks flush, and I shake my head. "Don't waste time. Let's go."

She stiffens, but nods back, resolve pushing aside her unease. She turns, gripping her horse's mane, and bends her leg, kicking her heel toward her butt. I grip the top of her boot and help her swing onto her mount. She settles, grabbing the closest horse's lead, and her emotions quiet as she focuses on the task at hand.

I swing onto Phoenix's back, and without another word, we head back toward the village.

The journey back is much longer due to the lack of the adrenaline that comes with the excitement of a hunt, and also because we have a string of horses carrying dead bodies keeping our pace slow.

The sun breaks over the horizon, bathing our faces in bright light as we finally enter Hillsound. Rydel pushes off the exterior wall of the tavern, striding across the small square, arms crossed over his chest. I press my lips together to keep my smile from surfacing at the look of indignation on his face.

But then a wave of relief and happiness slams into me. Quinn runs from the tavern, his mother shouting after him, "Quinn, slow down! Your head!"

I hop from Phoenix's back, and Quinn slams into my legs, arms wrapped tight around me. My clothing muffles his voice. "I'm sorry, captain. I shoulda been more careful. Ya trusted me. Tha village trusted me. I failed, and ya went into danger because of me."

I pat his back, then grip his shoulders, pulling him back. I step back, crossing my fist over my heart in salute. His eyes go wide, and his shock and wonder flutter through my chest. I keep my face hard, though my smile is trembling behind my lips as I say, "It's a soldier's job, his duty, to go into danger when called to do so. You did well, Quinn. Your task was to retrieve the healer and bring her to Hillsound. You did, even at risk to yourself. Well done. I'm glad to see you up and about. Do others still need help?"

He nods, tears rimming his eyes, but he blinks them away.

I jerk my head towards the tavern. "Well, then soldier, best go make yourself useful."

He nods, saluting me in the most adorable way before running back into the tavern. His mother gives me a grateful smile before following him inside.

Zinnia takes Phoenix and the string of horses back to the barn. Villagers appear to help unload the bodies, some loading the dead into a cart to take to the pyre in the far field, others work to undo the tack and get the new horses settled. We have an overflowing stable at this point.

Rydel walks up to me, barking at me as he passes, "With me, captain."

His tone is angry, but his lust slithers through my body, collecting in my balls, stirring my cock. I do as I'm told and follow. We pass a few houses, all quiet, and then Rydel pushes through a painted gate, walking up a manicured path to the front door of a small house. My brows pinch together, but I follow. The door swings open at Ry's push, and he enters, holding the door open for me. I cross the threshold, soft firelight greeting me from a fireplace in the single room house. A threadbare couch separates a sitting area from the tiny kitchen and open bath area, and a dispro-portionately large bed sits in the back corner.

"Whose house is this?"

I jump as the door slams shut. Rydel shoves his emotions at me, and a breath-stealing wave of desire is my only warning as he grabs my shoulders, spinning me around and slams his lips to mine.

Fire and starlight. That is what his kiss feels like. Our tongues immediately tangle, and I grip his hair to deepen the angle. He groans, and my eyes fly open, and I rip myself from his hold, panting, "Ry, your wound. You're still hurt. You need rest."

He stalks me. "Sam tended me. And what I *need* is you."

My eyes flit to the door, and he sighs. "One of the villagers gave us his home for the day and overnight if we want. I don't remember his name." I'm not surprised in the least. "He and his husband are staying with one of their friends between shifts patrolling the village. Happy now?"

The corner of my lips twitch, and I reach for him. "Yes. Very."

I groan as his desire curls through my gut, and his lips crash back to mine. My hand tangles in his hair as my other presses to his back, holding him against me. Our cocks brush through our clothes, and Rydel's hips rock into me. My body is on fire as he backs up, pulling me with him until we reach the bed. My eyes fly open as he grips me, spinning us. The backs of my legs hit the edge of the bed, and when he shoves, I fall back with a chuckle.

Propping myself on my forearms, I scoot back, kicking my boots off. Bending one knee, planting my foot, I smirk up at him. He crawls onto the bed, bracing his arms on either side of me. I fall back, meeting his heated gaze.

I can't believe we're still alive. I can't believe we're ... us ... together.

My heart beats for him. My fingers brush along his cheek, and he leans into my touch. Laying my palm against his face, I cup his jaw, gently pulling him down for a kiss. His heavy weight presses me into the lumpy mattress, but our touches remain light.

We take our time, undressing slowly, taking care with our many injuries, kissing each one. Fire light flickers over the cut plains of Rydel's body, and I worship him. There's so much emotion between us my throat threatens to close as tears prick the backs of my eyes.

With his next pass over my lips, his beard scratches my face as his breath ghosts over my skin. "Uh sahe'a iyai." *I love you.*

I hold his gaze, our bodies stilling, our breaths shallow. "Uh sahe'a iyai, saa." *I love you, too.*

His cock jumps against my thigh, and when I roll my hips, he groans, using his knees to push my legs wider. His beard scrapes my skin as he works his way down my body, my cock aching with each inch gained. When his breath shivers over my length, I shudder, my head falling back, my hands fisting the bedding.

"Eyes on me, Lucaryn."

I tuck my chin, gazing down my body, meeting his stare as he slowly closes his lips over the head of my weeping cock, hollowing his cheeks, sucking me down.

Fuck. This is how I'm going to die.

I try to buck into him, but his hands hold my inner thighs wide, pressing me into the bed. Pleasure curls through me as I watch Ry's mouth slide up and down my cock, saliva pooling at the base, dripping down my balls.

My hand snaps out, and my fingers scrape his scalp before I grip his hair, holding him deep. He chuckles, the sound vibrating up my cock, tingling up my spine. He swallows, and I see stars.

"Fuck, Ry. You feel so good. Fuck."

One of his large hands leaves my thigh to grip me ... hard. His mouth and hand move in sync, his wet mouth sucking me deep, his tongue swirling along my hard length. His hand squeezes in a pulsing rhythm, and my eyes nearly roll back in my head. But I don't want to miss a moment.

His other hand crawls up my body, his nails scratching my nipple before a sharp pinch draws a gasp from my lips. Without his hands holding me down, my hips are free to punch into his mouth. I feel his teeth hit his hand as he moves to keep up with my pace. Sparking pleasure gathers, and I know I'm close, but I'm not ready. Not yet.

I force my hips to stop pumping, and I pull his head from my cock. A line of saliva drips from his lips, and I pull him up my body for a greedy kiss, tasting myself. His thick cock slides against mine, and we both groan.

My voice is a mere whisper. "I need you, Ry. I need you

to come inside me. I want to feel your cum dripping from me and sliding down my thighs."

His eyes flare, and a deep growl rumbles from his chest. "Yes, sir."

Gods, I love when he calls me sir.

He reaches between us, gripping my cock, collecting his saliva before stroking himself once. My stomach clenches at the sight, and I want more. Sitting up, I lick my lips as he pumps himself again. I roll my tongue, gathering saliva in my mouth before spitting. His grip tightens, his eyes fixed to where my spit gleams on his length.

"Fuck, Sir. Again."

I swallow, gather more saliva, and spit again. His cock jumps in his grip. He pushes me back, lining himself up. Slowly, inch by inch, he slides inside me. The stretch is only a little painful, but the sheer bliss that shoots up my back chases away any discomfort. When he bottoms out, he holds himself deep, his eyes climbing my body before meeting my gaze. We stare at each other as he pulls out, almost withdrawing completely before slowly pushing back in.

His jaw flexes, and I have a moment of anticipation before he spits. The wet glob lands on my cock, and a second later, his calloused hand wraps around my cock, pumping in time with his steady thrusts. His gravelly voice sends gooseflesh across my entire body. "I can't wait to get my hands on more of Clara's lubrication."

I lift my hips with his next stroke. "This is working just fine, Ry." He rubs his thumb over the head of my cock, and my stomach clenches. "Just fine."

My entire body rolls, abs flexing, thighs bunching to experience every slick glide of his cock in my ass and his hand on my length. Reaching up, I press a hand to his chest, careful of his injuries. My fingers caress his skin, my touch moving over his shoulder, tracing the dark lines and swirls of his tattoo.

"Feel what you do to me, Rydel. Know the depth of what I feel for you."

His eyes soften, and his hair sways as he nods. I open myself to my magic, sending everything within me to him. His nostrils flare, and his pace picks up. His jaw flexes, and he nods again.

"Yes, Luc. I feel it. I feel you." His free hand presses to my chest over my heart. "This is mine." I nod, and he moves his hand over mine, shifting it so he presses my palm over his heart. "And this is yours."

"Always."

His hand drops back to my chest, and I keep mine pressed over his heart as he drives into me. Sweat slicks our bodies, and his giant body gleams with perfection, each swell and cut of his muscles in sharp relief. With his next thrust, he rolls his hips, hitting me deeper as his hand tightens on my cock.

"Ry!"

His words stutter with each strong pump of his hips. "Yes. Luc. Fuck. Yes. Come. Come now. Paint us with your seed." His eyes find and hold mine. "Sir."

The flood gates crumble. Pulsing pleasure explodes between my thighs, shooting tingling bliss up my body and down my legs until even my toes flex with pleasure. My cum splatters against my chest, then Rydel tugs me so the remainder of my release coats his abs.

I slowly come down, my hips still rocking with his thrusts. His hand remains pressed to my chest, but his other hand leaves my cock, his fingers trailing through my cum on his chest. When he brings his fingers to his mouth and sucks them deep, a groan rumbles up my throat. My hips buck, another short orgasm surprising me as more of my hot cum splashes on my stomach.

He pulls his fingers from his mouth, smearing his hand over my abs, rubbing my cum into my heated flesh. His voice is so deep, his eyes eating up every inch of me. "Perfect, Lucaryn."

His thrusts stutter, and he falls forward as his orgasm rips through him. His pleasure screams through my magic, ripping yet another orgasm from me. We both roar, our bodies pressed tight, my cum sticking between us. Gripping his face, I kiss him, licking his tongue as his thrusts slow, then stop.

We break the kiss to catch our breath. Ry's cum leaks from my ass, dripping between my cheeks, pooling on the bed. He peppers my face with soft kisses, and I run my fingers up and down his back.

Hot liquid drips onto my stomach, and I don't have to look to know Rydel's stitches have popped.

"Rydel—"

"I know. It's fine. Just ... let me hold you for a while longer."

I force myself to relax, hugging him with one arm as my other caresses his scalp. His head drops to my shoulder, and we just hold each other in this perfect moment. Time slips by, and his breathing starts to slow.

I wiggle, shoving him gently. "Ry, before you fall asleep on me—not that I'd mind—but I have to pee, and I'd like to wash at least some of my cum off my body."

Rydel groans, rolling to the side. His eyes are closed, but a small smile curves his lips. "Hurry back, and don't worry about cleaning too thoroughly. I plan to have you again."

I chuckle, shaking my head as I pad to the small kitchen. "Tend your wound, Ry."

He grunts again, but rolls over, sitting up to do as I asked. I relieve myself then pump water into the large sink, splashing water down my front, hissing as I cup water in my hand and bring it to my balls and cock.

On my way back to the bed, I lift the lid of a large chest at the foot of the bed, finding more bedding. The lid thunks closed as I release it. Good. I'd feel ... awkward leaving these people's bed in its current state. I'll change the bedding before we leave.

A new bandage covers Ry's side, but his skin still gleams with my cum. It doesn't seem to bother him though, as he rolls back into the bed. Holding the blankets up, he waits for me to crawl in beside him before tucking us in.

Our legs tangle, and we press close together. My fingers trace little circles over the design of his tattoo, and I imagine his marriage ink marking my hand. I can't wait. My eyes slide closed on a sigh, and I realize I didn't coordinate with any of our people to set up watches and patrols. I try to relax, knowing our soldiers will take the necessary precautions.

I worry for another minute before sleep claims me.

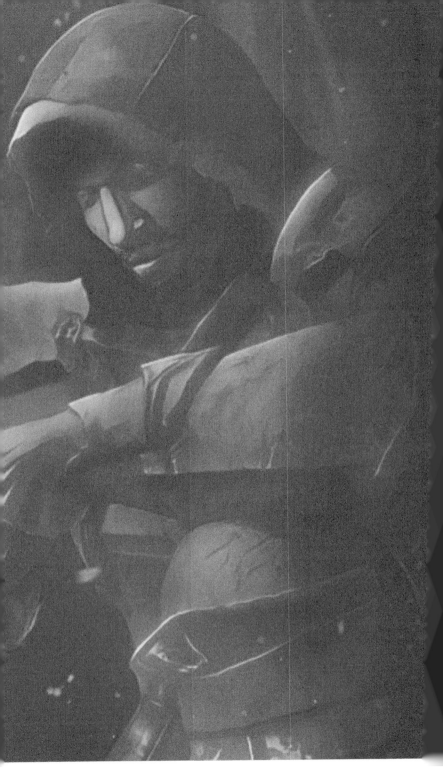

36

LUCARYN

I tighten Phoenix's girth, giving him a little pat on his side. A smile curves my lips as I recall Rydel waking me with his mouth around my cock. The sun was setting, and the fire had burned low. I took Rydel slow at first, reveling the feel of his tight ass and his deep grunts of pleasure. But before long, I was driving into him with powerful strokes, biting the flesh at the base of his neck. His ass slammed back into me as I drove my hips forward. We came together and fell back into the rumpled sheets. I slid into sleep again as Ry pressed a kiss to my temple, and I didn't wake till this morning.

I check my saddlebags and nearly jump out of my skin when Rydel slaps my ass, chuckling in my ear, "Such tasty thoughts, Lucaryn."

Amusement rolls through me, and when I look around,

a few of our soldiers busy themselves saddling their horses, but conspicuous smirks tell me they saw Rydel's act of affection. When I dig deeper, I'm relieved when all I feel is ... satisfaction, happiness, and relief. They're ... glad Ry and I are together.

A soldier leans into Zinnia's space, whispering loudly, "Finally."

She shoots a glance at Rydel and me before dropping her gaze with a smile. "I think it's been going on for a while."

I shift in place, busying myself with rechecking Phoenix's tack as the soldier replies, "Whatever, I'm just glad they're acknowledging it. We've been betting on that relationship for years." He scratches the back of his head. "I wonder who won the pool?"

Rydel chuckles behind me, slapping my back before gripping Kahar's reins.

I move to mount Phoenix, keeping an eye on Mica as he shuffles from the tavern. One of our men helps him mount up. Mica's pain is much less than it was just yesterday, but his body is still terribly weak. He rubs his chest, his eyes glancing around the group before landing on me. He grips his reins, attempting to sit taller as he nods at me, determined.

Before I can swing onto Phoenix's back, the sound of several horses and footsteps draws my attention toward the tavern. More than half the village stands before us, packs secured to horses, a few small carts hitched to mounts. Bellrain steps forward, head bowed slightly toward Rydel. "Your Majesty, we'd like to come with you."

Rydel doesn't respond, but he takes the time to look at each person, and the way they tense tells me he's picking through their minds. A swirl of emotions fill me, but none are hostile or even angry. They are anxious that Rydel might not let them come, but there's excitement of a new adventure, some nerves at the unknown, but mostly hope—hope of a new beginning.

Rydel plants his hands on his hips, his eyes sweeping the villagers. "You have lived in relative solitude your entire lives. There are a few villages in Lieren that will offer you similar seclusion, but life in the north is ... challenging."

Several people shift, and anxiety creeps into me as a few begin to rethink their decision. But Bellrain lifts her chin. "Those of us here are looking for change. Change is coming, regardless. You have been kind to us."

Rydel's face remains blank, but I almost laugh out loud as Rydel's horror hits me. I don't think he realized his actions would be looked at as kindness. His discomfort is adorable.

Bellrain continues, "We talked through the night. You have earned our loyalty. If you'll have us, we would be proud to call ourselves Lierens."

I step forward. "What of your tavern?"

She shrugs. "Father is staying." I glance over her shoulder, through the small crowd, and see Killock leaning against the door of his tavern, a small frown on his face. When he catches my eye, he nods, his resignation and approval slipping through me before I refocus on Bellrain as she says, "I have some money saved, we all do. We will find our way."

I don't bother to tell them that eventually this will all be Lieren, because I can't promise *when* that will happen. And in the meantime, the country is going to be embroiled in violence and turmoil.

Movement brings my gaze to the small boy standing in

front of his mother, his eager eyes wide and trained on me. Quinn is practically vibrating with his excitement and anticipation. I lift my gaze to his mother, asking, "Are you sure about this? The journey is long, and—"

She nods, dropping her hand to Quinn's shoulder with a smile. "This one would have found a way to follow you, regardless. We're going to Lieren."

A ripple of annoyance comes from Rydel, and I know he's concerned with how much slower our journey will be, but I feel him the moment he decides, and I smile. They're coming with us.

He takes another step toward the group, his voice ringing out in the tone he reserves as his 'king voice.' "Then you are Lierens. May the north welcome you in her cold embrace, and may you find warmth in her people."

Relief and excitement slam into me, and I sway, steadying myself against Phoenix. Quinn grins up at me, his fist tight against his heart. I return his salute, and he stands even taller.

Rydel turns, striding to Kahar, his voice sounding through my mind. "*It is going to take us weeks to get home now.*"

My lips twitch. "*We can always ride ahead.*"

His steps falter, and he smiles at me before swinging gracefully into his saddle. "*True. In fact, I think we shall, once we get closer to home.*"

I shake my head, rubbing my chest. It's adorable that he didn't even think about the option of leaving this group behind to get home faster. He's becoming a softie.

His head snaps in my direction, and I didn't realize I'd been projecting my thoughts, but I smile at him. "*It's okay to care, Ry.*"

I bite my cheek to keep from laughing at his scowl.

Without another word, our group heads out, heading north. I nudge Phoenix to come alongside the horse Quinn rides—one of the dead soldier's mounts from yesterday. "Quinn, is there a way we can travel unseen?"

His brows furrow, and his teeth bite his lower lip before he nods. "I haven't explored too far north, but I can get us a day's ride north on paths that should be empty ... especially this time of year."

His serious tone is cute, and I nod, making eye contact with his mother, who rides behind her son. Her worry for him claws at my heart, so I hold her gaze as I say to Quinn, "You and I will ride at the front." His mother relaxes slightly, and I look at the boy. "Lead the way, soldier."

I almost dance in my saddle as his pride and excitement flood my body. He nudges his horse forward, and I keep Phoenix close. Rydel nods at Quinn as we pass, his deep voice commanding. "We're counting on you."

The level of determination coming from Quinn straightens my shoulders, and I let a small smile slip as I look at Rydel. He smiles back, his voice amused in my mind. *"His thoughts are so excited and determined, it's all a jumble. I don't remember the last time I was that excited about something."*

His eyes travel down my body, and his gaze heats. *"Never mind. Yes, I do."*

My body stirs at his attention, and I let my love and desire for him leak out of my magic. He inhales, like he's breathing in my feelings.

Quinn and I take the lead, and true to the boy's word, we travel the entire day and into the night without passing another soul. My chest aches from pushing my magic out as far as it will go all day. But I never detect anyone beyond our group.

As the child moon sets, and the edge of the sky starts to

lighten, exhaustion from the group pulls harder at my magic —especially from Mica. Rydel must hear their tired thoughts because his magic caresses my mind. *"We should stop soon."*

I turn to Quinn. "Where is the closest village or town?"

I know the answer, but I give Quinn what he wants, a chance to prove himself. He looks west, then north. "There's a small town that way." He points west. "But if we keep going north for another few hours, there's a smaller village that way." He looks at me. "At least, that's what the maps say. I haven't been this far before."

His honesty is refreshing, and I nod, unable to keep myself from ruffling his hair. I know he hates it, the action making him feel like the little boy he is, but I do it anyway.

"We'll go west to the closer town. Thank you, Quinn. You did well today."

His annoyance melts away as pride takes its place. I let Quinn lead, keeping my magic attuned to any danger. Before long, a low stone wall comes into view, low roofs peeking from inside the town. As we draw closer, four people draw up outside the open gates, and their fear slams into me. I keep my eyes on them as I say to Quinn, "Let me take the lead."

Quinn salutes, pulling his horse back, and I smile. He's already more obedient than some of my soldiers.

The men standing at the gate lift their weapons. They don't wear the armor or colors of Adren, and their emotions are too chaotic to be trained for combat, so they're not soldiers. But sometimes that can be worse—untrained people driven by fear can do a lot of damage.

I'm about to send a wave of compliance through them, but before I get the chance, their eyes glaze over, and their weapons clatter to the ground. I feel a pinch of Rydel's pain.

"*I could have handled it.*"

He laughs in my mind. "*I know. But I've missed it.*"

"*Maybe don't kill them?*"

"*We'll see.*"

37

RYDEL

I didn't kill them. Boring. But I did knock them out with my magic, just to keep the voices in my head to a minimum. Luc used his power to calm the townspeople and secured us all lodging with ease. Luc and I took turns keeping watch, letting the people of Hillsound as well as our soldiers rest. Mica needs it more than anyone. I would have left him in Hillsound, but he insisted he could make the trip to Lieren without being a burden. I clapped his shoulder, admitting to myself I actually consider the Shadow Lord as a ... friend.

The next day we left, continuing on our way north.

Village by village, town by town, city by city, we have moved through Adren and into Lieren. Then, one day, one measly day from Farden, and I finally hear the thoughts I've been waiting for.

"He will pay. He won't get away with this. His evil stops here."

I roll my eyes, and Luc turns in his saddle. I nod at him, knowing he's picked up on the anger and rage coming from the three, no, four people hiding in the forest to the west. They're about two miles away, their position selected to keep them out of range of my magic. And if this had been a month ago, they would have been out of range, but now, I pick them up with ease.

I pull Kahar's reins, turning us west as I push my thoughts at Luc, the action becoming less painful and easier to do each time I speak in his mind. *"Stay with the group. I'll be right back."*

"Call if you need me."

I chuckle in his mind, loving the way it stirs his arousal as I say, *"So needy."*

He sends me a mental eye roll, and I peel off from the group. A few whispers, both mental and audible, carry from the villagers, wondering at my sudden departure, but my soldiers just shrug it off. They know something has snagged my attention, and unless ordered to do differently, they are to stay with the group.

I keep Kahar's pace slow, but the giant horse feels my anticipation, his tail flicking, his head tossing with impatience. I pull back on the reins, tightening my thighs, ready for his bucking hop as he tries to get the bit between his teeth. Nope. Not this time, devil horse. He snorts, and I laugh out loud. The sounds echo through the woods, and beautiful fear lights up the Adren soldier's minds. Mmmm. It's been a while. I crack my neck and shove my voice into their minds. *"You've come for revenge? Come. Try to claim it."*

"Fuck." ... "Shit." ... *"No! He's found us."* ... *"Now. Now's the time!"*

Hmm. Seems only one has the resolve to face me. I don't give them a choice. With a swift kick to Kahar's sides, he leaps forward, and we thunder into the small clearing where the Adren soldiers scramble to mount their horses. I laugh at their panicked thoughts, and one misses his stirrup three times as he hops around trying to get on his horse. He gives up, grabbing his sword, and faces me. Only one soldier is mounted, but all hold their weapons raised.

Terror stalls the thoughts of three of them, but one, the man closest to me narrows his eyes, and flexes his arm, pointing his ax at me. His mind is clear, his only thought focused on the royal crest of Adren. His loyalty to Erathan is commendable, but his king is dead. It's time for him to move on ... or die.

I keep my weapons sheathed, raising a brow at the leader. "What do you hope to gain here?"

"Your death." "Justice."

My lips press together, and I sigh. "Disappointing."

I keep my eyes on the scowling man, but I push my magic at the other three. Little gasps puff from their mouths before their arms lower and their shoulders slump. The woman smiles as I put her in a memory of the first time she saw her wife.

Mentally, I smirk at myself. Luc was right. I am going soft. He's made me ... happy. Ugh.

The male next to her goes blank as I trap him in a white space. No color, no noise, no touch. And the final soldier grunts then passes out as I stab his mind with the magic. I watch as the sparking lights in his brain flicker out.

I wave at them. "Three soldiers. Three punishments. Which do you think *you* deserve?"

The leader swallows, his focus wavering as fear begins to override his anger. Delicious.

I see the action before he moves, but I stay still as he flicks a small blade into his free hand, throwing it right at my face. Just to show off, I snatch the blade by the hilt, the point a mere inch from my nose.

His rage and fear mixes, his mind turning in a rush to try to find a way to win against me.

I laugh, flipping the blade in my hand. "You really should know better by now."

The knife sails through the air, and the loud click of metal striking metal sounds between us as he deflects it with his ax. Nice.

He sneers. "Coward. You can't beat me without your magic, so you use it like a crutch. You're a weak man."

I shrug, not rising to the bait. "Your opinion doesn't matter to me." I lean forward, and Kahar stomps loudly. "*You don't matter!*"

His eyes go wide, and then his mouth opens to release a beautiful scream. It's guttural, the sound coming from his very soul. He doubles over, then falls to the ground, thrashing in the crunching leaves. The two other soldiers don't move, completely unaware of their leader's plight. The man groans between screams until his voice cracks. Tears stream down his face, and snot bubbles from his nose. His back spasms, arching his spine. His head smacks against a small rock, and it comes away covered in blood. But he barely notices.

Kahar snorts, his tail flicking, occasionally slapping me in the back. I watch as the man rolls and bucks and screams, trying to get away from the pain. It goes on and on. I vaguely register the headache starting behind my eyes, but the joy of watching this man suffer under my power drowns it out. My cock starts to harden, and I adjust myself, wishing Luc had come along to this secluded section of the woods.

Mmmm.

Eventually, the soldier's screams die off as his voice goes hoarse, wheezing sounds still pushing from his throat. Then, his eyes go wide, he clutches his chest, and falls still.

I tsk, talking to Kahar. "Shame. Seems the pain was too much. I suspect his heart gave out. I thought he'd last longer."

Kahar snorts again, tossing his head. I look at the two remaining soldiers. "What should we do with them?"

I chuckle as Kahar dips his head, pulling against the reins in a motion that looks oddly like he's nodding.

"Yes. I agree."

My hand brushes his muscled neck as I turn him around. The lights in the soldier's mind flicker then go out. Twin thuds sound behind me as they fall to the ground, their minds dark, void of life.

I stretch, cracking my back as my ragged group comes back into view. Luc's gaze finds me immediately, checking me over for injury. I smile. *"I never got off Kahar. Easy."*

"Sounded like you had fun."

I shrug, flicking my dagger into my left hand, spinning it through my fingers. *"Not as much as I'd hoped."*

"So violent."

"You love it."

"I do." His desire slams into me, and my cock goes rock hard. Fuck.

"Home. Today."

Luc looks over our group before nodding at me. *"Agreed."*

I turn Kahar in a circle, then bring him to face the crowd. "The Captain and I are riding ahead. Stay the course. At your current pace, you should reach Farden tomorrow as long as the weather holds. Our soldiers will protect you, and the captain and I will take care of any 'obstacles' between you and the capital."

I look at Runic, trying to block out the excruciating memory that plays on a loop in his mind. "The group is yours, Runic."

I hear his objections as they spool through his mind. I wait. He can accept this task or pass it off. It's up to him how he moves forward from here. Everyone is silent for a long moment, each understanding the weight of Runic's pain since they were there to witness it.

He presses his lips together, sits taller, and nods.

I nod back, relieved. I don't know how to help him other than to make him do his job. It's up to him to figure out how to move past what Adastra did to him. Honestly, I don't know if he will ever be able to get past it.

That fucking woman. If I could, I would present Rannae to Runic so he could pull her apart piece by piece as I've seen him do in his mind over and over.

Lucaryn's quiet voice slips into my thoughts. "*His pain is … can he do this?*"

"*We have to let him try. Reena and Zinnia will help if needed.*"

With that, Luc turns Phoenix and kicks him into a controlled canter. His absolute faith in me is … I don't know what to do with Lucaryn. He feels so deeply. He's strong and protective, domineering, sweet and caring. And despite what I did to him, he's stuck by me. I know I don't deserve him, but I'll fight to the bitter end to keep him.

All it takes is a slight loosening of the reins, and Kahar jumps forward, thundering after Phoenix. I lean over the steed's neck, whispering to him through the whipping wind. "Let's see how quickly you can get us home, you crazy devil horse."

38

RYDEL

ONE MONTH LATER

My head roars with the collective noise of everyone gathered in the giant dining hall. Every soldier not on duty fills the long wood tables in the back of the room, their boisterous conversation and laughter echoing off the tall ceilings, filling the space with friendly camaraderie.

High lords and ladies from all over Lieren as well as some from Adren and even Trislen are in attendance tonight as well. Their jewel-colored dresses and tailored jackets stand out against the simple clothes of my soldiers and my servants—several who are off duty tonight and are here simply to enjoy the festivities.

I love a good party, even with the pain it brings through my magic.

My leg bounces where I sit at the head table, my legs crossed. I can't help but dart quick looks at Lucaryn sitting to my right. What's he thinking? A small smile catches on my lips. It's nice not knowing ... but still.

A woman barks a loud laugh from the back of the room as one of the female soldiers pulls her into her lap and kisses her. Several other soldiers down the table cheer them on, one grabbing a woman of his own, grabbing her ass before she slides onto the bench next to him with a giggle. A high lady at the next table down from where I sit shoots disapproving looks at the rowdy soldiers, her lips pursed, her hand clutching the low neckline of her bodice as if she fears someone might grope her at any moment. I almost laugh at her obvious discomfort. There are more than a few people here tonight who'd be happy to give her a little love, but only if she wanted it. My brow raises as her lips part slightly as she watches a man pull another into the not-so-dark shadows along the wall. He trails his fingers up the man's arm, their eyes heating before the man nips the other on the mouth before shoving him in the chest and grabs a mug of ale off the long table before rejoining his friends. The lady watches the whole exchange, and I'm not sure she's taken a single breath. Hmm. Her thoughts are deliciously carnal. Seems someone may want a little attention, but she'd never be so bold to venture beneath her station.

Shame. There's so much fun to be had tonight.

Sweat coats my gloved hands, and I wipe them down my pants, though it doesn't help at all. I want nothing more than to rip these gloves off and roll up my sleeves. Instead, I take a sip of red wine. Lifting my cup in salute, I nod at the newest high lord in my court. His brown eyes hold mine for a moment, and his wary thoughts spool through my head. He knows his choice wasn't a choice at all. It was inevitable.

When Luc and I returned ahead of our group, there was already a small stack of letters from high houses across Adren and some parts of Trislen, all requesting help and protection. Which I'm more than happy to provide—at a cost of absolute fealty.

Trislen is still embroiled in chaos and violence. Floods of Trislenians have been pouring into Adren, seeking refuge. We've even received a few small groups here in Lieren. Luc and I talked and decided to let Trislen suffer for a bit longer. They will beg for law and order when I offer it.

And it's getting worse. There are reports from my spies of unrest and even small riots erupting in Adren as the refugees grow restless and discontent. The people of Adren have started pushing back at the Trislenians living off their land and labor. And as the violence builds, more and more villages, towns, and cities turn to me. How sweet it is to sit here in my castle as the rest of the country comes to me on their knees.

My chest expands on a great inhale, and I plant both feet on the floor, pushing myself to standing.

The room goes quiet, all eyes slowly turning toward me. Luc stands at my side, tall and broad, seemingly unmovable, face stern, eyes watching the room. My voice carries easily over the crowd.

"Tonight, we celebrate the security of Lieren as well as our continued expansion. Lieren is strong. We hold and protect what is ours."

Luc steps forward, raising his cup in his gloved hand.

"All hail Lieren!"

403

The crowd raises their arms, holding their cups and mugs high.

"All hail Lieren!"

Luc calls out, "All hail the king!"

The crowd grows louder. "All hail the king!"

I lift my cup to my lips. The sweet burn of the wine slides down my throat, and from the corner of my eye I watch Luc's throat bob as he swallows. I wonder if his tongue is stained red from the wine? I'll find out later.

Lowering my cup, I raise my free hand, quieting the room once more.

"But, that is not all we are celebrating tonight."

Curious thoughts crowd my mind, everyone hanging on my words, wondering what I'm about to reveal and if it will be good or bad for them. I almost chuckle. One never knows with me. And that's the point.

I slide the gloves off my hands, and Luc does the same. Those closest to us stare with wide eyes. Their shock tingles up my arms. I glance down with shock of my own as Luc threads his hand with mine. In private, Luc is domineering, but in public he is reserved, stoic, harsh. The fact that he made the move to take my hand nearly robs me of breath. And when I move to raise our hands, he comes willingly.

I thought the room was quiet before, but now the silence is almost a physical presence pushing in on my ears. Even the crash of thoughts has stalled as everyone stares at our joined hands raised high.

Then, the room erupts in cheers, shouts, hoots, and hollers. Cups slam against tables, fists punch the air, and whistles shriek to the rafters. The noise crashes into me like a wave as everyone celebrates the new marriage ink covering Luc's and my hands.

Luc smiles at me, his face lighting up as he lowers our hands. My eyes go wide as he steps into my space, the toes of his boots kicking mine. He fists my shirt, pulling me into a kiss.

The crowd gets even louder.

I'm stunned for a long moment before I join the kiss, sucking his bottom lip into my mouth. Our hands are still clutched tight, the pressure burning slightly from the still healing tattoos. It's the most beautiful pain I've ever known.

We pull apart, and the crowd slowly calms from a torrent of noise to a raucous celebration. Luc and I sit, our hands slowly peeling apart, neither of us wanting to cut the contact. As I scan the large room, smiles and cheers greet me, but I pause on Runic. He's at the long table with the rest of the soldiers, a tired smile on his face as he raises his mug in my direction. I return his gesture, and we drink together even as his thoughts crowd out the others.

"Don't think about it. Shut it out. Forget it. This is a happy day. Don't bring it down. Don't think about it. Don't. Don't."

His smile never changes as he turns, accepting a clap on the back from one of his compatriots, the soldiers around him still yelling their congratulations for all the kingdom to hear.

Servants pour through the side door carrying platters heaping with aromatic food. The smell of spices floats through the air as roasted vegetables are placed on the table. Perfectly cooked venison arrives next, then boar, pheasant, and goat. Steamed grains and creamy oats join the heavily laden table.

When I look back up, Runic is gone, and I catch Reena slipping out the door, her thoughts concerned, sending her after her friend and fellow soldier.

405

Luc leans over, speaking loudly to be heard over the added sounds of plates scraping tables, utensils clinking on plates, and cups slamming down with demands for more. "It's up to Runic to find his way through this."

I nod, not sure if he *will* find a way, but I focus on Luc, on the festivities, and on the heaps of food before me. I have a little of it all, laughing around bites as soldiers approach our table, slapping Luc on the back, toasting their congratulations. He's going to be drunk in no time. A female soldier clicks her cup to Luc's, her broad shoulders flexing with toned muscle. Her grin lights up her face as she flicks her long red braid over her shoulder. "Perfect timing, captain. I won the pool."

Luc groans, and I laugh, asking, "How big was it?"

She smirks at us. "I could retire if I wanted." She lifts her cup in a salute to Luc, takes a drink, then pounds her fist to her heart, eyes on me. "But I love my job."

I salute back, taking a drink, and the group heads back to their table.

Mica steps in front of our table, bowing. He's still pale and too thin, but there's a healthy pink tinge to his cheeks, and his eyes are clear as he says, "Congratulations, your Majesty, Captain."

Luc smiles. "Thank you."

I nod, thankful the Shadow Lord chose to stick around. His contacts in Trislen have been invaluable. Since we arrived home, his people have kept us well informed of every fallen village, and of every rebellion against the quickly drowning dredges of the Trislenian army. It's been a pleasure to read every letter Mica brings to me.

I wave my hand at the revelry. "Enjoy yourself, Mica."

He grins, bowing again. "Thank you, your Majesty. I will."

I catch his slight limp as he makes his way back to his seat at a table near the middle of the room, right in the center of the room—where the Shadow Lord likes to be. He slides onto the bench, bumping Carelle with his hip, causing her to slosh her ale down her chest. She shrieks, spinning, and dumps the rest of her cup in Mica's lap. They both roar with laughter as their friends plunk two new mugs down in front of them.

My view is blocked when the large frame of Casin steps in front of our table. His muscular arm drapes over the shoulders of a tiny woman with long brown hair hanging nearly to her knees. Their interlaced hands proudly show off their own marriage tattoos, and they both smile at us.

"Congratulations, your Majesty, Captain."

Casin's deep voice carries laughter in his words. Luc and I both nod, raising our glasses for what feels like the hundredth time. And while Luc takes a large gulp, I only pretend to take a sip. I don't want to be too far gone tonight to forget what happens on our wedding night come morning.

The pair turn, Casin shouting at one of the soldiers with a barked challenge, and his wife beams up at him. I lean toward Luc, whispering, "She's such a small thing. How has Casin not split her in two?"

Luc throws back his head with a roaring laugh, his wine sloshing over the rim of his cup, splashing all over his pants. He doesn't even notice.

With a smile on my face, my eyes travel up our table and back. My finger taps a quick rhythm on the wood surface. A feminine voice whispers over my left ear. "Looking for these?"

Asha sets a large plate piled high with apple tarts in front of me. Luc snatches one, popping it in his mouth. Asha smiles, and I pull her into my lap, kissing her cheek. "I've missed you."

She swats my chest, trying to get out of my hold. "You've missed my cooking. You're a married man now, Rydel. Quit pawing at me."

I poke her side, causing her to squirm with a giggle. "Oh, come on."

Luc shoves another tart into his mouth, flaky pastry clinging to his beard. I lean over, licking him clean. Asha groans as I sit back, her thick ass pressed to my hips in that familiar way of hers. I hear her thoughts before she voices them. "If you two ever want a third ..."

I start to laugh her off, but a tickle of interest comes from Luc. Interesting. Maybe. Someday. I'm not ready to share him ... yet.

Asha laughs at us, scooting off my lap, brushing down her skirts. "Congratulations. Both of you. I've left you some ... treats in your rooms, your majesty."

Oh, I cannot wait to see what delectable morsels she's left us. But what I want most is sitting to my right.

The night crawls on. Most of the high lords and ladies have excused themselves for the night as the revelry got more ... rowdy. But a few have stayed, much to my delight. Jackets have been discarded, shawls and wraps tossed on the nearest chairs. Wine and ale flow, laughter rings out, kisses are stolen, and the occasional moan or muffled shout can be heard from darkened corners where torches have been extinguished.

For the third time, I glance out the large window, tracking the descent of the mother moon—the child moon crossing her path on their way to the horizon. Luc leans over, his inked hand gripping my thigh in promise of what's to come.

"Can we leave yet?"

His smile is wicked, but there's strain behind his eyes, and there's a slight tremble in his touch. I often forget he hasn't had the magic for very long. He's handled it so well—much better than I did at the beginning.

I grab his hand with a nod. We stand, a few people taking notice, but the celebration is in full swing, and Luc and I slip out. I hardly notice the guards along the long hall, flanking the stairs to our wing and barring the way at the end of the hall. It's all a blur in my rush to get to my rooms and get Luc naked.

His large hand wraps around the handle, his ink moving with the movement. Gods, those marks look so good on him. The door swings open, slamming into the wall with Luc's drunken eagerness. I laugh as I kick the door shut, stalking my husband across the room as I pull my shirt over my head. I catch the rich scent of chocolate and spy the dark tarts on the table by the window. But I ignore them as Luc's fingers caress the back of my hand, following the new designs over my wrist, up my forearm, across my bicep to blend into my older tattoos.

His eyes gleam with a wicked promise of what's to come, and when he fists my hair, yanking my head back so his teeth can sink into my flesh, I know I'm in for a wild night.

Luc's head rises and falls with my breath from where he's using my stomach as a pillow. His brows are pinched in thought as he reads the letter in his hand.

There's a soft crinkling as he finishes the page and flips it to the next.

The movement draws my eyes to his hand, his fingers flexing as he shifts the pages and starts reading again. I can't help myself. I reach out, lightly tracing the dark lines dancing over his brown skin. He sets the papers on his lap— his very naked lap and threads his hand through mine. Our marriage ink swirls and loops, blending together perfectly. Luc lifts our joined hands, pressing a soft kiss to the back of mine.

I shiver as Luc's touch absently feathers over my shoulder and across my chest, tracing his new favorite design—a scrolling arrowhead. I had it added when we had our marriage ink done in honor of Luc, and as a reminder of how I almost lost him.

Never again.

I smile as the papers on his lap shift, and I know his cock wants to play. The fluttering of desire starts to build, but I do my best to tamp it down. I'm still a bit ... sore from Luc's attention last night. It was rough, brutal, and exquisite. The two empty bottles of lubricant on the bedside table are a testament to our wild night.

There are dozens of those bottles within the table drawer. Clara, the owner of The Broken Mountain laughed as I made my request, nearly cleaning her out of her magical heating lube. She promised to keep me well stocked, and I promised her coin ... lots of coin. That stuff is ...

My ass clenches uncomfortably at the memory of Luc spreading the lubricant around my hole before slamming into me, the heat and pain striking pleasure up my spine. Luc used his magic to share our emotions, taking us both to the edge over and over, but kept us from falling until we were both sweating and trembling with need. He held my orgasm at bay, pulling out of me only to insert a glass plug that made me see stars. He then stroked himself with the lube until he released his cum all over my chest, twisting the plug as he did so. My body was molten under his, my wrists and ankles bound to the bedposts. He sucked me. He bit me. He choked me. And then he yanked the plug out and fucked me ... hard.

Luc's groan draws me from my sweet memories of last night. "Rydel, I may not be able to read your thoughts, but your desire is coming through loud and clear. Cut it out unless you want a repeat." He smirks up at me. "And I don't know if your ass can handle that right now."

Unfortunately, he's right.

To distract myself, I point at the papers now tented in his lap. "So?"

He picks up the top page. "Another city in Adren," —his fingers trail down the page, landing on a word— "Silvant, is requesting we make them a part of Lieren."

I smile. Another one falls into place.

I draw myself back to the letter in Luc's hand—his beautifully tattooed hand. "Their terms?"

He flips the page, reading on. "Their high families will swear fealty."

"Obviously."

"Their garrison will stand down."

"Again, obvio—"

He smacks me in the chest. "Quit interrupting."

I take his hand, nipping his fingers. "Sorry. Please, go on."

He tugs his hand free, pouting before a small smile cracks his stern look. Turning back to the letter, he reads on in silence. His brows climb his forehead, and he chuckles.

"They have already sent half of this season's taxes to Farden as a show of good faith."

"Eager."

Luc shrugs, the movement tickling my abs with his hair. "Understandable. Erathan's captain of the guard has stepped into the role of keeping the peace, and his head advisor is trying to rule, but neither is suited to handle the responsibility. The people are panicking. You and I are the strongest people in Imoria. We're the obvious choice for stability ... no matter how scared of us they are."

I laugh, sending Luc's head bobbing. I comb my fingers through his black hair, and he relaxes into my touch.

"So true. How nice it is to sit here in our castle and let the rest of the country submit themselves to us."

Luc hums.

I take the letter from his hands, reading over the terms again before asking, "With Silvant, how much of Adren will we have absorbed?"

Luc stretches, sending the papers sliding off his lap. "The entire northern region, and two of their northern ports."

A knock draws our attention to the double doors out in the receiving area of my rooms. Luc shoves up and off the bed, crumpling the papers before I can lift them out of his way. He's such a mess. He snags a pair of pants from the back of a chair on the way out of the bedroom, hopping into them as he makes his way to the doors. Cracking them open, he speaks with ... I listen in on the thoughts, identifying Casin as the person on the other side of the door. Luc and Casin talk for a few minutes before Casin's thoughts fade, and Luc closes the door.

He kicks his pants back off, waving another letter in his hand. He crawls across the bed, and my cock stands at eager attention for him. He looks down at me with a hungry look, planting his hands on either side of my hips before running his tongue from my balls to the tip.

"Fuck, Luc."

He looks up at me, his tongue flicking over my head, lapping at the pre-cum. "Not right now, your Majesty. We have a request from the capital of Adren." I sit up, thoughts of Luc sucking me off forgotten—for now. Luc smiles. "I hold in my hand a letter from the captain and advisor." He crawls up my body, the letter crinkling in his hand. His lips peck my own, and I taste and smell myself on his breath as he whispers, "What do you suppose they want?"

I fist his hair, pulling him in for a bruising kiss. I bite his lip, tasting blood, and he groans. I shove him back, ripping the letter out of his hands. He smirks, licking the blood from his lip, straddling my stomach. He watches me as I open the letter and start reading. My growing grin gives me away, and Luc leans forward, making to grab the letter, but I hold it out of his reach.

He smacks my chest. "Well?"

"Adren is ours."

Luc throws his head back and laughs, his erect cock bobbing over my stomach. I wince as my ass clenches. I flip us, papers scattering. Luc keeps laughing as I prop myself over him.

"The details need to be worked out, and we'll need to go down there before long."

Luc quiets, but his smile remains. "Was there a particular reason for their request?"

"The details were vague, but apparently there was a small riot in the capital. Trislenian refugees protesting the rations the captain put into place. Adren citizens angry at having their city overrun by Trislenians eating their food and staying in their taverns and inns for free. It took even less time than I thought for tempers to boil over and explode." My hand slides up his chest, and my fingers circle his throat. "And like you said, we're the obvious choice to bring them the law and order they need."

He arches into my touch, and I squeeze just enough to bring him that heady rush he's craving. His voice is deep and dark with promise as he says, "Yes, we will bring them to heel. How soon should we leave?"

"Not too soon. I'm in no rush. You can meet with our unit leaders later today and assess how many we can send down there. Our soldiers will help 'keep the peace' until I can get there myself." I roll my hips, his cock sliding between my cheeks.

He growls. "Until *we* can get there."

"Yes. Together."

His eyes go distant, and I let him mull over whatever he's thinking. He looks at me, eyes shining with determination. It doesn't matter what he asks, it's his.

"I'd like to take Quinn with us."

Ah, yes. Whenever possible, the young boy from Hillsound has stuck by Luc's side. Luc arranged for a small apartment for Quinn and his mother to stay in, and his mother got a job at one of our larger fabric suppliers. Though every time I see her, her hands are chapped and stained with fabric dye, there's always a smile on her face. Quinn tugged at Luc's heartstrings until my captain gave him a job cleaning the barracks and polishing the weapons —under supervision. That boy has Luc wrapped around his finger, and I love it. Quinn has potential, and he brings out a fatherly quality in Luc that makes me go soft inside. I'm making sure the boy is attending classes, playing the bad guy to Luc's good guy. Quinn will definitely keep us on our toes.

I pull myself from my thoughts, nodding at Luc's request. "Good idea. It will do the boy good to see more of the county. I'm thinking maybe we will leave at the start of the spring planting. We can do a tour of our farms, make sure the fields are sufficiently prepped and ready to handle a larger yield this year. We can take the time to stop at our newly acquired territory in Adren, and then make our way to the Adren capital."

"The spring planting isn't scheduled to start for another few months, Ry. Should we wait that long?"

Keeping my grip on his throat, I crawl up his body until my cock brushes his beard. He licks his lips, and I growl down at him. "I'm fine right where I am. I'm in no rush." I squeeze a little tighter, and he opens his mouth. My cock slides between his lips, and he swallows me down. My stomach flutters. "I have everything I need right here." I roll my hips, forcing him to take me deeper, feeling my cock under my grip on his throat.

He grips my forearm, the sting of my new tattoos lighting up my skin. With a quick thrust and twist, he reverses our position again. His arms thread under my thighs, hands planted on my hips, and he proceeds to suck me down until I'm shouting his name to the ceiling, stars exploding behind my closed eyes, my cum shooting down his throat and dripping from the corners of his mouth. As he pulls off me with a grin, licking his lips, I yank him to me, kissing him with everything I have, with everything I am.

I recall the saying I've often laughed at ... 'It is said evil will inevitably fall to the good deeds of men.' Well, most people consider me evil, and I enjoy being the bad guy—there's freedom in being the villain.

And here I am.

Here I'll stay.

I cup Luc's cheeks, staring into his bright blue eyes. "Uh sahe'a iyai. Surh iyai as suiyuhr iy niy ruhse'a." *I love you. Thank you for staying by my side.*

"Uszuiyr." *Always*

"Asahe'as." *Forever*

ALSO BY T. B. WIESE

Scan the code below for links to my Amazon author page where you'll find all my latest books as well as my website for signed books and swag.

Thank you so much for taking a chance on my villainous bad boys. I hope you had as much fun reading them as I did writing them.

This is the end of their story ... that's planned anyway. There's a whisper of an idea to write Quinn's story, but I don't know if it will solidify or not.

So, what's next?

Well, if you haven't read my first series, you can find The Elemental and The Dragon King on Amazon & my website. The Elemental is an epic fantasy that starts on present day earth and jumps to a couple different realms. There's fae, dragons, magic, dual POV, Slow burn in the Elemental, and insta-lust in The Dragon King with fated mates. The Elemental contains enemies to lovers, and both books have spice—The Dragon King more so than The Elemental.

New books coming? Of course.

I'm drafting my next series as we speak. It will be epic fantasy—more on par with The Elemental. Multiple POV with magic, conspiracy, friendships, found family, magic contests, political intrigue, betrayal, love ... it'll have it all. To get the latest updates, subscribe to my newsletter here.

Once again, thank you so much for coming along on Rydel and Lucaryn's journey. Don't forget to leave a review here. Good, bad, or indifferent, reviews help drive views on Amazon, and each one is appreciated.

ABOUT THE AUTHOR

T. B. Wiese is a military spouse, dog mom, photographer, Disney nerd, and lover of spicy fantasy. She loves animals (She grew up with dogs and working with horses, including working at the Tri-Circle D Ranch at Disney World), so don't be surprised when you find yourself reading lovable animal characters in her novels.

If you'd like to keep up to date with future releases as well as new swag and sales, sign up for her newsletter:

https://www.tbwiese.com/subscribe

SCAN THE CODE WITH YOUR CAMERA APP FOR HER SOCIAL LINKS

Made in the USA
Middletown, DE
18 September 2024